BACK IN HER HEART

The phony smile froze on Crista's lips as she attempted to slam the door in the wolf-dragon's face. The toe of his scuffed boot, attached to a long, muscular leg, intruded and Nash barged inside.

"I'm calling the cops," Crista said.

Nash's hand fastened over hers. "I came to apologize."

Crista jerked her hand away as if she'd been burned. "Fine. You're sorry you're an SOB. Apology accepted."

"I have to talk to you."

"Then call me."

"I already tried. You hung up on me. I have one less eardrum, thanks to you."

"You had it coming," she flung at him.

"What? You'll have to speak into my good ear."

For a long moment, Crista was silent.

His hand dropped away from hers and he flexed his lean fingers, as if they'd been too tightly clenched.

Crista frowned, wondering why she was still tingling in each place his fingers had touched. Moving a safe distance away, she tried to compose herself. Then, through a tunnel of half-forgotten memories, she heard his rich baritone laughter rolling toward her. The sound nearly brought her to her knees—the same place she'd been at age twelve when Nash had scooped her off the turf at her very first rodeo.

Taylor-made Romance from Zebra Books

WHISPERED KISSES   (0-8217-5454-8, $5.99/$6.99)
Beautiful Texas heiress Laura Leigh Webster never imagined
that her biggest worry on her African safari would be the handsome Jace Elliot, her tour guide. Laura's guardian, Lord Chad-
wick Hamilton, warns her of Jace's dangerous past; she simply
cannot resist the lure of his strong arms and the passion of his
Whispered Kisses.

KISS OF THE NIGHT WIND   (0-8217-5279-0, $5.99/$6.99)
Carrie Sue Strover thought she was leaving trouble behind her
when she deserted her brother's outlaw gang to live her life as
schoolmarm Carolyn Starns. On her journey, her stagecoach
was attacked and she was rescued by handsome T.J. Rogue. T.J.
plots to have Carrie lead him to her brother's cohorts who murdered his family. T.J., however, soon succumbs to the beautiful
runaway's charms and loving caresses.

FORTUNE'S FLAMES   (0-8217-5450-5, $5.99/$6.99)
Impatient to begin her journey back home to New Orleans,
beautiful Maren James was furious when Captain Hawk delayed
the voyage by searching for stowaways. Impatience gave way
to uncontrollable desire once the handsome captain searched
her cabin. He was looking for illegal passengers; what he found
was wild passion with a woman he knew was unlike all those
he had known before!

PASSIONS WILD AND FREE   (0-8217-5275-8, $5.99/$6.99)
After seeing her family and home destroyed by the cruel and
hateful Epson gang, Randee Hollis swore revenge. She knew
she found the perfect man to help her—gunslinger Marsh
Logan. Not only strong and brave, Marsh had the ebony hair
and light blue eyes to make Randee forget her hate and seek
the love and passion that only he could give her.

*Available wherever paperbacks are sold, or order direct from the
Publisher. Send cover price plus 50¢ per copy for mailing and
handling to Penguin USA, P.O. Box 999, c/o Dept. 17109,
Bergenfield, NJ 07621. Residents of New York and Tennessee
must include sales tax. DO NOT SEND CASH.*

RIVER MOON

CAROL FINCH

ZEBRA BOOKS
KENSINGTON PUBLISHING CORP.

ZEBRA BOOKS are published by

Kensington Publishing Corp.
850 Third Avenue
New York, NY 10022

First Printing: June, 1996
10 9 8 7 6 5 4 3 2 1

Printed in the United States of America

*This book is dedicated to my husband, Ed,
and our children, Kurt, Christie, Jill, and Jon,
with much love.*

*And to our new son-in-law, Jeff Walls.
I wish you love, laughter, and happiness.*

Prologue

Over the past ten days in December, Las Vegas—the city of neon lights and casinos—had become the cowboy capital of the world. Country and western music wafted from the showrooms of every hotel, and bands in every nightclub crooned cheatin' songs. Blazing marquees flashed images of spurs and saddles.

When the National Finals Rodeo hit town, the Nevada city *went country*.

Sixteen thousand fans—decked out in cowboy hats, jeans, and boots—were packed into Thomas and Mack Arena to watch the best cowboys in the country pit themselves against the wildest broncs and bulls the rodeo stock companies had to offer.

Intently focused on his upcoming ride, Nash Griffin pulled himself onto the platform behind chute number seven. He hoped it was his lucky number. Nash stared down at the powerfully-built black bronc called Exorcist. According to the other cowboys who had drawn Exorcist in earlier go-rounds, the gelding had lightning feet and the bucking force of a NASA rocket.

From his position on the rail behind the chutes, Nash caught a glimpse of his brother Hal, who nodded encouragement. Uncle Jim Pryce, who traveled the circuit with the Griffin brothers, hauled himself onto a nearby fence to watch the last of the saddle bronc competition. The expression on Choctaw Jim's weather-beaten features indicated the utmost confidence in his oldest nephew's skills.

"Hang tight, Good Time," Choctaw Jim called out.

"Exorcist is a mover and shaker and he'll knock the hell out of you if you give him the chance," Hal Griffin warned. "After his leap from the cage, he takes two straight jumps before doubling back hard to the right. Then he'll bury his head and turn his heels to the sky. After that, nobody knows what he'll do. No cowboy has lasted more than five seconds—me included."

Hal gestured toward his bandaged right arm. "Exorcist dropped me on my ass in the dirt, like I was a damned brick."

Nash took a steadying breath and concentrated on the horse stamping restlessly in its cage. Inch by inch, Nash lowered himself until denim met leather. The horse quivered beneath him and Nash resituated himself, trying to get just the right fit.

Exorcist was reported to be an outlaw—vicious and spooky. The rank bronc had catapulted Nash's brother through the air and into the restraining wall the previous day. To add insult to injury, Exorcist had kicked Hal while he was down—a favorite tactic of the unruly bronc.

This blazing-quick animal was guaranteed to deliver a wild ride. Half the points scored for a rodeo ride were credited to the horse. If Nash could keep his seat for eight seconds and make a respectable showing, this bucking horse could earn Nash the title of All-Around Cowboy—for the third consecutive year.

Eight seconds—which always seemed an eternity—was every cowboy's dream, Nash reminded himself.

"Watch him close, Good Time," Choctaw Jim cautioned. "That mean bastard will deliver a good scoring ride, but he'll make you earn every point."

Nostrils flared, teeth bared, and hooves slamming against the chute, Exorcist assured Nash he had his work cut out for him—as if Hal's injured arm wasn't testimony enough.

"Son of a bitch," Nash hissed when the wild-eyed horse slammed against the metal cage, trying to break his rider's leg before the chute gate swung open.

Repositioning himself, Nash clamped his gloved fist around the braided rein, feeling Exorcist tense up like a mountain of granite—ready to blow sky-high.

"Show that head-hunting bronc who's boss, big brother," Hal murmured as he eased off the railing. "That ornery son of a bitch owes me."

Nash glanced at Hal's bandaged forearm and then stared at the jam-packed arena. Determinedly, he took another deep breath, vowing not to come unglued from this hell-on-hooves until the buzzer sounded.

"Ladies and gentlemen, you're in for some real bronc-bustin' mastery tonight," came the announcer's booming voice.

Nash sure as hell hoped so! There were so many butterflies fluttering around his stomach he could barely breathe. Exorcist stood between Nash and his third All-Around crown. Blazing a path down the nation's highways, eating at truck-stop diners and sleeping in cheap motels, Nash had hung tough on the rodeo circuit. He had worked hard all year to keep the lead in the standings.

This devil horse could make or break him.

"Good Time Griffin of Kanima Springs, Oklahoma, will be riding Exorcist," the announcer informed the crowd. "This cowboy's only eight seconds away from his third world title."

Jaw clenched and body taut, Nash nodded to the chute boss. When the gate swung open, Exorcist bolted toward the blaring lights like an exploding cannonball.

Nash was convinced some prankster cowboy had slipped amphetamines into Exorcist's feed trough. The gelding's first leap took Nash fifteen feet in the air and nearly tore his arm from its socket. Nash's chin snapped against his chest, and it was a miracle he didn't bite his tongue in two. It damned sure felt as if he had.

Nash could taste blood—he wondered if Exorcist could, too.

Exorcist crashed down on all fours, slamming the vertebrae in Nash's spine together like an accordion. Nash reached a little deeper into himself when Exorcist screamed like a demon from hell, promising more fury. All four hooves left the ground, whipping Nash's head back, sending his hat cartwheeling off his head.

"Two seconds and counting," the announcer called out.

The crowd cheered Nash on, but he was past hearing anything except the creak and pop of leather, the shrill whinny of the devil horse taunting the newly damned.

Exorcist, eyes wild with rage, executed a series of body-punishing dives and swoops that had hurled his other riders after their hats.

Nash didn't budge, but every bone and muscle suffered from the effects of jarring, whiplashing motion. When the bronc wheeled sideways, trying to hurl Nash off balance, Nash gritted his teeth and skillfully matched the bronc's erratic rhythm. With his back held straight, his free arm waving in the air, and his spurs thrusting over the break of Exorcist's muscled shoulders, Nash countered every move with practiced efficiency.

The horse's next stiff-legged landing sent pained vibrations through the tail pad that protected Nash's hips, putting another wrinkle in his backbone. Lord, this horse was one of the most physically abusive creatures Nash had ever mounted! Choctaw Jim was right—Exorcist was going to make Nash earn every damn point.

"Four seconds!" the announcer shouted enthusiastically. "Ladies and gents, Good Time is halfway home. If he manages to stay put, he'll be the first cowboy to ride Exorcist this year!"

Four seconds? Nash was sure he'd been on this screaming demon for an hour. Exorcist was skewing himself up like an unleashed hurricane, pulling out all stops. Hooves shot skyward, and a flying mane of black flashed across Nash's line of vision.

The horse changed direction in midair, tossing Nash sideways. His grip slipped on the rein, but he clamped hold. Nash was losing sensation in his fingers, which were knotted around the braided rein. He didn't dare look down to see if his hand was still attached to his arm, for fear he'd break his concentration.

Carol Finch

Shit, Nash thought when Exorcist nearly bent in half and then swallowed his head, hurling Nash forward. Nash was not about to land on his butt and let Exorcist make mincemeat of *his* arm. He could be as mean as Exorcist when he felt like it!

"Five seconds down! It looks like you're in for a rare treat, friends," the announcer roared in excitement. "To date, no other cowboy has ridden all ten of his horses in this event."

Nash felt himself being shaken loose when Exorcist sprang in the air and then swan-dived into another stiff-legged landing that vibrated through every fiber of Nash's body. Bright lights and dust swirled in front of Nash's blurred vision. He was gripped by the impulse to grab the mane or neck—anything to anchor himself to hell's fury-in-horseflesh. But experience and determination prevented Nash from touching any part of this wild bronc and being disqualified.

He had to gut it out. Damn it, he'd sell his soul for the chance to become the three-time All-Around champ. He could nurse his bruises and sprains later. But until then, he'd stick to this goddamn horse as if they were physically joined at the saddle!

"Six seconds . . ."

Holy shit! The numbness ran clean up to Nash's shoulder. He couldn't even feel his arm. This fourteen-hundred-pound thunderbolt was aggravating every old injury he had. The crazed maniac threw itself sideways and Nash felt his shoulder being ripped from its socket. Pain shot through his shoulder and he hissed another curse through clenched teeth.

"Seven seconds!"

Nash spurred like a wild man, but on the next plunge he felt himself separating from the hellish horse. He almost welcomed the jarring thud of leather against denim—proof that he hadn't taken flight . . . quite yet.

"Eight seconds! He's done it, ladies and gents!"

The sound of the blaring horn was sweet as Nash unclamped his hand from the rein and hurled himself toward the pickup man, who closed in beside him. Legs and body adrift in space, Nash stretched himself toward the passing rider.

When Exorcist wheeled to thrust out his back hooves in one last defiant kick, Nash fastened his numb arms around the pickup man's waist. He groaned in pain when a flying hoof caught him in the hip. Exorcist obviously had no intention of exiting the arena without leaving a souvenir. The devil bronc may have been ridden for the first time all year, but he damn well hadn't been beaten.

Exorcist sped away, his hooves arching into the air, until the second pickup man leaned out to loosen the flank strap. The bronc took off at a dead run, and Nash wished the devil a hearty good riddance.

"You okay, Good Time?" the pickup man questioned as Nash dropped to the turf.

Nash took quick inventory to make sure his bones weren't protruding anywhere. "Yeah, I'm okay." Nash gritted his teeth and grabbed his throbbing arm. "Or at least I will be in a minute."

With one quick thrust Nash shoved his dislocated shoulder back into its socket and swallowed a howl of pain. He wasn't sure which felt worse—having it jerked out or slamming it back in place.

"I knocked my arm loose at a rodeo a couple of weeks ago," the pickup man empathized.

"Yeah?" Nash grunted as he came from his knees to his feet.

The pickup man nodded and spit an arc of tobacco juice as he watched Nash's bronze face twist with pain. "But I didn't have the guts to shove the damned thing back in place myself.

"That was one helluva ride, Good Time. Congratulations . . . and take care of that arm."

Nash's abused body was still vibrating as he wobbled over to retrieve his hat and then raised it to the applauding crowd. His left hand and arm burned like fire, but he managed to work the dents out of the dusty crown of his hat before replacing it on his head.

"With a score of eighty-seven, Nash Griffin has not only won this go-round, but also clinched the saddle bronc event for the third straight year. He has enough points to earn himself the title of All-Around Cowboy—again. This is rodeo's equivalent of the Olympic Decathlon. Ladies and gents, this is one mighty fine cowboy. You'll be hearing from Good Time Griffin for a long time to come!"

Although Nash felt as if he'd had the hell beaten out of him, the crowd's standing ovation kept his adrenaline pumping. He walked—half limped was more accurate—to the fence. Cowboys surged toward him from everywhere at once, slapping him on the back, congratulating him on conquering the wild bronc.

"Lucky son of a bitch." Levi Cooper chuckled, edging up beside his mentor and friend. "The news media and the women will be crawling all over you again. You really hit the jackpot in Glitter Gulch. You'll have so many offers to endorse products you'll have to rent a U-Haul to carry all your loot home."

Before the younger cowboy could get off a few more teasing comments, Nash was shepherded toward the locker room. Two microphones were shoved in his sweaty face before he could find a place to sit down and catch his breath.

Nash fielded the questions from the first newsman with a grin and a chuckle, even though his thigh and shoulder were throbbing worse than a toothache. When a red-headed female reporter started yammering about rodeo events being cruel and inhumane to the animals, Nash lost his good disposition.

"Lady, rodeos happen to be tame compared to equestrian shows where horses are occasionally rope-whipped and their tender underbellies are slammed with poles to force them to make higher jumps. And I've seen those Tennessee walking horses shackled during their training, so don't talk to me about rodeo abuse, because you don't have your story straight."

Although Nash could laugh and joke with the best of them—he hadn't acquired his nickname by accident—he could also drive a point home when necessary. He wasn't about to take any guff from this snobby reporter.

The redhead glared at Nash, her back conveniently to the camera. "No abuse? I've heard that you cowboys use sharp tacks to jab the broncs when you ride—"

"And that flank straps squeeze the poor animals' balls off?" Nash cut in, taking supreme satisfaction in watching his antagonist's face turn the same color as her hair. He lifted a booted foot for her flustered inspection. "You can check the rowels on my spurs, if it makes you feel better. But I'm here to tell you that rodeos are the only places where bulls and horses are given a sporting chance.

"In case you weren't watching, the rough stock around here has knocked half the contestants on their asses. That's certainly more than I can say for horses that get their tails broken for appearance and have their manes braided with ribbons."

Nash flashed a grin at the camera. "Around here, any cowboy or cowgirl caught mistreating any animal is dismissed from the rodeo association and barred from competition—forever. There are also veterinarians in attendance to keep close watch on the rough stock. The animals are only allowed to perform twice a day—which is not a privilege granted to cowboys. We're the ones who have to take what these bulls and broncs dish out."

Nash worked the last kink from his spine and nodded his raven head toward the pens filled with broncs. "Why don't you go ask those horses if they're giving a helluva lot more kicks than they get. I'll bet the whinnies will be unanimous."

The crowd of cowboys surrounding Nash snickered. Politely touching the brim of his hat, Nash surged forward, forcing the prissy news reporter to step aside and let him pass.

It was with supreme satisfaction that Nash strode off—without hobbling. Every square inch of flesh and bone ached. But at the moment, the pain was overshadowed by elation—and a sense of accomplishment. He had earned his triple crown by winning the saddle bronc and placing high in the bareback riding and calf-roping events.

Once inside the locker room, Nash sighed with relief. He had been on the suicide circuit for two hundred and thirty days the past year and he had seen more of the country than most folks had in a lifetime. He'd netted one hundred and fifty thousand dollars before the National Finals, and he'd been riding so high—here in Glitter Gulch— that even Exorcist hadn't been able to bring him down.

And now, by damn, he was going to let his hair down and celebrate.

Grabbing his gear, he stepped outside to find a crowd of eager females flashing come-hither smiles and stuffing phone numbers in his pockets. He was more than ready to drown the pain in whiskey . . . and hold onto something softer and safer than three-quarters of a ton of fury-on-the-hoof . . .

Good Time Griffin had it made. He was the toast of the town. He had bought the customary round of drinks in the bar after the show and had amused his acquaintances with the tales and the usual antics.

The world—no, the universe—was at his fingertips. Phone calls, offering endorsements, commercials, and requests for TV appearances, had forced Nash to rise earlier than he had intended. Sleep had been the only luxury he'd been denied.

Despite a headache, nothing could burst the bubble. Nash stumbled out of bed and stood under the shower to clear his brain. Then, he

dressed for the day and headed to the rodeo
arena. The applause of sixteen thousand fans still
echoed in Nash's head—just behind the thud of
the jackhammer, compliments of too much whiskey . . .

"Hi, Nash."

Nash glanced into the grandstands to see the
same bottle blonde who had pawed at him at the
nightclub where he'd celebrated his victory.
She'd been wearing painted-on jeans and a T-shirt
that read: FORGET THE BRONCS AND RIDE THE
COWBOY.

She had.

Nash had been drinking to excess, and he
hadn't been the least bit particular about the
company he kept. She had looked a helluva lot
better at closing time than she did now.

God, he hadn't been that drunk in months! He
couldn't even remember how he and the blonde
had gotten back to his hotel room—at the crack
of dawn.

"Are we still on for tonight, cowboy?"

Nash tilted his head back just enough to stare
at the buxom blonde through red-streaked eyes.
Today her T-shirt read: WRANGLER BUTTS DRIVE
ME NUTS.

Last night, under the influence of too much liquor, Nash had been amused by T-shirt slogans and
the willing flesh beneath them, but today he was
stung by repulsion. The aggressive jean-chasers who
flocked around rodeo cowboys were as shallow as
the makeup that caked their faces . . .

And so was *he* for yielding to the temptation of
strong liquor and wild women.

Nash had been living in the fast lane so long
that he'd lost his perspective, not to mention all

the common sense he'd been collecting for twenty-eight years. Choctaw Jim had warned Nash and Hal that rodeo cowboys put more stars in a woman's eyes than the flashing neon of casinos.

Of course, Nash's uncle was a walking encyclopedia of proverbs. Jim Pryce had ridden the circuit in his younger days and had a quote for every occasion. Too bad Nash had been so full of himself the previous night to remember Choctaw Jim's advice.

"Well, Nash?" the busty blonde prompted, striking a provocative pose that displayed her silicone breasts to their best advantage. "It's not like you're the *only* cowboy around here who's interested, you know."

Damn, Nash thought as he ambled toward the chutes. He could tolerate that female better when he wasn't sober. The word *bitch* quickly sprang to mind. So what did that make him for messing around with her? He obviously hadn't been very discriminating last night.

The blonde's upper lip curled in disdain when Nash casually dismissed her. "Screw you, Griffin."

"You already did, ma'am," Nash said in his best drawl. "But Exorcist rated a higher score for performance—"

Nash bit down on a curse when the box of popcorn in the woman's hand sailed through the air and hit him between the shoulder blades. Kernels fell like snowflakes on the dirt.

"You can go straight to hell, Good Time," the blonde snarled. "And you weren't such a great time yourself. I've had better rides in my Toyota."

With a caustic smirk, Nash half turned to see his brother striding toward him.

"What's your problem?" Nash muttered.

Hal Griffin ambled up beside his surly-looking brother. "You're the one with the problem. You forgot the two rules a cowboy should live by: Never squat on your spurs and steer clear of women. I keep telling you females are nothing but trouble, but you were too drunk last night to care." He appraised the hard lines of Nash's face, lines emphasized by lack of sleep. "Why don't you let me haze for Levi on this last go-round today. You look like death warmed over."

Nash snorted. "You don't look much better. How's your arm feeling?"

Hal shrugged his good shoulder. "I can rein well enough to keep the steer on line while Levi's bulldogging."

"Nash! We're up in the third slot," Levi called as he trotted his wild-eyed gelding toward the chutes.

"What the hell are you doing on Blue Duck?" Nash questioned gruffly. "I told you that horse is still too green for this kind of crowd. I'm supposed to be *hazing* on Blue Duck and you're supposed to be bulldogging off Popeye."

Levi flashed his famous boyish grin and resituated himself on the saddle. "This horse is good at lightning-fast starts. I'm trying to hold onto third place. I can use all the help I can get if I'm going to win some money."

Levi Cooper—or Dogger, as he'd been called since he'd begun traveling the circuit with the Griffin brothers three years earlier—had a determined glitter in his eyes that belied his easy-going smile. Nash knew he should have insisted on exchanging mounts. But the damnable truth was, Nash had his work cut out for him just standing on his own two feet and keeping down the five cups of coffee he had for breakfast.

Nash had promised to haze for Dogger during the steer wrestling event and he was going to remain true to his word. Afterward, Nash vowed faithfully, he'd crawl back into bed and wake up next Wednesday—at the earliest.

"Let me do the hazing," Hal insisted. "You still look green around the gills, Good Time."

"No way, not with that arm of yours, Hal," Dogger scoffed. "I've got to have this steer wrestled to the ground in under ten seconds if I'm going to walk out of here with some prize money. Good Time's the one who's had all the luck this week. I'm hoping some of it will rub off on me."

When Blue Duck shifted sideways at the sound of a chute gate slapping open and cheers erupted from the crowd, Nash grumbled under his breath. "You'll likely break your neck on that skittish horse, Dogger. Then it won't matter where you are in the standings or how much prize money you had a shot at."

Dogger flashed another grin. "Come on, Good Time, I just want a little glory. I've been standing in the shadows of the famed Griffin brothers since the two of you took me under your wing. I wouldn't mind walking away from Vegas with a little pride intact. Now, are you going to haze for me or do I have to do this all by myself?"

Hal scowled sourly. "I knew we shouldn't have agreed to train this bullheaded kid. He's got more brawn than brains."

Nash strode toward the bay gelding that had carried many a cowboy to the purse during the rodeo circuit. If Dogger had a lick of sense he would have climbed on the other bay, Popeye.

Hal and Nash had specifically trained him for roping and bulldogging. But Dogger had obviously decided Popeye had been overworked after so many trips into the arena during the week. Dogger wanted a fresh, rested mount so he could chase down the steer faster.

When Nash opened his mouth to make one last plea to exchange mounts, Dogger threw up his hand. "I'm riding Blue Duck and that's that."

"Fine. Go ahead and break your damned neck. See if I care," Nash grumbled as he piled onto the horse.

After cramming his hat down around his ears, Nash reined Popeye into the designated space to the right of the chute, beside the seven-hundred-pound steer ramming its horns against the rails and bellowing in outrage.

Nash's attention shifted from the rangy steer in the chute to the shrill voice in the stands above him. The spiteful blonde in her skin-tight T-shirt made an obscene gesture with her middle finger. Nash ignored her, longing for a bottle of aspirin and a soft bed instead of the hard saddle beneath him and the glaring lights above him. He just wanted to get this over with and then get the hell out of here.

His duty as hazer was to gallop his horse alongside the fleeing steer, keeping it running in a straight line so Dogger could launch himself off Blue Duck, lock his arms around the steer's horns, and wrestle the animal to the ground in as few seconds as possible.

Just one more short ride and Nash could drag his butt back to the hotel to recuperate. Groggy and sluggish though he was, he could handle the hazing, even while nursing a tender shoulder. Besides, he wasn't in as much pain as Hal, who had muscle ripped away from bone. Hell, he could probably haze in his sleep, since he'd done it a thousand times for his brother and Dogger.

Nash tried to settle himself comfortably in the saddle, but he couldn't seem to find the right fit. That was never a good omen for a rodeo cowboy. Nash squirmed again, while the bay chomped on its bit.

The veteran cow pony was accustomed to carrying a bulldogger alongside the thundering steer and peeling sideways after the leap was executed. Popeye was jittery as a grasshopper, finding himself on the wrong side of the chute. The horse seemed as awkward as Nash felt.

"Calm down," Nash murmured, stroking the bay's taut neck.

Eyes wide and ears pricked, Popeye reluctantly backed into the box across the chute from where Dogger was trying to get Blue Duck to settle down.

"Damned stubborn rookie," Nash muttered. Dogger wasn't going to wind up in the money, he was going to land on his ass. Nash should have been more insistent about switching horses . . .

Nash focused his attention on the wild-eyed Mexican *corriente* steer that scraped its ten-inch horns against the metal bars of the chute. The steer looked like trouble waiting to happen. The animal kept bolting backward against the rails and then slamming forward into the closed gate. On the left side of the restless steer, Dogger was still trying to maneuver Blue Duck into position—and not having much luck.

According to the rules of the event, the steer would be given a ten-foot head start when it came roaring from the chute to cross the designated score line. The bulldogger and his horse had to start from a standstill—or as close as Blue Duck could come, what with all his sideways prancing, tail-swishing, and head-tossing.

While the rodeo attendants set the barrier rope across the bulldogging box and tied one end of the tripping twine to the steer's horns, Nash watched Dogger focus his attention on the turf in front of him.

"Steer's ready," the chute boss called.

Dogger glanced over the top of the chute, waiting for Nash to nod. When he did, Dogger gave the chute boss the signal. "Let 'im rip and sign my paycheck!"

The gate flipped open and the *corriente* let out a bellow as he raced toward the far end of the arena.

Still inside his designated box, Dogger jerked back on Blue Duck's reins. The horse had tried to bolt forward prematurely, as he was accustomed to doing when he was used for hazing. Dogger, holding Blue Duck back, estimated the split second when the steer would hit the score line and reach the end of the twine that tripped the barrier rope, allowing the contestant a legal start.

Gouging in his heels, Dogger urged the jittery mount forward. Horse and rider reached the barrier a full second after the twine flicked away. Dogger was muttering curses while the barrier judge dipped his flag, signaling an acceptable— but late—start.

Nash swallowed a scowl when Popeye hesitated, just as he had been trained to do when he saw the steer bolt off. Both horses' timing had been thrown off when they exchanged positions in the

event. Both the contestant and hazer were a jump
behind the rangy steer that had shot off like a
pistol.

Digging in his heels, Nash tried to compensate
for lost time—hoping to put the veering steer
back on a straight course so Dogger could make
his leap.

"Come on, you fool horse," Dogger growled
when Blue Duck swerved to the left rather than
to the right—at the wrong time.

The gap between bulldogger and steer should
have been little more than three feet when Dogger made his move. But Popeye didn't bookend
the steer as well as he should have, forcing Nash
to cut sideways to pin the animal into proper position for Dogger to slip his boot from the stirrup
and drop onto the steer at a dead run.

The first wave of disaster struck when the left
stirrup slapped against Blue Duck's ribs and the
horse caught sight of Dogger plunging off his
right side. Blue Duck cut to the right—as a properly trained *hazing* horse should have done. Unfortunately, Blue Duck was supposed to cut left.
The horse slammed into the steer that Dogger
was trying to bring to the ground. Before Dogger
could dig in his heels and halt the steer, Blue
Duck stumbled sideways.

Nash heard the crowd shriek in alarm and he
reined Popeye away, hoping to give Dogger
enough space to recover. But Nash's reflexes were
sluggish. Too much whiskey and not enough
sleep had stripped away his edge. He could do
nothing but watch helplessly as catastrophe struck
a second time.

The steer balked beneath Dogger's weight.
Finding itself sandwiched between two horses, the

steer instinctively flung its head sideways, ramming a sharp horn into Dogger's shoulder. His groan mingled with Blue Duck's shrill whinny.

Blue Duck's legs tangled with the steer's hooves and Dogger's booted feet. Nash cursed, trying to give Dogger the space he needed, but he felt as if he were reacting in slow motion.

Blue Duck stumbled and fell on his rider, trapping the hapless cowboy against the steer . . .

Suddenly, the thrill of notching a third consecutive world title at National Finals swirled off in a cloud of dust. All Nash could see was the bloodstained rip on Dogger's shirt and the horrified expression that claimed the younger man's handsome features.

Nash grimaced when Dogger was crushed beneath twelve hundred pounds of horseflesh, his body twisted and pinned at an unnatural angle across the downed steer. Dogger's scream echoed around the lighted arena, bringing the crowd in the grandstands to their feet.

A look of horror on his face, the field judge tossed his stopwatch and clipboard aside and sprinted toward the wreck that had taken place in the middle of the arena. Hal Griffin leaped the fence and came running, while Nash bounded from his mount to grab Blue Duck's reins, forcing the downed horse back to its feet.

"No . . . !"

Nash heard his own voice reverberating around the suddenly silent arena as Blue Duck came onto all fours, leaving Dogger in a tangled mass of flesh and bone. The horse shook off the dust, its bridle jingling like the tolling bell of doom.

Nash swore that if he lived two centuries he would never forget the terror etched on Dogger's dirt-stained face. The young cowboy was draped across the steer, his denim-clad legs sprawled as if he had done the splits, his upper torso twisted like a cork stuck in the neck of a bottle.

"Get the ambulance in here!" Nash called to his uncle.

"Good Time . . . ?" Dogger's dusty lashes fluttered up to focus on his idol and friend.

"Don't move, Dogger," Hal instructed as he positioned himself across from his brother. "Sit tight while we get this steer out from under you."

Hal and Nash clamped hold of the wild-eyed Mexican steer's horns, dragging the animal forward until it could gain its feet.

For the space of a heartbeat Nash reflected on the snooty redhead journalist who had accused cowboys of mistreating livestock. It was the cowboy who bit the dust. The seven-hundred-pound *corriente* steer and twelve-hundred-pound horse had trotted away, virtually unscathed. More often than not, that proved to be the case.

Nash looked down at his younger friend who had propped himself on a skinned elbow. When Dogger stared up at him in a pained daze, Nash felt his heart shrivel in his chest like a raisin.

Go ahead and break your neck. See if I care . . . See if . . . I . . . care . . .

Nash cringed when his words came back to haunt him. He *did* care. Levi Cooper was a close friend, his traveling companion, his protégé. The orphan from Boys Town, Nebraska, had no family except his rodeo family. Nash was responsible for Levi and he had let his friend down when Levi needed him most. Nash had selfishly, drunkenly celebrated his own victory and arrived at the

arena sporting a hangover that left him unreli-
able in a crisis.

One thought rang loud and clear: Nash was to
blame for this. He had reacted too slowly, hadn't
paid enough attention, and he should have demanded that Dogger ride the veteran bulldogging horse. Both horses had been on the wrong
side of the steer chute, making the wrong moves
with dangerous precision. It was Nash's negligence that had caused Levi Cooper's ride to end
in calamity.

"Get me up," Dogger demanded, snatching in
shallow gasps of air. "I swore I'd never let myself
be carried from an arena, especially not the big
show. I may have fallen out of the goddam money,
but I sure as hell plan to leave here with my pride
intact."

"I admire you for trying to *cowboy up*, Dogger,"
Nash said, "but you're going to have to swallow
a little of that Nebraska pride this time."

Nash stared at the approaching ambulance and
then refocused on his friend. "There's times
when walking away isn't the smartest thing to do.
You might make matters worse."

"Fine, then I'll goddam get up by myself," Dogger hissed through the pain and humiliation.
When he tried to curl his legs beneath him, his
battered body refused to respond. A glaze of terror settled on Dogger's features. "Shit, I can't
move!"

Nash staggered back, as if he'd taken a punish-
ing blow. In shock, Nash and Hal watched the
medics shift Dogger onto the gurney and carry
him toward the ambulance.

"I never should have let him climb on Blue
Duck," Nash whispered in anguish. "That horse

wasn't ready for the pressure of a must ride. I should have been more insistent that Dogger mount Popeye."

"We both should have," Hal murmured bleakly.

Dogger stared back at Nash and Hal while he was being placed inside the ambulance. He raised his bloodied arm in a frightened, beseeching gesture. "Help me! I can't move my goddam legs . . . !" he wailed before the door closed behind him . . .

Dogger's hysterical words sliced through Nash like a knife. The bright neon of Glitter Gulch—lights that blinded a man into believing every day was a holiday in Vegas—flared in Nash's mind and then turned pitch black. The party was over for Good Time Griffin. His triumph had turned to torment. He was responsible for his friend's plight.

My fault, Nash chanted miserably. *My fault . . . !*

Nash made a pact with himself, there and then. The cowboy's creed stated that you never let a friend down. Nash had committed the cardinal sin. And until Levi Cooper could stand on his own two feet again, Nash was going to take care of him, provide every necessity and convenience. Nash owed Levi that—and more.

One

Crista Delaney shoved her reading glasses into place as she carefully studied the patient evaluations and staff visitation schedules. It had taken her the entire morning to familiarize herself with the last of the patients receiving physical therapy and home health nursing care. As the new departmental head of Kanima County Hospital, Crista was determined to treat each patient as more than just a name and statistic. Once she had made visits to each patient in rehabilitation she would feel settled and comfortable in her new position—a job that had been her godsend.

Three weeks earlier, Crista had loaded up everything she owned and driven away from her unpleasant past. Taking I-35, heading south from Oklahoma City, Crista had fumbled her way through several small rural communities to the hospital that served Keota Flats, Kanima Springs, and Hochukbi.

The area, which had been part of Indian Territory before the turn of the century, was noted for its rolling hillsides, wooded creeks, and sparkling rivers abundant with fish and wild game. It was a hunters' and ranchers' paradise, isolated by rugged terrain.

The locale reminded Crista of the ranch where

she had grown up in northern Oklahoma. The only difference was that her father wasn't standing over her shoulder, forcing his opinions and demands on her every time she drew breath.

And neither was Jonathan Heywood III . . .

Willfully, Crista stifled the turmoil of emotion associated with her ex-husband's name. Past was past, she reminded herself. She had made a mistake by marrying Jon—a costly one—but now she had begun a new life. She had her independence and a challenging job, away from the hustle and bustle of the city.

Crista had rented a cozy, partially modernized farm home west of Kanima Springs—population eight hundred thirty-seven and boasting a restaurant, a beer joint, two gas stations, and two small grocery stores. The community was an hour's drive from Oklahoma City if you were heavy-footed, an hour and twenty minutes if you weren't.

This was exactly where Crista wanted to be— needed to be. She was putting her life back in order and she was satisfied with the results.

Crista was two-thirds of the way through the time logs for the employees on staff when Jill Forrester poked her head inside the door.

"You better polish up on your salute, boss," Jill advised quietly. "The inspector just marched down the hall."

Crista groaned inwardly. Daisy Darwin, the retired navy nurse who had acquired the position of inspector—because of her military credentials—was a stickler for protocol and organization. Crista had discovered that at their first encounter. The old battle-ax didn't know a thing about physical therapy, but she expected the department to keep detailed records on every pa-

tient—past or present—in the office files. Crista
barely had room to turn around in the small cu-
bicle as it was, what with file cabinets brimming
with medical forms and patient evaluations in
triplicate lining every wall.

Vowing to be polite, she listened to Daisy's orthopedic shoes squeak against the freshly waxed
floors. Crista discreetly appraised Old Ironside's
hefty frame when she appeared at the door. She
even managed a cordial smile when Daisy glared
at her.

"How are you, Daisy?"

The cast-iron Daisy looked down her nose and
sniffed. She was not a woman who wasted time
with amenities. Her chalky face and sagging jowls
knew only one kind of expression—a disapproving frown. Crista doubted Daisy knew how to
smile. The persona of a caring, compassionate
military nurse in combat zones simply did not fit
The Admiral—as Crista often referred to her. Put
quite simply, Daisy Darwin was nobody's daisy.

"You've been here for three weeks," Daisy said
without preamble. "The honeymoon is over, Delaney. I expect your files to be in perfect order
by now. And why the hospital administrator gave
you the position of department head—at *your* age,
with *your* looks—seems obvious to me."

Crista's fingers curled into fists around the
evaluation file. She had the insane urge to squeeze
something. Daisy's bushy, gray head—for starters.
Crista had not gotten where she was by flashing
winsome smiles at administrators and strutting her
stuff. At twenty-eight, not only did she have exten-
sive education in her field of expertise and years
of experience, but her organizational habits had
been referred to as impeccable. Despite what the

damnable Daisy preferred to believe, Crista had
come highly recommended to this position.

Curbing her tongue, Crista watched the retired
military nurse wheel like a soldier on parade and
then march toward the file cabinets, intent on
finding at least one patient evaluation form out
of chronological order, one staff report incomplete. To Daisy's obvious disappointment, every
form was filed in triplicate and every patient's vital stats and medical record was updated and precisely documented.

Daisy's Brillo Pad head swiveled on her wide
shoulders, her dark eyes narrowed in begrudging
acceptance. "Everything seems to be in place
here."

Performing a perfectly executed about-face,
Old Ironsides crossed her arms over her flat
bosom and stared at the attractive blonde behind
the desk. "Don't think for even one minute that
I'm going to ease up on you, just because you've
apparently started off your new job with a bang."

Now why, Crista wondered—would anybody be
stupid enough to think *that*?

"You may as well know that the *older* woman
you replaced left this position because of my recommendation. She didn't run a tight ship. She
was too informal and lax with her staff. This is a
professional office and I'm a stickler for proper
procedure."

No kidding, thought Crista. Only problem
was that Crista's time could have been put to
better use in more frequent supervisory visits
to out-patients, rather than making copies of stuff
for the files because Admiral Pain-in-the-Ass liked
to shuffle papers.

Nodding curtly, Daisy wheeled starboard and

then marched aft. She halted at the door, flinging a parting shot over her rigidly aligned shoulders. "I'll be keeping my eyes on you, Delaney. Don't think I won't."

Crista silently hurled several non-regulation oaths at the retreating inspector. Daisy Darwin was about as pleasant as a plantar's wart. She never looked to give praise, only find fault. Crista wondered if she should match Daisy up with her widowed father. They had a great deal in common, which was why Crista had managed to hold her tongue. Crista had eighteen years of experience being dressed down and taken to task without the luxury of speaking in her own defense.

Jill Forrester materialized at the door, her blue-eyed gaze monitoring Daisy's retreat. "Admiral Darwin managed to fire off a couple of torpedoes before she set sail, I see."

Crista half collapsed in her chair and sighed audibly. "Sheesh! What's her problem anyway?"

Jill ambled into the room and perched on the vacant chair. "No love life," she diagnosed playfully. "It would be hard for a man to put the moves on Old Ironsides and salute her at the same time."

Crista chuckled at the image that leaped to mind. Before she could comment, Wendy York strolled inside to drop another evaluation file atop the stack.

"How is Daniel Riggs progressing?" Crista asked the young P.T. technician.

"Slowly but surely. I think he's ready for a visit from the occupational therapist. Daniel should be in better spirits when he learns dressing and bathing skills so he can begin functioning independently."

"He has regained upper body strength?"

Wendy nodded her strawberry blond head. "Enough to tackle the next phase of rehab."

While Crista and the technicians were discussing the teenage boy's progress, Wilma Elliot burst into the office. Eyes red from recently-shed tears, the middle-aged therapist slammed a file down on the desk, startling the three younger women.

"That's it. I quit!" Wilma burst out. "You can't pay me enough to go back out there. I have tolerated that guard dragon's snide insults for the last time. I want off this case or I'm going to resign—today, this minute, this second!"

Crista glanced down at the name on the file. She had yet to make a thorough study of Levi Cooper's case. She didn't recall much about the patient, except that his bulging file logged five years of physical and occupational therapy and that he had progressed as far as his medical condition would allow.

There was nothing in the report about a guard dragon. But then, Admiral Darwin wasn't interested in that sort of details, only medical forms and by-the-minute updates—in triplicate.

Wilma burst into tears. "I didn't even have a chance to give my examination before he shoveled me out the door," she said between sobs. "What does he think I am? A miracle worker? Damn it, I can't stimulate irreversibly damaged nerves and muscles. When is he going to get it through his thick skull that Levi has gone as far as he can go?"

Wilma braced her hands on the desk and stared at Crista through blurred eyes. "Either you find somebody else to make visitations to Levi Cooper or I'm walking out of here for good."

Crista glanced beseechingly toward Jill Forrester.

"Not me, no way," Jill declared. "I did combat duty at Chulosa Ranch once and that devil shouted me off the premises. He refused to let me set foot in the house and wouldn't let me examine Levi. That fire-breathing dragon won't let me take Levi's case, even if I wanted to, which I don't."

Crista turned to Wendy York. The strawberry blonde flung up both hands, as if she were being held at gunpoint. "I was restricted from setting foot on the property, too, right after Jill was told to get out and never come back. And he didn't put it that nicely, either."

"Well?" Wilma demanded between sniffs. "Are you going to find a replacement or not?"

Crista wasn't about to lose a perfectly good therapist because of some cantankerous old grouch who was probably related to Old Ironsides. "Consider yourself released from the Cooper case."

Wilma exhaled an audible sigh of relief. "Thank you, Crista. If I never have to see that maniac again it'll be fine by me. And if he ever finds himself in need of my medical skills he can damned well sit on his ranch and rot!" Wilma lurched around and stalked out to punch the time clock.

Crista plucked up the file and scanned the evaluation sheet. According to the well-documented reports, Levi Cooper had suffered a rodeo accident five years earlier. A fracture of the lumbar vertebrae had required strenuous, aggressive rehabilitation. The patient was now able to sit independently in a wheelchair. He had retained control of most basic bodily functions, had entered gait training after a year of therapy, and had shown little or no progress. He had quickly terminated the hospital therapy.

Levi Cooper's paralysis was irreversible. Every facet of therapy the department had to offer had been administered. The ADL—Activity of Daily Living—technician had worked with Levi, along with physical and occupational therapists.

Levi's home had been equipped with all sorts of exercise paraphernalia to improve and maintain upper body strength. Obviously no expense had been spared in providing an environment that allowed Levi Cooper to function within the limits of his abilities.

Crista glanced up from the detailed file. "So what's the scoop? Who is this fire-breathing dragon who sends P.T.s running for their lives?"

Jill eased back in the chair and crossed her legs at the ankles. "He's the handsomest devil you'll ever come across but he's mean as hell.

"He can rip you to shreds with a tongue like a whip. He pulls no punches—and he intimidates without even laying a hand on you. If he ever did, you would probably be in need of physical therapy," Wendy put in.

"He *who*? Does this monster have a name?" Crista demanded impatiently.

"Yeah, the SOB of Kanima Springs, that's who," Jill grumbled, half under her breath. "And to think I even found him attractive at first glance. But he cured me of that for life."

"He *who*?" Crista repeated emphatically.

"Nash Griffin," Wendy finally supplied.

Nash Griffin . . . The name skittered through the corners of Crista's memory like a shadow.

Her expression must have given her away, because Jill's blue-eyed gaze narrowed curiously. "You know him?"

Crista smiled enigmatically. "Let's just say I know *of* him. Anybody who knows anything about rodeo remembers the Griffin brothers."

Wendy and Jill stared at their boss in stunned amazement. "You know rodeo?" they asked in unison.

Crista didn't bother to elaborate, but simply nodded affirmatively.

"Good, then maybe you can relate to that oversize bully. The rest of the P.T. staff has had its fill of Nash Griffin. He's been on the warpath for five years, taking every scalp within reach."

Crista wasn't sure she wanted to meet the older version of the young man whom she'd had her first crush on at the tender age of twelve. The image of Nash Griffin was one of the few unblemished memories of her childhood—a memory her father hadn't managed to tarnish, since he was unaware of his daughter's secret infatuation. If Cole Delaney had known, he would somehow have played the fascination to his advantage. He was a master at that sort of thing.

Better to let the past remain where it belongs, Crista reminded herself. That had become her motto, especially now that she had divorced Jonathan, had pulled up stakes in Oklahoma City, and made a new life for herself in Kanima Springs.

Unfortunately, Crista would not be allowed to practice her sensible policy in this instance. First of all, her obligation and responsibility as P.T. department head was to coordinate the home health care and out-patient visitations for Levi Cooper. This was exactly why she was getting paid the big bucks, Crista reminded herself. She could handle this situation—no sweat. Dealing with her domineering father and an ex-husband like Jonathan was the additional experience not included on her résumés.

When Crista glanced at her watch and rose from her chair, both younger women stared at her.

"You aren't going out there, are you? The beast will eat you alive," Jill warned. "I'm not kidding. In Nash's eyes, no one can do anything well enough or often enough when it comes to Levi Cooper. The only one Nash wouldn't object to paying a visit is God Himself."

"Nothing you ever do is good enough," Wendy chimed in. "And everything you do is *never* enough."

Crista scooped up her purse, grabbed the incomplete evaluation chart, and then shooed the technicians from the office. "I'll need directions to Chulosa Ranch."

"That's easy," Jill smirked. "Take a right turn at the hospital parking lot and drive straight toward hell."

"You'll be able to smell the smoke and see the flames from here," Wendy added.

Crista chuckled in amusement. Despite her dealings with Admiral Darwin and the excessive red tape, Crista was exceptionally fond of the staff and her new job. "Come on now, Nash Griffin can't be *that* bad."

"Worse than the witch-admiral," Jill quickly confirmed.

"Twice as bad," Wendy seconded.

After Crista finally coaxed directions from her well-meaning staff, she headed for her car.

"Don't forget I'm bringing my brother out to meet you tonight," Jill called after her. "Wear something seductive!"

Crista smiled to herself. For two weeks Jill Forrester had been hounding Crista to meet her older brother, Jack. Crista had finally agreed, if only to end the constant badgering. Crista could politely but firmly refuse an invitation if it were offered—and then she could get on with business as usual.

After her disappointing marriage, Crista was reluctant to become involved in any kind of relationship—not for a good long while. She was just beginning to try her wings and it felt damned good to answer to no one but herself.

Marriage to Jonathan Heywood III was reason enough to be sour on men. Who needed the hassle and frustration? Who needed to be cheated on, lied to, and used? Crista had been too generous of spirit, too trusting. Who would have thought those qualities would turn out to be the curse of her life?

Two

Nash Griffin stood in the shadows of the barn, scowling as he watched the shiny red sports car kick up dust and stir the fallen autumn leaves as it sped along the bluff. The path leading down to Chulosa Ranch was better suited for pickups, not flashy, low-slung automobiles. This out-of-the-way ranch house was situated at the end of a winding maze of gravelled roads skirted with cottonwoods, cedars, and redbud trees. At the bottom of the sloping hill the hay meadow stretched toward Fire River. The house, barn, and sheds were protected by the high ridge to the north that blocked icy winter winds, and the breeze skimming the river provided a cool breath of air during the hot summer months.

This was Nash's Chulosa—the Choctaw Indian word for peaceful retreat. It was part of his Native American heritage, his private domain. But from the look of things, his haven was about to be invaded—again.

Probably the head honcho from the hospital, Nash speculated as he reached down to pet Leon, his cow dog that sported a red bandana around his neck rather than a collar. After Nash had sent Wilma Elliot scuttling off in tears earlier in the afternoon, she had probably tattled to the department head, who was undoubtedly coming out here herself—driving a fancy new car.

Well, she was about to get an earful. He'd had it with that damned P.T. department. They weren't making any progress with Dogger, not as far as he could tell. Hell's bells, Levi Cooper should have been dancing by now, considering all the therapy he had undergone.

Nash was convinced that Wilma Elliot and the home health nurses who came and went had simply been punching their time clocks and going through the motions. Considering the price Nash and Hal had paid for Dogger's rehabilitation, the hospital and its staff could damned well get some results!

When the sports car rolled to a halt and one long, well-shaped leg appeared, Nash frowned. Either the department head had her entire body lifted or this intruder wasn't here on hospital business after all.

Pushing away from the barn door, Nash strode off to intercept the shapely, blond-haired female dressed in a three-piece silk business suit—and no wedding ring . . .

His most intimidating snarl intact, Nash growled, "What the hell do you want?"

Crista stared up at six feet, three inches and two-hundred-and-some-odd pounds of rock-hard muscle in faded Wranglers and leather chaps that called even more attention to his masculinity. The dusty chambray shirt and scuffed cowboy boots completed the ensemble.

The raw masculine power was as strong as Crista remembered from her youth. Despite the scowl puckering Nash's sun-bronzed features, he was still the kind of man who was instinctively and instantaneously attractive.

Nash Griffin's Native American heritage had always been apparent in his coal-black hair, high cheekbones, the chiseled lines of his mouth, and his bronzed skin. Only those tawny eyes, surrounded by sooty black lashes, revealed his mixed heritage. He was definitely a man's man—and a woman's secret dream. He was tough, invincible—and overwhelming.

At age twelve, Mary Crista Delaney had fallen head over heels for those golden eyes that could twinkle with teasing amusement. Nash had been her instructor at one of the many rodeo clinics her father had shipped her off to. She could faintly remember his deep, ringing laughter, too. It had been a warm, rich sound that carried across the arena, a sound that turned heads, provoked smiles, and uplifted the spirit of the fuzzy-headed blonde who had idolized her instructor.

The sight of Nash Griffin—even the older, obviously more cynical version—triggered another memory. Crista could see herself sprawled face-down in the dirt, trying to wobble onto all fours, her wild hair tumbling over her eyes and shoulders.

Blinking back the stars that revolved around her head after a brain-scrambling fall to the turf, she had peered up into that young, handsome face and felt the world come to a screeching halt. Playful laughter had accompanied Good Time Griffin's approach. He had swaggered over to pick her up when she fell—and there was always that familiar jingle of spurs, Crista recalled. It was part of the image and sound she associated with Nash Griffin.

"Hey, Orphan Annie," Nash had said as he steadied Mary Crista on her noodly legs. "The idea here is to make the cut *with* your horse, not part company at the saddle." Nash had reached out to retrieve the lariat she had abandoned when the turf came flying up to slap her in the face. "If you wanted to try bulldogging that steer instead of settling for casting a loop around him, you should have said so."

Burying his hands in that mass of unruly blond hair, Nash had playfully pretended to set her head on straight. Plucking her up in a brawny arm as if she were a misplaced pillow, Nash had toted her back to her horse.

"It's okay, Orphan Annie. A little dirt between the teeth never hurt anybody. My uncle, Choctaw Jim, always did say that you know you're a full-fledged cowboy or cowgirl when the taste of rodeo grit becomes as familiar as toothpaste."

Even at twelve, Mary Crista had been mature enough to distinguish the difference between Good Time Griffin's teasing and her father's constant, ridiculing criticism. Cole Delaney would have crawled all over Crista for forgetting to clamp her legs against her saddle when the horse cut sideways to move into position alongside a thundering steer.

Mussing Mary Crista's long blond curls once again, Nash had set her on her saddle and then handed her the reins and lasso. "This horse is trained to perform automatically. Hell—heck, Orphan Annie, I trained this one myself, with a little help from Choctaw Jim and brother Hal.

"All you have to do is move with this horse and he'll take care of you. I've been watching you. You've got skills aplenty, little lady," he said with a wink and an encouraging pat on her knee. "I've got boys older than you, sitting over there on the fence, who haven't gotten the hang of roping and riding as quickly as you have."

Nash had turned the horse toward the chute where another steer waited to be released. "Go back over there where Hal is standing by the box and tell him I said I wanted you to try it again. Make these would-be cowboys look bad for me, will you? Then maybe I can get their attention. You know how guys are. They never want to be razzed because they've been bested by a girl. I want you to do just that."

He had tossed her another wink and a dazzling smile—something Mary Crista had never received from her slave-driving, fault-finding father. "You're the little lady who can show those boys how it's supposed to be done. So help me out here, will you, Annie? I've got to find a way to inspire those lazy clowns."

As Crista recalled, it was that wink and blinding smile that had inspired her during her next attempt at calf roping. Her horse had matched the calf's every move, positioning itself a body length behind and a little to the side. Crista had cast her loop over the calf's head and clamped down with her legs when the horse applied the brakes.

Nash Griffin had cheered the loudest and longest and Mary Crista's young heart had burst with pleasure.

When she had climbed up to perch on the fence, Nash had ruffled her hair once again and given her a quick, one-armed hug. Then he had bestowed another heart-melting smile on her and Mary Crista had never forgotten it.

Of course, Nash was just encouraging another

Little Britches contestant to live up to potential, but he had a way of making her feel special. Little Mary Crista Delaney had loved that amber-eyed cowboy for encouraging her.

Too bad the scowling giant who blocked her path at this moment was shattering those cherished memories.

"You got a tongue, honey?" Nash smirked disdainfully. "Or are we going to have to communicate through smoke signals?"

Crista tilted her head upward to compensate for the difference in their height. She tucked the past into the past where it belonged and concentrated on the business at hand.

"I am here to complete the bi-weekly visitations from Kanima County Hospital," she informed Nash. "May I please see Levi Cooper?"

"Who the hell are you?"

"The new P.T. supervisor."

"Well, damn."

"What is that supposed to mean?"

Nash grumbled under his breath. "Doesn't Dogger—?"

"Who's Dogger?"

"Levi Cooper. Doesn't he have enough problems without you making things worse?"

"I'm not following your train of thought."

"Yeah, right," Nash snorted sarcastically. "Next, I suppose you're going to tell me you don't have any mirrors in your house."

For the life of her, Crista couldn't imagine what mirrors had to do with making a P.T. visitation. "I presume Dogger is in the house—" When she tried to step around him, he shifted to block her path. The Border collie growled at her a moment after Nash did.

Crista had already dealt with one human battleship that afternoon. What was left of her cheerful disposition was being destroyed by this cowboy who obviously didn't remember her. Crista couldn't decide if she was disappointed or relieved. But she reminded herself, she had changed drastically in the past sixteen years. So had Nash Griffin!

"If you will allow me to do the job I'm paid to do, I'll be out of here in less than twenty minutes," she said crisply.

"No way, lady," Nash sneered. "I've spent damn near five years safeguarding him from women like you. And furthermore, I have a few things to say about the inefficiency of the staff in your quack department. I'm sick and tired of shelling out hard-earned money without noticeable results. You and your staff don't give a flying f—"

"Nash? Who's here?"

When Nash glanced over his shoulder to see Levi Cooper's shadowed profile behind the screen door, Crista took advantage. She surged around man and dog, smiled, and ascended the porch steps.

Levi sat in his wheelchair, smiling cordially. Before the fire-breathing guard dragon could cremate her, Crista whipped open the door, purposely catching Nash in the chin.

"Argh!"

"Ooops, sorry." Her tone of voice indicated she was nothing of the kind.

A snarl rumbled behind her, but Crista ignored the threat and sallied forth. "For some reason"— she said, as if she didn't know why—"Wilma Elliot was unable to complete her examination this afternoon. I stopped by on my way home to follow up."

"Send somebody else to do it, lady," Nash said menacingly. "If the *somebody else* meets with my approval, I'll be all too happy to cooperate."

Purposefully ignoring Nash Griffin and his growling dog, Crista turned Levi's wheelchair around in the wide entryway and surveyed the modernized ranch house. "Lead the way, Levi."

"The only way you're going is the same way you came in." Nash clamped his hand over hers, holding the chair in place. "You're either stupid or stubborn, lady, and I don't really give a damn which. I said I want you out of here, *now*, and that's exactly what I mean!"

Crista remembered that sugar drew more flies than vinegar and that tact and politeness tamed more beasts than sarcasm. Unfortunately, her temper had been tested to its limits by Admiral Darwin's highhanded threats. Crista had held her tongue for as long as she could.

Besides that, the wolf-dragon of Chulosa Ranch was spoiling her sweet childhood memories so fast it was heartbreaking. Her knight in shiny spurs—the idol of her adolescent dreams—had evolved into a monster. Nash was behaving just like her father and her ex-husband—two negative influences she couldn't forget fast enough.

Crista's good disposition snapped when Nash squeezed her hand until her knuckles popped. Hissing, she wheeled to place one well-heeled foot atop Nash's battered boot. Ramming her hip between him and the handle of the wheelchair, Crista blocked Nash skillfully. Then she took time to silently commend her high school basketball coach for teaching her the skill. It had become quite useful in her chosen profession.

"Damn it! Get the hell out of my house!" Nash roared from behind her. "I don't want you within five feet of Dogger!"

Crista was vividly aware of why Wilma Elliot had sobbed her way back to the hospital, demanding to be replaced. Furious, she rounded on the man breathing down her neck and shattering her fondest memories in one fell swoop.

"In the first place, cowboy, I did *not* acquire this position by giving joy rides. I passed anatomy, kinesiology, physiology, physics, and chemistry with flying colors. I happen to have a B.S. degree and a master's in physical therapy. I am also a registered nurse and have been working in every facet of rehabilitation and therapeutical exercise since I was a senior in high school.

"I was also the department assistant at a notable hospital in Oklahoma City before I accepted this job. And believe me," she fumed, matching him glare for glare, "I don't feel the least bit intimidated by you, so back off!"

Nash's black brows flattened over flashing amber eyes. Not to be outdone, she glowered back at him. Crista heard Levi Cooper camouflage a chuckle behind a cough. He was obviously the only one around here who found amusement in this battle of wills.

"And furthermore," Crista plowed on, "despite your rude, obnoxious comments to the contrary, I *do* care about every patient in the home health care program. I want the absolute best for Levi and so does the rest of my staff. If you think a few obscenities are going to keep me from my appointed rounds you are sorely mistaken!"

Never taking her eyes off Nash Griffin, Crista gestured toward her patient. "Take a hike, Levi. I'll catch up with you in a minute. I'm not quite finished with Nash yet."

Crista thought she heard another muffled snicker as Levi rolled himself toward the wide doorway to the right of the entryway, but she remained focused on Griffin.

"As for you," she continued in a quiet hiss, "I don't give a shit what *your* problem is, either. You aren't my responsibility, but Levi Cooper is. You may be looking down your nose at me because I don't dress in boots and jeans, but I've chewed as much grit as toothpaste in my time."

Nash's brows rose like exclamation marks at the unexpected comment.

"Don't let my appearance throw you, cowboy. You may have earned the name of SOB of Kanima Springs—and damned proud of it—but I happen to be Queen Bitch around here now. I can file charges against you for harassment, if I have a mind to. And I happen to know of one law firm in particular that is suit-happy."

Crista snatched a quick breath and continued, "Now, unless you want a restraining order filed against you, crawl back in your cave. Do you understand me?"

Nash was still stuck on the comment about grit and toothpaste. How the hell had this gorgeous package become familiar with an expression from the rodeo world?

Leaving the brawny cowboy standing there, staring at her, Crista spun on her heels and marched off in the direction Levi Cooper had taken. She paused to shut the door to what looked to be the personal quarters of her patient.

From the look of the spacious living area, which allowed Levi to come and go without banging into walls and furniture, Nash Griffin had done everything possible to accommodate his friend—or whatever relationship he was to Levi. Crista didn't know because the medical files didn't say.

She pulled up short when she reached the doorway that opened into a huge bedroom equipped with every therapeutic device under the sun, plus a whirlpool and mechanical lift that enabled the paraplegic to function as independently as possible.

The double bed was rigged with suspended rings and hand bars that allowed Levi to maneuver himself around and sit up. No expense had been spared. The personal quarters were bright, airy, and stocked with every conceivable convenience. Crista was impressed.

After taking careful inventory of the room, she focused on the sandy-blond man whose powder-blue eyes were twinkling up at her. Levi was a big, athletic-looking individual who practically dwarfed his wheelchair. He wore a multicolored Mo'Betta shirt, neatly creased Wrangler jeans, and polished lizard boots.

Of the two men, Levi appeared to be the one with taste and a good disposition. Crista would have expected it to be the other way around.

If the depression Levi was reported to have suffered during the first year of rehabilitation still plagued him, he hid it well. He appeared to be in positive mental spirits and he remembered how to smile.

Obviously Nash Griffin didn't.

"I'm sorry I lost my temper with your . . .

um . . . friend," Crista apologized. "It has been a trying day and Nash was the frosting on the battleship."

A bemused frown claimed Levi's brow. "Battleship?"

"The Admiral-inspector, to be specific," Crista clarified. "We call her Old Ironsides—not to her face, of course. I'm ready to swear she's somehow related to Nash. If she isn't, I'm thinking of introducing the wolf-dragon to the Admiral. They should get along splendidly."

With practiced ease, Crista took vital stats and tested the spasticity of Levi's legs. She pushed up the hem of his jeans to inspect his skin tone and fluid retention. Every report she had read on this case confirmed her own examination. Levi was making use of the exercise devices and keeping himself physically fit. He had obviously learned to function with his impairments. His neurostimulant treatments and daily activity were maintaining his muscle tone—upper and lower body. His handsome face boasted a tan, indicating he was getting his daily doses of fresh air and sunshine.

In short, Crista couldn't fathom what Nash's beef was all about. Everything that could be done was being done in Levi's ongoing rehabilitation.

Levi settled himself in his chair, bracing his elbows on the padded arm rests. "You're to be commended. Not too many people, especially women, get the drop on Good Time."

"Good Time?" Crista sniffed. "Seems to me he's been misnamed."

Levi's smile faltered momentarily, but he quickly recovered. Crista suspected he had gotten very good at concealing the feelings behind that carefree grin.

"The truth is that my rodeo accident affected Nash's personality as much as it did my legs. He holds himself responsible."

Levi gestured toward the suspended and stationary exercise devices that encircled his bed. "Nash and his brother, Hal, provided all these. I had insurance through the rodeo association, but not nearly enough to cover all these extras. The Griffin brothers remodelled their own house to accommodate me. Nash may be hell-in-spurs where you're concerned, but he treats me like God's brother."

No joke, thought Crista. Everything Levi could possibly want was at his fingertips—the remote control to a big-screen TV, a CD system with speakers large enough to blast eardrums, a library, and enough home video movies to satisfy every whim. Crista had never seen anything like it. Levi was definitely being treated royally.

"If I want something all I have to do is mention it to Nash or Hal and they move heaven and earth to get it."

Crista's gaze narrowed. Those words had been spoken like a man who had been spoiled excessively and was well aware of the power he wielded. Levi may have been confined to a wheelchair, but he knew he ruled the roost. Her ex-husband, Jonathan Heywood III, had spent his adult life in quest of this kind of power and position. Ironic, wasn't it, that Levi Cooper had what Jon had sold his corrupt soul to acquire?

"The Griffin brothers have been exceptionally generous," Crista acknowledged.

Levi nodded in agreement. "I'll see to it that Good Time doesn't give you any more grief."

"No need." Crista told him. "I have learned to take care of myself."

"So I noticed."

"Wilma Elliot has refused to make visitations while Nash is underfoot. I'll have to find a replacement," Crista informed him.

Levi smiled enigmatically. "Don't worry about it. I'll take care of Nash and his objections. But the truth is I was thinking of asking for a replacement myself."

Crista jotted down the necessary information on the evaluation chart, bade Levi good-bye, and then strode toward the door. To her relief, the wolf-dragon was nowhere to be seen. She did, however, encounter a stocky, weather-beaten cowboy carrying a supper tray toward Levi's private quarters.

"What are you doing in here?"

The older man's startled reaction drew Crista's bewildered frown. "I'm the head of P.T. at the hospital."

Bernie Bryant looked her up and down, like a veteran cowboy appraising a horse. "I can't believe he let you past the front porch!"

There was no question about who *he* was. The wolf-dragon again. Crista still couldn't puzzle out why she was considered to be public enemy number one. She was new in Kanima Springs, after all. She hadn't been around long enough to step on too many toes. With the exception of Old Ironsides', of course.

When Bernie turned sideways to ease past her, Crista noticed the unnatural bend in his left elbow. Bernie also noticed that she noticed.

"The rodeo," he said by way of explanation.

He smiled, calling attention to the gap between his teeth.

"One rank bull busted my arm at Mesquite, Texas," he elaborated. "I wasn't carrying insurance. Couldn't afford it. I could barely pay rodeo entry fees. The arm mended crooked on its own and the tooth didn't grow back. I was down on my luck when Choctaw Jim and the Griffin brothers offered to give me a ride out of town. I've been with them ever since, in one capacity or another."

Crista glanced at the tray in Bernie's hand. "As a cook these days?"

Bernie nodded his salt-and-pepper head. "For a while, when the boys were working the circuit to qualify for the National Finals Rodeo, I tended their chores on the ranch and worked part-time at the tavern outside of town."

"At Mangy Dog Saloon?"

Bernie nodded again. "Chief cook, specializing in ice cold beer, fajitas, and fried onion burgers. The place was more respectable in those days, but it's gone downhill since then.

"When Dogger had his wreck in Vegas, I quit at Mangy Dog so I could be here full-time." He smiled as he inched past Crista. "Sorry I have to cook and run, but Good Time gets his feathers ruffled if Levi's steak isn't served piping hot. He hovers over that boy like a guardian angel."

Levi was no boy, thought Crista. He was a full grown man—five months older than she was, according to medical records. And Nash Griffin was nobody's definition of a good time or a guardian angel! He had become a rude, hard-nosed bodyguard with the temperament of a rodeo bull. *Caged rage,* that's what cowboys called the danger-

ous beasts. The description fit this new version of
Nash Griffin to a T.

Well, there goes little Mary Crista's last precious
memory down the toilet, she thought as she let
herself out the front door. Meeting Nash Griffin
after sixteen years was proof positive that dwelling
on the past was a shortcut to disappointment. She
and Nash had both changed drastically.

Crista would have to bribe, blackmail, and cajole
one of her staff into taking Levi's case. The technicians would have to come here with whip and
chair to beard the beast of Chulosa Ranch. Maybe
a restraining order *was* advisable, she mused.

Crista halted momentarily when she saw Nash
Griffin on a stout roan quarter horse, charging
after a calf loping across the private arena beside
the barn. The roan kept breaking stride and tossing its head.

From the look of things, Nash was training the
pony for roping competition. The mount had a
ways to go, Crista decided. The horse overtook
the calf too quickly, leaving no room for a roper
to cast a loop, especially when the mount positioned itself behind its moving target rather than
shifting alongside the steer.

Instead of cursing the horse—as Nash had
soundly cursed her—he simply reversed direction
to begin the procedure again, using the second
steer in the chute. Crista watched Nash trip the
chute gate by means of a pulley and rope attached to the top of the metal cage, allowing him
to release the steer without dismounting.

With a snap of the rope, Nash freed the calf
and kept the cow pony well to the side by nudging
the horse with his spur. The lariat—like a magic
wand in the hands of a master—sailed through

the air and dropped over the calf's horns, bringing the animal to an abrupt halt. When Nash
bounded off the right side of the horse, the roan
backed up, keeping the rope partially but not
completely taut.

The roan gelding was slightly lacking in that
skill, too, Crista noted. The slack in the rope allowed the calf room to shift position while Nash
was taking it to the ground to hobble its hind
legs.

From the distance Crista could hear Nash's
deep baritone praising the horse, even if the roan
gelding hadn't kept the rope as tight as it should
have. Still, the horse got an affectionate pat on
the neck for taking its cues.

There was even the semblance of a smile on
Nash's tanned face . . . before he caught sight of
Crista. Nash's countenance changed instantly.
She obviously had the ability to spoil his mood
by her mere presence on his private stomping
ground. *Why* she drew such a hostile reaction,
Crista didn't have a clue.

Crista strode toward her car and sank onto the
seat. When she twisted the key, the sports car
growled to life. Her gaze instinctively drifted back
to the sinewy man and his faithful dog silhouetted
in the fading sunlight. Beneath that hard, cynical
veneer were lingering traces of the fun-loving,
warmhearted young cowboy who had scraped Orphan Annie off the turf, dusted off her smudged
dignity, and given her a wink and smile that made
her world seem twice as bright. But Levi's accident in Las Vegas five years earlier had obviously
burned a hole in Good Time Griffin's soul.

Crista wondered what role Nash had played in
the tragedy. During her monthly visits to Chulosa

Ranch she vowed to find out. Maybe it would be easier to deal with the wolf-dragon if she understood the circumstances of the incident.

Crista drove away, following the snakelike path from the obscure ranch house nestled beside Fire River. Her rented farm home was only five miles west of this peaceful retreat. She appreciated the country setting, even if the man who turned out to be her nearest neighbor was so unsociable.

Although her new home was a far cry from the ultra-modern condo on Oklahoma City's north side, Crista was enjoying the country atmosphere. Her only difficulties these days were dealing with the cranky hospital inspector and her grouchy neighbor. Things could be worse, she reminded herself optimistically.

Crista accelerated to make the steep grade that flattened out beside another sprawling hay meadow. The past was dead, she reminded herself. Little Orphan Annie was all grown up, and her knight in shining spurs had turned into a snarling monster.

"Should've known my first bout with puppy love would give me a nasty bite," Crista said to herself as she veered onto the highway and headed toward home. "And thank you, Nash Griffin. My transformation is now complete. Now there is absolutely *nothing* I want to remember about the past."

Three

Bernie Bryant moseyed from the barn to watch Nash put the roan horse through its paces. "How's Bowlegs coming along?"

Nash stepped from the stirrup, patted the roan on the neck, and led the horse to the fence. "Slowly but surely. Hal wants him to make his professional debut during the next rodeo. I want to be damned sure Bowlegs is ready."

"Still has a few rough edges, does he?"

Nash nodded as he stroked the horse's muscled shoulder. "He's just beginning to get the hang of backing up to hold the downed calf while the roper ties the pigging string."

"Well, you've got a couple more weeks to work with him," Bernie pointed out. "If I know you, you'll have Bowlegs performing like a pro."

Nash frowned. "I'll have to try him at night, surrounded by pickup headlights, to get him accustomed to the glare. I don't want him breaking from the box, turning tail, and heading for cover when he hits the bright lights of the big time."

"I'll help you set everything up," Bernie volunteered. "With lights flashing and music blaring, ole Bowlegs will outgrow his stage fright."

Bernie glanced toward the house. "Levi wants to see you when you can spare the time."

As had become his custom, Nash dropped whatever he was doing when Levi summoned him. "Can you unsaddle Bowlegs for me?"

"Sure thing, Good Time."

"Stop calling me that," Nash growled.

"Sure thing, boss," Bernie accommodated. He flung Nash a sidelong glance as they both climbed over the top rail of the fence, headed in opposite directions. "Your sour mood doesn't happen to have anything to do with that stunning blonde who was here earlier, does it?"

Nash's reply was a disgruntled snort.

Bernie grinned, displaying the gap between his teeth. "I'll take that as a yes. I may be on the back side of forty with two failed marriages to my discredit, but I'm here to tell you that therapist can still put the spurs to my male hide."

"Put a lid on it, Bern," Nash grumbled without a backward glance.

"Consider it done, boss. But you know me, I always did like to yammer."

"Yeah," Nash threw over his shoulder. "I recall it was your best rodeo event."

"Well, as I see it, most everything in life demands commentary. I was always the kind of man to oblige. And it wasn't my failure to communicate that cost me two wives," he called after Nash. "It was that damned rodeo. It gets in your blood and won't let you stay home. That's probably why you've turned so surly over the years. Hal and Choctaw Jim are still traveling the circuit and you're tending the home fires. If you'd break loose and pay your entry fees—"

Nash wheeled around, halfway between house and barn. "When the hell are you going to learn that you should never bypass the chance to shut

up? We've already got every damned kind of therapist trooping down here to write up reports that
don't change a thing. I don't need a self-appointed
cowboy psychologist checking for the *rodeo* in *my*
blood."

Nash flung his arms in an expansive gesture
and glared at Bernie. "Just unsaddle the horse
and give him a good rubdown and plenty of
feed."

"Geez, boss," Bernie chuckled, undaunted by
Nash's outburst. "It's a good thing I've developed
an elephant's hide the last five years. Saves wear
and tear on a man's feelings when you get all
bent out of shape. But if you keep this up much
longer, I might just quit you."

"Mangy Dog Saloon is waiting for you," Nash
flung back.

"That's where you should be going occasionally. A little distraction wouldn't hurt, and some
female companionship—"

Nash muttered in a muffled oath that Bernie
didn't ask him to repeat. He stalked toward the
house in clipped strides, his spurs clinking in stac-
cato. It had been a lousy day, all the way around.
Two explosive confrontations with the staff of the
P.T. department and he was ready to bite the
head off whoever was unfortunate enough to
cross his path.

Nash halted on the porch and manfully reined
in his temper. Levi would not now—or ever—become Nash's scapegoat. Levi was the only one on
the planet who received preferential treatment,
the only one who ever would. Nash owed Levi all
the courtesy and consideration he could provide.

On that thought, Nash breezed into the house,

trying to muster a pleasant smile. But these days, frowns felt more natural.

"How's the steak?" Nash asked by way of greeting.

Levi glanced up from his plate. "Cooked perfectly—medium rare. Just the way I like it."

"Good." Nash ambled into the room and plunked into the vacant chair. "If it's ever less than perfect, let me know. I'll make it right."

Levi chuckled at his haggard-looking friend. "You always make everything right, Good Time."

"This isn't the rodeo circuit," Nash said with a meaningful glance. "The name these days is just plain Nash."

"We have to talk." Levi pushed his plate aside and then wheeled around to confront the brawny cowboy face-to-face. "This is about Crista."

"Who?" Nash asked, as if he couldn't guess.

"You know, the new department head at the county hospital. You were a little hard on her, don't you think?"

Nash set his jaw stubbornly. "Nope. I had legitimate reason for saying what I did. We've spent a helluva lot of money on equipment and therapy sessions. I expect to see results. It seems you're getting nowhere fast, and I didn't mind telling Wilma Elliot and the new department head that in plain English."

Levi's pale, blue-eyed gaze skipped to the exercise machines, dodging Nash's penetrating stare. "I'm told these things take time, Nash. Lots of time."

"And I think we should just purchase a gait machine—or whatever the hell they call that contraption you drive to the hospital to work with twice a week. Then I can monitor your progress personally."

"No," Levi quickly objected, refusing to look Nash directly in the eye while he was lying through his teeth. "Those visits to the hospital get me away from the ranch for a change of scenery. I look forward to them. The therapists say I'm right on schedule, in fact."

Nash sighed tiredly before murmuring his customary reply. "Whatever you want, Levi."

Levi rolled his chair directly in front of Nash. "What I *want* is Crista Delaney on my case."

Nash's tanned features closed up instantly. "No way in hell—"

"She's got class and style and she ain't bad on the eye, in case you didn't notice," Levi cut in.

Nash had definitely noticed. Hell, he'd have had to be dead a week not to notice. Nash's body had gone on red alert the moment one well-proportioned leg protruded from the open door of that shiny red sports car.

Oh yeah, Nash had noticed what terrific condition the head honcho was in—from the top of her curly blond head to the toes of her navy blue shoes.

And those cedar-green eyes! Gawd, they were fascinating. A man could get lost in *that* forest. Crista Delaney was an easy look, all right.

That was the problem—a definite problem . . .

Leaning forward, Nash rested the threadbare elbows of his shirt on the well-worn knees of his faded jeans. "Levi, take my word for it, having that woman on your case is a very bad idea. I'll go to the hospital and find someone who'll suit

you better. Besides, I suspect that head honcho
has already seen more than she wants of me."

Levi nodded thoughtfully. "I expect you're
right."

"Good, then that's that." Nash rose from his
chair.

Levi reached out to stuff Nash back in his seat.
He stared at him, eyeball-to-eyeball. "No, Good
Time, that is *not* that. Look the lady up and apologize for jumping down her throat. She's got
spunk and style and I like her. The whole house
practically lights up when she walks in. Just having
her around makes me feel good."

"Right," Nash muttered. *Feeling good* in the
most sensitive places would inevitably lead to frustration for Levi. Obviously he hadn't thought that
far ahead. Well, Nash sure as hell had, years ago.
Five years ago, to be exact. Nash had vowed never
to throw temptation in Levi's path.

"I would like you to track Crista down and tell
her you're sorry you blew up," Levi insisted.
"And then you can ask her to take my case—bi-
weekly. If it puts her too far behind on paperwork
at the office, maybe we could pay her a little extra
for her overtime."

Nash sat there like a slab of stone. His mind
rebelled at the inevitable complications.

"I'm sorry, Levi, I just can't do that."

Levi's back went rigid and his chin jutted out.
"Fine, then you can haul all this damned equipment to the dump, because I'm not going to
bother using it anymore. Either I get a change of
scenery in the form of Crista Delaney or I'll sit
here until I rot."

He flicked Nash a quick glance, noting that he
had dropped his dark head against his chest, and

heard him hiss a curse. The tactic was working splendidly. Levi pressed harder, preying on Nash's sense of guilt and his sympathy.

"What the hell's the use anyway? It's been five years since the accident and I'm not back on my feet. Like you said, progress is slow. Maybe I should just give it up—"

"All right, calm down, damn it," Nash interrupted hastily. "I'll go talk to Crista tomorrow—"

"No, tonight," Levi insisted, refusing to budge an inch.

"We play poker together tonight," Nash reminded him. "Just like we do every Friday night— you, me, and Bernie."

"Every Friday night except tonight," Levi amended. "Tonight you're going to shower, shave, and put on some respectable duds before you track Crista down. I don't want her sitting around all weekend, steaming about the tongue-lashing you gave her. By Monday, you may never be able to convince her to come back here."

"Oh, for God's sake," Nash growled in exasperation.

"I'm serious about this, Good Time." Levi rolled back, lifting himself on his arms to resettle the lower half of his body. "I don't care if you have to sweet-talk her, just get her to come back." He paused strategically before flashing Nash his best boyish grin. *"Please . . ."*

Nash rose to his feet—something he wished Levi could do. Aw, damn it, he'd been catering to Levi so long he knew no other way to handle his friend, especially when the chair-bound cowboy started spouting off the way he had during the first year of rehabilitation.

Nash didn't want to endure those bouts of de-

pression again. There had been days when Levi
drew so far into himself that there seemed to be
no way to reach him. If not for the parties Nash
had given, inviting old friends from the rodeo
circuit to the ranch to cheer Levi up, there was
no telling what might have happened.

And if Crista Delaney caused a setback by her
mere presence at the ranch, Nash would have
her head as the hood ornament on his battered,
broken-down pickup!

"Thanks, Good Time, I really do appreciate
this. In fact, I'm already looking forward to
Crista's next visit." Levi beamed like a flood light.
"I think I'll go pump some iron."

Inevitable disaster.

The words hummed through Nash's brain as
he made his way through Levi's private quarters.
He was very much afraid Levi had taken one look
at that blond bombshell and begun fantasizing
about things that would never happen. Nash had
to devise a way to defuse this situation without
leaving Levi in a tailspin.

"Our supper is on the stove," Bernie announced as he strode through the front door.
"I'll bring the cards and poker chips and we can
get started after we eat."

"There won't be a poker game tonight," Nash
grumbled crankily.

Bernie stopped short, his maimed left arm jut-
ting out from his hip. "Of course there will be.
It's Friday. We always play poker on Friday, dominoes on Wednesday, and pitch on Monday. How
else do you think I keep the days of the week
straight?"

Nash heaved an enormous sigh and began unsnapping his pearl-studded shirt. "Levi wants me

to apologize to the new therapist I took apart this afternoon."

Bernie blinked. "He does?"

"He wants Crista on his case."

Bernie broke into a wide grin.

Golden eyes flared ominously. "Just shut the hell up, Bern."

"I didn't say a damned word, did I?"

"You were thinking it. Same thing."

When Nash headed toward the shower, Bernie followed. "What about your steak?"

"I'll grab a sandwich in town."

Nash closed the bathroom door and permitted himself a string of colorful curses. Bad news in a beautiful package, that was Crista Delaney. Big trouble waiting to happen. It was the same feeling Nash got when he sank down onto a wild bronc and couldn't seem to find the right fit.

Usually, that feeling came immediately before one flying leap sent a cowboy the same way as his hat—a scratch ride and no paycheck. In a manner of speaking, that was what Levi would encounter if he became fixated on that attractive therapist.

In less than five minutes, Nash had showered and was parading around naked in the upstairs bedroom he shared with his brother when Hal was between rodeos.

He reached for a clean pair of jeans, his hand stalling on the hanger. His dress clothes looked pretty much the same as his work clothes. He hadn't spent a dime on his wardrobe since Levi's accident. Every cent had gone to exercise machines, hospital visits, and the handicap van equipped with a hydraulic lift and hand-operated brakes and accelerator.

Nash had wanted Levi to enjoy all the independence he possibly could—sparing no expense
or personal sacrifice. All the profit from his ex-
tensive winnings, all the endorsements, TV commercials, and appearances plus the profits from
the cattle and horses paid Levi's staggering bills.

He had even refused to hire help on the ranch,
opting to do everything himself—with the help
of the best cow dog in the county.

Nash pulled his Wranglers off the hanger and
grabbed a faded blue shirt—the best of the lot.
As for his dress boots, they had lost their shine
years ago, but what did he care? How fancy did
you have to dress when you groveled? It wasn't
as if he would mean anything he said to Crista.
It was just a formality to appease Levi.

Nash could say he tried to persuade Crista to
come back, but he would neglect to mention that
he hadn't tried very hard.

Snatching up the phone book, he looked for
the number before he recalled that Crista was
fresh from the City. She wouldn't be listed yet.

He dialed the operator.

"What's the address for Delaney?" Nash inquired as he stuffed his foot in his boot. "West
of town? You're a lot of help."

He was west of town, sitting on two thousand
acres of prime pasture and wheat ground. So
where was Delaney camped out? "Just give me
the number then," he demanded impatiently.

When Nash dialed the number, a soft, sultry
voice came over the line, triggering an image that
had stuck in his mind like a cocklebur. "Crista?
This is Nash Griffin."

Nash winced when Crista slammed the receiver
down so hard she nearly blew a hole in his ear-

drum. "This should be fun," he muttered sarcastically.

Raking his fingers through his damp, black hair to comb it into place, Nash appraised his reflection in the mirror. He looked presentable, tired as hell but presentable. These twelve- and fifteen-hour days working the ranch, baling hay, and training rodeo mounts were wearing him down. Unfortunately, he couldn't afford to slow his pace.

Wearily, Nash descended the steps and grabbed the cleanest hat from the hooks beside the door. Once inside his rattletrap pickup, he jiggled the key in the faulty ignition until it made good connection. The engine snarled to life, sputtered, choked, and then settled into an erratic hum.

As had become the Border collie's habit, Leon came running at the sound of the idling farm truck. Nash leaned over to open the passenger door, allowing Leon to hop onto the seat and then plop on his personalized, braided mat.

Maybe Nash would take Bernie's advice and stop by Mangy Dog Saloon to sip some suds. While he was there, wolfing down a greasy burger, some of the regular clientele could point him in Crista's direction. Either that, or Nash would have to send Leon to sniff Crista out. He was too tired and unenthusiastic to do the legwork himself.

Thirty minutes later, Nash strode inside the local watering hole. The tavern, with its saddles for bar stools, mason jars for mugs, and western paraphernalia lining the walls, was filled to capacity. Young single males were sipping beer and hollering at each other above the blaring jukebox. The

voice of Garth Brooks—Oklahoma's native son—
crooned about being too young to feel so
damned old.

Nash could certainly relate to that.

A waitress in skin-tight jeans and a bosom-
hugging knit blouse was sauntering among the
tables. Her chest shook like Jell-O. So did her
hips. Nash scowled in disgust.

The woman reminded him of the glossy groupies who hovered around the beer stands at rodeos, waiting to latch onto lonely cowboys who
were far from home. This waitress had "available"
printed all over her, and she seemed to invite
every pat on the fanny, answering every wolf call
with a wink and an accommodating smile.

The days Nash had spent bellying up and frol-
icking with the barflies were over and done. That
side of life was partially responsible for his inability
to come to Dogger's assistance that fateful day in
Vegas. A wild night and too much whiskey had cost
Nash his edge and put Dogger in that wheelchair.

Since Nash had quit the rodeo circuit to care
for Levi, his social life was practically nonexistent.
Only when a few of the cowboys stayed over at the
bunkhouse at the ranch, paying visits and checking on Levi's progress, did Nash run with the
crowd and let his hair down the way he'd done in
the old days. He wasn't the life of anybody's party
anymore. Good Time Griffin had vanished from
the rodeo scene completely. These days, Nash kept
his nose to the grindstone at the ranch.

"Nash Griffin, is that you?"

The booming voice of a neighboring rancher's
oldest son brought several cowboy hats around.
Nash managed a faint smile of greeting.

"Come sit down and I'll buy you a beer."

That used to be Nash's line. A round on him.
Let the beer barrel roll. He'd tell a joke—or
three—to liven the place up, grab a bride-for-
the-night at some far-flung rodeo, and ride into
alcohol-induced dreams . . .

Once upon a time, but never again . . .

"Thanks but I'm kinda in a hurry." Nash straddled the saddle stool and bought his own beer.
"Anybody here know where I can find the new
hospital employee? The blonde?"

Roy Chester—a would-be rodeo cowboy who
held his own calf-roping, beer-drinking blowouts
in the corrals on his ranch—rocked back in his
chair and grinned. "You mean that well-stacked
knockout?"

Wolf calls and uproarious laughter resounded
around the smoke-filled room when Nash nodded affirmatively.

"Got a hot date, do you, Good Time?"

Several beer mugs rose in salute. Nash scowled.
It seemed he scowled a lot these days, for one
reason or another.

Dave Higgins's lopsided grin and glazed eyes
revealed he'd been drinking hard since sundown.
"Mind if I come along with you, Good Time?"

Nash swallowed a sip of beer. "This happens to
be business."

The comment drew a round of horselaughs.
Nash gritted his teeth. Uncle Jim always did say
you had to be three sheets to the wind to appreciate the humor of a drunk.

"Give me a break here, fellas. This has to do
with Levi's therapy."

The crowd quieted down immediately, each
man silently studying the contents of his Mason
jar.

"Hell, Nash, you ought to know where Crista lives," Dave Higgins remarked. "Choctaw Jim rented his farmhouse to her. Sounds as if your uncle and your brother aren't home long enough to fill you in on what goes on outside Chulosa."

Nash nearly choked on his beer. Crista was his closest neighbor? He had driven all the way into town just to reverse direction? Well, hell's jingling bells!

"While you're out there, put in a good word for me," Roy called out. "It's been a long, dry spell since my wife moved out on me. I could use a little action."

"I'll take a piece of that action," somebody hooted from the corner booth.

Nash left his half-finished drink on the counter and stalked out. He felt like an idiot. Hell and be damned, the little lady had camped out at his uncle's place and nobody had bothered to tell him. Choctaw Jim would hear about this when he got home!

That's what you get for isolating yourself, Griffin. The whole damned town could burn down and you wouldn't know it unless you happened to see the smoke.

Plopping beneath the steering wheel, Nash revved the engine and sped off. Leon sprawled on his rug, resting his head on his paws. Maybe Nash would drop back by Mangy Dog to unwind, after he apologized to the head cheese . . .

And maybe he wouldn't . . .

Since the disaster in Vegas, Nash never drank more than one beer. He refused to dull his senses or let his reflexes be impaired. Levi Cooper was living proof of what life in the fast lane could do to a man and his best friend.

"Shit," Nash muttered as he drove toward his

uncle's house. He hoped he could figure out how to deal with this situation before he reached the ranch.

Crista grumbled when the doorbell chimed. Jill-the-marriage-broker was so anxious to match Crista up with Jack Forrester that she was leaning on the doorbell.

"I'm coming!"

On her way down the hall, Crista smoothed her form-fitting black dress over her waist and hips. The bell was still chiming when she whipped open the door.

The smile froze on Crista's lips as she attempted to slam the door in the wolf-dragon's face. The toe of a scuffed boot, attached to a long, muscular leg, intruded as Nash barged inside. He glanced at his surroundings, then sank down on the blue-and-white striped sofa as if he owned the place.

"I'm calling the cops," Crista threatened, making a beeline toward the phone.

Nash bounded up to intercept her. His hand fastened over hers, slamming the receiver into its cradle before Crista could dial.

"I came to apologize," he said gruffly.

Crista jerked her hand away as if she had been burned. "Fine, you're sorry you're an SOB. Apology accepted." Her arm shot toward the door like a speeding bullet. "Now get out of my house."

"I have to talk to you."

"Then call me."

"I already tried. You hung up on me. I have one less eardrum, thanks to you."

"You had it coming," Crista flung at him.

"What? You'll have to speak into my good ear."

"I'd rather box both of your ears, so don't push it, Griffin," she sniped, refusing to be amused.

When Nash pivoted on his heel, Crista sighed with relief—until he parked himself on the couch rather than making his exit. "I'm expecting company," she informed him stiffly.

Nash glanced at her, his eyes aglow like a wolf's reflecting moonlight. Predatory, Crista thought to herself. All-powerful, ominous when he was angered, threatening when he wasn't.

The image of the young man she had loved in days gone by clashed with the callous, cynical rancher she had tangled with earlier in the day. Two entirely different men, Crista reminded herself. And don't you forget it!

"Expecting a date, Crista?" Nash asked with a smirk as he thoroughly assessed her seductive attire.

Her chin thrust upward. "If I am, it's certainly no business of yours."

"I didn't say it was." Nash settled himself more comfortably on her sofa, his long, muscled legs sprawled in front of him. "I was only making conversation."

"I don't like conversation. I don't like *you* and you made it crystal clear that you despise *me,* so there is nothing left to be said."

For a long moment, Nash was silent. Then he stood to loom over her. Somehow she expected he would do something like that. Intimidation at its finest, she thought. One twist of those beefy hands and her head would roll across the carpet. She should have studied martial arts instead of physical therapy.

"I was rude, disrespectful, and obnoxious this afternoon," Nash blurted out.

"You can say that again."

"I was rude, disrespectful, and obnoxious this afternoon."

Crista tried not to grin, but her lips curved upward, just enough to assure Nash that he had managed to amuse her.

Nash didn't change expression, simply stepping backward. "Thanks for that, at least, *Curly.*"

The nickname prompted Crista to comb her fingers through her unruly mop, which streamed over her shoulders and tumbled to her waist.

"It's the humidity," she said lamely. "I should move to a drier climate."

"Yes, you should. I'll help you pack."

Crista bit down on a grin. No way in hell was she going to afford Nash the satisfaction of thinking he had amused her twice in the same evening.

"Are you here for a repeat performance of this afternoon's verbal boxing match?" she asked warily.

"Why do you want to know? Do you need time to return to your corner before you come out swinging?"

"No, actually I'm light on my feet and reasonably quick." His masculine aura was beginning to get to Crista, and she wanted none of it. She swerved around the human blockade, adding, "I simply don't have time to go several rounds with you. As I said, I'm expecting someone—"

When his hand grasped her elbow, Crista flinched. She was entirely too aware of this man, even after she had sworn that she wasn't allowing another man in her life for at least a year—or ten.

"We have to talk," Nash insisted. "I'll be brief."

His hand dropped away and he flexed his lean fingers, as if they had been too tightly clinched around a bull rigging. He sucked in his breath, then glanced away from Crista. She frowned at his odd behavior, and at the same time, found herself wondering why she was still tingling each place his fingers had touched.

"I'm here because Levi wants you—"

The doorbell clanged. Crista drew a shaky breath and moving a safe distance away, tried to compose herself. If she'd had the equipment she would have checked her blood pressure. It was probably shooting through the roof, and had been since she found Nash on her doorstep.

Go figure . . .

Crista reached for the doorknob as if it were her salvation. She hoped the Forresters had arrived to provide a distraction. She definitely needed one. Nash Griffin, even the more cynical version, was disturbing her. That was the last thing she wanted . . . or expected . . .

Four

"Hi, Crista. I'd like to introduce you to—" Jill's voice dried up when she noticed the looming figure casting an ominous shadow across the living room.

A one-time victim of Nash Griffin's tirades, Jill automatically retreated a step, colliding with her brother.

Crista gave them a cheerful smile—the kind she used on her patients. "Come in Jack and Jill."

"Christ," Nash smirked, for Crista's ears only.

Crista glared him into silence before turning her back. "Nash Griffin was just leaving."

"No, I wasn't," he contradicted—almost pleasantly.

Evergreen eyes zeroed in on Nash. He didn't budge from his spot, but he came dangerously close to smiling when his gaze slid down Crista's shapely backside. He met the fierce glower she flung over her shoulder, reminding him of what Levi had said about spunk and spirit. Crista Delaney certainly had that—and more.

That glorious tangle of blond curls made a man's fingers itch to bury themselves. Nash had come dangerously close to yielding to the temptation a few minutes earlier—too damned close. And, if he'd had to stare at that sensuous mouth of hers much longer, he shuddered to think what might have happened.

Crista Delaney was a vivid reminder that Nash hadn't been with a woman for a long, *long* time.

And it will be a good while longer, too, Griffin, so don't get any crazy ideas.

While Jill Forrester stood there indecisively, Nash appraised her tall, lean, brown-haired, and very dignified-looking brother. Sister and brother bore a strong family resemblance. They were clean-cut, wholesome, and attractive.

Jack simply wasn't Crista's type, Nash decided. Probably a nice guy, but . . . Hailing from hardy rodeo stock himself—with Choctaw blood bubbling in his veins—Nash had never had all that much use for his more civilized, sophisticated counterparts. No pizazz.

Nash appraised Jack's trendy attire and then silently smirked. A pleated monkey suit would never have suited Nash's tastes. And that gaudy tie! *Dogs* wore collars. Horses wore halters and bridles. Intelligent life forms were supposed to object to ropes around their necks, even if they *were* made of silk. Hell, Nash wouldn't have worn a tie to his own funeral.

"So . . ." Crista said, attempting to break the ice. "Jill tells me you're an accountant in Keota Flats."

When Crista gestured toward the sofa, Jack took his cue and shepherded his wary sister alongside him. "Yes, I've been with the firm for six years." He smiled charmingly.

Nash rolled his eyes and wished Jack would fall down and Jill would go tumbling after.

"If you need an accountant to handle your taxes, I would be happy to take you on."

While Crista led the conversation, Nash propped himself against the wall like a prison guard overseeing an inmate's visitation. He supposed he should make himself scarce, but he had promised Levi that he would talk to Crista and he wasn't leaving until he had accomplished his mission.

When Crista offered to fix drinks for her guests, Nash followed her into the kitchen. "I'll help you," he insisted.

Crista wheeled around, her curly hair tumbling over one stiff shoulder. "I don't need any help—I simply need you to leave. In case you haven't noticed, my usually talkative technician can't find her tongue."

"So what am I supposed to do? Help her look for it?"

Crista gnashed her teeth. "I was told that you jumped down Jill's throat a couple of years ago. Obviously, you made a vivid impression on her and she's uncomfortable around you."

"Her problem, not mine." Nash reached around Crista's half-bare shoulder to grab a glass for himself. "I told her to vacate my property and she resisted. But I never laid a hand on her."

"No need, not when you can flay flesh with your rapier tongue." Crista grabbed two glasses from the cabinet. "Jill is only twenty-five, for heaven's sake, and hardly worldly enough to handle an ex-rodeo champ who has probably forgotten more curse words than she has ever heard."

"How do you know that?"

"I heard you curse a blue streak this afternoon. The foul cloud is probably still hanging over Chulosa Ranch."

"Not that, the part about the rodeo," he specified.

Crista avoided his tawny-eyed stare. "I've done my homework, Griffin. You were at the top—All-Around Cowboy, three years running. Now, why don't you saddle up and ride off into the sunset while I entertain my *invited* guests."

Nash spun her around, sandwiching her between him and the counter. Without further ado, he cut straight to the heart of the matter. "This is the deal, Curly. Levi wants you on his case. He's got some crazed notion that you would be good for his morale. I tried to convince him you would be nothing of the kind . . . Hold still, damn it."

"Back off, Griffin," Crista said.

"Not until you hear me out—"

"Crista? Is everything okay in there?" Jill called from the living room.

"Everything is fine," Nash answered for Crista. "We'll be out with the drinks in a minute."

"Make it fast," Crista demanded. "You have fifty-nine seconds . . . fifty-eight . . ."

Nash spoke in a quiet rush. "I've spent five years making double damned sure that every woman who comes near Levi is absolutely harmless."

"We're all harmless—" Crista tried to protest.

"Not the ones like you and Jill and that other blonde on your staff," Nash corrected. "Before the accident, Levi was a virile man with plenty of women chasing after him. He may be confined to a chair now, but that doesn't mean he doesn't have urges. He's got some kind of fixation for you that could lead to trouble."

When Crista stopped resisting him and started listening, Nash eased his grasp on her arm and made the most of the minute she had granted him. "I was supposed to come over here to beg you to make the bi-weekly visits. Levi says he'll quit using the exercise equipment and write himself off as a hopeless cause if you don't agree. But if you do, and if you show him anything more than simple kindness, he will latch onto it like a fish to a baited hook. And when he starts getting the kind of ideas he can't finish, you'll back off and maybe even walk way from him. He'll be devastated, and I can't bear to see him wallowing in depression again. The first year was living hell. Now, how are we going to handle this situation, Curly? *You* tell *me.*"

Crista peered up into Nash's stormy amber eyes, the light of understanding finally dawning on her lovely features. "So that's the reason for your fierce protests and concerns. That's why you wanted no one but Wilma Elliot coming out to the ranch, until even she somehow managed to set you off."

Nash nodded his raven head. "You don't wave a lollipop in a baby's face and then cruelly jerk it out of reach. Maybe Levi needs female companionship, but I've made sure he remains in an all-male environment, with the exception of women old enough to be his mother—which he doesn't happen to have, by the way. The men at the ranch are all the family Levi has."

"So what are you suggesting? That you and I pretend some romantic interest in each other to discourage his fixation on me?" she smirked caustically.

Nash's gaze dropped to her inviting mouth. For sure and certain, he'd need a cold shower when he got home.

"No way, Curly. I would never stand in the way of anything Levi Cooper wanted. He knows that. Whatever Levi wants, I make sure he gets."

Crista eyed him for a moment. "What about what *I* want? What if *I* had an interest in you instead, not that I really would, you understand."

"He knows that wouldn't matter. I would never cross the line, never betray a friend."

"Then what do you expect me to do? Come tramping out to your ranch dressed like a bag lady?"

Nash muttered under his breath as he surveyed Crista's curvaceous figure. "I doubt you could pull that off, but it's a thought."

"I suppose I should be flattered."

"You should be paying attention," Nash grumbled. "My minute is almost up—"

"Crista?" Jack called before he stepped around the corner.

Scowling at the interruption, Nash pivoted around to glare into Jack's awkward smile.

Stuffing his hands in the pockets of his loose-fitting slacks, Jack shifted from one foot to the other. "Jill and I decided it would be better if we came by some other time for a visit."

"How about Saturday night?" Crista suggested. "I'll fix dinner."

Jack glanced uncertainly at the formidable figure in faded denim.

"This isn't what you think," Nash assured him. "We're discussing one of her patients. And no, I won't be coming to dinner."

"Well then . . . if you're sure . . ." Jack said hesitantly.

"Very sure," Crista replied. "I'll expect you around seven tomorrow night."

While Jack and Jill let themselves out, Crista tossed ice cubes in her glass and poured herself a drink.

"Have you got anything around here to eat? I bypassed a steak when Levi insisted I track you down."

"By all means, make yourself right at home," Crista said in a tone that negated the offer.

Nash opened the refrigerator and poked his head inside. "This place *is* like home, actually," he said. "This is my uncle's farm. He's been living at Chulosa since the accident and renting out his house. Jim Pryce is my uncle."

Crista sank down at the kitchen table and sipped her drink, watching Nash build himself a Dagwood sandwich that would have lasted her a week. "You and the cows appear to have four stomachs," she said with a shake of her head.

Balancing his sandwich in one hand, Nash eased down into a chair. "I never pegged you as an authority on cattle."

"Probably not. Like most men from the Stone Age, you don't give women much credit." She raised her glass. "Welcome to the 90's."

Nash munched on his sandwich in silence while Crista nursed her Diet Coke. After a moment, she braced her arms on the table and stared at him curiously.

"Would you mind telling me what your connection is to Levi Cooper?"

"I already did. He's like my adopted brother."

"I meant your connection to the accident," she specified.

Nash ignored the comment. But Crista, he had quickly discovered, was nothing if not persistent.

"You were there in Vegas when Levi took his fall, right?"

When Nash refused to reply, Crista stared him squarely in the eye. "Look, Griffin, you want my cooperation, but I need to understand the entire situation. I want to know my patients—emotionally and physically. And, while we're on the subject of Levi, it's my professional opinion that he's handling his disability better than *you* are. You treat him like a child, protecting him from every conceivable difficulty, even before it happens. He's living in a glass bubble you've created. It isn't healthy to let him depend on you for everything, expect everything from you. Will you always be there for him?"

"Yes," Nash said quickly, irrevocably. "Always."

Crista shook her head in dismay. "In that case, I don't think I want to take Levi on as a patient, not when you obviously don't intend to let him lead a normal life. I think I should find someone else to make the visitations and restrict myself to monthly evaluations."

"Fine—then you deliver the news to Dogger. Find somebody who won't pose the slightest temptation." Nash frowned curiously. "Don't you have any male therapists around that hospital?"

"At present, no."

Nash guzzled half his Coke and slumped back in his chair. "So now what, Curly?"

"Good question."

"You're supposed to have a good answer. You're the expert, or so says your title."

Crista bared her teeth and shook her finger in Nash's face. "Don't start with me. I've had a bad day. And thank you so much for your contribution to it."

Nash pushed away from the table and then rose to his feet. "You've got until Tuesday to figure something out. I'll tell Levi that you're considering his request. That will buy you some time."

He paused at the kitchen door to fling her a meaningful glance. "But if you do decide to take his case and come waltzing out to Chulosa looking like a fashion model, I'll meet you on the porch for advanced classes in conjugating four-letter verbs. You ain't heard nothin' yet, Curly. I was just getting warmed up this afternoon."

"If I visit Levi, I'll wear a modest dress. Does that make you happy? Will anything make you happy?"

Nash sighed. "You just don't get it. Come here, Curly."

Bemused, Crista followed Nash into the living room. When he veered down the hall toward her bedroom, she screeched to a halt. "Where do you think you're going?"

"To your room." Nash flipped on the light, taking quick inventory of the frilly bedspread, lacy curtains, and feminine paraphernalia. "There's something in here you need to see."

"I'll just bet there is!" Her face flushed with irritation. "That has to be one of the most pathetic come-ons I have ever heard . . . !"

Through a tunnel of half-forgotten memories, Crista heard that rich baritone laughter rolling toward her. The sound nearly brought her to her knees—where she had been at age twelve when Nash had scooped her off the turf.

Crista was still trapped halfway between the past she vowed to forget and the present, when golden eyes twinkled down on her.

"All I want is for you to take a good look in

the mirror. Then I'm leaving. And," he added wryly, "I'd like to think I could devise a better come-on than that if I tried."

Not sure she could trust him, Crista hesitated a moment, then forged ahead. Halting in front of the mirror, she appraised her reflection. "Okay, I'm looking. So what am I supposed to see?"

Nash positioned himself directly behind her. Without actually touching her, he sketched the fullness of her breasts, careful to keep a three-inch separation between the tempting curves of her body and the itching palm of his hand. Meticulously, he outlined the trim indentation of her waist and the provocative flair of her hips.

When he finally spoke his voice sounded as if it had rusted. Even *not* touching her was more stimulating than he would have preferred. "A man, any man—even the meanest SOB in Kanima County—would have to be blind in both eyes not to notice the way you fill out a dress. And this hair—" Nash stilled his hand when it involuntarily moved toward the shining mass.

Mesmerized, Nash monitored the rise and fall of her breasts, watching her nipples pebble beneath the clinging fabric. He groaned inwardly when his traitorous body reacted. This demonstration had only succeeded in heightening his awareness of the woman he found himself unwillingly attracted to.

So much for good intentions, Nash thought to himself.

"Sex appeal," he said huskily. "obvious, noteworthy, and impossible to ignore."

Crista met his gaze in the mirror, fascinated by the hypnotic ripples in those eyes, experiencing unwanted sensations. She swallowed visibly and strived for a light tone of voice. She almost succeeded.

"Okay, Griffin, I'll see what I can do about my appearance, but I'm gonna feel pretty foolish when I clomp to your doorstep with my hair in curlers, dressed in a terrycloth bathrobe and fuzzy house shoes."

His deep skirl of laughter sent tingles down Crista's spine. She and Nash stood there, both of them gazing at the man and woman behind the mirror, feeling the mounting physical attraction radiate through the room. The electricity between them fairly crackled.

"I better go," Nash rasped, stepping away.

Crista cleared her throat. "Yes . . . um . . . you should." She nearly ran toward the front door. "Try not to drop by tomorrow night. My matchmaking friend has high hopes for me and her brother, the accountant."

Nash plucked his hat off the end table and ambled through the door Crista held open for him. "Maybe that's the answer. If you pretend interest in the number pusher, Levi might take the hint that you're unavailable."

"What makes you think I'll have to *pretend* interest?" she challenged.

"Because Jack's too predictable, too regimented. Being with someone *nice* would be downright boring for someone like you."

"Someone like me?" Crista sniffed, highly affronted. "You don't know me well enough to psychoanalyze me. After several rounds with you, being with someone *nice* sounds extremely inviting. Maybe I could get used to it!"

"You would tire of him in a week," Nash predicted. "Think about it, Curly. The man balances books for a living. If everything doesn't come out *nice* and *even*, he slaves away until it does."

Crista clenched her teeth. "Maybe I'll fall for Jack and prove you wrong. That would certainly discourage this lovesick admirer you claim I have."

"That's your business, Curly. My business is keeping Levi in prime mental and physical condition. I promised to give him whatever he wants, whenever he wants it."

"What about you, Nash Griffin? What do you want?"

"That doesn't matter. I stopped living five years ago. Now I just exist to pay the bills and care for Dogger."

"Trapped in the past is no place to be. You can't be objective, rational, or sensible about Levi and what is best for him."

Nash half turned, his eyes clouding with inscrutable emotion. "If I need advice I'll go see a shrink."

Nash strode out and climbed into his truck, where Leon patiently awaited his return. Nash didn't appreciate the fact that he actually enjoyed sparring with Crista Delaney. She was quick-witted, intelligent, and too damned attractive . . . And there was something about her that left him with the niggling feeling they had met somewhere before.

But how could that be? Nash would have remembered a woman like Crista. She wasn't the kind a man could easily forget. So why did he have the unshakable feeling that he had known her forever?

Nash shrugged off the thought and drove

home to take a cold shower. He called himself nine kinds of crazy for dragging Crista in front of the mirror to make his point. That had turned out to be one of the worst ideas he'd ever had.

Jack Forrester poked his head hesitantly inside Crista's front door, checking for signs of uninvited guests. Crista chuckled at the precautionary measure. "I suggest you come in before you sprain your neck. There's no one here but me."

"Good." Jack heaved a sigh of relief and whipped his arm from behind his back, revealing a bouquet of roses.

"My, aren't we gallant," she teased playfully.

Grinning, Jack handed her the flowers. "I also have a gold-plated cross out in the car, just in case the werewolf is lurking about."

"He's probably down by the river, howling at the moon. Last time I looked, it was hanging in the sky like a glowing ball of fire."

Crista turned away to fetch a vase. "I thought Jill was coming with you tonight."

"She had a date. I guess she decided to give us some privacy. Little sisters can sometimes be as bad as meddling mothers, you know. Jill was none too happy to find Nash here last night. All the way home she kept referring him to him as 'the Dragon.' "

Jack ambled into the kitchen at Crista's heels. "Personally, I thought the werewolf persona fit him better. I kept expecting him to throw back his head and howl, but Jill was betting he would breathe fire."

"He's not all that bad," Crista surprised herself by saying. "For some reason—about which he re-

fuses to elaborate—he is fiercely devoted to the
paraplegic patient living at his ranch. If Nash
thinks Levi's best interest isn't everybody's foremost concern, he goes ballistic."

"Well, I guess no one can fault him for that.
It's reassuring to know he cares so much about
something." Jack paused to inhale the tantalizing
aroma that filled the kitchen. "Smells good. It
seems you cook as well as Jill claims you supervise
the P.T. department."

"Jill exaggerates." Crista placed the bouquet on
the table. Tossing Jack an elfish smile, she strode
over to retrieve the casserole from the oven. "Or
maybe not. According to your sister, you're the
best accountant in the firm—and in the Midwest.
You should be making senior partner any day now.
She has assured me that you have enough clients
singing your praises to form a choir."

Jack chuckled as he retrieved the iced tea glasses
from the counter. "Jill obviously does exaggerate."
Seating himself, he glanced curiously at his dinner
companion. "So tell me—now that you've spent
three weeks in the Oklahoma outback, are you
longing for life in the fast lane again?"

Crista served her guest a heaping portion of
chicken cacciatore. "No, actually I prefer to remain off the beaten path."

For more reasons than one! Crista certainly
wasn't going to elaborate about her reasons for
reclaiming her maiden name, dropping her first
name, and leaving no forwarding address with
the post office when she moved to Kanima
Springs.

Jack sampled the casserole and nodded approv-
ingly. "This is good stuff. You're a woman of
many talents, obviously."

"Thanks. And what about you?" Crista quizzed. "Are you satisfied with life in Keota Flats?"

"Being a city slicker at heart, I find myself making the drive to the metropolis a couple of times a month. Maybe we could take in a movie and dinner sometime. I'd enjoy the company."

Crista didn't accept or decline. The jury was still out on Jack Forrester. True, he was pleasant company, and he came highly recommended—by his sister. He was . . . *nice* . . .

Crista winced. That was exactly what Nash Griffin had said about Jack. Nice . . . predictable.

Well, what was wrong with *nice?* She wasn't looking for serious involvement, after all. An occasional dinner date with a successful accountant certainly couldn't hurt. *Nice* was fine with Crista. A lot Nash Griffin knew about her needs and desires!

Two hours and an old classic home video movie later, Crista bade Jack good night.

And it *had* been a good night, damn it, Crista thought defensively. Okay, so there were no sparks. And so what if the brief touch of Jack's hand on hers, the incidental brushing of their shoulders while they sat side by side on the couch, didn't make her fizz.

It was . . . nice . . .

"Gawd," Crista muttered as she closed the door behind Jack. "I really hate you for being right, Nash Griffin. Really I do!"

Nash had managed to avoid Levi and the topic of Crista Delaney for a full day. He had risen at the crack of dawn to swath hay and hadn't finished until long after dark. When Nash finally returned to the house, he found Levi camped out in the entryway, an open book in his lap, his blue eyes intently curious.

"Well, is she coming back?" Levi asked without preamble.

"She's thinking about it," Nash replied as he dropped his hat over the hook beside the front door.

Disappointment furrowed Levi's brow. "That doesn't sound very definite."

Heaving a tired sigh, Nash walked toward his friend. "There are some things a man can't control, you know. A woman is one of them. You said yourself that Crista has grit and gumption, and she doesn't like being told what to do. I expect she'll make up her mind in her own good time."

Levi peered solemnly at Nash. "Did you apologize for what you said?"

"Yep."

"Nicely?"

Nash bared his teeth. "As nicely as I know how."

Levi stared at him skeptically. "That's what I thought. You simply went through the motions—and not very sincerely, I suspect."

Nash had decided it was best to nip this ill-fated infatuation in the bud. Maybe Levi could deal realistically with Crista if he knew she had a romantic interest in someone else.

"Last night wasn't a good time to talk to her," he explained. "She was expecting a date—an accountant from Keota Flats, to be specific. I was interrupting."

Nash stared down at the open book in Levi's

lap, hoping to change the subject. "What are you reading, Dogger?"

Levi shrugged a broad shoulder. "I asked Bernie to pick up a library book on money management last time he was in Keota Flats."

Nash's brows rose in surprise. "Money management? What the hell for? You've been doing a good job with expenses and budgeting on the ranch all these years."

"Hell, Good Time, I want to be the best at whatever I do. That was always my problem, you know. The habitual over-achiever. I want this ranch to run like a well-tuned pickup.

"Since you and Hal deeded a third of the property over to me and put me in charge of the bookwork, I want to know all the ins and outs of accounting . . ." Levi frowned. "Just who is this accountant who has the hots for Crista?"

Well, damn. So much for avoiding the topic of Crista Delaney, thought Nash. "Some guy named Jack Forrester. His sister is on the P.T. staff."

"Is he good looking?"

"How the hell should I know?" Nash muttered grouchily. "I'm not an authority on that."

Levi's sandy head tilted to survey the scowl Nash wore so well these days. "You've been in a rotten mood since yesterday. I suppose it's because of Crista."

"I'm as happy as a pig in shit," he countered sarcastically. "I've been swathing hay all day, I ate lunch—on the go—on the tractor, and have another hay meadow to bale up tomorrow. I need to spend more time working with Bowlegs before he makes his debut. There are calves to be separated, inoculated, and branded. I didn't get to take a breather last night because I had to go apologize to your therapist while her boyfriend was lurking around. I'm also dead on my feet, so why wouldn't I be the epitome of good humor?"

"You need to get away from the ranch more often," Levi insisted. "Why not travel with Hal and Choctaw Jim and enter one of the rodeos?"

"No." Nash's voiced pounded like a gavel—hard and final.

"Bernie and I can take care of things. You'll have the weaning calves worked and moved to separate pastures before Hal and Choctaw Jim get home. There's no reason why you can't hustle the next couple of rodeos."

Nash snorted. "You sound as if you're trying to get rid of me."

Levi looked away, fidgeting. "No, certainly not."

"Well, I'm not hustling any rodeos unless you're with me. End of discussion."

An enigmatic expression claimed Levi's handsome features before he glanced back at Nash. "I'm not quite ready for that yet, Good Time. But soon, I hope."

What Levi meant—but didn't say, Nash presumed—was that he wanted to attend a rodeo when he could *walk* to one, *ride* in one. Nash was beginning to think that was never going to happen, no matter how long and hard he prayed for that day. And damn it, what was with those therapists anyway? They only had Levi on the gait machine twice a week. They should double the time.

When Levi wheeled his chair toward his private quarters, Nash stared after him. "Need any help getting ready for bed?"

"Yeah, but unless you're a curly-headed blonde, you wouldn't be of much help to me. I could use a relaxing massage to soothe cramped muscles."

The parting remark hit Nash like a doubled fist in the solar plexus. Sure enough, Crista's appearance had triggered fantasies that he'd spent five years trying to avoid.

"Well, hell," Nash muttered, spinning toward the door.

Maybe he couldn't restore the use of Levi's legs, but Nash could grant one small request. It would probably be a mistake, but Levi was tearing Nash's heart out by the taproot.

It was that dejected tone of voice Levi had used as he rolled away that got to Nash—as nothing else could. It also kept Nash moving when he was tired enough to drop in his tracks.

"Where are you going at this hour?" Bernie questioned from the kitchen door, a bowl of popcorn tucked in his crooked arm and a Coke in his right hand.

"To grant a wish."

Bernie snickered. "Take my word for it, you ain't anybody's idea of a fairy godmother these days."

"Don't you ever get tired of shooting off your mouth, Bernie?" Nash grumbled as he snatched up his hat.

"Nope." He grinned unrepentantly. "Like you said, I was always a better bullshitter than bullrider—"

Bernie wasn't allowed to finish his sentence before Nash slammed the door behind him.

Five

The flash of headlights swept across the bedroom wall and the crunch of gravel brought Crista straight up in bed—only minutes after she'd sprawled out. Grabbing a robe, she sped down the hall. Whoever had leaped onto the porch was now hammering on the doorbell.

When Crista swung open the door to see Nash Griffin, her shoulders slumped in exasperation.

"Now what?"

Nash muttered at the picture Crista presented in the shimmering silk nightgown and thigh-length robe. "Shit, Curly, is that your idea of a robe?"

Crista bristled immediately. "Look, Griffin, what I choose to sleep in is none of your concern."

She thrust out her chin. "Now what do you want?"

Pure spunk and spirit, Nash reminded himself. Crista Delaney was an expert at giving as good as she got.

"Levi needs you."

Crista's countenance changed abruptly. "Did he fall? Is he having muscle pain, spasms?" she asked before she scurried off to change clothes.

"Something like that." Fascinated, Nash as-

sessed her long, well-contoured legs as she retreated into the shadows.

"I'm ready." Crista re-appeared in the living
room, carrying what looked to be a medical bag,
dressed in high-top Nikes, an oversize sweatshirt,
and sweatpants blotched with white paint.

Nash glanced at the recently painted wall. It
was obvious this industrious renter had taken
brush in hand to renovate the place herself, since
her landlord wasn't home long enough to do it
for her.

Once outside the house, Nash didn't bother
scurrying to open the door of his truck for Crista.
The greater the distance between them, the better off he'd be. Besides, things would run
smoother if he remained more an antagonist
than a friend.

Crista settled herself beside the dog. A frown
knitted her brow when she heard Nash suck in
his breath. "Are you okay?"

"An old rodeo injury acting up," Nash lied as
he jiggled the ignition switch.

"Where?"

"Where what?"

"Where is your injury?"

"A dislocated shoulder, to name one."

"So name two," she insisted as he whizzed off
in the jalopy—complete with a steel hay fork
bolted to the bed.

"Two bad knees that don't have enough carti-
lage left to fill a thimble, plus ligaments and tendons torn loose so often they're nothing but scar
tissue," Nash rattled off. "Then there's the floating rib that was hooked by a steer horn. But that
happened in my own corral while I was working

cattle. The big red Salers bull and I don't get along too well."

"You've had a great many falls, Humpty Dumpty. You should marry a doctor to save yourself some money."

Nash stared straight ahead. "I'm not planning to marry anybody—doctor, nurse, or otherwise. And I rarely bothered with hospitals while I was on the suicide circuit. I put myself back together with Ace bandages and adhesive tape."

Jonathan Heywood III should take lessons from Nash Griffin, Crista decided. While Nash was scraping himself off the turf, without complaint, Jon whined about nothing more serious than a hangnail.

Too bad Crista hadn't noticed what a big baby Jon was before she married him. And too bad she hadn't noticed all his other flaws before she made the crucial mistake of thinking Jon could be the answer to her problems. As it turned out, he was just another problem she had to resolve.

Distance and divorce had been the only solutions.

"You know something, Griffin?" Crista murmured, watching the silhouettes of electric poles fly past the side window.

"What's that, Curly?"

"I'm not planning on getting married, either. Once was plenty."

Nash glanced in Crista's direction, studying her in the dim glow of the dashboard lights. He had wondered about her marital status, but he hadn't asked. Now he knew. Not that it mattered, of course. He wasn't going to become involved with Crista Delaney. That's all there was to it.

Nash faithfully repeated that vow as he weaved down the path leading to Chulosa Ranch.

"Crista!"

The look of surprised pleasure on Levi's face gave Crista an unexpected sense of gratification.

"You put yourself to bed, did you?" Crista asked as she ambled into the room with a cheerful smile. "Glad to see it, Levi. I always appreciate self-reliance."

Crista was aware that Nash Griffin was behind her, monitoring every nuance, every comment, waiting to jump down her throat.

Levi chuckled as Crista eased a shapely hip onto the side of his bed. "Nice outfit."

"And no makeup," she didn't hesitate to point out. "What you see is all there is. Sorry, pal, without the cosmetics and designer clothes there isn't much. And this hair leads a life of its own."

Crista pulled back the quilt, leaving the sheet as a shield over Levi's legs. She flashed him an impish grin to put him at ease. "And just between you and me, I can be a real bitch before I've had my morning toast and coffee."

Levi glanced over Crista's curly head at Nash, smiling like a cowboy in rodeo heaven. "I doubt that."

"Do you? Then maybe you need to consult my ex-husband. He'd be happy to verify it."

Levi's blue-eyed gaze darted back to Crista while she massaged his legs. "The man must have been a fool if he gave you walking papers."

"Mutual disenchantment," Crista said matter-of-factly, her hands working in practiced rhythm. "I have to be charming and cooperative all day at the office, and during private visitations with patients. After five—if I'm lucky to get off that early—is another story." She glanced up, flinging Levi a mock glare. "So don't press your luck with me, pal. I let your friend Griffin off easy the other day, only because I was punching a time clock. I'm on *my* time right now."

Levi's laughter resounded off the metal exercise equipment and vibrated through Nash's heart. It had been a long time since he had heard that sound. In fact, Levi hadn't been so amused since the last time several cowboys had laid over at Chulosa for an old-fashioned outdoor barbecue.

In silence, Nash watched Crista work her magic. All the while, she drew Levi into casual conversation. As he had hoped, she had downplayed her appearance and listed all her failing graces—in an attempt to create the effect Nash had asked for.

Crista was definitely a pro. And after the rude remarks Nash had made to her, he felt the need to apologize—in earnest.

"Turn over, Levi. I want to massage your back," Crista requested.

"I'll help—"

Crista tossed Nash a glance that stopped him in his tracks. "No, Levi can do it by himself, and he should do it each time he wakes during the night. There's no need for you to do what he's perfectly capable of managing by himself."

Nash nodded mutely and backed off.

"Oh, Good Time, I forgot to tell you that Hal called while you were gone," Levi reported, contentedly resting his cheek against the pillow. A sigh escaped his lips as Crista kneaded his shoulders and spine.

Nash crossed his arms over his chest and propped himself against the wall, refusing to let himself speculate on how those hands would feel on his body. He didn't want to know.

"How are the go-rounds coming along at the rodeo?" Nash inquired.

"Hal's leading the saddle bronc competition. He's second in the standings in bareback riding."

"What about calf roping?" Nash prompted.

"He said he caught a hoof in the ribs, but he managed to throw and tie his calf with a respectable score. Hal says he's sore as hell, though.

"Hal and Choctaw Jim should be back in a couple of weeks, after they hustle small-time rodeos in New Mexico and Texas. Hal said to tell you that you better have Bowlegs ready, because Popeye has gotten a rigorous workout lately. Every cowboy wants to lease him. Since we're getting twenty-five percent of the winnings for the use of the horse, Hal and Choctaw Jim are coming out way ahead on expenses."

Nash smiled faintly at the news. Popeye more than paid his feed bill and the long hours spent training the horse were worth the time invested. Blue Duck was also being ridden by a number of cowboys, as well as the lightning-quick Arabian and quarter horse that Nash had trained specifically for calf-roping events. With three horses in contention for Roping and Bulldogging Horse of the Year, plus Bowlegs as promising potential, the Griffin brothers were making good money off their livestock on the rodeo circuit . . .

A pang of longing assailed Nash. Somewhere between his heart and soul he felt the tug to revisit the world he had known. Although he had vowed to God—and himself—that he would walk away and never look back, there were times when the craving for the old life was so strong he could almost taste it.

He would never again get caught up in the raucous night life of his younger years, but deep down inside, Nash missed the thrill, excitement, and challenge of rodeo.

Nash focused on the alluring woman whose soothing voice had nearly lulled Levi to sleep. The younger man's eyes were at half-mast, a dreamy expression on his features.

Nash may have complicated matters by dragging Crista to the ranch, but seeing Levi's contented smile somehow made it worth the repercussions that would inevitably follow.

"You made my day, Crista," Levi murmured drowsily. When she rose from the bed, he pried one eye open and smiled up at her. "Thanks, angel."

"You're welcome, Levi. Get a good night's sleep."

"Will you be back Tuesday?"

Crista darted a quick glance at Nash. "I'll have to think about it. It would have to be after my regular hours—when I'm customarily in my worst moods. It wouldn't be fair to unleash my problems on you."

"I'll take my chances, every chance I get," Levi sighed groggily.

Like a shadow, Nash followed Crista through Levi's private quarters. The ever-present wolf, she caught herself thinking.

"Thanks, Curly. Dogger needed that."

"I didn't feel any spastic tension," Crista remarked. "He really is in good physical condition, the best I've seen in a while. Levi didn't really need me tonight."

"Yes, he did," Nash contradicted. "He needed a woman's tender touch, the sound of a feminine voice." Then Nash made the mistake of staring into those evergreen eyes, and words he hadn't meant to say tumbled out. "So did I, Curly. I just refuse to let myself remember there's more to life than work."

To Crista's startled surprise, Nash reached up to ruffle her unruly curls, and even cracked a rare smile. "There's something about you that reminds me of a kid I once knew—a long, long time ago, when I was giving rodeo clinics in college. She had a head full of the blondest curls I've ever seen. A couple of shades lighter than yours."

Crista stopped breathing. She wasn't sure she wanted Nash to remember little Mary Crista Delaney—the lonely, isolated tomboy who had lost her heart to a secret fantasy. She didn't want Nash to touch her, either. There was an earthy sensuality about Nash Griffin, and it took voluntary effort on her part to resist what seemed to come naturally around him.

Resolutely, Crista retreated into her own space. Survival instinct warned her not to venture any closer to the fire she sensed within him.

Nash dropped his hand to his side, unconsciously brushing away the feel of those silken curls sliding over his callused palm. He stared at the air over Crista's left shoulder. It was easier to talk to her that way—avoiding those eyes and that beguiling face.

"I'm sorry about what I said to you yesterday afternoon. You were right. I was way out of line."

When Nash pivoted and ambled toward the dimly-lit living room, Crista frowned, puzzled. "Aren't you going to take me home? Or am I supposed to walk?"

"I think it best if Bernie drives you back," Nash replied before he disappeared around the corner.

After a moment, the sturdy-looking cook strode into the hall, smiling like a beacon in the darkness. "Well, of course I'll give the little lady a lift. It'll get me out of this house. I've been stuck here so much lately I feel like an overworked housewife." His dark eyes twinkled with ornery amusement. "Wanna stop by Mangy Dog for a nightcap?"

"Better take a rain check, Bernie. I left my boots and jeans at home, so I would probably stick out like a sore thumb."

"A sore thumb? Not hardly," Bernie chuckled as he clamped his hand around her elbow to steer her toward the door." But you're right about one thing. Nobody wears Nikes to a cowboy honky-tonk, unless he's itching for a good fight. I'd hate to break my other arm trying to protect you."

When Bernie scurried to open the door, Crista glanced back at the looming shadow. Dim light reflected off those golden eyes, again reminding her of a watching wolf. She caught herself wondering what Nash was thinking, how he perceived her. Then she quickly told herself she didn't care what he was thinking. He had made it clear that he intended to keep his distance. She sincerely hoped he did—or so she tried to convince herself.

Without another glance, Crista walked toward the battered truck, vowing she wasn't wasting time or emotion on Nash Griffin. He had his life to live and she had hers. They were going to continue leading separate lives, even if her sessions with Levi forced them to cross paths. And that, she assured herself, was exactly the way they both wanted it.

"How did everything go Saturday night?" Jill Forrester demanded the instant she appeared at Crista's office door.

Crista took a cautious sip of steaming coffee—she'd already scalded her tongue once—and then smiled. "Fine. How was your date?"

Jill picked up her schedule for the day, glancing mischievously at her boss over the top of the clipboard. "I didn't have one. I lied so you and my big brother could have some privacy."

Crista clucked her tongue playfully. "Scheming doesn't become you, Jill."

Jill frowned in disappointment. "You aren't going to tell me any more than my close-mouthed brother did, are you? You're spoiling all my fun, you know."

"Your brother is very . . . nice." Crista groaned inwardly when the word tripped off her tongue.

"I can tell you for sure that it's a far better match than The Dragon."

Crista glanced up, feigning shock. "You considered matching Jack up with The Dragon . . . I mean Nash?"

Jill rolled her eyes. "Stupidity doesn't become *you,* boss," she flung back playfully. "I had Old Ironsides in mind for The Dragon."

Crista had harbored the same spiteful thought. But the better she got to know Nash Griffin, the more she believed he needed someone to understand his situation, someone who appreciated his strong sense of responsibility to his friend.

But, Crista hastily reminded herself, that *someone* wasn't going to be her. She couldn't be as objective as she needed to be if she was fighting like the very devil not to take Nash Griffin personally.

Jill stopped smiling when she noticed the name of a patient on her schedule. "I've been concerned about the little girl who was admitted after the auto accident."

Crista nodded. "Crushed right femur, shattered radius and ulna. Dr. Peters did reconstructive surgery to piece Lisa Chandler's arm and leg together. I checked on her Friday afternoon. We'll treat her with aggressive rehab."

"It's her emotional state that worries me most," Jill confided.

"Like minds must run on the same track," Crista murmured. "I stopped in to see her again this morning. Too bad her mother didn't think to make the same effort before she sauntered off to work. Janelle Chandler is treating Lisa's injuries as if they were an imposition. The poor kid is barely thirteen and her face is marred by lacerations and bruises. She's getting no sympathy from home, and I'm not so sure I believe that story about one of Janelle's boyfriends driving the car when Lisa was injured. It all sounds fishy to me."

"It sounds a little fishy to me, too, especially since this supposed boyfriend wasn't at the scene of the wreck."

"That's because he went for help," Crista said with a smirk. "Or at least that's Janelle's story. Lisa must have been ordered not to discuss the incident, because I can't pry any information out of her."

Jill glanced wryly at Crista. "The bouquet you gave Lisa was a nice touch, by the way. It looked amazingly familiar. It didn't happen to be the one Jack gave you, did it?"

Crista squirmed awkwardly. "I decided Lisa might appreciate them since her mother didn't bother to bring her anything."

"And what about the musical jewelry box with the ring and two expensive necklaces?" Jill prodded.

"My ex-husband gave those to me," Crista explained with a shrug. "I figured his girlfriend received the same gifts on birthdays and Christmas, so Jon wouldn't forget *what* he gave to *whom*. Lisa needed something that sparkled and chimed to perk up her spirits."

"You're very generous, boss."

Crista smiled cryptically. "That little girl reminds me of somebody I used to know."

A knowing grin pursed Jill's lips. "It must be that curly blond hair. One of these days, we'll have to sit down and have a nice long chat about your mysterious past over a few cocktails."

Gesturing toward the door, Crista prompted Jill to begin her appointed rounds. "You really should adopt half a dozen kids," Crista advised. "Your mothering instincts are being wasted on me and your brother. And just so you know, I'm not one to dwell on the past. Too much time wasted on things that can't be changed, I always say."

Jill took her cue and strode off, pausing just outside the open door. "Who's getting stuck with the Levi Cooper case?"

"Yours truly."

"And when do you think you'll find time—in between monthly supervisional visits, scheduling, and evaluations?"

"I'll make time after my regular hours."

"I'll call the fire department," Jill volunteered. "Maybe they'll loan you a fireproof suit so you can escape from the dragon's den alive."

Crista chuckled in amusement. "Jack and I believe the wolf persona suits Nash better. Your brother advocates carrying a shiny gold cross and I tend to agree."

"There, you see? You and Jack do have a lot in common!"

"Get to work, Forrester," Crista demanded, giving her best impersonation of the admiral-inspector.

"Yes, ma'am." With a snappy salute, Jill clicked her heels together, wheeled around, and marched off in crisp, military-regulation strides.

Nash walked into the spacious office beside Levi's living suite to see the younger man hanging up the phone. "Who was that?"

Levi flinched, unaware that he had company. "You startled me, Good Time. I didn't hear you come in."

After tossing the endorsed check on the desk, Nash dropped into the empty chair. "I sold one of the three-year-old colts to the rancher who lives near Lawton. He wanted a fast-moving mount for his son to train for the high school regional rodeo."

Levi picked up the check and glanced at the

amount, whistling appreciatively. "The rancher didn't mind paying a pretty price, did he?"

"It's a good horse—"

"Worth every cent," Levi broke in, smiling. "Yeah, I know. I used to ride the ones you and Hal trained."

Nash shifted in his chair. He, too, remembered those days when Levi roped, bulldogged, and rode with the best of them.

How could Nash ever forget?

"Did Hal and Choctaw Jim get off all right this morning?" Levi questioned as he shuffled the papers on his desk, concealing the legal document that had been on top of the pile.

Nash nodded. "We had a little difficulty loading Bowlegs in the stock trailer with the other horses. But Bowlegs is off to the rodeo under my protest. I still don't think the horse is ready, but Hal wants to give Popeye a rest. They were headed to a small-time rodeo in Texas that uses lighter-weight rough stock. The competition shouldn't be as fierce as it has been the past few weeks."

"Hal can handle Bowlegs," Levi said confidently. "I've watched both of you give new mounts crash courses and on-the-job training during competition. You can make a horse perform for you even if the mount isn't quite ready."

"That was when Hal and I were younger, and more daring and foolish," Nash contended as he rubbed his aching shoulder. "These days the ground seems to be getting harder than it used to be. And previously injured body parts wake up slower and don't loosen up until after a hard day's sweat."

Levi stared out the window, surveying the herd

of horses grazing on the thick carpet of grass. "And some parts never wake up at all . . ."

Nash soundly cursed his careless tongue. Here he sat, complaining about a few measly aches and pains while Levi simply *sat*. Damn it, Nash swore, he had the sensitivity of a fence post!

"I'll stick the plastic steer skull on a hay bale after lunch. Why don't you come down to the barn and cast a few loops while I'm trimming Popeye's hooves."

"Not today." Levi turned his chair toward the bedroom, tucking the document beside him. "I changed my hospital visitation from tomorrow to today. I'll be gone most of the afternoon."

Nash watched Levi roll away. Those long sessions at the hospital never seemed to do much good. Several times Nash had offered to go along, just to see what those expensive rehab sessions entailed, but Levi insisted on going alone.

Levi hadn't managed to stand on his feet at home so what the hell were those physicians doing at the hospital?

Not a whole hell of a lot, he was sure. But then, he wasn't about to let Levi give the sessions up. If there was even a remote possibility that Levi could learn to walk again, Nash vowed to pay for it.

"Oh, before I forget," Levi called from the bedroom, "I have a medical form for you to sign. Hal signed his John Hancock last night before he turned in."

Before Nash could pry his weary body from the chair, Levi reappeared. Levi laid the medical form—with its concealed document taped beneath it—on the desk. With a stack of stapled medical evaluations camouflaging the information on the legal paper, Levi handed a pen to Nash.

"It's just more of the same red tape for the insurance company and hospital business office," he said with a dismissive shrug.

Nash trustingly placed his name above his brother's and dated the protruding form on the bottom page. "Anything else, Dogger?"

"Nope, that covers it," Levi said, turning away with a secretive smile. "I'll drop the papers off on my way to therapy."

"Do you have plenty of gas in your van?" Nash asked as he rose to retrieve the cellular phone he insisted Levi carry with him at all times.

"Fueled and ready," Levi confirmed, stuffing the phone in the pouch beside him. "I'll deposit this check in the bank on my way through town."

"Are you sure you don't want me to ride along with you? I could—"

Levi waved Nash into silence. "No need for that. This is my contribution to the ranch, after all. You and the other men supply the brawn. I have to settle for running errands in my van." He tossed Nash a breezy smile. "Besides, I enjoying getting out of the house. The therapists say activity is essential. And Crista advocates independence, you know."

Nash rolled Levi outside and then backed the handicap van from the garage. Levi insisted on tucking his file inside his chair and handling the loading procedure by himself. Once he had rolled onto the hydraulic lift that elevated him into the van, he moved forward to lock his chair into position behind the hand-operated brake and accelerator.

Nash watched Levi drive away. If the situation

were reversed, Nash knew he would be every bit as insistent as Levi about operating his own vehicle and making a personal contribution to the ranch. The human need to be needed was good for the soul, Nash reminded himself.

However, overwhelming guilt and regret prompted Nash to leap into action at the slightest indication Levi might need assistance. It had become reflexive.

"I'm ready!" Bernie called as he sailed out the front door. "Let's go halter-break a few colts, Good Time."

Nash watched the fire-engine-red van disappear over the rise to the north before he pivoted toward the barn. It was going to take a hard day's sweat to lubricate his tendons and muscles. He had been so tired the previous night that he felt as if he had slept under his bed rather than on it. Nash suspected Levi awoke feeling that way, every morning of his life.

"So keep your damned trap shut in the future and don't complain, especially to Levi," Nash scolded himself on his way to the barn.

Six

Crista had settled into the routine of visiting Levi on her way home from work. She and Nash had been taking a wide berth around each other. She had seen him in the corrals, training horses or trotting off across the pasture to check cattle. Leon, the cow dog wearing a red kerchief instead of a collar, was Nash's constant companion.

It was as if the prowling wolf—and Crista definitely agreed with Jack Forrester's comparison— was roaming his territory, allowing Crista to intrude while he kept a distant vigil.

Levi, on the other hand, was always eager to see her, always greeting her with a cheery smile. Crista was being particularly careful around Levi. Her touch was strictly therapeutic and her conversation intimated nothing more than friendship and professional concern.

Levi had adapted well to his limitations. Crista's only concern was his remarks about Nash's and Hal's insistence on granting him every whim. Levi Cooper was being spoiled worse than a newborn infant, and in Crista's opinion, it was an unhealthy situation.

When she questioned Levi about the rodeo accident, he refused to elaborate, merely mumbling about a bad night in Vegas. Crista still didn't have a clear understanding of why the Griffin brothers—Nash in particular—had become so dedicated to Levi's rehabilitation.

Crista finally decided to pose questions to the only resident in this all-male community who had the gift of gab. Bernie Bryant, she had noticed, enjoyed talking about anything and everything. Crista's opportunity to quiz Bernie came one evening when Levi received a phone call and sent Crista away with a request for privacy.

Bernie was in the kitchen, preparing supper, when Crista sought him out.

"Something wrong?" Bernie inquired when Crista appeared at the door dressed in a shapeless flannel shirt and baggy jeans, her hair piled atop her head.

"No, Levi is just taking a call."

"Again?" Bernie glanced up from the stove. "That man has been on the phone more than he's been on the exercise equipment lately. I wonder what's going on."

Crista wandered over to pluck up a slice of tomato from the salad on the counter. She was famished.

"I need some background information about the accident," Crista said between bites. "I don't want to upset Levi by recalling bad memories, and I haven't been able to ask Nash since he's always busy."

That wasn't exactly the truth, but she didn't figure Bernie needed to know that.

"Well, it isn't something either of them wants to discuss," Bernie replied. "I wasn't there when it happened, you understand, but I've picked up bits and pieces."

Eavesdropped was more like it, Crista suspected. Bernie, it seemed, was as curious as she was.

"I know Nash feels responsible. He's said that much. His sense of obligation is more than obvious."

Bernie flipped the chicken fried steaks in the skillet and then glanced over his bulky shoulder at Crista. "Well, it all goes back to the first year when Levi started traveling the circuit. He was raised at Boys Town in Nebraska, you know. His folks had abandoned him when he was barely two years old. Rumors were that his parents were part of some weird religious cult." Bernie snorted. "I can't imagine anybody running off and leaving their own kid."

Neither could Crista. It was a concept she had never been able to grasp.

"Levi grew up, hankering to rodeo," Bernie continued while he cooked. "He showed up at a couple of benefit performances and clinics the Griffin brothers gave for underprivileged kids. Levi was quite an athlete and a fast learner, I'm told."

Levi's athletic prowess was evident, Crista reminded herself. He was built like a football player, with shoulders like a bull.

"Hal and Nash pulled a few strings to make sure Levi got a rodeo scholarship. The kid was good and he was tough. Sometimes he was a little too aggressive in the arena, but Hal and Nash coached him. Levi quit college a year early to turn pro. He traveled with Nash before and after Hal suddenly decided to join the service. The three musketeers followed the circuit together when Hal came back."

Bernie paused and shifted awkwardly.

"They . . . um . . . were known as the Wild Bunch during their heyday. The night life on the circuit can be . . . er . . ."

"I get the picture, Bernie," Crista assured him. "Good Time Griffin and Company, right?"

"Er . . . right. Anyhow, Levi liked to stick with the best. Nash was just that, and Hal was making his comeback after he . . ." Bernie cleared his throat and shrugged enigmatically. "Well, that's another story."

From what Bernie had said, Crista was able to put two and two together. "So Levi idolized Nash and was determined to follow in his footsteps. Did Levi become too daring in the arena, trying to match Nash's accomplishments?"

"Yeah, the kid definitely had stars in his eyes. He also had a longing for All-Around Cowboy titles, silver belt buckles, and hand-tooled trophy saddles."

"Nash had already clinched his third straight title, after his closest competition scratched during a saddle bronc ride. From what I've been able to piece together, Nash's winning-night celebration was nothing short of a bash. He was supposed to haze for Levi during the last bulldogging go-round. Levi wanted to finish in the money so bad he could taste it. At the last minute he decided to bulldog off one of the horses the cowboys used for hazing in that event."

Crista picked up a stalk of celery and chewed on it. The picture forming in her mind was becoming grimmer by the minute, especially since she was already familiar with rodeo and she knew the tragic outcome.

"Since Nash was still groggy from too much whiskey and not enough sleep, he didn't offer

much protest about switching mounts. He just
climbed aboard the horse to keep the steer on
line for Levi. But the horses were out of their
usual positions and they cut the wrong directions
at the worst possible time. Levi took a headlong
dive for the steer anyway. The livestock collided
and Levi was pinned between the steer and the
falling horse. I guess Nash's reactions weren't
what they should have been and he couldn't give
Levi the space he needed to recover."

Crista winced. She had taken enough falls beneath thundering hooves to realize a pile-up like
the one Bernie described could be disastrous. "So
Nash shoulders the blame for Levi's paralysis because he had celebrated his own glory so hard
he was of no use in a crisis."

Bernie nodded. "Hal wasn't much better. He
felt guilty as hell, too. Hal had been at the chutes
before the last go-round and had offered to take
Nash's place, even though Hal had injured his
arm during a saddle bronc ride.

"And if you'd been here the first year after the
accident, watching Levi's mood swings and bouts
of depression, you would realize why Hal and
Nash got accustomed to doing his bidding. They
were willing to do almost anything to boost Levi's
spirits.

"They were all the family the kid had. The Griffins even went so far as to deed an undivided
third of this ranch to Levi, just so the kid would
feel he really had a home of his own."

Crista frowned pensively, but she didn't inter-
rupt since Bernie was on a roll.

"The whole bunch of us have done everything
in our power to keep Levi's morale up. Choctaw
Jim started renting out his farmhouse and moved

in here to lend a hand. The extra cash helps pay the expenses."

Crista admired the cowboys' dedication, and she understood why Nash had become so fiercely protective. She also knew what those bouts of depression could be like, because she had witnessed them firsthand with other patients. It wasn't something easily forgotten.

"Since the accident Nash ramrods the ranch while Choctaw Jim and Hal follow the circuit," Bernie elaborated. "Hal even hires himself out to ranchers who have problems rounding up wild strays, and Nash trains and sells horses in his spare time."

Spare time? Crista hadn't noticed Nash having much of that. To date, she hadn't seen Nash Griffin sitting in one place long enough to gather dust. Usually, he was so tired that he leaned on the nearest wall, when he did take time to catch his breath.

"I keep telling Nash he needs to enter a rodeo, but he won't leave the ranch for more than a few hours at a time—"

Bernie slammed his mouth shut when he caught sight of Levi rolling through the dining room. "You had another phone call, Dogger? I hope you haven't started dialing those weird 900 numbers."

Levi chuckled as he wheeled into the kitchen. "Naw, I've just been visiting with a few friends I've met in town."

When the back door creaked open, Crista glanced up to see Nash—in his customary ensemble of faded jeans, shirt, and chaps. Her gaze lingered on him momentarily, before she looked the other way. Neither of them offered a word of greeting.

Levi glanced back and forth between his therapist and his friend and smiled secretly to himself. "Stay for supper tonight, Crista," he requested. "This is our pitch night, but since Hal and Choctaw Jim are on the road, we could use an extra card player." His gaze darted back to Nash, who looked none too pleased. "Ask her to stay, Good Time. Dinner would be our way of thanking Crista for the extra hours she's been spending here."

"I really should go," Crista insisted, well aware that she had already overstayed her welcome where Nash Griffin was concerned.

Levi rolled forward, blocking her path. "Aw, come on, Crista. Say you'll stay. We would enjoy the company, wouldn't we, fellas?"

Crista was certain Nash would enjoy nothing of the kind. She waited, wondering if the brawny cowboy would bend to Levi's will the way he usually did. Sooner or later she was going to have to broach the subject of catering to Levi with Nash again. That should be loads of fun, she predicted. The wolf-dragon would probably singe her ears with curses before he chewed her up and spit her out. Hazards of her job, Crista reminded herself grimly. Telling people what they would rather not hear was never easy.

"Ask her to stay, Nash," Levi prodded. "I really would like a little female company. It's been a while, you know."

Crista decided, right there and then, that Nash bent to only one man's will—Levi Cooper's. When Levi flashed that boyish grin of his—a tactic he had mastered when he wanted to wrap someone around his finger—Nash was hooked, reeled and landed.

Nash sighed and then stared over the top of Crista's head. "Stay for supper, Curly. We would enjoy it."

"No, I really can't. I brought some evaluation files home to complete tonight. I've been running behind lately."

Her visits with Lisa Chandler had put her even farther behind schedule. In addition, Admiral Darwin was due for a surprise inspection any day now. Daisy Darwin was itching for the chance to criticize Crista's efficiency and tattle to the administrators.

"You have to eat somewhere, don't you? Why not here?" Levi persisted.

Scowling, Nash surged across the kitchen, his spurs clinking against the ceramic tile. "Sit down, Curly. Like Levi said, we owe you a few meals for service above and beyond the call of duty."

Avoiding his touch, Crista sat down before Nash could physically plant her in the chair.

Dinner was a treat for Crista. She had been existing on microwaved entrées for more days than she cared to count. Levi and Bernie competed to take control of the conversation in order to entertain her, while Nash ate in silence. He glanced everywhere except at Crista.

"Did that black mare ever have her foal?" Levi asked after he polished off his first mountain-size helping of mashed potatoes and gravy.

"Yep. Right before I came in for supper," Nash said.

"You should take Crista down to the barn to

see the latest arrival," Levi suggested. "I'll help Bernie clear the table and set up for our pitch game."

"I need to—"

Before Crista could object to going anywhere alone with Nash, Levi interrupted her. "There's nothing more amusing than watching newborn foals try to gain their feet. Nash wouldn't mind taking you to the barn. He's probably going to check on the foal again anyway."

Crista muttered silently at another of Levi's manipulative techniques. He was an absolute marvel.

Out of habit, Nash did Levi's bidding, she noted. Nash swallowed down his last mouthful of steak—the man ate like a starved elephant—and then led the way to the kitchen door.

In resignation, Crista followed him. As they ambled down the moonlit sidewalk Nash had constructed to accommodate Levi, Crista studied his broad silhouette.

"How long do you intend to keep this up?" she asked.

"Keep what up?"

"This beck-and-call routine with Levi."

Nash pulled up short and rounded on her. His glittering golden eyes reflected the light that beamed though the kitchen window. "You made it clear a couple of weeks ago that your business was strictly yours. And my business is definitely mine," he snapped. "How I handle Levi isn't your problem. You may be a hot-shot physical therapist, but you're not my shrink."

Crista didn't back down one inch. "Can't you see what Levi is doing? He's soaking up your sympathy and preying on your guilt. He may be confined to a chair, but he sure as hell has plenty of power and influence around here."

Nash growled several foul oaths, then stormed off.

Crista tramped after him with all the tenacity of a pit bulldog. "Since you think you're responsible for his accident, you bend over so far backward it's a wonder you haven't fractured *your* lumbar vertebrae—"

Nash halted so abruptly that Crista smashed her nose against the rigid wall of his back. When he lurched around, snarling, she braced herself. She had known this would be no picnic. Sure enough, it wasn't.

"Let's get one thing straight here and now, Curly," Nash sneered. "The only reason I've allowed you to come here is because Levi has been in an exceptionally good mood since you started showing up. I sure as hell don't like having you around and I'm sure this is going to cost him dearly. I believe I've made that clear enough already."

"Yes, you have," she threw back at him. *"Blunt* is your middle name, after all. But just because you ended up with a headache the size of Chulosa Ranch the day you hazed for Levi in Vegas—"

His hand shot out, clenching painfully around her elbow, jerking her close enough for her to feel his hot breath on her cheeks. "Who the hell told you that?"

Crista grimaced when his vise-like grip cut off the circulation in her arm. "It doesn't matter who."

"It does to me, damn it. It couldn't have been Levi. He doesn't want to discuss the incident any more than I do. We made a pact years ago to let it lie." He glared suspiciously at her. "Unless you charmed it out of him. I warned you about personal remarks."

"And I warned you about spoiling Levi beyond repair." Crista wrenched her arm free and shook it until the blood began to flow normally. Damn, the man didn't know his own strength, especially when his temper was high. "All you've succeeded in doing is teaching Levi lessons he shouldn't have learned. You'll make a monster of him, if you aren't careful—"

"Something wrong out there?"

Nash and Crista simultaneously pivoted to see Levi poised in the doorway, smiling his charismatic smile.

"Everything is just fine," Nash managed in a reasonably civil tone. "Come on, Curly."

Crista found herself propelled down the sidewalk at such a swift pace that she had to trot to keep up. She was all ready to launch into another heated debate . . . until she entered the barn to see the coal-black foal struggling to its feet. The mare nickered encouragingly, nudging her awkward offspring to stand and nurse.

Chuckling in amusement, Crista strode over to watch the foal's bony legs fold up like a lawn chair, dumping it in the straw-lined stall. Patiently, the mare repeated the procedure.

"She's breathtaking," Crista murmured.

She had forgotten the simple pleasure of childhood on her father's ranch. Despite the conflicts of later years, there had been many peaceful, enjoyable moments. Many of them centered around events like this, watching life beget new life and offering a gentle, coaxing hand to the new arrivals.

Watching the birth of calves, lambs, and foals had always fascinated Crista. Just seeing newborns struggle to achieve what she often took for granted could mellow her worst moods.

"It's a stud colt," Nash corrected, smiling despite himself.

"Have you named him yet?"

As if invisible tentacles had grasped her, Crista was drawn toward the lighted stall—and its beckoning gate. She was accustomed to horses and quickly entered the stall to stroke the sleek head that was two sizes too big for the rest of the foal's spindly body.

Nash blinked in surprise. "What are you doing?"

"Getting acquainted." When the mare stamped nervously, Crista reach up to stroke her quivering neck. "It's okay, girl. I just want a closer look at your baby. No harm intended."

One of Crista's daily chores—if one could call something this pleasurable a chore—was to teach the colts not to fear human touch. Part of the training program her father practiced was rubbing down and physically handling foals from the moment of their arrival. The procedure, known as imprinting, made breaking and training easier.

The instant Crista set her hands on the wobbly creature she realized she had been practicing forms of physical therapy since she was a child. Cole Delaney had unknowingly taught her what he later objected to as her chosen profession.

Before Crista was aware of what she had done, she had braced the colt on its stilt-like legs and turned mother and foal nose to nose. Her practiced hands swept from forelock to rump, gliding down both hips to each tiny hoof.

God, how long had it been since she had bathed a foal with her scent and her touch? Too long, Crista decided.

All the while she was reassuring the leery creature that there was nothing to fear from the human hand, she spoke to the mare and foal in hushed tones. Every now and then she reached up to assure the mare that no harm would come to her fragile offspring.

After a few minutes, Crista remembered she wasn't alone. Abruptly, she glanced up to see those penetrating amber eyes boring into her. Nash was propped against the railing and he spoke not one word. He simply watched her work with the colt. Another minute elapsed before Crista heard his muffled footsteps retreating through the hay-lined barn.

This was much-needed therapy for her, Crista realized, smiling contentedly. Her conflict with Nash seemed days ago rather than minutes.

Since there were unused corrals behind Crista's rented farmhouse, she wondered if Jim Pryce would mind if she stabled a horse there. Riding for pleasure rather than competition, without her father standing over her, criticizing every mistake, would be . . .

Crista sighed heavily. "God, Dad," she murmured, "I've been carrying around a lot of angry baggage all these years. Just one word of praise or encouragement from you could have made a world of difference. Just once, I wish I could have done something right in your eyes."

Crista cut a glance over her shoulder when she heard the gate creak open. Nash had reappeared from the tack room, carrying cotton swabs and a bottle of iodine to clean the foal's navel—a precautionary measure to prevent infection.

Reflexively, Crista took the antiseptic from Nash as she had often done under her father's orders. She felt Nash's curious gaze, the silent questions her behavior prompted. But he didn't ask and she didn't volunteer information.

Why should she? She could be as stubborn and uncommunicative as Nash when she felt like it. Besides, exchanging information might lead to friendship and Crista wasn't sure that was such a good idea. Better to harbor fantasies from the past than become emotionally involved with the man Nash had become. Too bad that fun-loving, good-natured cowboy she once loved had turned into such a sourpuss. He might have been her dream come true.

Yeah, right, Crista thought with a grin.

"Something amusing about doctoring a newborn foal, Curly?" came the quiet baritone voice beside her.

Crista willfully put the past back where it belonged and glanced at Nash. When his hand brushed across hers, holding the newborn at bay when the wobbly creature stamped too close, Crista withdrew. She shrugged nonchalantly, forcefully ignoring her reaction to what should have been a harmless touch.

"I'm simply enjoying myself. Is that a problem for you?"

Nash completed his ministrations and came to his feet, his free hand gliding absently down the colt's sleek back. "Nope. Would you like to tell me where you learned about gentling foals, a trick that is usually known only to horse trainers?"

"Nope." She grinned elfishly. "You want to tell me this foal's name?"

"Curly Sue," Nash decided on the spur of the moment.

"A stud named Sue?"

Nash broke into an uncharacteristic grin. "It will make him tough as hell."

"You might regret it when the time comes for you to break Curly Sue to saddle and bridle."

"It shouldn't be a problem, not if you're hanging around here, practicing *imprinting* techniques on him."

When Nash strode back to the tack room to replace the supplies, Crista let herself out of the stall. Leaning against the rail, she watched the foal make its instinctive search for nourishment. Crista stood there for the longest time, picking and choosing memories from the past, gathering a select few that had been untainted by her domineering father.

Cole Delaney had always pushed too hard and Mary Crista had inherited or developed—she wasn't sure which—one helluva stubborn streak. But one thing was for sure: despite the conflicts between widowed father and daughter, Crista was still a country girl at heart. Moving to Kanima Springs was like a pilgrimage, and she had discovered this was exactly where she needed to be. She kept remembering the sweet simplicities of life that had somehow been submerged in sea of disappointments.

Nash set the medication in the cabinet and glanced back to study the shapely profile beside the stall. From the doorway he could stare at

Crista without having to guard his expression.
Damnation, he had watched her smooth her
hands over the colt and found himself wishing
they were gliding over him.

Nash had been avoiding Crista, trying not to
notice her when she paid visits to Levi. He had
ridden miles inside the corrals on raunchy horses
and thundered off to check cattle and fences—
anything to stay out of her path. But the mere
thought of her, the forbidden urges, the scent of
her, always caught up with him. It was insane, un-
productive, and frustrating.

Nash had tried to leave the impression that he
had no interest in becoming closer to Crista. He
kept repeating all the necessary platitudes to ward
off the attraction he didn't want to feel.

And still the thought of her burned his mind
like a brand, and passion sizzled through his veins
like fire.

"Damn, Griffin," Nash grumbled at himself.
"You know the rules better than anyone. Hell,
you made the rules. Hands off her—and every
other female on the continent. What Levi can't
have, you can't either. That's the deal. You're the
one who put Levi in that goddam wheelchair."

Nash was, however, curious to know where
Crista had learned so much about handling
horses. He stamped back across the stall.

"Come on, Curly," he muttered as he strode
down the aisle. "Let's get one game of pitch over
with so you can go home—"

Nash didn't know whether to call it bad luck
or bad timing when Crista spun around at the
same instant he surged down the narrow lane.
They collided like meteors. His forward momen-
tum sent Crista stumbling backward. Years of ro-

deo experience and reflexive instinct prompted Nash to grab Crista's arm to steady both of them. Unfortunately, Nash missed his intended target. His hand clamped around one full, firm breast nestled beneath the baggy flannel shirt.

Nash wasn't sure who gasped the loudest. It was too close to call. As for himself, he could feel his breath vibrating past his clenched teeth.

Now he'd really gone and done it. He had touched what he had outlined that night in front of the mirror . . . And found himself dreaming about every night since. Damn . . .

Nash heard himself groan when his arms involuntarily contracted, pulling Crista closer, wishing he had the good sense to push her away. His willpower had completely deserted him at the moment when he needed it most.

And suddenly, it was as if he were about to cartwheel off the side of a wild bronc in a rodeo arena when his lips made the softest landing imaginable.

Nash found himself standing flush against Crista, absorbing every curve molded to him like a soft leather glove. And damn it to hell, it was that same perfect *fit* that every veteran cowboy sought when he eased down—inch by inch—onto the back of a bull, bronc, or onto his own saddle.

And if ever there was a right fit, this was it . . .

Nash heard the forbidden truth echoing somewhere in the back of his brain. He held Crista so close that he could feel her breath catch at the same instant his did, feel her body arching up to him when his hand slipped down from her waist to splay across the rounded curve of her bottom.

His deprived body reacted violently in the space

of a heartbeat. He was so hard he ached, and his chest burned as if it were clogged with dust.

When Crista's arms slid over his chest, her nails anchoring on the rigid slope of his shoulders, Nash reached down to pull her legs around his hips and braced her against the wooden rails of the stall. Although there were jeans and zippers between his flesh and her soft warmth, it didn't stop him from thrusting instinctively against her, leaving no question as to what his body wanted, needed . . . demanded . . .

The hot, pulsing realization prompted his feverish kiss, the plunging motion of his tongue. It was a poor substitute for the intimacies Nash wanted, but as Levi had said: Sometimes you have to take what you can get, whenever and however you can get it.

And Nash wanted Crista in the worst way.

Nash closed his eyes and savored the taste of her, the delicious feel of her body against his, knowing he was asking for trouble, knowing he was tormenting himself . . .

God have mercy! Nash thought when his mind began to whirl. A deep shudder rippled through him, nearly bringing him to his knees. He scrambled for balance as he had a thousand times when he felt his control slipping with every high-flying leap on the back of a bronc.

Nash was a creature of old habits. He held on tight, because it was second nature not to let go, not to take that embarrassing fall to the turf. Every rodeo instinct was suddenly conspiring against him as his mouth slanted over her parted lips and his body melted into hers, as if they were sharing the same skin—and still couldn't get close enough to satisfy the craving that consumed him.

Let go! the sensible side of his mind screamed as he tasted her, absorbed the luscious feel of her.

Hold on, no matter how it hurts, no matter what happens, the voice of years of rigorous training shouted in contradiction. *Don't ever let go . . .*

When Crista answered every kiss and caress with the same uncontrollable hunger that was driving Nash to the brink, his whole body shuddered in helpless response. Her fingers slipped into his hair, sending his hat tumbling to the ground. Her tongue speared into the recesses of his mouth, matching each ardent thrust of his. Her legs clenched around his hips and he drove against her in something akin to fiendish desperation.

Nash was out of control, craving what he knew he couldn't have.

Only divine intervention would prevent him from making one of the worst mistakes of his life . . . Divine intervention or the unexpected roar of a pickup barreling down the driveway toward the barn . . .

Thank God—or whoever had showed up before Nash forgot every vow he had ever made, forgot everything he ever knew and yielded to overwhelming temptation . . .

Seven

The flare of lights and roar of an engine jerked Nash back to reality so fast he nearly dropped Crista—and himself—in the straw. Gravel crunched beneath tires and horses stamped in the metal trailer hitched to the extended cab pickup that had rolled to a stop outside the barn.

Nash swiveled his head around to see headlights spearing through the floating dust particles, spotlighting him and Crista as if they were on center stage. Nash stepped back, bracing an arm on the top rail of the stall to be sure he *could* still stand. His encounter with Crista left him more shaken than he wanted to admit. Hell and damnation! Nash felt as if he was plugged into an electrical socket!

"Nash, is that you?"

Nash sucked in a breath and willed himself to speak over the thunderous pounding of his pulse. His heart was beating against his ribs like a drumstick on a xylophone. "Of course it's me. Who the hell did you think it was?"

Was that his voice? He sounded like a croaking bullfrog.

Inhaling deeply, Nash made his way to the barn door on what felt like two left feet. "Hal? What are you doing home already? I thought you were hustling two rodeos this week."

Hal Griffin braced his shoulder against the passenger door of the truck and sprawled on the seat. He shifted carefully, hoping to find a position that didn't hurt. There wasn't one—and hadn't been for the last two hundred miles.

"I got run over and stomped on," he called out the open window. "The ribs I bruised at—" Hal glanced at his uncle, who sat behind the steering wheel.

"Where the hell did I catch the flying hoof? We've been on the road so much lately I can't even remember what happened where."

Choctaw Jim stepped down from the cab and circled around to Hal. "Damned if I remember. All the arenas are starting to look the same."

Concern etched Nash's features when the light flicked on inside the cab. Hal was propped up like a rag doll. Nash darted outside to support Hal when Choctaw Jim eased open the door.

"Can you stand up?" Nash asked worriedly.

"Hell no, don't you think I already would have if I could?" When Nash reached through the window to grab his arm, Hal slapped his fingers away. "Just get the horses unloaded. I may decide to spend the night where I am." He sucked in a shallow breath, his bronzed face twisting with discomfort. "I might not have a choice about moving until the pain wears off."

A muddled frown furrowed Hal's brows when a curly head and shapely body swished through the headlight beams. "God, I'm in worse shape than I thought. I'm seeing angels."

"Better than circling buzzards," Nash insisted before glancing back at the object of Hal's hallucination. "Would you take a look at him, Curly, while I stable the horses."

Crista tried to smile and eased closer to the sturdy cowboy who held himself so rigidly that he looked as if he would break to pieces with one false move. "Hal Griffin, I presume."

"Last time I checked. That takes care of me, now who are you?"

"Crista Delaney. I'm a physical therapist," she said before tending to the business at hand. "Have you experienced shortness of breath?"

"Yeah, just now." Hal tried to smile but never made it. He melted back against the seat when Crista's hands sped over the snaps of his tattered shirt and then swept off in hurried inspection. "Go easy on me, honey. I'm one giant bruise."

When Choctaw Jim climbed back into the cab to drive away from the unhitched trailer, Crista bounded into the pickup bed. The truck bounced over the rough path leading to the house and Hal cursed colorfully. By the time Jim stopped beside the porch, Levi and Bernie were awaiting them.

"Bernie, call the hospital and tell—" Crista wasn't allowed to finish.

"This is the end of my trail," Hal interrupted in a pained growl. "No hospitals. We've already spent a fortune on them."

Crista gnashed her teeth and slid off the side of the truck. "Damned bullheaded Griffins—both of them."

Crista took command of the situation when Choctaw Jim, Bernie, and Nash rushed forward to unload Hal. "Keep him braced, so he doesn't have to move his upper torso. Don't put any unnecessary pressure on his ribs and abdomen."

"Shit, that hurts!" Hal hissed through his teeth when Nash tried to prop him upright.

"Spasms," Crista said. "I've got some medication in my bag that will relax the muscles. If you can hang on until we get you in bed, I'll have you on cloud nine before you can blink."

Very carefully, Hal turned his head toward his brother, who had his arms clamped to Jim's, forming a makeshift chair. "Why in the hell is this woman here, anyway?"

"Because she's Levi's new therapist."

Hal cocked his brow in surprise. "Oh, yeah? Did we have a change of policy about that sort of thing while I was gone?"

"You might say that," Nash muttered as he and his uncle eased Hal onto the porch and through the door Crista held open. "And by the way, Uncle, why didn't you tell me you had rented your farm to the little lady?"

Choctaw Jim shrugged and smiled mysteriously. "I guess I just forgot."

Nash snorted, then stared at the mountain of steps to be scaled. Hal was two-hundred-some-odd pounds of solid weight. Maneuvering him upstairs to the bedroom they shared would be no small feat. "Ready, Choctaw?"

"Ready as I'll ever be," Choctaw Jim Pryce replied. "I wish I were twenty years younger and Hal was twenty pounds lighter."

"I'll bring up the rear," Bernie volunteered, positioning himself behind Hal to steady his back.

With extreme care, the cowboys toted their patient upstairs. Under Crista's instruction they placed Hal on the edge of the bed and piled a mountain of pillows against the headboard.

"Nash, bring my medical bag from Levi's quarters,'' Crista ordered as she unbuttoned Hal's soiled shirt.

Nash watched those skillful hands glide over Hal's broad chest and then quickly spun away when Hal managed a pained but devilish grin. An unfamiliar knot coiled in the pit of Nash's belly. Damnation, if he didn't know better—and if he did, he wouldn't admit it to himself or another living soul—he would swear he was jealous of his own brother! Scowling, Nash stalked off to fetch the supplies.

"What's eating him?" Hal questioned between ragged breaths. His pensive gaze drifted from the curvaceous blonde to Bernie Bryant.

Bernie shrugged his bulky shoulders.

Choctaw Jim's bushy gray brows furrowed as he, like Hal, studied the attractive female who had invaded their all-male territory. An enigmatic smile pursed Jim's lips as he glanced toward the door through which Nash had disappeared with noticeable haste.

"Bernie, I could use some hot towels and antiseptic," Crista requested when she spied the red welts and purple bruises that discolored Hal's belly. "Does it hurt to breathe?"

"Yeah." He braced his arms on the bed and grimaced. "You aren't going to tell me that if it hurts, don't do it, are you?"

Evergreen eyes twinkled when Crista smiled down at Hal, nearly stealing what was left of his breath. The room suddenly seemed to light up like a rodeo arena on opening night.

When Nash barreled back into the room, still scowling, Hal had the feeling he knew what was wrong with his brother. It was the age-old prob-

lem that had been the curse of men's lives since
time immemorial—*women!*

"Are you all right, big brother?" Hal inquired,
his gaze bouncing suspiciously between Nash and
Crista.

"I'm not the one whose health is in question
here," Nash muttered.

The gruff tone of his voice, as well as his thunderous expression, caused the other three men
to exchange curious glances.

"Well, actually, it is," Hal contended, trying to
ease into a more comfortable position while
Crista gently pressed her fingertips into the tender ridges of his abdomen. "Choctaw Jim and I
were thinking you might be able to take the
horses back to the rodeo in the morning. Several
of the other cowboys are leasing from us. I've already lost the money I paid for entry fees at
Wichita Falls, but the horses can cover it. You
could take my place in the events at Fort Worth
since the first go-round doesn't begin until tomorrow night."

Nash was all set to decline . . . until his gaze
drifted to Crista, as it had the infuriating habit
of doing when she was around. Considering that
humiliating fiasco in the barn, maybe a few bone-
jarring bucks on the back of a wild bronc would
knock him back to his senses. For sure, he needed
to put some space between himself and temptation.

Although all three men were staring at Nash,
awaiting his decision, Crista's head was bent
downward, concealing her expression as she silently continued her examination. Nash suspected she would welcome his absence. Crista
Delaney didn't seem any more thrilled with the

attraction between them than he was. Although
Nash had vowed not to attend rodeos until Levi
was ready, he was seriously considering breaking
that promise now. And for a damned good reason: self-preservation. He simply could not keep
his hands off Crista Delaney. He had proved that
beyond all doubt tonight.

"I'll take care of the chores while you're gone,
Good Time," Choctaw Jim spoke up.

"And I'll help when I'm not tending Hal and
Levi," Bernie volunteered.

"We could use the extra cash—ouch!" Hal
choked on his breath when Crista located the tenderest spot on his belly.

"Sorry," she apologized quietly.

"Luckily, you're gentler than the horse that
used me for a doormat," Hal said before refocus-
ing on his brother. "It's time for you to get back
on the circuit, Good Time."

Nash stared at his injured brother, wrestling
with conflicting feelings of frustration and guilt.
"You know the deal, Hal."

"Yeah, and we both know the number and
amount of the bills that keep this place in operation. You could walk away with a rodeo purse, no
sweat. The competition shouldn't be too tough
at Fort Worth this year. The leading contenders
are planning to sit these two rodeos out to prepare for the world championship roping and
steer wrestling in Guthrie in a couple of weeks. I
was the projected leader, and you were always better than I was. You'll be a shoo-in."

"Maybe in the old days," Nash amended. "But
I'm out of practice and you've been on the rise
since you came back from the army."

Choctaw Jim studied his older nephew astutely.

"We all know you're still in good condition for roping and riding. You do the same thing for a living that you'll do if you return to the circuit."

When Crista finally lifted her head to peer at him, Nash felt as if he had taken a doubled fist in the gut. He had gotten tangled up in those green eyes and forgot everything except the hunger that had devoured him. For the first time in five years Nash had placed his own needs above Levi Cooper's. If Nash remained at the ranch he would risk succumbing again. He couldn't afford to stay here, even though he had vowed not to go.

"Okay, little brother. I'll haul the horses for the other cowboys and compete at Fort Worth while you're laid up."

Hal nodded—carefully. "Good. Now what about the second rodeo I was planning to hustle next week?"

Nash dragged his gaze away from Crista and stared at his brother. "Fine, but I'll probably bust my butt since I'm out of practice. Then we'll both be flat on our backs, counting the cracks in the woodwork. Now are you happy?"

"Delighted," Hal insisted with a pained grimace.

When Bernie strode off to fetch the supplies Crista had requested, the other men filed out behind him. She focused absolute attention on her patient—a much safer prospect than centering her thoughts on the man who had crumbled her defenses with one kiss.

Crista willfully concentrated on her ministrations. Strange, she thought. Although Hal Griffin could have passed as Nash's twin brother—except for Hal's obsidian eyes—touching him didn't trigger the sparks she had experienced in the barn.

Damn it, she could almost feel his hands roaming over her, gliding over her hips to bring them into contact with . . . She and Nash had been like two nuclear warheads colliding in space . . .

"Hey, lady, take it easy, will you?" Hal snorted. "I've already got bruises on my bruises. Where's that painkiller you were bragging about?"

Crista grabbed her bag to retrieve a syringe. "This will take effect quickly," she assured him. "When you're resting more comfortably, I'll wrap your ribs for support. That will make it easier for you to breathe." She glanced back at her patient. "Have you eaten anything the past couple of hours?"

"Beside the grit in the arena?"

Crista grinned. "That doesn't count as nourishment."

"No, I haven't. I just wanted to get home as fast as I could."

"I'll have Bernie fix you something. This medication will make you sick if you don't have food in your stomach."

"Sicker than the pain?"

"Afraid so," Crista confirmed. "And believe me, cowboy, you won't want to be upchucking while your abdominal muscles are in spasm."

"I'll eat whatever Bernie decides to serve." Hal braced on an elbow and eased onto the pillows. "Go ahead and stick me. I live for pain, you know."

Crista was beginning to believe it. The rough and tumble life of a rodeo cowboy wasn't for the faint of heart. The word *tough* had been invented to describe this particular breed. Nash and Hal

Griffin were prime examples of gritty, bold, and tough individuals who had pushed themselves to their physical limits—and kept going back for more.

In Crista's glory days of high school rodeos, she had developed that same attitude, driven by a need to acquire her father's affection by meeting his constant demands for perfection. But she was just a novice compared to Nash and Hal Griffin. Although her present job required physical strength, it was mere child's play compared to the brutality of the arena.

"I suppose you aren't too thrilled about me sending my brother off to ride the circuit again," Hal presumed.

"Actually, I think it's for the best." Crista gave Hal the injection before he even realized it. He barely had time to flinch. "Your brother's blind focus on Levi isn't particularly healthy for either of them."

"It's complicated," Hal assured her with a dark look from even darker eyes.

"It's still unhealthy," Crista persisted as she replaced the syringe in the leather bag.

Hal's eyes narrowed appraisingly. "Is there something going on between you and Nash that I need to know about? In the first place, I'm not too keen on—"

"Nothing is going on," Nash growled as he strode into the room, bandages and antiseptic in hand.

Hal watched Nash and Crista glance everywhere except at each other. Something *was* going on, he decided. And whatever it was, neither Nash nor Crista wanted to discuss it. Good, Hal thought. Maybe they both had enough sense to back off before they messed up each other's lives. Hal had been burned—and badly—in his younger years. No way was he going to play Cupid for his older brother.

In Hal's opinion, women weren't to be trusted. They were—by nature—scheming and manipulative. He'd learned that the hard way. Besides, things were running smoothly on Chulosa Ranch—without women underfoot. Hal preferred to keep it that way.

"Would you ask Bernie to bring Hal something to eat," Crista requested, staring at the air over Nash's broad shoulder.

"Sure thing, Curly."

When Nash wheeled away, Crista went to work on her patient, relying on the professional efficiency that had become second nature. Hal posed no problems while she stabilized his ribs and abdomen.

The painkiller had taken instant effect, and he was becoming groggy. When Bernie appeared with a tray of food, Crista left the cook to spoon-feed Hal, who was losing his coordination—compliments of the sedative.

Crista descended the steps to see Choctaw Jim, Nash, and Levi waiting for a report on Hal's condition.

"I'm not a doctor," she was quick to remind them, "but I think Hal cracked a rib. The muscle spasms should subside in three or four days, depending on how much he limits his activity. I'll alternate hot packs and cold compresses each time I come for my sessions with Levi."

"You don't need to bother paying next month's

rent," Choctaw Jim, put in. "Provided the rent covers your medical fees."

Crista studied the crusty older man whose Native American heritage was even more evident than that of his nephews. The first time Crista had met Jim Pryce she had taken a liking to the older man. His wise, dark-eyed stare left her feeling that he knew more than he would ever bother to say.

Jim had been exceptionally easy to deal with when negotiating the contract to rent the farmhouse. Crista had asked for paint to redo the living room and bedroom and he had bought the needed supplies and even offered to do the job for her. Crista had insisted on doing it herself, since Jim had already replaced the leaky kitchen faucet and faulty light switch in the dining room.

Jim Pryce was a jack of all trades, Crista had concluded. She had the feeling that her landlord—or Choctaw Jim, as he was called by his closest friends and family—had taught his nephews the art of self-reliance. Crista didn't know what had become of Nash's parents, but it was obvious Nash and Hal had been placed in competent hands. Crista wished she could say the same for young Lisa Chandler, the accident victim under her care.

"A month's rent more than covers it," Crista objected. "Half the rent would be—"

Choctaw Jim flung up a callused hand. "Even trade," he declared in a tone that invited no argument. He wasted his breath.

"I hardly think—"

"Uncle Jim said it's an even trade and that's that," Nash cut in without so much as a glance in Crista's direction. He headed for the stairs. "I

need to pack for my trip. Thanks for taking care
of my little brother, Curly."

"You're welcome," Crista said to the entryway
at large.

Medical bag in hand, she bade the other men
good night and drove home. She wasn't thrilled
about being alone with her thoughts, which kept
circling back to the incident in the barn.

In stubborn defiance, Crista turned up the vol-
ume on the radio, only to hear Oklahoma's own
Vince Gill crooning about calling out names
when nobody was there. Grumbling, she switched
stations and listened to some self-important news-
caster spout commentary on the disgraceful state
of national politics.

When Crista entered the house, the light on
the answering machine winked at her, indicating
a string of messages. The first three were from
callers who refused to leave a name or number,
one of Crista's pet peeves. It was also cause for
concern when living alone on an isolated ranch.
In this day and age, thieves often checked out
residences before swooping down like buzzards
to pick a place clean.

The fourth message was from Jack Forrester,
inviting her to a movie and dinner in the city that
weekend. Crista decided to shower and treat herself to a glass of wine before accepting or declin-
ing the invitation. She could definitely use a safe
distraction after her embarrassing encounter with
Nash.

"Big mistake, Delaney," Crista chastised herself
before she held her head under the shower noz-
zle.

The last thing she needed right now was an
exasperating relationship with a man who would

inevitably use her the same way her father and
ex-husband had. Nash's loyalties were to Levi and
she could never be more to him than a place to
ease his physical urges.

No way, Crista told herself sensibly. She was going to steer clear of Nash Griffin.

In Crista's opinion, loyalty, fidelity, and devotion were the best indicators of a man's worth.
But then, she had never considered herself an
authority on men—which was a good thing since
she already had one failed marriage and broken
ties to her father to her discredit.

Crista dried herself off and abandoned any
hope of figuring out what made men tick. With
a silk robe wrapped haphazardly around her, she
padded barefoot to the kitchen, towel-drying the
heavy mass of hair. Wine bottle in one hand and
glass in the other, she reversed direction and then
parked herself on the sofa in her darkened living
room.

Ah, the welcome sound of silence. After a long,
hectic day, it was good to take a breather and
relax—as long as her thoughts didn't drift down
forbidden avenues.

Crista sipped her wine and focused her
thoughts on Lisa Chandler. The little girl nestled
in the west wing of Kanima County Hospital really
got to her. While Lisa was recovering from her
first reconstructive surgery, her mother rarely
came to check on her. When Janelle did show up,
Crista had noticed the glazed eyes and lack of
coordination that hinted at drug use—illegal va-
rieties, Crista speculated. She shuddered to think
of the home life Lisa endured. Judging by Janelle's skin-tight blouses and jeans, the woman

spent her spare time attracting and accommodating men.

What kind of chance would Lisa have in life with a role model who spent more time buying cosmetics than visiting her injured daughter? And why, Crista wondered with a shake of her head, did people even *have* children if they weren't prepared to make a commitment to raising them? Children needed love, encouragement, and direction.

Of course, Crista mused, the opposite could be just as damaging. Having a parent dictate a life for a child wasn't the answer, either. She had lived through the pressure and constant criticism of that until she finally rebelled.

Too bad newborn babies didn't come with instruction manuals. God never should have given parents the right to make their own mistakes when it came to children . . .

The hum of an engine and the flash of headlights put Crista on alert. She hoped the three missing messages on the answering machine weren't a forewarning of thieves to come. Here she sat in a darkened house, ingesting enough wine to make her reactions sluggish. She was in no condition to thwart a robbery, and she certainly wasn't dressed appropriately, either!

Her heart thumped in rhythm with the footsteps pelting across her front porch. To her relief, the prowler had the decency to knock on the door.

"Who is it?"

"Me," came the gruff reply.

Crista was beginning to wish her visitor had been a prowler. He would have been less dangerous than Nash Griffin.

"I thought you were packing to leave."

"Open the damned door, Curly."

Crista stumbled to her feet, shoved the mop of damp hair over one shoulder, and guzzled a quick drink for courage. If Nash Griffin had come to say good-bye, he need not have bothered. And if he was coming to request her services for Hal or Levi, then . . .

Grumbling, Crista approached the door. If her medical expertise was needed, she would go. She only wished her chauffeur could be anyone but the impossibly cranky, dangerously attractive Nash Griffin.

She also reminded herself that one's fondest wishes rarely came true.

Eight

When Crista opened the front door, Nash forgot why it was so all-fired important to breathe. Her slinky, hunter-green robe crisscrossed over her breasts, just loose enough to expose a bit of cleavage. The hem of the short garment left plenty of bare thigh and calf exposed to his hungry gaze.

Crista clutched a wine bottle in her left hand—a hand devoid of those acrylic dragon nails some women considered appealing. Nash appreciated her wholesome, natural look. Crista Delaney was that, all right—and more, God help him. She radiated spirit and possessed a gorgeous body that Nash had allowed himself to become a little too familiar with earlier that evening. The cold shower he had taken before driving over to her place had been a waste of soap and water. Everything in him reacted to this lovely female.

"Is Hal or Levi having a problem?" Crista questioned, clutching self-consciously at her robe.

Her attempt to conceal her femininity only drew Nash's attention to the green silk and bare skin beneath it. "No," Nash muttered. "I'm the one with the problem."

"My therapeutical expertise will cost you double," she said, striving for a teasing tone to camouflage the fluttering sensations the sight of him evoked.

Nash invited himself into the house and closed the door behind him with a decisive snap.

"Wine?" she offered.

Lord no, thought Nash. The last thing he needed was to take the edge off his willpower—something that had turned out to be flimsier than he used to think. He stood there, itching to tunnel his fingers through that glorious tangle of damp hair and tip her head back to accept his kiss. Nash forced himself to discard those thoughts and concentrate on the purpose of his visit.

"I only came by to tell you that what happened tonight won't happen again," he blurted out with customary candor.

"I'll drink to that." Crista lifted the glass to her lips and took a swallow.

Nash scowled sourly. "For the record—"

"We're keeping records?" she asked flippantly.

Nash glared her into silence. "For the record," he repeated slowly and deliberately, "you weren't exactly an unwilling participant. I distinctly remember you kissing me back, damn it."

Crista finished off her wine and then pivoted to set the bottle and glass on the end table. When Nash cursed under his breath, she tugged modestly at the hem of her robe. As she recalled, Nash had an aversion to her skimpy attire—and most everything else about her.

"Is there anything I do that pleases you?" she muttered in frustration.

"Very little." Nash forced himself to stare at the shadowed room rather than Crista's profile. "I didn't like what happened tonight."

"Neither did I," Crista informed him as she sank down on the far side of the sofa, maintaining a safe distance.

Nash plopped down on the opposite end of the couch, as close to the armrest as he could get without actually sitting on it. "I have obligations that consume all my time and effort."

"And I have no desire to get involved with another man after my failed marriage," Crista declared. "I'm enjoying my independence."

"That makes two of us. I don't want to find myself at the mercy of my hormones just because I find you attractive."

Crista nodded in agreement. "I'm not particularly proud of the fact that I'm physically attracted to you, either. Luckily, things won't progress any farther than they already have. Since your motto is: *What Levi can't have, you can't, either,* what happened in the barn won't be repeated. We'll just chalk it up to a momentary loss of sanity on your part and mine."

"Fine with me," Nash said firmly.

"Then we're in total agreement," Crista replied, staring at the wall. "I've always thought sex was overrated, anyway."

Her cynical comment brought Nash's head up in a hurry. His gaze was fixed on Crista's profile. "Your husband obviously wasn't much of a lover," he said with characteristic bluntness.

"He wasn't much of a lawyer, either." Crista reached over to pour herself another drink. "Jonathan couldn't acquire enough clients fast enough or get rich quick enough to prove himself more successful than his almighty father. He dipped into the trust funds of some of his clients, as well as the compensations from insurance settlements, and invested heavily in the stock markets.

"Unfortunately, one of his clients did him the discourtesy of dying earlier than Jonathan expected and the heirs demanded their trust funds. Jonathan was caught short and scrambled to cover his losses by relying on loan sharks, whom he arrogantly thought he could outsmart. Jon only wound up outsmarting himself."

"And did you approve of his unscrupulous tactics?" Nash questioned, watching her closely.

Crista sipped her wine, wondering why she was spilling her guts to a man who didn't really care all that much about who she was or where she came from. The wine, she decided. It had loosened her tongue. But what the hell? Talking about Jon was safer than dwelling on her mental and physical lapses with Nash.

"I didn't know what was going on until charges were brought against Jon. The loan sharks started leaving threatening messages on the answering machine."

Crista managed to hold her head up with a degree of dignity, adding, "I'm sure the woman Jon was involved with was more upset that he would be doing time at a minimum security prison than I was. Both of them were living off the money I had in savings, without my knowledge. When Jon went to trial I decided I wasn't all that enthusiastic about supporting both of them so I filed for divorce."

"Did you know he was seeing someone else?" Nash asked, silently admiring Crista's attempt to convey the story without reducing herself to tears. It must have come as a blow to her ego to realize she was the last one to know her ex-husband was embezzling money—including hers—and screwing around with another woman.

"It seems I never knew what Jon was doing until after the fact. As it turned out, there were actually three somebody elses during our two years of marriage." Crista cut Nash a quick glance before looking the other way. "So it shouldn't be too difficult for you to understand why I'm no more interested in getting involved with you than with any other man who puts everything first in his heart, except me. I've been used all my life—by my father and then by Jon—and I have no intention of finding myself in that position again."

Against his better judgment, Nash found himself reaching across the space that separated them, drawing her closer. "You didn't deserve that, Curly. No woman does."

The husky tone of his voice, compounded with the effects of the wine, crumbled Crista's resolve. It had been a long time since a man had bothered to show her concern or compassion. Crista found herself curling up against Nash, as if she belonged there—which of course she didn't and never would.

His arm folded around her, drawing her head to the solid wall of his chest. Crista leaned against him, amazed at the comfort she derived from a man she wasn't sure possessed an ounce of sympathy for anyone except Levi Cooper.

"I think they should have thrown the book at your ex-husband," Nash grumbled in disgust. "Minimum security? Hell, a thief is a thief. Three-timing thieves are even worse. What kind of justice is that anyway?"

"The kind you get when your daddy is a hot-shot attorney who socializes with the judge who tries your case. The Honorable Daniel Prescott and Jonathan Heywood II were in the same college fraternity and occasionally double-dated while they were cheating on their wives."

"Son of a bitch," Nash muttered.

"Son of a genuine bastard," Crista corrected. "Jonathan's dear ole daddy taught him that it was important to keep a wife for social and professional pretense while he ran around on the sly."

"How did you get tangled up with the likes of Jon Heywood III anyway?"

Crista pushed away from his chest, raked her hair from her face, and smiled regretfully. "Because I wanted to get away from *my* dear ole daddy and I thought marriage would break the influence he was trying to keep over me when I graduated from college. I've made a study of dysfunctional families by living in them. That's why *independence* has such a nice ring to it. I've been in too many situations where the woman tries to please, hoping to be loved just for herself, while the man takes what he wants, without the slightest concern for the woman's feelings."

Nash decided, there and then, that he could cope far better with this striking female when there was conflict between them, not tranquillity. He shouldn't have pried into her past, shouldn't have cared that Crista had such a hard go of it. And for sure and certain, he shouldn't have been so comfortable, having her nestled beside him, his arm wrapped around her shoulders—as if that was the most natural and expected place for his arm to be.

They had really done it now, damn it. They were sharing confidences as best friends would. They were coming to understand what made one another tick. That wasn't a good thing for two people who could no longer conceal the fact that they were physically attracted to each other, certainly not after they had clung to each other in the barn like drowning cats going down for the third and final time.

"I better go," Nash murmured, marshaling the will to leave. "I have a long day ahead of me. I'm already getting the pre-rodeo jitters, after a five-year absence from the circuit."

Crista nodded in understanding, having been there a few times herself. "Worse than the actual ride itself, in most instances. Easier to do it than wonder how it will turn out."

Her perceptions were right on the mark. Nash wondered how she knew so much about such things, wondered about her familiarity with training horses. But he didn't ask. He and Crista had already shared too many private moments.

When Nash rose to full stature, Crista glanced up at him. "One question, Griffin, *just for the record.*"

Nash smiled faintly when she tossed his words back at him. "What's the question, Curly?"

Curious green eyes met his level stare. "Do you think it's *me*?"

Nash frowned, unable to follow her train of thought. Perhaps she'd had one too many glasses of wine. "You lost me, honey."

Crista curled up in a tight ball, her arms wrapped around herself, her legs drawn up beneath her. "I never could please my perfectionist of a father, no matter how hard I tried. And obviously I couldn't please my husband who—"

Nash's index finger settled on her lush lips, shushing her. "A husband would be every kind of fool not to appreciate the best thing he had going for him."

Her thick lashes fluttered up, and Nash felt himself trapped by his own intense longing, yet tormented by the fierce sense of responsibility he had accepted five years ago. "Damn you, Crista Delaney," he muttered just before his mouth dipped downward. "You're turning me into a worse hypocrite than I already am . . ."

Nash felt his arms contracting as he sank down beside her. He pulled her onto his lap, settling her rounded bottom against the throbbing rigidness in his jeans.

Now, as before, his instantaneous reaction— and hers—swept them both up in a torrent of need. Nash drank in the taste of her like a dying man quenching his thirst. His hands glided beneath her flimsy robe, peeling away the fabric to caress her silky flesh with thumb and fingertips.

When Crista gasped in response to his touch Nash groaned aloud. He memorized the satiny texture of her skin, felt her body quivering beneath each caress, felt her moving instinctively closer.

Nash closed his eyes and gave himself up to defeat. He had been fighting Crista, tooth and nail, for all the good it had done him. He had purposely provoked her every chance he got, hoping to drive wedges between them. He had treated her disrespectfully and ignored her. And for what? He still couldn't keep his hands off her, because she was the sweetest taste of heaven he had ever known.

His fingertip circled the pebbled crown of her breast and he heard her breath hitch, as his did. With the gentlest touch, he brushed his thumb over the dusky peak before his moist lips followed.

Her fist clenched his forearm. The more pleasure he offered her, and himself, the tighter her grasp. Her helpless reaction was an intriguing challenge to arouse her until her nails dug so deeply they could break the skin. Nash told himself that he wanted that, welcomed it. The biting pressure was vivid testimony that he affected her to the same degree that she affected him. At least he wasn't alone in this.

While his lips feathered over one taut crown and then the other, his hand ventured off on a journey of pure pleasure. The brush of his hand over Crista's flat belly left her gasping for breath. Intrigued, Nash's palm splayed lower and Crista all but melted in his arms. He wanted to feel the fires of her desire bathing his fingertips, to taste the very essence of her, to know every intimate secret of this woman who destroyed his self-control as if it never existed.

"Oh, God . . ." Crista whimpered as his hand glided between her thighs, gently urging her legs apart. Splinters of fire hit her like a barrage. "Nash—?"

Her moan of pleasure was his name—an enticing incantation that drew Nash deeper. He had the unmistakable feeling that Crista's ex-husband had been so impatient and so intent on his own pleasure that he hadn't bothered to arouse her or acquaint her with her own sexuality. Jonathan had probably led her to believe *she* was the reason he sought satisfaction elsewhere.

Well, if nothing else, Nash promised himself, Crista would become aware that she was more than capable of mindless passion—if and when she decided to become involved with a man who truly deserved her.

As for himself, Nash was discovering new dimensions of his own desire. Watching Crista come alive in his arms gave him a unique kind of pleasure that flowed through her and into him.

He wondered if, in his past, there were shades of Jonathan Heywood III. Had he been the same kind of insensitive bastard? The thought made Nash feel ashamed, shallow, selfish.

Well, he wasn't like that now, he realized. He was vividly aware of Crista's needs and desires— more so than of any woman he had ever taken to his bed. Nash was a changed man in a dozen different ways, all because of this spirited woman whom he wanted like hell burning but knew he could never have, not when his loyalties had to be elsewhere.

What Crista wanted most, Nash couldn't give her. But he could teach her that she was a woman capable of deep passions, despite her ex-husband's spiteful claims to the contrary.

With infinite care, Nash traced her softest flesh with thumb and fingertip, feeling the warm rain of her desire flowing over him, through him. His questing fingertip delved deeper and he felt the secret shudder racing through her. When he felt her pulsate around him, felt her nails digging into his arm as if she were holding on for dear life, he lifted his head to gauge her expression. Lightning bolts of pleasure sizzled through Nash when he saw the stricken expression on her face, witnessed the glittering sparks of passion in those green eyes.

"Damn you, Nash Griffin," Crista gasped as he

caressed her. "I wish I didn't know it could be like this."

"And I should have been more careful what *I* learned," he mused aloud. Nash didn't need to know how intensely satisfying it was to pleasure her. But now he knew, and he was lost.

Nash took her mouth with slow penetration and languid retreat, imitating the erotic probing and withdrawal of his fingertip. Each sensuous gesture had Crista gasping helplessly.

His mouth abandoned hers, hearing her ragged breath tear in and out as he brushed his lips along the column of her neck. His hand retraced its erotic path up her belly to her breast, bathing the erect nipple with the sultry heat of her desire. His dark head descended, tasting the evidence of her passion that he had painted on her breast.

When her breath broke, Nash lifted his hand to limn her parted lips. His mouth returned to hers, sharing the taste of her passion, lost to a need so profound that they both shook with it.

"You make me forget every vow I ever made, woman," he whispered against her lips. "I want you until hell won't have it."

When Crista arched toward him, Nash felt his entire body fill with intolerable longing. His hand moved downward; he inserted two fingers into her secret warmth, at the same instant plunging his tongue into her mouth. Nash knew the exact moment when the tremors consumed her, how long they lasted, and when they subsided. Not only were Crista's fingers biting into his arm so tightly that she nearly cut off circulation, but her body responded to the wild intensity of her pleasure with every quiver and gasp.

She was like a wildfire burning him alive! Nash could think of nothing more vital than having her wrapped around him, more necessary than burying himself so deeply inside her that he couldn't tell where her passion ended and his began.

It had been so damn long since he had been with a woman. He ached from eyebrow to ankle and everywhere in between. He was holding more woman than he had ever known—too much woman, too much temptation.

Nash had thought hell had little left to teach him after the tragedy of five years past. Well, he had been wrong. He wanted Crista Delaney with every fiber of his being, every beat of his heart.

But he couldn't have her, because he had nothing to offer her that really counted, not when his future might forever be linked to his past, not when he couldn't give her the kind of devotion she had never known, and rightfully deserved. He couldn't make her an important part of his life— what she wanted and needed most.

That was the hell of it. Nash knew he had to back away—just as soon as he took care of a few of the sensations tormenting him . . .

Nash half twisted on the sofa, ignoring his own voice of reason. He eased Crista beneath him, letting her absorb his weight, letting her feel the burgeoning evidence of his need.

While she moved restlessly beneath him, he pressed closer, cursing the denim that separated them and yet thankful he hadn't breached the last barrier that would most assuredly take him over the brink.

His big hands framed her face—staring into her lovely features as they twisted with frustrated passion, knowing her expression mirrored his own. His mouth melted over hers, savoring her response.

Nash molded her body into his hard contours, and felt his profound hunger combine with hers. Yes, he knew he was making a mistake that would haunt his days and disturb his sleep, but he let himself enjoy her for just a few more moments. He would stop soon, after one last kiss, one last caress. He had to . . .

Her responses nearly unhinged him. Nash couldn't recall deriving such pleasure with a woman, even when he had refrained from taking her completely. But if he did, it would be absolute heaven. Yet, heaven wasn't something he was intimately acquainted with. Nash was more familiar with the torments of hell, and that's where he'd wind up if he didn't get himself in hand while he could still remember that he had to do exactly that!

Nash forced himself to do what he knew he had to do—he braced his arms and hauled himself to his feet, putting the space between them that he never should have encroached upon in the first place.

"There's nothing wrong with you, Curly," Nash said as calmly as he knew how. "You can get as hot and bothered as any woman I've ever been with. One of these days the right man will come along to show you what you've been missing. But I'm not the right man. I have nothing to give, at least not what you need to make you happy."

Nash anticipated her reaction. In fact, he had counted on it to break the spell. His casual tone produced the results he wanted. Crista clutched her robe and coiled up on the sofa, glaring at him.

"Now that you think you've proved I'm not made of ice, get out!"

Nash frowned, unsure of what she meant. *"Think?"*

Crista breathed raggedly, her face flaming with humiliation. "You could have had whatever you wanted just now, and I might have discovered what all the fuss was all about."

Unshed tears clouded her eyes as she glowered at him. "But you aren't interested enough to follow through." She clamped her mouth shut and looked way.

Nash could have kicked himself for having to be cruel. But Crista had gotten this all wrong.

When he hadn't allowed himself to finish, she presumed he didn't find her appealing enough. Well, hell, he had endured all this frustration for nothing!

At least she would be mad enough to stay the hell out of his way in the future. There was that, Nash consoled himself. He was certain he couldn't survive having Crista so close again. He knew his limits. Nash had reached them with Crista Delaney—here, tonight.

When he turned away to scoop up his hat, Crista hissed at him. "I hope some bronc busts your ass, Nash Griffin."

Nash shoved his hat into place and pivoted to face her, mustering a half smile. "I'm gonna miss you, too, Curly," he said in his best drawl.

On his way to his rattletrap truck, Nash asked himself at what moment he had lost his good intentions. He had somehow managed to screw up—in reverse—with Crista. He was beginning to think that was his mark of distinction. He had meant to reassure her about her femininity, and he wound up undermining it—and frustrating the hell out of both of them.

His only consolation came in knowing Crista would go out of her way to avoid him in the future. When he returned from the rodeo, she wouldn't give him the time of day, but at least she would realize he wasn't the kind of man she could ever rely on. Nash was the kind of man who believed in telling it like it was.

"Bastard," Crista muttered when she heard the jalopy drive away. How could she want a man so desperately one minute and wish the same man would burn in hell the next? The guy was obviously making her crazy!

Swearing under her breath, Crista snatched up a glass of wine, hoping to drown the scent and taste of Nash Griffin. By God, she wasn't going near him again! And she really did hope he got dumped on his butt on the first buck out of the chute. It would serve him right if he hurt half as much as she was hurting now!

"Nash, are you okay with this?"

Although Nash had tried to tiptoe quietly around the room he shared with his brother, Hal had awakened at dawn.

"I'm okay enough with it, I guess." Nash plucked two of Hal's western shirts from the closet. "Can I borrow these for the rodeo? Mine look too much like rags."

"Sure, take whatever you need." Hal shifted uncomfortably and groaned in pain. "Damn, who would've thought muscle spasms could hurt so bad. I hate to think what shape I'd be in now if your girlfriend hadn't—"

Nash whirled around. "She's not my girlfriend, she's Levi's therapist."

"Down, boy. I *thought* I was kidding. Obviously there was more truth to it than I first suspected. I must have hit a nerve."

Nash unzipped his duffel bag and hurled the shirts into it. He missed. He did not, however, miss Hal's smirk. "Now you listen to me, little brother, if I had my way, Crista Delaney wouldn't set foot on this ranch. As far as I'm concerned, she's a constant reminder of what Levi is doing without. But Levi insisted on having her take his case."

"And you couldn't refuse him."

"No, I couldn't. But I warned Crista to keep her distance and guard against any situation that might give Dogger the wrong idea."

Hal braced his brawny arms for support and carefully scooted back against the pile of pillows. "I just wanted to make sure I knew exactly which way the wind blew before you left for the rodeo. I didn't think you were stupid enough to get involved with a woman, even a knockout like that. Women will tear your goddam heart out if you let them."

Nash was well acquainted with his brother's opinion of women. After Hal's betrayal, he had joined the service, hoping to vent his anger and frustration.

Having never been head over heels—with the exception of being catapulted off a few wild broncs—Nash couldn't understand how a man could become so soured by a relationship with a woman. True, he was feeling the effects of his attraction to Crista, but he had chalked his loss of self-control up to his long abstinence, not to mention the challenge Crista presented without even trying. Nash had always been a man who enjoyed challenging himself. Why else would he have spent so many years on the rodeo circuit?

Now, if Hal and everybody else would just back off and leave him alone maybe he could get on track. If there was one thing Nash had learned, it was that he could still function normally when he remained a safe distance from that curly-haired female.

Out of sight, out of mind, Nash convinced himself. A few wild rides in the rodeo arena and he would come home and settle into business as usual.

When Nash turned away to retrieve his gear, Hal's comment stopped him cold. "Crista said it was a good idea that you were spending time away from Dogger. She thinks you're spoiling him rotten—or words to that effect."

Scowling, Nash jerked up his duffel bag. "I don't need a damned therapist dictating what's best for me and neither do you. It seems to me that we would all be back to normal around here if God's sister minded her own damned business!"

Hal watched his brother stalk away. The name Crista Delaney—whether spoken in seriousness or jest—turned Nash right side wrong in the blink of an eye. Hal would have to make double-damn certain Crista harbored no secret fantasy about Nash.

There was no way Hal would let Nash suffer

through a humiliating affair. If Crista was looking
for security she had better look elsewhere. Chulosa Ranch was male territory. If not for Levi's
need of home health care nurses and physical
therapists to make occasional visits, he would
have posted the place off limits to women.

Hal grimaced and shifted position on the bed.
If he hadn't been in so much pain last night,
eager for the relief Crista's skillful hands had provided, he might have been less civil toward her.
But he wasn't going to let his older brother make
the same mistake Hal had made at the foolish
age of twenty. No woman was going to break Hal's
heart, because he would never let one close
enough.

The same held true for Nash, Hal vowed determinedly. Hal was going to do his older brother
a favor and make sure some scheming woman
didn't cut his legs out from under him and trample on his heart. Crista Delaney was nothing but
trouble. Hal would remind Nash of that, every
chance he got.

Nine

Crista pulled her sunglasses off the bridge of her nose to check her appearance in the rearview mirror. Sure enough, red streaks still made her puffy eyes look like a road map.

"Thank you, Nash Griffin," she muttered bitterly.

Because of that jerk she had polished off the remainder of the wine and was *still* awake half the night. She was wound tighter than a clock.

Crista pulled into her parking spot at the back of the hospital and headed for the door. It was going to be hard to be the cheerful therapist while her spirits were scraping rock bottom. She had lost all respect for herself the previous night. She had responded to Nash as she had responded to no other man, and it still wasn't enough.

Perhaps spending Saturday with harmless Jack Forrester would lift her flagging spirits. Crista sure as hell wasn't going to mope around the house, feeling sorry for herself. She had discovered—to her shame and humiliation—that she had no willpower when it came to Nash Griffin. No matter how much he infuriated her at times, she was hopelessly attracted to him.

Crista had just stepped inside the hall when

Wendy York buzzed around the corner, nearly colliding with her.

"Good, you made it on time."

"In time for what?" Crista questioned.

"Lisa Chandler is being dismissed this morning. Her mother wants to drop the poor kid off before she goes to work. Lisa has been anxious to see you before she leaves."

Crista discarded her own frustrations, reminding herself that there were those in this world who had honest-to-goodness problems. Mustering a smile, Crista strode toward her young patient's room.

"So you're headed home today, are you?"

A frizzy blond head nodded glumly. Settled in her wheelchair, Lisa reached out with her good arm to lift the jewelry box in her lap. "I want to give this back to you."

"But I gave it to *you*," Crista insisted, kneeling in front of the young girl. "I want you to keep it."

Lisa adamantly shook her head, her blond hair tumbling around her in ringlets. "I might . . . lose it."

In other words, Crista presumed, Lisa's mother might find the need to pawn it to support the habit Crista was suspicious that Janelle Chandler had.

"I'll tell you what, Lisa. Why don't I keep the gifts in my office until you return for your next surgery. Then we won't have to worry about your things getting misplaced."

Lisa smiled tentatively. "At least I'd have them for a little while . . . um . . . before they get lost."

Crista flashed her patient her brightest smile and made a mental note to contact the social worker in Keota Flats. If her suspicions were correct, she would need the kind of proof that would remove Lisa from a destructive environment. Crista had two weeks before the next scheduled surgery—two weeks to save this lonely, mistreated little girl from future misery.

"I'll take good care of your gifts until you come back," Crista promised, "and I'll stop in to see how you're making out at home. Wendy and Jill will be dropping in to check on you, too."

"I wish . . ." Lisa compressed her lips, handed over the jewelry box, and glanced away.

Crista gave the girl's hand a fond squeeze. "You just take good care of yourself, young lady. I've gotten pretty attached to you the last couple of weeks, you know . . ."

Her voice trailed off when Janelle Chandler sashayed into the room to retrieve her daughter. If Crista was any judge, Janelle was a part-time bar maid and part-time . . . Crista cringed inwardly at the prospect. She preferred not to speculate on where and how Janelle made extra money, but it was hard not to notice the way her clothes hugged her skin like a body wrap. The layers of makeup coating her face were thick as mud, making her look cheap and easy.

"Let's go, Lisa," Janelle insisted, glancing at her watch. "I've got to get to work."

When the nurse rolled Lisa to the exit door, Crista stared after her. If something wasn't done about Lisa's situation, the poor kid wouldn't have a chance in life.

Lost in thought, Crista ambled toward her office, toting the jewelry box. Crista set it on her desk and opened the lid. Both necklaces had been carefully arranged so their gold chains wouldn't tangle.

"You have nothing better to do than decide

what accessories to wear for the day?" Admiral Daisy Darwin harrumphed from the doorway.

Crista gritted her teeth at the inspector's sarcastic tone. "Good morning, Daisy."

Daisy marched into the office, looking down her long snout. "I'd prefer that you put the jewels away and get to work. You're hardly making a good impression, fiddling around in here, as if this were your private wardrobe closet."

While the cast-iron Daisy tramped over to inspect the file cabinets, Crista silently tucked the jewelry box in the bottom desk drawer.

She had just dropped into her chair when Daisy rounded on her, waving an incomplete evaluation sheet like a banner. "I see we're getting lax with our work," she declared triumphantly.

"No, we are not," Crista contradicted as pleasantly as possible. "That file belongs to Levi Cooper. I have taken his case as an extra duty—after my normal work day. His guardian can be very difficult to deal with. The last therapist on his case requested a transfer and Levi's guardian demanded it."

"And how are you managing with this cantankerous guardian?" Daisy wanted to know.

Crista focused her attention on the evaluation sheet rather than Daisy's condescending stare. "We have an acceptable working arrangement," she replied. "My patient has no complaints, either."

"Well, he *should*," Daisy snorted. "You have failed to complete his paperwork after your visitation. You know I expect every case to be updated immediately so no vital information is forgotten or omitted."

"That was to be my first order of business after seeing one of our patients off this morning."

While Daisy rummaged through the files, hoping to find another example of incompetence, Crista completed the report and handed it over for the inspector's perusal.

"Don't you think this particular case could be handled by regular hospital visits?" Daisy inquired.

"Probably, but as I mentioned, Levi's guardian is paying the additional costs for home visitations and he has provided all the exercise equipment necessary."

"Well, I don't claim to be an expert in physical therapy—"

Like hell she didn't! Daisy considered herself an expert on everything, even when she didn't know beans about anything except military protocol. Inspecting files and nitpicking were Daisy's fortes. She simply didn't function well in the civilian world.

"—But it seems to me that this patient has been rehabilitated as far as his disability will allow. I don't see the need to continue wasting our therapists' time."

Crista had heard enough. She had also had a rotten evening and a frustrating morning. She rose to her feet and planted her hands firmly on the desk as she confronted the sour-faced inspector.

"I do not consider any patient a *lost cause* or *waste of time*. In this business, it's the anticipation of therapeutic visits that often boosts a patient's spirits. We provide an important lifeline that prevents some patients from falling into depression. We have to be extremely careful to be sure our patients receive personal attention instead of reducing them to a name and number on a file in these cabinets. I don't know about you, Daisy, but my conscience will not allow me to dehumanize patients."

Daisy stepped back apace, clearly annoyed by Crista's directness. She was, however, having difficultly formulating a reply. Wheeling away like a soldier on parade, Daisy thrust back her shoulders and marched from the office. "Just make sure you keep the evaluations updated," she tossed over her stiff shoulders.

After Daisy's spectacular exit, Jill and Wendy scuttled into the office, smiling in immense satisfaction.

"Well, I guess you drydocked Old Ironsides," Jill said with a snicker. "If Daisy dares to contest you, she'll come away sounding like the most inhumane creature on the planet."

"You were eavesdropping," Crista said accusingly.

"Of course we were," Wendy replied, undaunted. "It isn't every day that we get to see and hear the admiral-inspector being put in her place. She used to give your predecessor hell—and then some. In fact, Daisy was one of the main reasons Margie took another position. She was fed up with dealing with Old Ironsides and listening to all her petty complaints."

"I have a feeling I could spend a week trying to please Daisy Darwin and receive nothing but more criticism for my efforts," Crista said, thinking instantly of her own father.

"You've certainly got that right," said Jill.

"Well, I'm going to get something else right." Crista handed Jill one of the files on her desk.

"I've heard there's a competent social worker in Keota Flats. I want her to keep track of Lisa Chandler and her mother for the next few days."

"Taking a personal interest, are we?"

"I take *every* patient personally," Crista clarified. "We're all human, after all, and we deserve the best we can get—especially a kid like Lisa."

"Gotcha, boss. I'll make the necessary call. Have you got something specific in mind to check into?"

Crista's smile evaporated. "Janelle's possible drug addiction. If she's dealing or buying, I want Lisa out of the home and placed in a safe, positive environment. I wouldn't put it past Janelle to coerce Lisa into selling some of that stuff to friends at school. The kid is too withdrawn. I think she's battling much more than injuries from the accident."

"I'll stop by and check on her after lunch," Wendy promised.

"I'll drop by on my way home," Jill offered.

"Good. Lisa is going to need constant supervision. I think Janelle plans to dump the poor kid off in her wheelchair and let her fend for herself for the rest of the day."

When the technicians scurried off, Crista sank down to study Lisa's file. Although Janelle had neglected to list the name of her employer, she had penciled in a phone number.

Crista snatched up the phone and dialed.

"You have reached Mangy Dog Saloon," said the recording.

Crista dropped the receiver in its cradle. It was just as she thought. Janelle, while drawing wages and tips as a barmaid, was probably making con-

tacts at her place of employment and lining up
private clients after hours . . .

"Boss?" Jill poked her mahogany-colored head
inside the door. "Are you going out with Jack on
Saturday?"

Crista nodded. "I left him a message before I
came to work."

Jill beamed in satisfaction. "Glad to hear it. I
think you're good for each other."

Crista picked up her files and strode off to
work. She had several supervisory visitations to
make with out-patients in the county. It was going
to be another long, busy day, guaranteed to keep
her mind off Nash Griffin—she hoped.

Nash fastened his protective vest and shrugged
on the flashy shirt he had borrowed from his
brother. The locker room beside the arena was
filled with the drone of voices and an occasional
outburst of laughter. Cowboys from all over the
country were preparing for competition, exchanging tidbits about the rough stock that might
keep a friend in the saddle long enough to hear
the buzzer that indicated a successful ride.

It felt odd to be back in the world he had
walked away from five years ago, but it was also
satisfying. There were a few familiar faces and several new ones in the cowboy crowd. Nash had
been instantly accepted and welcomed back. He
had also been given informative tips about the
saddle bronc he had drawn for the first go-round.

According to Pepper Sloan, who had ridden the
same horse the previous week at the Heart O'
Texas Rodeo in Waco, the mount called Hell and
Gone took two straight-up leaps the instant the

chute gate opened. Then the powerful bronc doubled back hard to the left, buried his head between his front legs, and kicked holes in the sky.

Nash inhaled a bracing breath, tucked the hem of his shirt, and grabbed his saddle. It was always easier to get into the swing of things after that first roller coaster ride into the lighted arena. He just hoped Crista's parting curse hadn't followed him through Wichita Falls to Fort Worth. He'd rather not find himself biting dust in the first go-round.

The chute boss, an old friend who had been around as long as Methuselah, grinned when Nash appeared in the lanes. "Glad to have you back, Good Time. The announcer has already informed the crowd that the three-time All Around Cowboy is going to make his comeback tonight. I guess the other cowboys gave you the word on Hell and Gone."

Nash nodded his dark head and shoved his hat in place.

"I have another word of advice for you—just in case Hell and Gone sends you flying before or after the buzzer. The word is *duck,*" Rocky Marshall emphasized. "That mean-tempered bronc likes to crack a few skulls with his heels. Flank strap or no, Hell and Gone will knock you senseless if he has the chance."

Great, thought Nash. If he did manage to hang on for the eight-second eternity, he could expect Hell and Gone to retaliate. The horse's tactics reminded Nash of Exorcist, the last bronc he had ridden.

"And now, ladies and gents," came the animated voice over the loudspeaker. "Turn your attention to chute number four and give the three-time All Around Cowboy a warm Texas wel-

come. Good Time Griffin has dropped down from
Kanima Springs, Oklahoma, to show us how it's
done."

Applause and cheers hung in the damp night
air as Nash climbed over the rail of the chute.
The raunchy bronc whipped its head around in
hopes of giving the rider a greeting nip.

"Here now, Hell and Gone," Rocky Marshall
snapped. "Behave yourself. You'll get your sporting chance, just like you always do."

Nash fastened his saddle in place and eased
down to find the right fit, and suddenly the years
evaporated. He may not have ridden in competition, but he had handled plenty of wild colts at
Chulosa Ranch.

"How does it feel, Good Time?" Rocky questioned as Nash settled on the saddle.

The faintest hint of a smile pursed Nash's lips.
"Like riding a bicycle. I guess it's true that there
are some things you just don't forget."

"You ready to let 'im rip?"

Nash inhaled a deep breath and nodded. The
chute gate swung open and the memories of his
title-winning ride in Glitter Gulch came whirling
back with each bonerattling jump. Every whiplashing dip and dive was accompanied by the whisper
of Bernie Bryant's words: *Rodeo get in your blood . . .*

Another voice intruded in Nash's thoughts as
he spurred the bronc and moved in rhythm with
each flying leap.

I hope you bust your ass . . .

Amid the cheers and round of applause that
serenaded each rip-snorting buck and jarring
thud, Crista's curse resounded, over and over
again.

Nash hung tough when Hell and Gone spun

like a food blender. "This one's for you, Curly," Nash chanted until he heard the anxiously awaited sound of the buzzer.

Nash heeded Rocky's advice as he leaped toward the pickup man. He ducked his head. Sure enough, Hell and Gone swerved in midair. Deadly hooves collided with the pickup rider's mount, missing Nash's skull by a scant few inches.

"Spiteful son of a bitch, isn't he?" the pickup man said around a wad of tobacco that looked to be the size of a golf ball. "Nice to have you back, Good Time. Helluva ride, too. I expect you'll be buying a round of drinks down at Hog Wild Saloon tonight, just like in the old days."

Nash dropped to the ground, listening to another round of applause erupt from the grandstands.

"Good Time Griffin is sure enough back in the saddle, folks," the announcer chuckled. "The cowboy just scored an eight-eight. That was one fine ride on one raunchy bronc."

Nash hopped over the fence to find himself congratulated by the crowd of waiting contestants.

"Thanks a helluva lot, Good Time," one of the bronc riders snorted playfully. "You didn't have to set the standard quite so high on the first ride of the first go-round, now did you? Hell, and here I was hoping not to scratch on my first buck out of the chute. Now I've gotta ride like a damned champion to place in the money."

"Which one of these broncs is your box seat?" Nash questioned as he pulled off his gloves.

"Bad Company," the rookie cowboy reported. "I'm hoping we don't *part* company too soon."

"Get the right fit," Nash instructed the blond-haired cowboy from Montana. "And don't quit shifting position until you do."

The young cowboy glanced over his shoulder and grinned appreciatively. "Thanks, Good Time. I can use all the advice I can get, especially when it comes from one of the best pros in the business."

Nash heaved a relieved sigh and watched the kid from Montana take Bad Company all the way to the buzzer. The lanky cowboy had potential, just like Levi Cooper . . .

Scowling, Nash wheeled toward the locker room to prepare himself mentally for the bareback competition. As Crista Delaney kept telling him: *You can't wallow in the past. You have to get on with your life and make the best of it.*

Rounding the corner of Levi Cooper's private suite, Crista pulled up short. She heard the phone ring, heard her patient's voice drifting through the living area from the office. Curious, Crista inched closer to the partially closed door.

"I told you not to call me. Everybody around here will get suspicious and start asking too many questions."

There was a pause before Levi continued in hushed tones. "Yes, I realize this is important, but you've got to wait for me to contact you from now on. Nash and the others are curious about all my phone calls. Did you get the rest of the money?"

Crista swallowed uneasily. The conversation sounded suspiciously like some of the ones she had overheard her ex-husband making behind closed doors.

Good Lord, was Levi embezzling money from

the very men who cared and provided for him? Crista wouldn't be surprised. She had warned Nash that he'd been overdoing it with Levi.

"I'll be there tomorrow to make the last of the arrangements and check the plans," Levi promised. "I'll call you later tonight, just in case something else comes up."

Crista reversed direction and tiptoed back to the doorway to make a noisy entrance. The last thing she wanted was for Levi to know she had overheard him.

"Levi? Time for your therapy session. Let's get the vital stats out of the way first."

The door to the office swung open and Levi greeted Crista with his customary charming grin. "Hello, good lookin', how's it going?"

Crista responded with a forced smile that concealed her concern. "Can't complain." Opening her bag, she retrieved the sphygmomanometer to check blood pressure and then took his pulse. Both were marginally higher than normal. Probably the excitement of scheming behind the Griffin brothers' backs, she speculated.

"Why don't you start your weight training circuit while I run up to check on Hal," Crista suggested.

"He could use another painkiller," Levi informed her. "He's been growling like a bear since breakfast. I could hear him from down here . . ."

Levi's attention shifted to the window and the view of the corrals, barn, and pasture. Crista followed his gaze to see Choctaw Jim casting his loop over a runaway calf that had apparently objected to being inoculated.

Despite Crista's wary suspicions, she noted the look of longing on Levi's features, the shadows in his powder-blue eyes. "You still miss it, don't you, Levi?"

Levi sighed heavily and gestured toward the hay bale that had a plastic steer head protruding from one end of it. "I went down this morning to toss a few loops while Bernie and Jim were branding calves. But it's just not the same as being in the saddle, feeling a horse gathering itself and lunging off in hot pursuit. I want to be one of them again, even when I know . . ."

His voice dried up as he turned his chair away from the window. "Go ahead and check on Hal. I'll get started on my exercise program."

Crista watched Levi roll toward his bedroom. She had the inescapable feeling there were two sides to Levi Cooper, each battling for supremacy. The cowboy who could no longer compete in bulldogging and roping still longed for yesteryear, for the career cut short by tragedy.

But there was obviously a resentful side, too. In light of the conversation Crista had overheard, Levi's concealed bitterness had manifested itself, probably in unscrupulous dealings. Whatever he was doing wasn't something the Griffins and Company would approve of—or were even aware of. That wasn't a good sign.

Between Crista's growing concern for Lisa Chandler and the gnawing uncertainty about Levi's secret agenda, she was feeling the stress. When she reached the head of the steps she overheard another conversation—*argument* was closer to the mark. From the sound of things, Hal's incapacity had increased his irritability. But then, she reminded herself, the brawny cowboy was a Griffin. She was beginning to think that a surly disposition went with the name.

"Damn it, Bern, I'm not going to eat this slop. And stop treating me like a baby. You're starving me to death with this diet. And if I see another bowl of Jell-O, heads are going to roll, starting with yours!"

"Crista suggested this diet until your spasms let up," Bernie informed him.

"Well fine, let *her* eat this crap. I want meat and potatoes. After rabbit food for the past few days and junk food on the circuit, I need some decent nourishment!"

"Just eat your applesauce and shut up about it," Bernie grumbled. "Between you snapping and snarling and Levi sending me off to fetch this and that every time he gets a phone call, I can't get a blasted thing done around here."

Crista frowned. She was reminded of her last few visits to the ranch, when Levi had sent her on an errand while he took a phone call. Apparently he had used the same tactic on Bernie. Crista's suspicions stirred once again. Although she had grown fond of Levi and had easily related to the personality he projected while she was underfoot, she wondered if she had yet to meet the real Levi Cooper. There seemed to be another man behind the quick, easy smile, a man who had the Griffins curled around his little finger and knew how to use his power to its best advantage.

It was obvious that some people changed drastically after tragedy touched their lives. Nash was a prime example of a fun-loving young man who had withdrawn into himself, simply existing rather than enjoying life. And Levi Cooper could be like Dr. Jekyl and Mr. Hyde. The phone conversation she had overheard, coupled with Bernie's comments, left Crista wondering if the men at Chulosa were in for a disappointing surprise when Levi concluded whatever secret business he was conducting . . .

"Go feed that crap to Leon and bring me some real food," Hal ordered gruffly.

Crista forged into the room. "You'll eat that *crap* and like it, Hal Griffin," she ordered in no uncertain terms. "In case you've forgotten, you have a body wrap around your midsection, including your digestive tract. Give your beat-up bod a break and treat it kindly for just a few more days."

"Lady, I hope you don't think you can act like you're my own dear, departed mother," Hal muttered at her. "And don't get the idea I feel the least bit obligated to obey your orders."

Boldly, Crista approached the bed, defying Hal's black scowl. She popped him on his bare shoulder, not hard enough to hurt, of course, but with enough force to get his undivided attention. "Now you listen to me, cowboy. I was the one who worked overtime to care for you when you were hurting so bad you couldn't even drag yourself out of your truck and up to bed. You were down to begging for painkillers, because just breathing was sheer torture."

Crista leaned down, her curly hair tumbling every which way, blocking Hal's view of everything except the stern expression on her face. "You've got a choice, sugar; you can eat your applesauce and Jell-O or take a chance on me tampering with that steak you keep demanding. I'll have you out like a bad lightbulb and put you on IV's in the hospital, before you wake up to realize where you are. So don't mess with me, buster."

One black brow shot up. "Do you talk to my big brother the same way you talk to me?"

"Yep," she affirmed.

"And he lets you get away with it?"

"He hasn't figured out how to shut me up. He also knows I carry a loaded syringe that can send him to never-never land." She smiled mischievously. "I have the fastest draw in Kanima Springs. I can lay you low with one shot, whenever I feel like it . . . Like now . . ."

Hal flinched when, to his shocked surprise, he felt the prick of a needle against his arm. He hadn't even known it was there—what with those beguiling green eyes distracting him.

"What the hell was that?"

"Painkiller," Crista reported. "Now don't get on my bad side, sugar. I'll have you looking like a pincushion before you know what hit you."

When Crista stepped away she raised the syringe as if it were a smoking pistol and blew breath on the tip. She wore an expression of triumph that had Hal muttering under his breath.

"Give him something to sweeten his disposition while you're at it," Bernie requested, grinning from ear to ear, exposing the gap between his teeth.

Crista took a threatening step forward and Hal flung up a bare arm—the same one she'd sneaked up to poke. "Okay, lady, you win this go-round. I'll eat the damned mush but I won't like it."

Playfully, Crista twirled the syringe over her fingers and stuffed it into the pocket of her medical jacket, as if she were holstering a pistol. "That's mighty gentlemanly of you, cowboy," she said in her best western drawl. "I aim to keep the peace on this here ranch, don'tcha know?"

In spite of his low opinion of women, Hal grinned reluctantly. It was becoming increasingly apparent why Crista Delaney was a sensitive subject with Nash. She had a natural charm and the kind of irrepressible spirit that drew a man against his will. Nash was in considerably more trouble than Hal first thought. The woman had way too much sex appeal and an irresistible sense of humor.

"You can get up tomorrow, if you feel up to it," Crista told Hal while checking his pulse. "But absolutely no exertion. Climbing the steps will be exercise enough for the next couple of days."

When the phone rang, Crista reached over to pluck up the receiver. "Chulosa Ranch."

There was a long, noticeable pause.

"Crista?"

She flinched. The sound of Nash's deep baritone voice evoked a riptide of sensations.

"How are your patients?"

"Fine," she said in a neutral tone. "How's the rodeo going?"

"You'll be disappointed to hear I didn't bust my ass as you had hoped."

Crista muttered under her breath. That had been a childish thing for her to say, even in a fit of temper. "I'm sure you'd rather speak to your brother." She shoved the phone at Hal, pivoted on her heel, and walked out the door to oversee Levi's therapy session.

Ten

Hal eased back on the pillow and swallowed his applesauce. "Is everything going okay in Fort Worth?"

"I'm holding down first place in bareback and saddle bronc," Nash reported. "Second in calf-roping."

"Not bad after a five-year layoff," Hal complimented.

"I'm thinking of inviting some of the cowboys to the ranch next week. I thought maybe Levi could use a pick-me-up. Do you feel up to organizing the party and getting the food?"

"Sounds good, big brother," Hal affirmed. "I'll ask Bernie to go shopping. He'll probably leap at the chance to get away from me."

"Ask Uncle Jim to spiff up the bunkhouse so the boys will have a clean place to sleep."

"Will do. How are the horses holding up?"

"They're carrying winners to the purse," Nash reported. "We should do all right here. I bought myself in the bulldogging calcutta yesterday. Some of the cowboys decided to have their own competition on the side."

"Who's hazing for you?"

"A rookie from Montana who shows a lot of promise."

"Justin Simms," Hal recalled. "He's got a lot of cowboy try. One of these days he'll be at the top of the rankings."

"Those were my thoughts exactly," Nash affirmed. "If I place in the calcutta, it should pay for this hoedown for Levi."

"He'll enjoy seeing the cowboys again. Bernie says Levi has been staring at the walls and keeping to his own quarters quite a lot the past few days. He went down to toss a lariat this morning, but it's the first time in a while."

"Let's keep this party a surprise," Nash requested.

"You've got it, big brother." Hal yawned broadly and released an enormous sigh.

"Are you sure you're feeling all right?"

"Yeah, but I just got tricked into taking a painkiller by that fiery therapist. I think it's starting to take effect. She promised to keep me sedated if I didn't behave myself. She's fast on the draw with that damned syringe."

"I better go. I need to exercise the horses before tonight's performance," Nash explained. "Take care of yourself, Hal."

"And you hang tough, big brother," Hal said drowsily.

"Get some rest."

"As if Crista gave me a choice." Hal hung up the phone and shut his eyes. He was asleep in less than a minute.

After Crista finished her session with Levi she found herself heading for the barn to check on the stud colt—as had become her habit after every visit. While Choctaw Jim was busy inoculating the calves he had caged in the squeeze chute, Crista let herself into the stall with the brood mare and foal. The process of imprinting the colt had a relaxing effect on her. It was heartening to realize there were some things about her childhood that she *did* want to remember.

Crista wondered how her father was managing at his ranch these days. Although she sent cards and gifts for his birthday, Father's Day, and Christmas, she never heard from Cole. All because she had refused the college rodeo scholarship and insisted on studying physical therapy. Lord, her father was as stubborn as a mule!

Crista sadly shook her head as she drew her hands over every inch of the colt's slender body. She wondered if Cole would ever come to regret his ultimatums. She certainly had. Since her mother had succumbed to terminal illness when Crista was in kindergarten, Cole Delaney was all the family she had left . . .

"You're exceptionally good at imprinting," Choctaw Jim noted as he leaned against the railings of the stall. "Plenty of practice, I'd say."

"Enough," Crista said evasively.

A wry smile quirked Choctaw Jim's lips. "My horse is still saddled. Would you like to take him for a spin?"

Crista glanced up into his onyx eyes, noticing the sly twinkle. "Now why would you think I might want to do something like that?"

He stepped into the stall to grab Crista's hand and then led her down the lane. "I've been around horses, cowboys, and cowgirls all my life. It isn't hard to spot someone who knows her way around animals as well as you do."

Choctaw Jim paused while the saddled mount

stamped restlessly in the corral. "I had been traveling the rodeo circuit, long before Hal and Nash's mother called to say that Barry Griffin had found someone else to take her place. My sister needed help raising two rough, rowdy boys, especially when she had been in ill health for years.

"Between working both ranches, attending rodeos, and checking my own livestock I've learned to recognize a kindred spirit at a glance. Besides that," he added with a wry grin, "I was the chute boss at the National High School Rodeo in Oklahoma City, while Hal and Nash were competing in college events."

"Is that a fact." Crista studied the sturdy gray gelding, avoiding Jim's mischievous grin.

"It's a fact." Choctaw Jim reached over to place the reins in Crista's hand. "When we made the arrangements for you to rent my place, I was instantly reminded of a curly-headed blonde who looked amazingly like you. She was one whale of a barrel racer in those days. There were a half-dozen young cowboys drooling over her while she was turning and burning barrels in the arena. Mary Crista was what they called her back then. She was damned good. I kept expecting to see her name in *Pro Rodeo Sports News* a few years later, but I never did. What happened?"

Crista swung into the saddle with practiced ease. "I believe I will take that ride after all."

Choctaw Jim chuckled at Crista's way of avoiding the question. "I don't have any barrels on hand, but wooden crates should suffice. Give ole Bandit a spin, but keep in mind that he likes to cut his corners short."

Crista trotted the gray gelding around the private arena beside the barn. The horse had an easy gait and, with the lightest touch of Crista's heels, Bandit responded like a patriot missile.

"How long has it been?" Jim questioned as he set the third and last crate into place.

"Almost six years."

"Then you better take the first round slow and easy, just to get Bandit used to the cloverleaf course. He's trained to get the jump on contrary calves, not crates."

Crista peeled off her white frock coat and tossed it to Choctaw Jim. "This is between you and me, okay? I don't want anyone else to know I've competed in rodeos."

The veteran cowboy nodded in compliance. "I can mind my own business when I'm told to, though I don't know why you would want to keep this a big secret."

"I have my reasons," Crista murmured as she focused her concentration on the crates that had been placed one hundred feet apart.

Her high-top Nikes felt awkward in the stirrups, forcing her to clamp her legs tightly around Bandit's belly to steady herself. Crouching down, Crista put her heels to him, feeling the horse explode in a surge of power. By the time they reached the first crate, Bandit was at full gallop. She reined him to the right of the crate and he broke stride, unaccustomed to making figure eights around objects rather than cutting a calf from the herd.

Crista gave Bandit time to collect himself before taking the clockwise turn. With a sharp jab of her heel, she sent the quarter horse thundering toward the second crate, banking left for the spin. The horse leaned too sharply, causing Crista's knee to collide with the crate. It rocked slightly but didn't topple as Bandit sprinted toward the last crate. Clamping her hand on the saddle horn, Crista pulled Bandit into a tight turn, and then raced toward Choctaw Jim.

Bandit put on the brakes at the first tug on the reins, his eyes wide with excitement, his head up as he rolled the bit in his teeth. Choctaw Jim's dark-eyed gaze swung from his snorting horse to the flush of unmistakable pleasure that claimed Crista's face.

"How long did you say it had been?" he asked wryly. "Seems to me you still know how to shave a few slices off the cutting edge. Why don't you give it another run, just for old time's sake?"

Crista couldn't resist the invitation. She had missed riding far more than she realized. In fact, she would have stayed until dark, putting Bandit through the paces, teaching him when to slow his gait and when to pull out all stops. Half the fun of riding barrels had been training a spirited mount to the point that it could run the course with the speed and precision that cut unnecessary seconds off a stopwatch.

While Choctaw Jim watched, smiling that enigmatic smile of his, Crista thrilled to the feel of the wind rushing past her face, the feel of the muscular gelding moving beneath her, racing at speeds that left her spirits soaring.

"Well, shoot me down and trample all over me," Bernie Bryant breathed in awe. He stared out the kitchen window, marveling at Crista's skills. Astonished, he watched her fly through the cloverleaf pattern as if she'd been born on the saddle.

He never dreamed they had a cowgirl in their midst. Nobody had said anything to him about it.

"Bernie?"

The cook nearly leaped out of his Wranglers when Dogger's voice boomed over the intercom. "I'm going into Kanima Springs, just to drive around. The walls are crowding in on me."

"You want some company?" Bernie asked as he washed Levi's supper plate.

"No, just some fresh air. I'll be gone a few hours."

"Don't forget to take the cellular phone," Bernie prompted. "If you have car trouble, give me a call."

"I've already got the phone tucked in the pocket of the chair."

Bernie rinsed the plate and set it in the dish drainer. "Are we still on for dominoes tonight?"

"I'll be looking forward to it, but I might be a little late getting home."

"I'm flexible."

When Levi signed off, Bernie turned his attention back to the window, watching Crista train Bandit. The gray gelding was a natural, possessing the speed, spirit, and quick reflexes required to negotiate sharp turns and cover ground at a thundering gallop . . .

Bernie tensed when Bandit became a little too cocky with his newfound skills and slammed against the crate. Crista went tumbling to the ground. Her high-top Nikes couldn't anchor her feet to the stirrups. To her credit, though, she knew how to drop, roll, and bound to her feet before Choctaw Jim could dart out to check on her. Breathing a sigh of relief, Bernie watched

Crista swing back onto the saddle, all body parts intact.

"Are you sure you're okay?" Choctaw Jim questioned as Crista trotted Bandit toward him.

Crista nodded. "Just remind me to dust off my boots the next time I decide to ride. These tennis shoes weren't meant for stirrups."

"Anytime you feel the urge to straddle a horse again, just let me know. If you don't want to do it here, I'll bring Bandit over to you," he offered generously.

Crista swung down, reflexively patting Bandit's neck in reward for a job well done—until he became too sure of himself. "Any particular reason why you wanted me back on a horse?"

"For the same reason I think it's good for Nash to get back on the rodeo circuit," Jim replied. "When you're good at something and you enjoy doing it, you should do just that—enjoy it."

"These days I don't have the time to keep a horse in good riding condition," she replied. "I don't have to tell you how undependable and cantankerous a horse can become when it doesn't get regular workouts."

"Bandit is always in good condition. I exercise him when I'm home and Nash occasionally uses him to work cattle. The horse is yours for free loan. You just say the word, Mary Crista."

Crista smiled at the kindly expression on Jim Pryce's weathered features. "I'll keep it in mind."

All the way home, Crista caught herself grinning. Suddenly the frustrations of a hectic day seemed miles away. It would be tempting to accept her landlord's generous offer. It would also be good therapy for an overworked therapist who probably got too involved with her patients and needed to find ways to release bottled-up emotion.

Levi Cooper maneuvered his van up beside the pay phone outside The Crawdad Hole Restaurant to place a call before returning to the ranch.

"J.C? Levi. All systems are go. We've got to move fast, though. I can't take a chance of anyone at the ranch finding out what's going down. You'll have to take care of the last of the arrangements for me."

For several minutes Levi listened to what his associate had to say. "Thanks, J.C. Now we can tie up all the loose ends at just the right time. If I can dream up another excuse to get away, I'll drive up in a couple of days to check things over. But it won't be as easy to sneak off when Nash gets home."

J.C. interjected a comment and Levi responded with a crack of laughter. "Yeah, well, Good Time will get *his* soon enough, and so will Hal. I've planned for this day for a long time. It can't get here soon enough to suit me."

The sight of an old model car parked on the grass path that led to one of the pastures near Crista's home drew her attention.

Out of habit, she stopped to check the vehicle. No one had collapsed on the front seat, thank goodness. And there were no signs of foul play.

Crista glanced around, wondering if a hunter might have been tramping around the thickets, scaring up game. If memory served, it was dove season. Abandoned cars and pickups were often seen parked beside country roads this time of year.

When Crista noticed the extra set of clothes on the back seat she presumed some city-dweller had driven out to hunt after work. With a shrug she turned back to her car and headed home.

It was dark by the time Crista strode up the steps. A wary frown knitted her brow the moment she stepped inside. There was an unfamiliar scent lurking in the house. Nothing obvious, but still . . .

The instant her gaze strayed to the sofa she recalled her encounter with Nash. It was humiliating to realize the man she had wanted to the point of desperation hadn't found her impossibly alluring as well.

"What did you expect?" Crista asked herself as she veered into the kitchen. She obviously lacked the kind of appeal that kept men coming back for more. Jonathan had taken his interest elsewhere. Nash Griffin had easily been able to resist her, even while he introduced her to sensations that overshadowed all thought.

"Just forget it, Delaney," she grumbled as she pulled open the refrigerator to scrounge up something for supper. "It's probably this tangled mop that repels men. You should keep it just the way it is, though, and be thankful you've got it. For sure, you don't need entanglements with men. You're obviously lousy at relationships."

The phone blared and Crista dashed off to take the call before the answering machine clicked on. "Hello?" she said breathlessly.

"Hi, boss. It's me, Jill."

"What's up?"

"I thought you'd want to know that I contacted the social worker in Keota Flats and asked her to keep a close watch on Lisa Chandler and her worthless mother."

That came as a relief. "Good. Thanks, Jill."

"The social worker has a heavy workload, but she's going to check on Lisa while making her rounds. I told her I had stopped by and checked on our recently released patient who had been left to fend for herself with a bum arm and leg. The house was a pit, just as you figured it would be," Jill confirmed with a disgruntled sniff. "Janelle hasn't been around much since Lisa was dismissed from the hospital."

"I'll call the sheriff's office to see if I can get a detective to keep surveillance on Janelle."

"Do you know where she works?"

"I called the number on the medical file to find out," Crista informed the technician. "She waits tables at Mangy Dog Saloon."

"Janelle also works part-time in a liquor store before driving down to Kanima Springs," Jill added.

"Wonderful."

"Before you hang up, Jack wants to talk to you," Jill put in hurriedly.

Crista waited for Jack to pick up the phone.

"I have reservations at a swank restaurant in the city. I thought we might eat early, avoid the crowd, and take in the theater rather than a movie this time."

"Sounds good," Crista said with more enthusiasm than she actually felt. "Would you mind if we made a detour on our way through the city?"

"Does that mean we'll be able to spend even more time together?" There was a smile in Jack's voice. "If it does, it's fine by me."

Crista wished she could be more responsive to

the compliment. But experience was teaching her
that the better men got to know her, the less they
liked her. Jack would stop asking her out once
the newness wore off.

"I need to pick up a piece of equipment for
one of my patients," Crista explained. "It will only
be a few minutes out of the way."

"I'll pick you up around three o'clock Saturday
afternoon."

"Better yet, I'll drive up to Keota Flats so you
won't have to drive in the wrong direction. I need
to check on Lisa Chandler while I'm in town."

When Jack hung up, Crista quickly dialed her
oldest and dearest friend. Within a few minutes
she and Cynthia Marrow had worked out the arrangements to borrow the item Crista had in mind
for Levi Cooper.

The next order of business was to place a call
to the sheriff's department, with the odd request
to tail Janelle Chandler. Before the dispatcher
gave Crista a long spiel about an understaffed
force, Crista shamefully used the power of her
position at the hospital to get the results she
wanted. All for a good cause, she assured herself.

Crista strode back to the kitchen to pop left-
over meatloaf in the microwave. When she had
eaten and showered, she strolled toward her
room, towel-drying her hair on the way. She stumbled to a halt when she noticed the closet door
standing slightly ajar.

Uneasiness skittered down her spine. Her gaze
circled the room, taking careful inventory of the
furniture and her personal belongings. Crista's attention fastened on the dresser, where the lace
of one of her bras peeked from the top drawer.

Hardly daring to breathe, she listened for the

slightest sound that might alert her to danger. But nothing stirred, not even a mouse.

"God, you're losing it, Delaney," she chastised herself.

Distracted by thoughts of Nash Griffin, she had probably been careless about cramming clothes in the drawer and closet while she hurriedly dressed for work. Now, she was allowing her imagination to conjure up scenes out of a horror movie—

Then Crista noticed that the latch on the bedroom window was unlocked. Surely she hadn't done *that!* She always kept the windows locked, unless she was airing out the house, which she hadn't done all week.

Her suspicions aroused, Crista checked her jewelry and valuables. Nothing appeared to be missing. Odd, she thought. If she didn't know better she would swear someone had been snooping around her house. Maybe that was the unfamiliar scent she noticed the instant she walked in.

After securing the deadbolts on the front and back door, Crista called it an early night and climbed into bed. She didn't bother watching the ten o'clock news, for fear the usual gruesome stories would feed her nightmares.

Trying to think optimistic thoughts, Crista closed her eyes and willed herself to relax. She could use a decent night's sleep, especially if she would be called upon in the middle of the night to defend herself against the unidentified mass murderer who had sneaked into her home to fondle her unmentionables—his sick mind twisted and hell-bent on returning to attack her while she slept . . .

Lord, Delaney, she thought, tugging the quilt protectively beneath her chin. *Pull yourself together and go to sleep!*

* * *

Nash peeled off his shirt—carefully. His left arm hurt like hell blazing. His old shoulder injury, aggravated by the new wound he had acquired while making a launch off Popeye to wrestle a steer, was throbbing with every heartbeat. Nash had managed to throw the steer to the ground, but not before the big brute swung its head and hooked him in the arm with a horn.

For all his aches and efforts, Nash was holding down a solid third place in bulldogging. Of all his rodeo techniques, his steer wrestling skills proved to be the ones most in need of polish. If not for his well-trained mount Nash probably would have landed in a tangled heap.

The door of his cheap motel room rattled beneath an insistent knock. "Hey, Good Time, some of the boys are headed to Hog Wild Saloon to sip some suds," the kid from Montana called to him. "Would you like to join us?"

Nash opened the door, keeping his scraped shoulder concealed by tossing his shirt over it. "Thanks, Justin, but a hot shower and a cold cola sound like my idea of a good time tonight."

Justin Simms grinned. "Well, anytime you want to join the fun, just let us know. We'd be glad to have a rodeo legend in our midst."

Nash returned the friendly smile before Justin swaggered off to catch up with his friends. Some legend, thought Nash. The other cowboys were looking for cold drinks and hot women. Nash would have gladly settled for a relaxing massage, like the ones Hal and Levi received from Crista . . .

An alluring image, boasting a saucy smile, picked one helluva time to bombard Nash. Too

bad he had practically turned himself into a
monk the past few years. Forgetting one woman
by losing himself in the arms of another had tremendous appeal right about now.

All that business about out of sight, out of mind
had been a lot of bullshit. Since Nash had heard
Crista's soft, sultry voice on the phone this afternoon, he kept remembering the intriguing
sounds he had drawn from her, discovering every
intimate place she liked to be touched . . .

Nash swore under his breath when his body began to respond to the memory. Damn, he could
have used a painkiller himself—and not just to
ease his shoulder wound.

Maybe he should call and apologize for the
things he had said to Crista the night before he
left for the rodeo. Hell, he had always been too
blunt for his own good. He never had acquired
the gift of tact. Probably never would, either.

Although he had tried to prove to Crista that
she was all the woman a man could ever want,
his good intentions had backfired. Nash hadn't
meant to hurt Crista's pride. He had only wanted
to get away from her while he still could, before
he crossed the line completely—mindlessly—only
to regret it later.

Nash absently reached for the phone, but his
hand stalled in midair. No, hearing Crista's voice
again would only torment both of them.

He may have sown a few wild oats in his
younger days, but he still had a few old-fashioned,
midwestern values where Crista Delaney was concerned. She wasn't like the camp followers
around rodeos, looking for one-night stands—
and the cowboys willing to deliver them.

From what Crista had confided—over one too

many glasses of wine—men had caused her a lot of misery. Her father sounded like an impossible tyrant and her ex-husband must have been a card-carrying jerk . . .

And Nash was another one . . . He had teased Crista with her newly awakened sexuality and then left her thinking he hadn't really wanted her.

Did she deserve that?

The answer to that question caused Nash to wince—and not from the painful throb in his shoulder. He was already carrying around a bucket of guilt because of Levi's tragic accident. He didn't need this ill-fated attraction weighing down his conscience, too. Especially not tonight, not when he was feeling tired, lonely, and more vulnerable than he had in years.

Nash took a fortifying breath and picked up the phone. It suddenly dawned on him that he had already memorized Crista's number, but he refused to dwell on the significance of that. He didn't have the slightest idea what in the hell he intended to say. Funny thing, though, she was the one he wanted to share his victories and defeats with. Deep down inside, he knew his intent to apologize was only part of the reason he wanted to call her. He wanted—needed—her voice to be the last thing he heard before he drifted off to sleep.

Nash didn't dare let himself dwell on the significance of *that,* either!

The shrill ring brought Crista awake with a start, her heart pounding crazily. She groped for the phone and knocked it to the floor. Muttering, she fumbled in the dark for the receiver.

"Hello?" she mumbled.

"I woke you up, didn't I? Sorry about that, Curly."

"That's okay," Crista said, yawning. "I had to get up to answer the phone anyway."

Nash chuckled.

The sound of his deep laughter scattered the cobwebs in Crista's brain. She sat upright. "Nash? Are you all right? You aren't hurt, are you? I'm sorry I put that spiteful curse on you. I was mad and humiliated and . . ."

Crista groaned when she realized she had forgotten to engage her brain before she freed her tongue. "What do you want?"

Nash snickered again. "I liked you better when you were half asleep."

The huskiness in his voice put a reluctant smile on her lips. "Your brother is doing fine, if that's what you called to find out. And Levi went through his circuit training without a hitch. Your uncle doctored a few sick calves and everything at the ranch is running smoothly. All you have to do is take care of yourself. No need to worry about anything else."

"That's nice to know, but that's not why I called."

Crista sank back on her pillow. She knew she shouldn't be enjoying the sound of his voice, the easy camaraderie that never seemed to last more than a few minutes at a time.

Nash cared so deeply and felt so responsible for his friend that he had devoted his life to providing for Levi. Crista wondered what it would be like to have a man that devoted to her—a man whose smiles had once been the highlights of her unhappy childhood. Try as she may, Crista couldn't seem to forget the lovable, fun-loving man Nash had been, the man he could be again . . .

"Crista?"

"I'm still here," she whispered, lost to fond memories.

"Good. I was afraid you had dozed off."

There was a noticeable pause. Crista waited, wondering what had prompted Nash to call.

"I'm sorry about that night before I left for the rodeo. When a man wants a woman as badly as I wanted you and he knows he can't have her, it plays hell with him. I wasn't trying to hurt or humiliate you. I only wanted to stop for your sake as well as mine."

Crista squeezed her eyes shut against the sensations his husky voice aroused. "I wanted you, too," she admitted. "Wanted you the way I have never wanted anyone else, the way I didn't even know it was possible to want a man. I didn't know I could respond like that."

Nash clenched his teeth as her words sizzled through him like electricity. All too clearly, he remembered how explosive their passion had been.

It was a damned good thing they were miles apart. If Crista was as vulnerable and susceptible as he felt right now, he would be buried so deep inside her . . .

Nash immediately stifled that tantalizing thought.

"I'm sorry I lashed out at you," Crista apologized. "Frustration does indeed wreak havoc. I suppose I should have thanked you for calling a halt that night. But I was feeling so much pleasure from your touch and I wanted—"

"Give me a break here, Curly," Nash quickly interrupted. "I'm scheduled for two rough rides tomorrow on Whiplash and Gone Wild. I won't make it to the buzzer if I'm in the same condition then as I am now. You're making me ache all over, just remembering what it was like."

Crista caught her breath. Was he experiencing the same torment that she was? It was consolation, at least, to know that he did find her desirable, that he hadn't teased her for his own ornery amusement.

"I didn't want to leave you with such a bad good-bye," Nash said after a moment. "You came away with the wrong impression of why I called a halt, and it's been weighing on my conscience. If I hurt your feelings, I'm sorry. I just never seem to say the right things when I'm with you. I guess I'm out of practice, after five years of living in an all-male environment."

Crista sighed, further tormented by the fact that Nash had devoted himself to a man who might not be very appreciative. It was on the tip of her tongue to reveal her suspicions about Levi, but Nash didn't need that right now, and probably wouldn't believe it, anyway. He had enough on his mind without her complicating the situation.

"I wish you luck tomorrow. Everyone at Chulosa is rooting for you."

"I better get some rest," Nash said tiredly. "Good night, Curly."

Crista replaced the phone on the nightstand and snuggled beneath the quilt. She almost wished Nash hadn't called, and yet she was glad he had. There was comfort in knowing they were both fighting the attraction, even if nothing could ever come of it. She only hoped to God that all Nash's generosity toward Levi wasn't wasted.

Eleven

"Levi?" Crista called from the door of her patient's private quarters. "Come outside. I brought an exercise device I want you to try out."

Frowning, Levi rolled through the living area and eased down the ramp Nash had built beside the front steps. His jaw dropped when Crista picked up the modified saddle she had borrowed from Cynthia Marrow.

Crista glanced over Levi's head to see the other three men staring at her in amazement.

"When I was here a few days ago, Levi mentioned that he missed horseback riding." She indicated the saddle, which was equipped with a back support, semicircular metal bars that stabilized the chest, and leather straps that secured the legs. "These special saddles are being used in various clinics for riding programs. They have been tested for safety and approved. If you can spare the time, I'd like you to see this demonstration so you can assist Levi when I'm not here to do it."

Choctaw Jim and Bernie clambered off the porch in nothing flat, ready and willing to help. Hal Griffin remained where he was, appraising Crista with an indecipherable expression in his glittering black eyes. Crista had the feeling Hal didn't approve of putting Levi back on a horse.

While Choctaw Jim lugged the saddle to the barn, Bernie clamped his hands on the handles of the wheelchair and rolled Levi away. Crista turned to meet Hal's piercing stare.

"I'm not sure *torment* is a satisfactory part of therapy," Hal snorted sardonically. "I don't want to see Dogger come to more harm than good with this harebrained experiment."

Crista tilted her chin upward. "Are you coming down to the arena to see for yourself how Levi manages on the back of a horse or aren't you?"

With his ribs still bound in protective wrap, Hal breathed a restricted sigh and reluctantly descended the steps. "I'll say one thing for you, lady, you've got gumption. You realize, I'm sure, that if anything goes wrong and Levi gets hurt, my big brother will take you apart with his bare hands. And I'll be there to help him, bruised ribs and all."

Crista smiled confidently. "I'll make you a deal, cowboy. If Levi doesn't enjoy every moment of this therapy, if he doesn't get thrills from becoming one of the gang again, I'll even hold still while you try to break me into little pieces. Fair enough?"

Frowning darkly, Hal muttered, "You damned well better be right about this."

Under Crista's conscientious supervision the modified saddle was cinched to the gentlest mare on the ranch. Then Levi was lifted into place and, in a matter of minutes, Crista had secured the support bands.

Beaming with unmistakable pleasure, Levi clucked his tongue, sending the sorrel mare off in a walk and then into a trot.

"Well, I'll be damned," Choctaw Jim murmured.

Bernie chuckled in delight. "That goes double for me."

Crista glanced sideways to gauge the cynical Hal's reaction. He was watching Levi with reluctant satisfaction. The tension that held Hal rigid decreased with each loping circle Levi made around the arena.

Levi's burst of laughter and whoop of excitement erupted as he galloped past the bystanders. Only then did Hal break into a full-fledged smile.

"Okay, little lady, so I owe you an apology," Hal begrudgingly admitted. "So what's it going to cost us to have a special saddle like this one made? I have a feeling Levi is going to want one of his own—there has to be a catch here somewhere."

"There's no catch. This saddle belongs to a friend of mine. She—" Crista smiled ruefully, remembering. "She doesn't have time to ride much these days. She's willing to sell the saddle to you for a reasonable price—after a lengthy trial period, of course."

"How can we thank you?" Hal asked in a humbled tone.

Crista turned to stare him squarely in the eye. "By *not* treating me as if I were some sort of dangerous threat all the time."

Hal's full lips quirked, his obsidian eyes twinkling. "It's nothing personal. It's women in general."

"I figured it was something like that. I had a tendency to judge all men by my ex-husband," she confided. "But that business about one bad apple ruining the whole basket doesn't always apply. I'd appreciate it if you cut me a little slack—"

"Okay, which one of you wants to ride out with

me to check the cattle?" Levi called out as he reined to a halt, his face flushed with pleasure.

"That would be me, Dogger," Choctaw Jim spoke up before pivoting around to saddle Bandit. "I need to check on the sick calves I doctored a few days ago."

Blue eyes sparkling, Levi glanced down at Crista. "How can I ever repay you?"

By not betraying the very men who've stood behind you, Crista thought to herself. Instead she said, "You just did, Levi. That smile is worth millions."

"When Choctaw Jim and I get back, I'm going to try roping off a horse."

"Now, slow down, Dogger," Hal insisted with a disapproving frown. "Let's take this one step at a time, shall we?"

Crista nodded. "Give yourself a chance to get the feel of riding without the use of your legs before you try roping. True, it is being done. In fact, I know of one cowboy in particular who suffered a similar injury. After adjusting to the modified saddle, he's been entering team roping competition with a friend. But it's going to take time. You'll have to be patient."

Levi grinned broadly. "When you're up to it, Hal, maybe we could give team roping a try. You could rope the steer's head while I take the back heels, at least until I get my timing down. Then we can switch off."

"I suggest you begin with the improvised steer-of-a-hay-bale." Crista gestured toward the plastic calf head. "Once you've mastered that, you can graduate to a real calf."

"I'll start practicing tomorrow," Levi announced.

"Ready, Dogger?" Choctaw Jim called out.

Levi reined toward the older cowboy, who had reappeared from the barn. "I've been ready for five years," he said, as he trotted away.

Satisfied, Crista watched Levi put the mare into a canter. She hoped that by giving him the chance to become one of the cowboys again, he would return the same loyalty the other men had generously given him. And even more, she hoped to God that this niggling feeling that warned her Levi was concealing something turned out to be false. She was going to work on Levi's conscience every chance she got, reminding him of all the sacrifices Nash and the other men had made for him. If he was half the man the Griffins and Company thought he was, he wouldn't betray the best friends a man could ever hope to have.

Nash heaved a weary sigh as he veered down the path toward the ranch, hauling the horse trailer behind him. The silhouette of the two-story, wood-frame home, barn, and outbuildings was set against a backdrop of a full moon. A fine mist dotted the windshield, assuring Nash he would arrive home just ahead of the rain.

As much as he had thrilled to the challenge of the competition that had once been an integral part of his life, he was glad to be home. He had also missed seeing . . .

Willfully, Nash squelched the memory of evergreen eyes. His attempt to practice that out of sight, out of mind philosophy hadn't worked worth a damn.

As soon as his headlights beamed across the lawn, dark figures poured from the front door.

Levi was easily recognizable as the lights reflected off the chrome of his wheelchair.

"Well?" Hal demanded immediately. "How did you do?"

"Respectably," Nash replied through the open window of the extended cab truck. "How are the ribs?"

"Which ones? The barbecued ones Bernie saved for your supper?" Hal questioned. "Not bad."

"Not bad, hell!" Bernie snorted as he propped himself against the hood. "You had three helpings, as I recall. I had to hide a few for Nash before you gobbled them all up."

Hal ambled toward the passenger-side and took a seat. "I'll help you unload the horses."

"Do you have permission to do that already?" Nash asked.

"I'm permitted limited activity." Hal absently braced one hand over his mending ribs to shift position. When Nash pulled away from the house, Hal added confidentially. "All the arrangements have been made for the wingding. Bernie bought the supplies while Levi was at the hospital doing his gait therapy. By the time he returned, he never even knew Bernie had been gone."

"Good. I made the invitations by phone from the hotel in Fort Worth and asked a few of the cowboys at the rodeo to come by if they had a chance. Most of them are planning to take in the competition at Guthrie, so they'll be in the area."

"The bunkhouse has been cleaned and readied," Hal added, smiling cryptically as Nash stopped beside the barn. "This should be a grand surprise, all the way around. A little friendly competition in our own arena should be fun. It'll give me a chance to work out the soreness before I enter the rodeo at Guthrie."

After Hal and Nash unloaded the horses they ambled side by side up the concrete sidewalk to find Levi waiting on the porch. Without ado, Nash pulled out his wallet and handed over the checks from his winnings and the leasing of their horses.

"Damn, Good Time, this is *better* than respectable," Levi hooted.

Nash shrugged his stiff shoulder. "Most of the top cowboys are saving themselves for next week's rodeo. I held my own against the rookies."

"Held your own?" Hal smirked, when he saw the amount of the check. "You take five years off and come back that strong the first time out of the chute? Hell's bells, you should be the one on the circuit instead of me."

"Beginner's luck," Nash said with a dismissive flick of his wrist.

"Yeah, right," Hal snorted.

"This is going to come in handy," Levi said, stuffing the check in his shirt pocket. "I got another bill from the hospital yesterday. I'm about ready to give up those sessions—they're just too damned expensive. I can't see that the gait machine is doing all that much good anyway."

"Wrong," Nash growled. "You're sticking with it, no matter how much it costs."

Levi smiled secretively and then gave a shrug. "Okay, Good time, if you say so. I just want you to know it's going to take damn near all of this check to cover the most recent expenses."

Nash muttered under his breath. It was impossible to get ahead when that hospital charged an arm and two legs for treatment. As of yet, Nash hadn't seen Levi on his feet—walking, or even standing up. And despite Levi's usual objections, Nash was seriously considering marching himself to the hospital to have a look at that fancy, computer-driven, electronic gait stimulator.

According to Levi, the program triggered electrodes for alternate step patterns that simulated walking. If Levi had been ambulating around the exercise room while the technicians pushed the computerized cart behind him for the past three years, why wasn't he showing progress?

Hal shook his dark head as he followed Nash and Levi through the door. "Two first places and one second in bulldogging? Damn, I'm impressed. I still think I should stay home to train horses while you follow the circuit."

Nash placed his dusty hat on the hook by the door and flung his brother a stern glance. "No way, Hal. You're the one who qualified for National Finals. If you drop out now, someone else will replace you in the standings. Besides," Nash added quietly, "we need your paychecks to cover expenses."

Hal nodded. "I guess you're right. The money flows out of here as fast as we can haul it in. It takes all you and I can collect to keep Levi functioning. If not for leasing horses, giving rodeo clinics, and selling the horses you train, we couldn't meet expenses."

Nash wondered how long he and Hal could continue this grueling pace. For Levi's sake, Nash hoped he and Hal could make ends meet for years to come. It sure as hell hadn't been easy the past five years, and it probably wouldn't get any easier, either.

* * *

Crista stood on her front porch, her arms crossed over her chest, the toe of her high-top Nikes tapping irritably in rhythm with the rain-drops that dripped off the eaves. After calling the sheriff's department nearly an hour earlier and being told Detective Pine "will be there directly," she was still awaiting his arrival.

Finally—finally!—a nondescript car slopped through her muddy driveway. A cloud of smoke rolled from its interior as the short, stockily-built detective emerged. With the thick stub of a cigar clamped between his teeth, Detective Pine care-fully veered around the puddles to join Crista on the porch.

"Are you Ms. Delaney?"

She nodded curtly.

The detective thrust out his stubby hand in greeting. "I'm—"

"Late," Crista finished for him.

The detective rocked back on his heels, clasped his hands behind his back, and smiled around his smoldering cigar. "I'm a busy man, Ms. De-laney, and this is a big county."

Crista didn't back down an inch. "I'm aware of all that, detective. We all have our problems. I was assured three days ago that my request for surveillance would receive priority, especially con-sidering the physical condition of one of my young patients."

"Well, as I said—"

Crista quickly cut him off. She was in no mood for excuses. "Since that time, I've gotten the royal runaround from headquarters. I should think the neglect and near-abandonment of an injured child should take some kind of precedence around here. Until you do your job, the social worker in Keota Flats can't do her job, and a very fragile, vulnerable child suffers greatly because of it."

Detective Pine chewed on his cigar. "I stopped by Mangy Dog Saloon to investigate your accusations, but there isn't a law against a waitress accepting dates with patrons after working hours. If that were the case, every single female in the county, you included, would be under suspicion."

Crista was fast losing patience with this insensitive, lackadaisical agent. "Janelle Chandler has a child at home recovering from a traffic accident which left her confined to a wheelchair until after a series of surgeries. Janelle has left her daughter unattended during the days and half the nights."

"How old did you say the kid was?"

"Barely thirteen."

Detective Pine shoved his hands in the pockets of his jacket and puffed on his cigar, staring at Crista through a cloud of smoke and squinted gray-blue eyes. "You do realize there are kids living in the streets who are used to fending for themselves, don't you?"

Crista gnashed her teeth, exasperated. "In casts and a wheelchair? That's a new one on me, detective. And as for the child's mother, I'm reasonably certain she's involved with drugs. That's another reason my patient needs to be removed from her dangerous situation."

"You have proof of this?"

"No, that's what I hoped *you* were collecting the past three days," Crista muttered.

"Well, I'm doing what I can."

Which was a big fat nothing, in Crista's opinion. Determinedly, she kept her simmering temper under control. It looked as though she would to have to shadow Janelle herself. Never let it be said that dealing with the families of patients was easy. One way or another, they could be genuine pains in the butt.

Crista glanced down at the muddy footprints she had discovered on her porch when she returned home from work that evening. The footprints were the second reason she had demanded to speak to Detective Do-Nothing. Unfortunately, she had come to the conclusion that this man was simply putting in his time until he could collect his retirement pension.

"While you're here I'd like you to make note of the footprints on the south porch. I think I may have scared off a prowler when I drove up."

"Are you sure those prints don't belong to you?" Pine asked with a skeptical smirk.

Crista's nails curled into her clenched fists. She wondered what the penalty might be for assaulting a shabby excuse for a law official. "I'm absolutely certain they aren't my prints," she assured him. "A few days ago, I came home to find three empty messages on the answering machine, an unfamiliar scent in the house, an unlocked bedroom window, and closet doors and drawers left ajar."

Detective Pine removed the flaming cigar from his froglike lips and smiled slightly. "I assume nothing was stolen during this alleged break-in."

His ridiculing stare made Crista feel foolish for even mentioning the incident. But the muddy prints had left her wondering if there was some connection between the blank messages and the opened drawers.

"I suppose you want me to keep surveillance on your place, too—just in case," Pine said in a tone that sounded suspiciously like sarcasm.

"And I suppose that since a crime hasn't actually been committed I can't expect protection."

"That's the law," he said with a nod of his bald head.

It wasn't the first time Crista had wondered if she should simply set flame to her wasted tax dollars that supposedly paid for the protections promised in the Constitution. The document was obviously idealistic or outdated. Protection seemed to be one of those marvelous theories that didn't work worth a damn in reality.

Crista had encountered similar frustration while living in the City. A juvenile had been caught and arrested when he broke into her car, attempting to steal the vehicle from the hospital parking lot. The boy claimed he had been chased by a street gang and was desperate to find a place to hide. He had been turned over to his mother's care, and Crista had been assured restitution would be forthcoming. That had been two years ago. Restitution still had not come forth.

Scratch another one up for the good old justice system and its incompetent handling of delinquents. Damn it, Crista was trying to prevent one child from following in her mother's footsteps and ruining her life. Did she have to take matters into her own hands and rescue the poor child herself?

Obviously.

The detective tossed an unconcerned glance toward the footprints and then pivoted toward his car. "I'll see what I can do about the waitress at Mangy Dog, tomorrow or the day after."

"Don't knock yourself out," Crista murmured, scowling as he zigzagged around the puddles.

As the mud-splattered, army-green car pulled away, Crista hurled several curses toward the man

inside it. So much for Detective Pine. She would
have to protect her own interests against possible
burglars and also make sure Lisa Chandler was
properly cared for.

Crista's first order of business was to flick on
every light in the house, switch on the TV, and
look very much at home—while she was gone. Her
main problem would be leaving her car in the
driveway when she needed it to reach Mangy Dog
Saloon. Perhaps Nash could give her a lift . . .

Crista immediately discarded the thought. She
wasn't even sure Nash had returned from Fort
Worth, and he had made it clear enough that
they should keep their distance. She decided to
beg a favor from her landlord. Hopefully, Choctaw Jim wouldn't mind hauling her into town and
picking her up a few hours later.

On the wings of that inspiration, Crista zoomed
through the front door to make her home look
occupied and place her phone call.

Twelve

When the phone jingled, Nash rose from the supper table to answer the call. "Chulosa Ranch."

There was a hesitant pause.

"Nash, this is Crista. May I speak with Choctaw Jim?"

Nash had purposely refrained from contacting Crista after returning from the rodeo, but the sound of her voice brought pangs of longing and regret. Although he had called her from Texas to smooth over a bad good-bye, nothing had changed. Nothing was ever going to change. When a man could offer a woman nothing of himself, he was better off letting go, before letting go became impossible.

It was a sensible philosophy, Nash assured himself, but knowing that he was doing what was best for both of them didn't ease the longing that gnawed at him.

"It's for you," Nash said, gesturing toward his uncle.

Choctaw Jim downed another bite of chocolate cake and rose from his chair.

"This is Crista. I would like to ask a favor."

"Name it."

"I was wondering if you could give me a lift to Mangy Dog Saloon."

Choctaw Jim's graying brows shot up like exclamation marks. "Are you sure you want to go there? Is something wrong with your car?"

"I'll explain everything when you get here."

"I'll be down as soon as I finish dessert."

When Jim hung up and returned to his chair, Nash eyed his uncle with impatient curiosity. "Well?"

Jim smiled slyly. "Well what? I took the call and now I'm eating cake. That's that."

Nash picked up the succulent ribs Bernie had heated up for him. "Is Curly having car trouble?"

"Nope."

"Then what did she want?" Nash muttered at his taciturn uncle.

"She wanted to talk to me."

Nash glowered lightning bolts when the corner of Jim's mouth kicked up in an ornery grin. "What's the big damn secret between the two of you?"

"There isn't one," Jim replied calmly. "What's the big damn problem with *you?*"

"Nothing," Nash scowled at his plate. When he glanced up, the other men at the table—his brother included—were trying to smother their amused grins. *"What,* damn it?"

Hal shrugged nonchalantly. "I thought you said you had no personal interest in Levi's therapist."

"I don't. I was only curious. Hell's bells, you clowns act as if it's a federal offense to ask what she wanted!"

When Jim polished off the last of his cake, he scuttled away from the table. "I'll be back in a half hour."

Nash watched his uncle stride off, then stalked toward the front door.

"Where are you going?" Hal called after his brother.

"To feed the damn dog."

"I already fed Leon the rib bones we ate earlier," Bernie piped up. "He's as full as a tick."

"Then I'm going to invite Leon inside to play dominoes, so what's it to you?" Nash threw over his shoulder.

The door slammed shut. Hal stabbed a chunk of cake and glanced at Bernie. "Is it just me or has anybody else noticed that Nash has had a shorter fuse than usual the past few weeks?"

"He has been more irritable than usual," Bernie agreed. "And, of course, tramping around in the rain isn't going to improve his disposition."

Hal wasn't sure the drizzling rain that had followed Nash home was the reason for his brother's short temper. Woman trouble, he concluded. The damn fool. Hal was vividly aware of how a woman could tie a man in knots. If Nash didn't watch his step he was going to wade in too deep. And considering Nash's devotion to Levi, he would drive himself nuts if he tried to divide his loyalty.

As usual, Hal reminded himself, loving a woman did crazy things to a man. Good thing Hal had learned his lesson when he was young. No one would ever accuse him of snapping everybody's head off, just because of a female! Yes indeed, thought Hal, he would have to sit his big brother down and have a long talk, before Good Time Griffin bought himself the worst of times.

A steady drizzle had turned Crista's driveway to soup by the time Choctaw Jim pulled up in the rattletrap pickup. Dressed in a hat, boots, jeans, and western blouse, Crista made a dash for the vehicle.

"Nice duds," Jim complimented as Crista piled into the cab. "Only problem is you've got your hat pulled down so low that it's hard to get a look at that pretty face."

Crista plucked off the felt hat, sending her curls tumbling to her waist. The hat was going to conceal her identity while she kept surveillance on Janelle Chandler's evening activities.

Choctaw Jim shifted the truck into gear and slopped through the mud. "Just why did you want to leave your car at home during this jaunt to Mangy Dog? Are you hoping to pick up a date?"

Crista scoffed. "No—I think someone has been casing my place for a robbery," she confided, noting Jim's shocked expression. "I left all the lights on, but it would ruin the whole effect if the car was gone."

"You've had a prowler?" he croaked. "I can't recall ever having trouble way out here. Most people have to have a map to find this place."

"Well, someone knows where it is. I saw an abandoned car parked by the road a few days ago. I presumed it might be hunters . . ."

Her voice evaporated when she realized it had been the same day she had noticed the unlatched bedroom window and open dresser drawer. Coincidence? Crista doubted it.

"It could have been hunters," Jim concurred. "During open seasons they leave vehicles everywhere and tramp around your property, tossing trash whenever they feel like it. They'll walk right past a 'No Trespassing' sign and thumb their noses at it. When you catch up with them, they'll swear they have the owner's permission to hunt, even when they don't have a clue that they're talking to the owner."

He snorted disgust, adding, "And just wait until the first day of quail season. You'll swear you're living in a war zone. Kanima County is quail paradise. Hunters migrate here in coveys."

After a moment of silence, Choctaw Jim glanced at Crista's striking profile. "I know it isn't any of my business, but is there a particular reason why you called me rather than Nash to drive you to a tavern I'd never recommend to a lady like you?"

Crista winced and glanced at the weather-beaten man whose Native American heritage was stamped on his features with vivid clarity. Those dark eyes always seemed to peer right through her and his cryptic smile suggested he already knew the answer to his question. He was only baiting her to see if she'd admit the truth. Jim was a most perceptive man, with fifty years of life experience to his credit.

Inhaling a deep breath, Crista confessed the truth—since Jim seemed to know it already. "I think it's best if Nash and I stay away from each other as much as possible."

Jim veered around another muddy curve, the headlights glistening on falling raindrops. Silence, measured by the steady thump of the windshield wipers, filled the cab of the truck for a long moment. Crista breathed a sigh of relief, assuming Jim was going to let the subject die.

No such luck.

"You plan to keep your distance from Nash, but not because you're afraid of the big bad wolf." It wasn't a question, but rather a statement of fact.

"The wolf?" Crista repeated. "Is that your perception of your oldest nephew, too?"

"*Nashoba* means wolf in the Choctaw language," he explained. "Hal is short for *Halupa—Nishki Halupa* to be more accurate. It means the eyes of an eagle."

Crista was amazed at how well the name fit the Griffin brothers. Hal had dark, penetrating eyes like an eagle while his older brother possessed the golden eyes—and sometimes the forbidding persona—of a wolf prowling at night.

"My totem name, which is also my middle name, is *Opah*—the owl." Jim chuckled in amusement. "Too bad I'm not that wise."

"Your family is obviously proud of its heritage and traditions," Crista noted, settling herself comfortably. "As I've heard it told, it's good to stand for *something* so you won't fall for *anything*.

"Your nephews appear to be living up to their totems. Nash growls when he's provoked, and Hal has the look of a man who misses nothing. And you," Crista added with an accusing stare, "seem to know what I'm thinking before I even say it. I feel I'm at a grave disadvantage because no Indian blood flows through my veins."

"You do okay for a white woman," Jim teased, chuckling. "You also gained a distinct advantage when you decided to pitch your teepee in this region, so rich in Choctaw heritage. The towns and landmarks all have specific meanings for our people."

Crista suspected as much. "Like Kanima?"

Jim nodded. "It means somewhere, or someplace, the place for which you search for the answers you seek. Keota Flats translates as fire-gone-out, and the little hamlet of Hochukbi, to the south of here, means cave."

"And Chulosa Ranch?" Crista quizzed.

"The peaceful retreat," he translated.

Crista nodded thoughtfully. The place had certainly become that, she decided. The panoramic ranch, nestled beside Fire River, which was lined with thickets of cottonwoods, elms, and sandplum trees, was tucked beneath the rolling hills. It was like a country all its own.

When Jim pulled onto the pavement and veered toward town, his gaze momentarily darted to Crista. "You haven't told me why you have a hankering to mix with the wild crowd at Mangy Dog Saloon. Being new here, you may not be aware that that tavern has a tough reputation. In Hal's and Nash's younger days, it wasn't unusual for them to have to fight their way out of the place. Too much beer and boasting makes for a bad combination. The lowlife patrons who hang around the place these days are always eager to prove their manliness by provoking fights."

Jim chuckled, remembering several instances when Nash and Hal were forced to take on lopsided odds and came away sporting bloodied lips and shiners. "You'd be surprised how many men around here are downright jealous of the Griffin brothers' accomplishments in pro rodeo. Their mentality must leave a man thinking that if he can whip a tough cowboy, it makes him the better man. Of course, those same troublemakers don't have the gumption to climb on the back of a rank bronc or raging bull for eight seconds."

"And there are those who can't understand why a man would risk those dangers," Crista inserted.

"Yeah, I know. It probably seems crazy to most civilized folks. I guess some of us are simply throwbacks to the Old West." He paused to toss Crista one of those enigmatic smiles that always left her wondering if this intriguing individual knew things the average mortal failed to comprehend.

"Either that," Jim added, onyx eyes twinkling, "or the Great Spirit keeps sending some of us back to Mother Earth to keep traditions alive from another time." Before Crista had a chance to thoroughly digest that thought-provoking comment, Jim questioned, "So what's the lure that draws you to Mangy Dog Saloon?"

Crista avoided his direct stare. "Business, of sorts. It has to do with one of my patients, in a roundabout way."

"In other words, I should mind my own business and keep my nose out of yours," Jim concluded.

"Now I know where Nash learned the art of blunt-and-to-the-point," she teased.

Jim's smile melted as he fixed his penetrating gaze on Crista. "There are times, Mary Crista, when having a confidante and friend are in your best interests. I realize you like your independence, but I'm here for you if you need me. I hardly think my knowing how you think and what you feel, and why you want to keep quiet about your one-time rodeo career will threaten your independence, now will it?"

Crista sighed. Okay, she asked herself, so what could it hurt to confide in Choctaw Jim, especially when he knew quite a lot about her already? He didn't appear to be the kind of man who blabbed everything he knew. And after all, he *was* doing her a favor.

"I have a very dear friend named Cynthia Marrow," Crista began, staring through the windshield as if it were the door to the past. "She's the one who lent me the saddle for Levi. Cynthia was the best friend I had as a kid, the only one my father would permit me to associate with, for fear other people with other interests might influence the career he had planned for me in rodeo and horse training. Since Cynthia also lived on a ranch near my home, I was allowed to practice riding with her."

Crista watched the windshield wipers slap rhythmically while Jim waited for her to proceed. "Cyn and I were top contenders in barrel racing all through high school. But her career was cut short, not because of a rodeo accident like Levi's, but because of a fall on a trampoline. Several graduating seniors were throwing a party that ended in disaster. My father hadn't allowed me to attend the party, but I was at the hospital every day with Cyn, helping her cope and recover from her accident."

"You were there for all her frustration and depression," Jim predicted quietly. "You provided the shoulder for your friend to lean on."

Crista nodded and swallowed the lump in her throat. "Yes, and I understand what you went through with Levi, because I lived through it with Cyn. She was as vital and active as Levi was. I was there through that first year of Cyn's rehabilitation, trying to encourage her, boosting her sagging spirits. I even volunteered at the hospital so I could help with her exercise sessions. It was during that time that I realized how much I needed to be needed, that I wanted to make a difference in people's lives, since I couldn't make a difference in my own father's . . ."

When Crista dropped her head, Jim muttered aloud. "I saw and heard the way your father treated you at the High School Finals. He was quick to criticize and slow to compliment—if ever."

"I could never do enough—well enough," Crista whispered as she fiddled with the hat on her lap. "My dad hit the ceiling when I announced I wanted to become a physical therapist rather than follow the rodeo circuit. But I knew I had found my true calling, despite his threats and outrage. Without his financial help, I enrolled in college and roomed with Cynthia. She decided to major in psychology, specializing in the traumatic effects of disabling disease and accidental injury, while I studied P.T. When Cyn went to graduate school at another college—"

"You felt lost and wound up getting married," Jim inserted, wearing that knowing smile. "Funny how often things like that happen. Sometimes a misdirected sense of timing overshadows what *should have been* deep affection—and isn't."

Crista glanced at Jim, giving her head a shake. "How did you figure that out?"

"I've learned to read between lines, Mary Crista. And," he added with noticeable remorse, "I discovered what love really was when I was twenty-five, what love should be. It doesn't come around often in a lifetime."

Crista swore she saw a flash of pain on Jim's shadowed features. "What happened?" she persisted.

"My wife was killed in an automobile accident and my world came crashing down around me. That's when I started traveling the rodeo circuit to fill the void. I rode the raunchiest bulls and the wildest horses. The injury a powerful animal delivered was easier to cope with than the pain that can cut the heart in two."

"It kinda makes you wonder if it's worth it, doesn't it?"

Jim took his eyes off the road and stared at Crista. "It is worth it," he assured her quietly. "And when I see two people who belong together, who really care about each other the way Kathy and I did, I like to think that part of what we shared is living in them."

"Interesting philosophy," Crista said with a grin, hoping to lighten the conversation. "This is part of your philosophy about old souls returning to Mother Earth to recapture what might have been lost forever, isn't it?"

Jim chuckled at her question and the glistening amusement in her cedar-green eyes. It wasn't difficult to understand why Nash had been mesmerized, in spite of himself, or why the cynical Hal had begun to soften slightly toward Crista. She had a natural charisma that intrigued men.

"So you were paying close attention to what I said earlier, weren't you?"

"Yep, when a friend talks I try to listen. It's becoming a lost art, you know."

"Then suppose you tell this new friend of yours why you feel the need to keep your rodeo background a secret from Nash and the others. I'll be a good listener."

"That," Crista answered, "is still very personal and private. I've spilled enough of my guts to you in return for you doing me this favor. You know more than I would have preferred. And if I didn't trust you I wouldn't have said as much as I have. I don't like to dwell on what can't be changed."

"Fine, mum's the word, if that's the way you want it."

"That's the way I want it," she confirmed.

Jim flicked on his blinker and turned into the tavern parking lot. "Watch your step in there,

Mary Crista," he warned in all seriousness. "You can get your business in bad shape—real quick—in Mangy Dog Saloon. If you'd like reinforcements, just in case things get out of hand, I'll be glad to—"

"No," Crista cut in quickly. "I'll call you when I'm ready to come home."

Despite the concerned expression on Jim's craggy face, Crista took a deep breath and stepped out into the drizzle that was fast becoming a steady shower. With her hat pulled down around her ears and her hair tucked beneath it, she made a run for the neon sign hanging above the door.

Choctaw Jim kept the truck idling until Crista disappeared inside. He had serious reservations about leaving Mary Crista Delaney in a bar teeming with rowdy cowboys and the riffraff that wandered into the place on rainy nights. Most of the clientele—by nature and habit—had more energy than common sense.

A slow grin worked its way across Jim's lips when an idea occurred to him. Whistling the melody from one of Garth Brooks' country hits about friends in low places, Jim headed back to Chulosa Ranch. The country music star, who hailed from Yukon, Oklahoma, must have paid a visit to Mangy Dog Saloon—or someplace just like it—somewhere along his way to stardom. The bar was a perfect inspiration for many a hard-living, beer-drinking song.

Nash glanced up from the table when he heard the rattle and creak of the front door. It was domino night at Chulosa, and he'd been losing steadily since his first draw from the "bone pile." His mind kept wandering, wondering what mysterious errand his uncle had run for Crista.

The instant Choctaw Jim materialized in the doorway, his denim jacket dotted with raindrops, Nash threw him a questioning glance. Alive with a curiosity he couldn't restrain, Nash watched his uncle saunter toward the table to pat Leon on the head. The dog was sitting in Jim's usual place, playing the "dummy" hand.

"Deal me into the next hand," Jim requested. "I won't play for points, only for sport, until it's time to leave again."

When Jim straddled an empty chair—backward—and draped his arms over the back of the seat, Nash glowered at his uncle's infuriatingly secretive smile. "What the hell's going on?"

Jim shrugged casually. "Nothing for you to fret about. I'm taking care of it."

"Taking care of what, damn it!" Nash erupted.

All four men at the table—and Leon—glanced up from the rows of dominoes. Nash scowled—at himself.

"Well, since you're so curious," Jim said, swallowing another smile. "Crista is having trouble with prowlers. Probably some perverted Peeping Tom who's got a thing for her, is my guess. With her looks it's hardly surprising."

"Prowlers?" Nash echoed.

"So it seems." Jim nudged his oldest nephew, who was too preoccupied to pay attention to the domino game. "Play your double-five, Nash. You've already screwed up the game bad enough as it is."

Nash glanced at his uncle's twinkling obsidian eyes and slapped down the suggested domino.

"So? Did you see anyone lurking around Crista's place?"

"Nope. I didn't look. She wanted me to take her to Mangy Dog Saloon."

"Why in the hell did you do that?" Nash snorted.

"Because that's where she wanted to go," Jim replied calmly.

"You left her there all by herself?" Nash exclaimed in disbelief.

"She assured me she was used to taking care of herself."

"Hell's bells!" Nash erupted, bolting from his chair. His thigh bumped the table, sending dominoes clattering, exposing every player's hand.

"Well, so much for that game," Levi grumbled. "And here I was with the perfect hand . . . Nash?" Levi stared after his departing companion, and so did the other men.

Out of habit, Leon hopped from his chair, following devotedly after his master.

"What's eating Nash tonight?" Bernie questioned no one in particular while gathering the scattered dominoes. "He's been fidgeting in his chair like a caged bronc."

Hal watched his brother disappear around the corner and heard the front door slam. "Definitely woman trouble," he said with certainty. "He's going to be sorry as hell if he doesn't find a cure, too."

"Now me, I like women just fine," Bernie remarked as he picked up his new hand of dominoes. "I just never could hang onto the good ones. I was too busy following the call of the rodeo . . ."

"Or maybe it was because you did too much talking at the wrong times," Levi smirked. "It's your play, Gabby. And for heaven's sake, pay more attention than Nash did. He sure fouled up the last game."

"Is that a fact?" Choctaw Jim chuckled. "Couldn't concentrate, you say?"

"Not worth a damn," Hal affirmed.

Choctaw Jim figured as much. His oldest nephew was showing all the symptoms of a man who had convinced himself that he couldn't have something he was beginning to want very badly. Nash had become as irritable as a wounded rhinoceros. A taste of the old rodeo life certainly hadn't cured him, and distance hadn't eased the craving.

Nash Griffin had it bad, Jim decided. And if he wasn't mistaken—and he doubted he was—the roar of the jalopy pickup and the blast of bad mufflers indicated Nash was on his way to make sure Crista wasn't getting more than she bargained for at Mangy Dog Saloon.

Thirteen

Crista tucked herself behind the only table available in a darkened corner of the crowded bar—the table near the emergency exit. Mangy Dog Saloon was a far cry from the cocktail lounge and elegant restaurant Jack Forrester had taken her to the previous weekend.

The Rowdy Bunch had swaggered in a few minutes after Crista arrived, easing their jean-clad rears onto the saddles that served as bar stools. Although the four woolly-faced men called for a pitcher of beer, Crista suspected they had downed a few cool ones before they arrived. They were loud and boisterous and had been flinging off-color remarks since they staggered in.

Most of the patrons paid the riffraff no attention, since they were engrossed in conversation and drinks at their respective tables. The blaring jukebox drowned out some of the noise the men at the bar were making. Crista ignored them as best she could, focusing her attention on Janelle Chandler. The sleazy waitress had made several drumroll walks past the Rowdy Bunch, and had received a couple of pinches on the fanny for her efforts. The primitive mating ritual was making Crista nauseous.

She muttered and slowly nursed her beer—not

her favorite beverage, by any means. The mere color of beer seemed as inviting as drinking from a toilet. Red wine was definitely more Crista's style.

For the past hour she had stuck to her secluded corner, her face shaded by her hat, monitoring Janelle's activities. Every time the waitress bent over to take an order or set drinks served in mason jars on the table, she offered patrons a view of cleavage showcased by her skin-tight, scooped-neck T-shirt. Janelle had *available* and *indiscriminate* stamped all over her. It was enough to make Crista ill.

While Lisa was managing alone as best she could, Janelle was strutting her stuff for anyone who cared to watch. Crista wondered how many times Janelle dragged her stud-for-the-night home while Lisa slept in a nearby room. The thought put a muted curse on Crista's lips. She wanted Lisa moved before something disastrous happened . . .

"Hey, sugar, what are you hiding under that hat?"

Crista groaned silently when she peeked up from beneath the felt brim to see one of the woolly-faced cowboys who had wandered away from the Rowdy Bunch and invited himself to her table. When he pulled out a chair, Crista flung up her hand to forestall him.

"Don't bother sitting down. You aren't staying."

Red Cameron snorted defiantly and plunked down across from her. "My, aren't we uppity."

"No, we aren't," Crista contradicted. "I'm not here looking for a good time, only a drink and the chance to unwind."

Red tossed Crista what she assumed to be his most disarming smile—it left a lot to be desired. The carrot-haired and carrot-bearded cowboy was as appealing as the wrong end of a horse.

"Come on, honey, loosen up a little. At least tell ole Red your name."

"Jane Doe," Crista replied before wetting her whistle with her drink.

"Cute." Red guzzled beer from his pint jar and then wiped his frothy mustache with his shirt-sleeve.

Crista rolled her eyes in disgust.

"Janelle, bring me another tall one, will ya? The lady and me are just getting around to the intimate details of *her* place or *mine.*"

Red's drinking buddies hooted in laughter. Crista swallowed an oath and ducked her head when Janelle slinked toward the corner table.

"I thought we had a hot date after I get off work, stud muffin," Janelle pouted as she set the beer in front of Red.

Stud muffin? Crista would have howled at the ridiculous endearment if she hadn't been afraid she'd blow her cover.

"Of course we do, sugar, but your shift isn't over for two hours. In the meantime, I'm looking for *free.*"

Red's comment confirmed what Crista suspected. Janelle Chandler wasn't beneath selling her wares for extra cash—none of which was used to care and provide for her invalid daughter.

Detective Pine was going to hear about this, and Crista wouldn't hesitate to testify in a court hearing to move Lisa to a better environment. The Child Abuse Rescue Team that had established a home-like center for needy children near

Hochukbi was going to have to make room for one more resident. Crista had seen the bruises on Lisa's cheeks and arms when she first arrived at the hospital. If they were the result of a recent traffic accident, Crista would eat her Stetson—brim and all.

When Janelle strolled away, one hip at a time, Crista raised her head, only to find Red leering at her.

"So what do you say, honey? Your place or mine?"

"You think there's room enough beneath the rock you crawled out from under?"

Crista immediately regretted her snippy rejoinder. Provoking a burly goon who had sex on his brain and beer on his breath was risky business. A meaty hand snaked across the table to latch onto her forearm, digging painfully into her flesh.

"Look, bitch, I'm as easygoing and fun-loving as the next man, but I don't have to take any shit from a snooty piece of ass like you."

"Let go," Crista hissed, trying to jerk her arm from his viselike grasp without calling unwanted attention to herself.

"Damn, you're a strong little thing, aren't you?" Red sniggered, leaning closer. "What do you do for a living anyway—?"

"She beats the living hell out of worthless pricks . . . and *I* help her." The low, menacing snarl came from behind Red's right shoulder.

Red swiveled his bushy head around, cocked a brow, and took the measure of the annoying intruder. "You talking to me, asshole?"

"Must be. You're the biggest asshole I see around here."

The jukebox was still blaring, but conversation died down when Nash Griffin loomed over the table like a wolf poised to attack. The patrons had turned their attention toward the corner.

Crista swore inventively when she peered up into those flashing amber eyes and the black scowl etched on Nash's face. The last thing she needed was to get tangled up in a brawl that might expose her identity. Janelle might become suspicious if she realized Crista was the woman under the Stetson.

"Let's go, Curly," Nash growled.

When Crista tried to rise, Red jerked her back into her seat.

"Get lost, pal, unless you want to meet the rest of my friends." Red hitched a thumb toward the bar.

Crista watched Nash calmly appraise the three men in flannel shirts and faded jeans as they climbed off their stools. If Nash was concerned about the lopsided odds, his expression didn't show it. Crista, however, suspected he was nursing a few sore muscles after his return to the rodeo circuit.

In hopes of avoiding a scuffle that might aggravate Nash's old injuries and whatever new ones he might have acquired, Crista tried to defuse the situation. "This is my date, Red," she insisted, trying to worm loose. "He may be late, but he's here now."

Red scoffed, refusing to ease his grasp. "Yeah, well, it's too bad your boyfriend had to go and offend me, isn't it?"

From the corner of his eye, Nash saw the three men close in around him. He sighed in resignation and pivoted to display what looked to be a gesture of surrender.

"I thought you'd change your mind, asshole," Red smirked. "Why don't you—argh!"

Nash's elbow jerked downward, smacking Red's face against the table—twice—before the bewhiskered man knew what hit him. When Red reflexively covered his bloody nose with the hand that had manacled Crista's wrist, Nash reached out to hoist Crista out of her chair and shove her through the emergency exit.

"Now you've done it, you sorry son of a bitch," Red snarled, vaulting to his feet. "We're gonna beat the living hell outta *you!*"

Crista squawked when Nash's attempt to shove her through the exit—and out of harm's way—left her stumbling for balance. Her booted feet skidded in the mud and then flew out from under her. Unconcerned about the muddied condition of her clothes, she twisted around to see how Nash was faring. Through the partially opened door she could see Nash poised and ready for Red's oncoming fist.

"Take it outside, boys, or I'm calling the cops!" the bartender shouted.

Red took it on the chin instead. With lightning grace, Nash shot sideways and then stepped back. He slammed the door into Red's menacing sneer, flattening his bloody nose on the right side of his face. Furious, Red tried to reach around the door to claw out Nash's eyes, but Nash trapped the bulky arm against the doorjamb, giving it a hard whack for good measure.

While Red howled in pain and outrage, Crista scrambled onto her hands and knees. Before she could gain her feet Nash swooped down to grab her elbow, uprooting her from the mud puddle and hauling her to safety. His long, swift strides left Crista jogging to keep up with him.

"Reminds me of the brawl at Calgary Rodeo," Nash recalled as he broke into a sprint. "A mob of Canadians decided to knock our Southern drawls right off our lips, even if they had to take a few teeth in the process. Hal, Levi, Choctaw Jim, and I found ourselves outnumbered . . ."

Nash's voice trailed off when curses rumbled through the pouring rain. He glanced over his shoulder to see the Rowdy Bunch hot on his heels.

"Get in the pickup, lock the doors, and crank the engine," he instructed, pushing Crista ahead of him. "Jiggle the ignition switch or the truck won't start."

"What are you going to do?" Crista asked anxiously.

"CYA," Nash replied, slapping the key into her hand.

"What?" Crista frowned, bemused, as Nash shoved her into the cab of the battered truck.

"I'm going to *cover your ass,*" Nash muttered. "Open the door and let Leon out," he added. "I might need his help."

Crista leaned across the seat to open the passenger door. With his red handkerchief tied around his neck, Leon hopped down to provide reinforcement while Crista struggled with the faulty ignition switch.

"Now calm down, fellas," Nash coaxed the approaching foursome. "You really don't want to piss me off."

"Like we give a shit," Red snarled. "I'm gonna break your fuckin' neck, cowboy!"

"Wanna bet?" Nash challenged, wishing Crista knew the trick to starting his contrary truck. As of yet, she hadn't managed to rev the engine. They were running out of time, and Red was clean out of patience.

Red halted abruptly when Nash reached into the bed of the truck to retrieve the tire tool. Leon bounded around the front of the truck—teeth bared, crouched to spring at the first sign of threat to his master.

All four men pulled up short and then scattered apart so Nash couldn't fell them with one blow. Nash ignored their crude expletives. When the men closed in on him, Nash gestured toward the dog.

"Before I sick Leon on you, I'm giving you fair warning that he has an odd quirk," Nash explained, bracing himself for the oncoming attack and praying Crista could start the truck before hell broke loose. "Leon always goes for the balls when he's working with cattle. He saves me the trouble of castrating cantankerous calves. So when Leon leaps at you, I suggest you protect your family jewels."

"Rush him!" Red snarled.

Nash heard the long-awaited growl of the engine while he fended off attack from the right flank. About damn time, he thought as he leveled a blow that caused Red to double over. Nash hopped in the bed of the truck as Red crumpled to his knees, holding his injured midsection and swearing in gasping breaths. A howl of pain erupted when Leon's sharp teeth sank into a vulnerable crotch.

"Told you," Nash smirked as he tapped on the back window. "Step on it, Curly!"

Crista shoved the jalopy into gear and whizzed
off. Bad mufflers bellowed and a raft of vile curses
hung over the parking lot. Nash's sharp whistle
sent Leon in hot pursuit. The dog leaped into
the truck bed before Crista veered onto the highway. The threesome sped away, accompanied by
another chorus of profane curses.

A half mile later Crista rolled to a stop to let
Nash climb inside the cab. She had debated
about driving all the way home, leaving Nash and
Leon in the pickup bed. She had the unmistakable feeling Nash was going to give her hell
sooner or later. If it hadn't been raining, Crista
would have preferred later to sooner.

Dripping wet, Nash plunked down on the passenger-side of the truck, ordering Leon to remain
in the back. Staring straight ahead, Nash's mouth
flattened out, matching the drooping brim of his
hat.

Crista heard him mutter several indecipherable
curses and she wondered why he hadn't said
them directly to her. Was he actually going to let
her off lightly, after he'd come dangerously close
to getting beaten to a pulp?

Crista mashed on the accelerator and cast Nash
an apprehensive glance. Still, he uttered not one
word to her. She wondered if he was too furious
for words.

"For what it's worth, thanks for helping me out
of a tight scrape," Crista murmured in her most
appreciative voice.

A second later, she wished she had kept her
mouth shut. Instead of easing the tension she had
set Nash off like a lighted fuse.

"Damn it! What the sweet loving hell could you have possibly been thinking?" His baritone voice reverberated around the cab like a sonic boom.

"I was thinking you would probably react exactly the way you did," Crista replied, breaking into an impish grin.

Nash took a steadying breath. It was evident that he was trying to get a grasp on his runaway temper—and barely succeeding. "What possessed you to go to Mangy Dog Saloon?" he asked between gritted teeth.

Crista glanced quickly at his rigid profile. Yep, he was still mad as hell, she decided.

"I was . . . um . . . keeping surveillance on the mother of one of my patients."

Nash gaped at her. "Now let me make sure I've got this straight," he said with deceptive patience. "Despite the fact that you were concerned about prowlers casing your house, you tramped off to the roughest bar in the tri-city area to shadow somebody's *mother*?"

Crista turned off the highway, sighing in exasperation. "It didn't sound quite so preposterous when the idea first occurred to me. And what would you have suggested I do? Hang around the house, waiting for whoever was prowling around my place to come back?"

"You should have called the sheriff."

"I did call the sheriff's department. Detective Pine—"

Nash's groan interrupted her momentarily, but she hurried on.

"—Came out. He was supposed to be trailing Janelle Chandler, the waitress at the bar. Pine was absolutely no help, by the way. While he was at the house, I showed him the mud prints on the porch and told him about the opened dresser drawer and closet door in my bedroom. He shrugged off my concern. It was apparent that if I wanted something done I would have to do it myself."

Nash laid his head against the back of the seat and muttered several expletives that Crista didn't ask him to repeat. She drove in blessed silence for two miles before approaching headlights nearly blinded her. The speeding vehicle whizzed past, splashing mud across the windshield of the truck. Crista swerved toward the ditch and stamped on the brake to avoid a head-on collision.

"The maniac!" she fumed. "He must have been doing sixty on this sloppy gravel road." She glanced over her shoulder, seeing nothing but the fading beams disappearing over the hill.

"Scoot over and let me drive," Nash demanded.

Before Crista could comply, he hooked his arm around her waist, yanked her out from under the steering wheel, and slid beneath her. Crista found herself sitting beside Nash—all too close. She quickly scooted over to hug the passenger door.

"I don't bite, Curly," Nash commented before he mashed on the foot feed.

"I thought we agreed it was best if we kept our distance."

Crista felt his penetrating gaze on her, but she continued to stare at the mud-caked windshield. It would be all too easy to cuddle up to the warm strength of Nash's powerful body, especially after the unsettling incident at the bar. But Crista knew where that could lead.

Nash sighed audibly. "Crista . . ."

"Just don't say anything, damn it," she cut in.

"Just let me out by the front door and let's call
it a night."

"I'm going to walk you to the door," he said
in no uncertain terms.

"I can walk myself to the door, thank you very
much."

Despite her protest, Nash killed the engine and
climbed down from the truck. Crista made a mad
dash for the porch, with Nash one splash behind
her.

"You can go home now," she insisted as she
fished into her pocket for her house key.

"Just shut up and open the door, Curly," Nash
muttered. "I intend to check the house to make
sure it's safe."

Crista unlocked the door and flung her arm in
an expansive gesture. "There, are you happy
now—?"

Her voice fractured when she noticed the medical journals scattered on the carpet. Frantic, Crista
made a beeline toward her bedroom to check on
the purse she had stashed under her bed.

"Son of a bitch." Nash halted at the bedroom
door when he saw the opened drawers, the wispy
lace of bras and bikini panties strewn around the
room. The closet door stood wide open and the
cosmetic table looked as if a miniature tornado
had scattered mascara, lipstick, and eyeliner everywhere.

Crista whirled around, her green eyes wide with
shock and confusion. "What kind of pervert
would do this?"

Nash turned back in the direction he had
come. "I'm calling the cops."

"Ask for Detective Pine," she instructed.

Crista stood in the middle of her disheveled

room, shivering from the dampness. The thought of some weirdo tramping around her private quarters unhinged her. Everywhere she looked her personal belongings were in disarray—fondled by some demented fiend.

When Nash abruptly grabbed her arm, she reflexively shrank away. "Easy, honey," he murmured, as if soothing a skittish colt. "I'm just going to get you out of here. Let's go into the kitchen. I'll fix us some coffee while we wait for Detective Pine."

Crista knew she shouldn't have leaned against Nash when he curled a supporting arm around her hip. He didn't really want her cuddling up against him, not for any reason. But she needed his compassion, the kind of sympathy she generously offered her patients and rarely received herself.

When Crista felt Nash give her a comforting squeeze, tears misted her eyes. "I'm sorry," she whispered miserably.

"For what, darlin'?"

She shrugged helplessly. "For everything, I guess. For dragging you out in the rain. For getting you into a fight." She inhaled deeply, marshalling her composure. "You can go on home. I'll handle it from here. I'll have a few minutes to pull myself together before the detective arrives . . ."

Crista flinched when she noticed the doors of her kitchen cabinets standing ajar. That was the last straw! Her fragile emotions shattered like glass.

"Well, damn it! Not the kitchen, too!" she railed.

Nash shepherded Crista to the kitchen table and settled her into a chair. "Just sit tight. I'll take a look around and see if any other rooms have been ransacked."

Dazed and frustrated, Crista nodded. Her gaze swung to the cabinets where dishes and food items had been shoved aside, as if someone had been in search of something. But what?

When Crista heard Nash's approaching footsteps she glanced up. "Well?" she questioned expectantly.

"Someone went through the bathroom linen closet and medicine cabinet," Nash reported grimly. "One of the closets in the spare bedroom was standing open."

Crista raked her fingers through her hair and then propped her arms on the table. "This makes no sense."

"Where's your purse?"

Crista winced, her wild gaze leaping up to Nash. "I put it under the bed after I tucked a ten-dollar bill in my pocket, and then left for town. Seeing my bedroom torn upside down distracted me. I forgot to check to see if my purse was missing."

"How much cash did you have?"

"About forty dollars, I think."

Nash reversed direction and returned a few minutes later, carrying Crista's purse. "The money is gone." Setting the purse on the table for Crista to inspect, Nash strode off to make coffee.

"Well, damn it," Crista said suddenly.

"You already said that. Now what?"

"My credit card and calling card were stolen."

"Anything else?"

"I don't think so."

"You want me to report it for you?"

Crista shook her head. "I'll do it."

She rose on unsteady legs to make the calls. Her

hands were trembling so much she had to dial the first number twice before she got it right. Once she had given the explanations, she returned to find a steaming cup of coffee awaiting her.

Every time she glanced around, anger, confusion, and frustration bombarded her. Tears welled up in her eyes, but Crista valiantly fought them back. She was going to hold herself together. She was going to . . . bawl her damn head off . . .

At first wail, Nash was beside her. "Come here, Curly. You might as well get this over with before the detective shows up."

With a gentle smile and tender touch Nash urged her onto his lap and into his waiting arms. It was more than Crista could take. In all her life, only one man had ever been there for her. It hadn't been her father or her husband. They had taken from her, making her do all the giving. It was this big, brawny cowboy, who had once lifted her off the ground and cheered her up when she was barely more than a child, who was offering comfort—now as then.

Crista made an absolute fool of herself. She flung her arms around Nash's neck and soaked the front of his faded shirt—worse than it already was . . .

Fourteen

Nash told himself not to get *too* comfortable while he became the shoulder Crista cried on. But it was damn hard not to enjoy the feel of her supple body molded against his. Holding her was as comforting to him as it appeared to be to her.

When she shifted position to soak another spot on his shirt, Nash's arm tightened reflexively. With his chin resting on the top of her curly head, he allowed himself a smile she couldn't see.

"Don't worry about it, Curly," Nash murmured as his hand absently glided down her back, settling familiarly on the curve of her hip. "I've wanted to cry my eyes out a few times myself."

"But you never cry, do you, Nash?" Crista mumbled against the side of his neck, her warm breath stirring against his skin like a lover's caress. "I wish I were as strong as you are."

The sound of a humming motor and the splatter of mud brought Nash's head around to see headlights flash through the windows. When Crista pushed away, wiping the tears from her cheeks, Nash made the mistake of staring into those eyes that reminded him of evergreens glittering with dewdrops.

He lost it—there and then. Before he could consciously restrain himself, he did what came all too naturally with Crista. His hand curled beneath her chin, tilting her face to his kiss.

Nash told himself he'd have been a helluva lot better off if he had simply devoured her in an act of sexual hunger. It would have assured him that what he felt was strictly physical. But he kissed her entirely too tenderly, giving far more of himself than he intended. And when Crista returned his gentleness so instinctively, it nearly did Nash in.

The kiss spoke of too many things Nash thought he already knew but couldn't afford to admit. Tonight's fiasco had brought them another step closer together—emotionally and physically. And it wasn't a good place to be while he was fighting himself, and his needs, on a daily basis.

The thought of this lovely, free-spirited woman—who saw herself as a champion of the less fortunate—caught up with Nash so many times in the course of a day that he was wearing himself out trying *not* to think about her . . . and failing miserably . . .

For a short time Nash forgot his vows and priorities. He simply enjoyed the intoxicating taste and feel of the woman in his arms. It was heady stuff, and only the sound of approaching footsteps prompted him to drag himself back to reality.

"Better hop up, honey," Nash urged, his voice rumbling with desire. "Detective Pine Cone has obviously arrived on the scene."

Crista stared at him with an expression of disoriented enchantment. Nash chuckled. He was nobody's Prince Charming, that was for sure.

Detective Pine, perpetually puffing on his stogie, wiped his feet on the mat and surged inside. His gaze circled the living area and he smirked. "According to the report I received, your house was vandalized. Did you find more muddy footprints on these strewn magazines, Ms. Delaney?"

Crista set her back teeth and forced herself to deal civilly with the detective. "We'll start in the bedroom and work our way through the house."

In swift strides, Crista led the way down the hall. Detective Pine took quick inventory of the bedroom before Crista motioned him into the bathroom. Then she led him into the kitchen where Nash waited with two fresh cups of coffee—neither of them for the skeptical detective, she was happy to note. She gratefully accepted the steaming brew while Pine completed his unenthusiastic investigation.

"Looks like nothing more than mischievous juveniles on the prowl," Pine concluded between puffs on his cigar. "They just scattered a few things around, especially your undies, and made off with some cash. You did say you lost forty bucks, didn't you?"

Crista wondered why Nash had even bothered calling the cops. It was obvious Detective Pine wouldn't take an interest in the incident, unless she was lying on the living room floor in a pool of her own blood.

"So essentially, you're saying there isn't much you can do, even now that a crime has been committed, as I suggested it might this afternoon."

Pine ignored the subtle rebuke and posed his questions. "I presume you were away from the house when this incident occurred. Is that correct?"

Crista's nails dug into her clenched fists as she struggled for some measure of control. She wanted to slug this guy. Knowing Nash was standing behind her, offering moral support without taking command of the situation, prevented her from losing her cool. It gave Crista an unbelievable amount of reassurance. She wondered if Nash even realized what a profound statement his mere presence made to her. Probably not. He had become a protector, a guardian angel, even if he was known to snap and growl like a wolf on occasion.

Crista gathered her wandering thoughts and focused on the overweight detective. "I was at Mangy Dog Saloon, keeping surveillance on Janelle Chandler, since you didn't have time to do it," she informed him crisply. "Janelle made arrangements to meet a *paying* client after hours. Said client told me so himself, though I doubt he will be able to keep his appointment this evening." Crista didn't bother to elaborate on that.

Pine's thin brows shot up. "You shadowed the Chandler woman?"

"Somebody had to. You can't seem to find the time," Crista fumed. "Janelle has a thirteen-year-old daughter at home recovering from a traffic accident that I seriously doubt was reported exactly as it happened. The girl should be in CART, not in her mother's negligent care."

"CART?" Pine repeated.

"Child Abuse Rescue Team," Crista said, as if he should know—and didn't. "I've already contacted a social worker to check the housing condition and home care. And since you obviously plan to shrug off the intrusion into my home, maybe you could use the extra time to put a tail on Janelle. I'm reasonably certain she's doing drugs. But until you catch her in possession or arrest her for prostitution it's going to be difficult to have her daughter removed to a safe environment."

"I'll see what I can do," Pine said, pivoting toward the door.

Crista stepped in front of him, blocking his retreat. *"Get it done,"* she demanded emphatically. "You may be all set to rock back on your retirement pension, but there's a kid in Keota Flats who is going to become a human sacrifice if you don't quit dragging your feet. At least there will be one little girl who will be rescued from impending disaster because of you, Pine."

Pine eyed Crista for a long, irritated moment, but she refused to back down or apologize for raking him over the coals. "Give the poor kid a break, Pine. It will be the first one Lisa Chandler has had in all her thirteen years."

When Pine walked away, Crista half collapsed against the wall. She hadn't realized how exhausted she was until she tumbled from her adrenaline high and her legs threatened to buckle beneath her.

When Crista heard Nash puttering around in her kitchen, she forced herself to move—while she still could. "Just leave it," she called to him. "I'll straighten things up when I get home from work tomorrow."

Nash pivoted around to appraise Crista's pinched expression. She looked beat. He could relate to that. "Let's at least put your bedroom to rights," he insisted.

When Nash ambled toward the hall, Crista remained rooted to her spot, leaning heavily on the nearest wall. She was beginning to understand why Nash found this position so appealing. It did wonders for those who were dead on their feet.

"I'm not sure I want to sleep in there," Crista mumbled. "I'll camp out on the couch."

Nash gave his head a shake. "No, Curly. I'm going to clean it up right now so you can get a decent night's sleep."

Crista sniffed in distaste. "That isn't likely to happen."

"You'll have more room to toss and turn on your king-size bed. "Come on, you've handled everything else this hellish day has dealt you. You can handle this."

When Crista hesitated, Nash strode toward the bedroom. He was folding the last of Crista's undies and replacing them in the drawer when she finally appeared.

"Nice skivvies, Curly," he tried to tease her.

"I refuse to be amused, though I do appreciate your efforts," Crista grumbled.

Nash grabbed a lacy black bra, held it up to his chest, and waggled his eyebrows. Finally, Crista broke down and grinned in spite of herself.

"And to think anyone would refer to you as a fire-breathing dragon or the big bad wolf," she said through her smile.

Nash folded the garment and tucked it away. "Go shower while I finish up in here. It will make you feel better."

Crista nodded and sighed audibly. "You're probably right." Her green eyes drifted to Nash and then skittered way. "Thanks for being here when I needed moral support. I know you're eager to get back home. Go ahead. I'll be okay."

Nash watched Crista walk away, her wet clothes clinging to her like a coat of paint. She still looked fragile and vulnerable, as if she were hanging by a thread. Nash wasn't sure she should be left alone . . . even when he was starkly aware of the

dangers of staying . . . Yet, he didn't really want to
go . . .

The sound of the spraying shower incited vi-
sions similar to the ones that had visited his
dreams the past few weeks. He didn't care to
count the number of times he had caught himself
fantasizing about having Crista's naked flesh beneath him, around him . . .

His entire body filled with tormenting sensations. Nash wheeled toward the door. If he didn't
get the hell out of here—and quickly . . .

"Well, shit," he muttered as he stepped into
the hall.

Crista had emerged from the bathroom,
wrapped in a towel, her shock at finding him still
in the house evident on her freshly scrubbed face.

All Nash's noble intentions abandoned him as
he helplessly devoured every bare inch of her exposed skin. He felt like a deprived child cherishing the sight of a long-awaited gift. The craving
to unwrap this pretty package sent another surge
of frustrated need thrumming through him.

Nash found his footsteps taking him toward
her. "Tell me to leave, Crista," he gritted out.
"Tell me you don't want me here."

"I can't tell you I want you to leave," Crista
whispered, staring at him too openly, too hun-
grily. "It would be a lie."

Nash felt himself reaching for her, lifting her
into his arms. He wanted Crista with every fiber
of his being, and he wasn't going to be able to
function normally until he'd had her.

When she nestled against him, Nash inhaled
the fresh scent of her hair, her skin. His senses
were filled to overflowing. He couldn't think ra-
tionally, couldn't move without wanting her to ut-

ter distraction. With a groan of surrender, he
sought her lips, and she gave herself up to his
kiss without hesitation or restraint.

Nash carried Crista to her bedroom, barely taking time to watch where he was going. His mind
was on the symbolic threshold he'd crossed at the
bedroom door, on the feast he was making of her
mouth, the feel of her body cradled in his arms.

Slow down, Nash told himself. *You're worse than a
stallion trailing a mare!* This was, after all, the very
same woman who had been led to believe she
wasn't worth a man taking the time for long, slow
lovemaking. Crista deserved to be pampered, to
know she was desirable, to understand that she
was a woman of remarkable passion and sensuality.

Despite his lecture, Nash felt a hungry impatience flaying him alive. When her fingers delved
into his hair, holding his head to hers, offering
and accepting the need that claimed them both,
he felt feverish sensations sweep through him.

Suddenly, he was adrift in the land of the lost.
He was nothing more than what this fiery female
had made of him—a man in the grip of desires
that had been held too long in check. A shuddering moan escaped him as his hand glided up her
silky thigh, pushing the terry cloth out of his way.
Crista was firm yet incredibly feminine to the
touch. Nash ached to explore every inch of her,
to pleasure her until the frustrations of the evening were a blur.

A fleeting thought broke through the needs
that assailed him. He could use a shower himself,
and as crazy as it probably sounded, he wanted to
come to Crista as appealing and desirable to her
as she was to him. If Nash was going to break his
vow, then, by damn, he was going to do it right.

"Nash?" Crista's breath wobbled in her chest when he set her to her feet and rewrapped the towel around her.

Nash could hear the confusion in her voice, the uncertainty. She was probably expecting him to leave her as he had once before. And though he knew it would be best for both of them if he did, he didn't have the heart. Once had been more than enough.

Without daring to look into those shimmering, evergreen eyes, Nash flipped back the bedspread and urged her between the sheets. "I need a shower. I smell like a lathered horse."

"I wouldn't mind—"

He looked down at her then, when she was tucked beneath the fluffy comforter, her wild mane flowing around her. *"I would."*

Before impulse need got the better of him again, Nash turned, peeling off his shirt on his way. He was headed for the fastest shower on record and into a night he would probably regret later . . . but definitely not now . . .

Crista's gaze settled on the muscled physique of the man looming beside her bedroom door. She honestly wondered if Nash's insistence on a shower was meant to give them both time to reconsider. For her, the past two minutes had not been spent in wary hesitation but rather in shivering anticipation. If nothing else, she had learned how it felt to desire a man—really desire him, with every part of her being—for the first time in her life.

Crista couldn't, wouldn't, lie to herself. She ached for Nash Griffin, longed to satisfy the fan-

tasy that meeting him again had inspired. If she
had learned nothing else, it was that this ruggedly
handsome cowboy was still the same caring, gen-
erous-hearted man she had fallen in love with
many years ago.

Her gaze moved longingly over him, marveling
at the pleasure she derived from studying his powerfully-built body. Although the human anatomy
had become a familiar sight in Crista's profession,
the overwhelming figure of the man who stood
before her stole her breath away. Nash Griffin was
utterly magnificent—a sculptured work of rippling
muscle and physical conditioning. Hard work and
rigorous activity showed in every sleek contour.

Crista caressed him visually, as her hands and
lips itched to do. She longed to trace every scar—
souvenirs of his battles in the arenas and the corrals. She wanted to hold him, to know—at last—if
intimacy between a man and woman could provide more satisfaction than she had previously experienced.

But still Nash lingered in the shadows of the
hall, like the elusive dream that had teased her
for years.

"I tried to give us both time to think this over,"
Nash murmured huskily. "You know I have very
little to offer. Have you changed your mind?"

A tender smile pursed her lips. She was touched
by his honesty and consideration.

"I think," she whispered, turning back the comforter invitingly, "that you should come to bed."

Crista drank in the wondrous sight of him as
he approached, confident in his masculinity,
treating her senses to the tantalizing prospects of
knowing him in the most secretive and intimate
ways. When Nash slid between the sheets, his

body gliding alongside hers, she burned in the very core of her being.

To her surprise, Nash didn't forcefully wedge his way between her legs to take his pleasure after a few hurried, meaningless caresses. That was what she had come to expect from her husband—when he spared time for her between affairs. To Crista's stunned amazement, Nash simply gathered her into his arms and dipped his head toward hers. His lips feathered over hers with a whispery touch. He surprised her, captivated her with his tenderness and patience.

"It's been five years," he confided softly. "I don't have any protection . . . because I hadn't planned on needing any."

Crista smiled at his concerned expression, and another corner of her heart began to crumble. She should have expected that a man who took his responsibilities so seriously would look before he leaped.

"I've had injections," she informed him quietly.

"They have shots for that sort of thing these days? I guess that shows how far out of touch I am."

With a playful grin, she sketched the creases that fanned from his eyes, the distinct lines that bracketed his sensuous mouth. "Considering the way you make me feel, I'd hate to have to count on remembering to cross my fingers at a time like this."

A low, resonant chuckle rumbled through his massive chest. Crista felt the pleasurable sound vibrate through her, bringing her to a higher level of sensual anticipation.

"So would I," he agreed. "I'm having enough

trouble trying to keep myself under control without worrying about crossing fingers . . ."

Nash stifled a groan when Crista sidled closer, settling in the crook of his arm. He was trying to proceed slowly, especially after he had come on to her like a wild man that night in the barn and then tormented her—and himself—on their second encounter. If he was going to make a mistake with this bewitching woman, Nash wanted it to be the best one he ever made.

This would be a night to cherish, a night of mutual discovery, because they both knew there could never be anything permanent between them. He had told Crista that in a dozen different ways and he knew she understood where his loyalties must forever lie. But there were times—like now, most especially now—that he wished for things that couldn't be.

"I want to be gentle with you," he told her as his palm drifted down her arm to follow the curve of her hip.

"You already have been, more than I'm accustomed to," she confessed in a ragged whisper.

Her comment made Nash wonder exactly what she *was* accustomed to. The possibilities didn't please him. Nash didn't know that Heywood character from Adam, but if the man had never given a woman like Crista what she needed and deserved, he must have been an absolute idiot.

When Crista's lips drifted down his throat to whisper over his chest, Nash couldn't contain his pleasure. His entire body was taut with self-imposed restraint, and every nuance brought him a step closer to the edge. Crista was killing him with her tender explorations—he wondered if she knew how devastating she was.

"Do you mind if I touch you?" she asked against the muscled plane of his chest.

"Be my guest," Nash croaked, his voice one octave lower than normal.

"Am I disturbing you, Nash?" she teased, arching sensually against him.

"Mmm . . ." was all he could manage while he fought the difficult battle.

"I hope that was a yes, because touching you gives me the most fascinating kind of pleasure."

Nash was sure he died and skyrocketed to heaven when her tender caresses swept from one male nipple to the other. And just when, he would have liked to know, had his skin become so damn sensitive? The flight of her fingertips left fires burning in their wake. Nash should have known those hands could work potent magic. He had witnessed their effects on Hal and Levi.

"Damn . . ." Nash hissed through his teeth when Crista's hand descended across his belly to trace the hard length of his manhood. When her fingertips enfolded him, he felt unruly desire spurring him like a merciless rider. "Easy, lady," he gasped. "Cowboys are only known for eight-second rides, you know."

Crista laughed at the comment, but she couldn't help but be flattered, knowing she was playing havoc with his self-control. She was the one he had chosen—after five long years. And for as long as it lasted, she was going to take this wild, heady ride.

When Crista tried to ease the quilt away to explore him with her lips as well as her hands, Nash curled his arm around her, restraining her. She gave her tangled blond head a shake, silently re-

questing that he ease his grasp and give her free
rein.

"I want you to know how I felt that night on my
couch," she insisted, breaking free of his grasp.
"I can't tell you—I have to show you how wonderful you made me feel, how you made me
burn . . ."

"I'm already burning alive," Nash assured her
hoarsely. "It can't get worse . . ."

When her lips whispered over his rigid flesh
Nash clenched his fist in the hem of the quilt. It
was an instinctive reaction. Holding on tight was
a practiced skill from his rodeo days, but the rides
he was accustomed to taking were worlds away
from the bone-melting caresses of her fingers and
lips. When she tasted the silver drop of need that
had escaped his willful control, Nash felt his body
trembling helplessly. The sheer intimacy was almost too much for him to bear. Damn it, he was
going to embarrass himself the first time out after
five long years.

"Crista, don't," Nash choked, clutching desperately at her roaming hands. "No more. I swear I
can't last when you're doing the things you're doing. I'm not made of stone."

"No? Feels like it to me," she assured him mischievously, reveling in her newfound ability to
make him shudder beneath her onslaught.

Before Crista knew what had happened, she
found herself on her back. Nash was propped on
his elbows, bending over her, the scant light revealing his rakish grin.

"Okay, little lady, you wanna play rough, do
you?"

Her hand lifted to limn the strong line of his

jaw as she smiled up at him. "No, not rough. I was just enjoying you. Is that wrong?"

Nash nipped at her fingertips, marveling at the maelstrom of indefinable sensations she drew from him. "I'm enjoying you, too," he admitted. "But not as much as I intend to . . ."

Feeling her instantaneous response to the flick of his tongue against the peak of her breast, Nash growled in pure satisfaction. When he aroused her he didn't have to hold anything back. He couldn't say the same when she was touching him.

Each little gasp and moan from Crista was un-adulterated delight to him. Her pleasure became his. He adored the way she arched into his hands and lips, giving so generously of herself, un-ashamed of her responses. She left him feeling as if he were the most skillful lover on the face of the earth, even though he was out of practice.

There was no pretense with Crista. Every wild response brought a satisfied smile to Nash's lips. He could caress her for hours, feeling her quiver and burn—for him, because of him. He would never tire of this kind of affection, though he had never spent so much time on a woman's needs. He had never wanted to until now. But with Crista, for Crista, he wanted to explore the height and depth of every conceivable sensation, to pro-long her pleasure and his own.

And he wanted her to want him in every way imaginable . . .

The hungry thought whispered through his mind as his hands and lips drifted lower, feeling her warm flesh responding to each adventurous touch. His caresses stroked from knee to inner thigh, sensitizing, teasing, arousing. His fingertips grazed her secret flesh, testing her dewy response, bathing in the hottest, sweetest kind of fire he had ever known.

"Nash . . . no . . ." Crista's voice frayed when his lips brushed over her inner thigh. "I've never . . ."

"Neither have I," he assured her. "But I want to taste you, all of you."

He pushed her hands away and felt her fingers clench on his shoulder as he feathered his lips over her with the gentlest care. He caressed her until she wept for him and then he offered her a lover's tenderest, most intimate kiss.

Nash couldn't begin to describe the overwhelming pleasure that coursed through him when he felt her contracting around his lips and fingertips, heard that sweet sound she made when passion burgeoned and consumed her.

Fascinated by the power he held over her, he brought her to another shuddering climax with the penetration of tongue and fingertips. When her voice shattered in a cry that was his name, Nash eased between her legs, sheathing himself in her soft warmth, feeling her answering caress of want and welcome.

Nash drew her legs around his hips, lifting her to him, sinking into her until they were rocking in a cradle of passion so deep and intense that he couldn't tell where the waves of splendor ended and the rolling sea of ecstasy began. With each driving thrust she came undone in his arms, arching eagerly toward him, asking for all he had to give, holding nothing back. He told himself to ease his grasp on Crista when he felt the first shudder of passion claim him, but he didn't know how to let go, had never learned. He simply held on for the duration of the most amazing ride of his life.

Immeasurable pleasure engulfed him. Nash uncurled above her, burying his head in the soft curve of Crista's neck. His pulse pounded like hailstones and he wondered if his heartbeat would ever return to normal without bruising his ribs. Willfully, Nash drew a breath, only to inhale the scent of her—a scent that, he was sure, would cling to him forevermore.

Sure enough, Nash thought as he drifted along in ecstasy. Making love—having sex, he quickly amended—with Crista was the most enjoyable mistake of his life. It couldn't get better than this. And being a veteran cowboy, Nash had always known when he had found the right fit . . .

The thought made him grin against the curve of her jaw.

"Is there something you find amusing that has escaped me?" Crista questioned in a noticeably thick voice.

He rose on his elbow and dropped a kiss to her lips. "Nope."

Her gaze narrowed thoughtfully. "You don't want to tell me what you were thinking, right?"

"Right," he confirmed. "Entirely too personal."

Crista flashed him a wry smile and moved languidly beneath him. "What could be more personal than this?"

"You might be surprised," he said, breaking into a naughty grin.

Crista playfully swatted his shoulder. "Okay, then I won't bother telling you what I was thinking."

"That's probably for the best. We're getting in too deep . . ." Nash chuckled at his unintended pun. Crista smiled impishly, sharing a moment of humor combined with the most intimate of all pleasures.

"It's late. I should go home," Nash murmured a few minutes later.

"Yes, you probably should."

Nash stared down into her face, watching the dim light shimmer in the her curls. Hell, who was he kidding here? He was nowhere near ready to leave. The pleasure they had given each other was a mere whetting of hungry appetites. Though he should have been sated, the fantastic splendor of the moment-out-of-time had only intensified his craving. He wanted her again—now—and his body was already showing signs of being willing and ready to take up where they had left off.

"Nash?" Crista's long lashes swept up, her eyes wide with surprise.

He knew she could feel him stirring within her. They were practically sharing the same body, after all. Grinning, he bent to kiss her forehead, her cheek, her eyelids.

"Helluva thing, lust," he murmured as his hands moved of their own free will. "You can barely understand it and sometimes—like now— you can't even control it. I thought I was made of willpower until I met up with you."

Nash stopped trying to ignore the sensations roiling inside him, stopped trying to engage in conversation. Waves of hunger were spiraling through him in rapid succession, making impossible demands. Passion billowed like a warm fog, consuming all thought—except one . . .

Crista was his perfect fit.

Nash wondered if he would ever be able to reveal such an intimate secret to Crista without embarrassing them both . . .

Fifteen

After Crista had drifted into exhausted sleep, Nash lay awake, listening to the patter of rain. He needed to leave, but the warm contentment surrounding him was like a cozy quilt that compelled him to linger—just a few minutes more.

He tried to tell himself that the incredible satisfaction he had enjoyed with Crista was a direct result of his long abstinence.

It was a logical explanation.

It was also the one Nash decided to stick with—for sanity's sake.

He couldn't become too attached to this curly-headed beauty, because if he did he would tie himself in knots. He would want things that conflicted with the sacrifices he had vowed to make for Levi.

That was the deal, Nash reminded himself grimly—and not for the first time since Crista had come into his life.

Quietly easing away, he scooted off the edge of the bed. Why he was trying to be careful not to disturb Crista he didn't know. She barely stirred even when he pushed a pillow under her head to replace his shoulder.

The perfect mistake, he found himself thinking as he tiptoed off to retrieve his clothes. But hell, if a man was going to blunder, it might as well be a doozy. Problem was, Nash wasn't sure he could watch Crista come and go from Chulosa Ranch without remembering every moment they'd shared, without wanting her all over again.

Stepping outside, Nash noticed that his Border collie faithfully awaited his return. Leon was tucked beneath the window to avoid the rain.

Nash glanced around the porch. Damn, he would like to get his hands on the pranksters who had invaded Crista's private domain. Something about the articles and rooms that had been ransacked niggled him. Nash had seen vandalism and had pulled off a few pranks himself during his rodeo days, but this case didn't fit the usual scenario.

Detective Pine had shrugged off the incident as mischievous juveniles pestering a pretty woman. Nash didn't buy it. He doubted Crista would, either, after she got over being upset and had time to think things through. This ranch was well off the beaten path, and Crista was new in town. Why would she be a target?

Nash made a mental note to keep close tabs on Crista for the next few days—just in case she was being stalked. In this day and age, you never knew. There were a lot of crazy loons running loose, even in this remote neck of the woods.

Calling to Leon, Nash climbed into the truck and jiggled the ignition switch. He drove home, hoping he could sneak into his house as easily as he had crept away from Crista's. But knowing Hal, it wasn't going to be easy. Hal's eagle eyes rarely missed much, and he'd become a light sleeper since the days he had flown 'copters into places he refused to name, into situations he refused to discuss.

This was one night Nash hoped his brother was sleeping soundly.

"I was beginning to think you'd forgotten where the hell you lived," came the raspy voice from the bed against the south wall.

Nash muttered under his breath as he unzipped his jeans. He had taken off his boots in the hall before he inched toward his bed. He needn't have bothered.

Nash eased onto his bed and stared at the ceiling. "Can't you sleep, little brother?"

"Nope, not when I have the unshakable feeling you went to bed before you came home. It's supposed to be the other way around. I thought you'd given up moonlight rodeos, Good Time."

Nash grimaced inwardly and quickly sought a safer topic. "I had a little trouble at Mangy Dog Saloon. Four goons were itching to take me apart."

"That place is nothing but trouble."

"Yeah, well, I had to help Crista make a fast getaway."

"Are you still in one piece?" Hal questioned.

"I'm fine."

"And, of course, you felt it was your duty to console the little lady afterward."

Nash noted Hal's cynical sarcasm. Because of his low opinion of women, he had little sympathy for anyone of the female persuasion. "I took Crista home, only to discover someone had broken into her house and scattered her belongings."

"What?" For the first time Hal sounded concerned.

"I think we should keep an eye on the place

for a few days. Whoever checks the cattle in Choctaw Jim's pastures needs to swing by to make sure no one's prowling around."

Hal was quiet for a moment. "Don't get too attached, big brother. It isn't worth the heartache. Granted, that blonde has spunk and style, but you'll waste a lot of perfectly good emotion if you think anything might come of it. I already learned my lesson the hard way. And believe me, if you aren't in it just for the sex, then you better get the hell out—fast."

With that cynical piece of advice, Hal turned on his side and went back to sleep. Nash tried to take his brother's words to heart, knowing it was for the best. The night he had spent with Crista would have to be a one-time deal. He had satisfied his curiosity and appeased his needs. He had to get back to business as usual, because it could be no other way.

Until Levi could stand alone Nash Griffin had commitments to keep.

Levi Cooper blinked in disbelief when a string of cowboys filed into his private quarters. It had been several months since the last rodeo union, and no one had bothered to inform him company was coming. If he had known, he would have made his secret arrangements around this wingding. Now he was going to have to make a private phone call to alter his plans.

"Hello, Dogger. You're lookin' good, buddy." Rooster Anderson, the sturdy bulldogger from South Dakota, led the group of cowboys into the room.

Within moments, Levi found himself surrounded by the crowd who had run with the Griffin brothers on the rodeo circuit. Some of the biggest names in the professional industry had arrived—at Nash's invitation, Levi suspected.

Levi glanced toward the door to see Nash in his familiar pose of holding up the wall, his arms over his broad chest, his battered boots crossed at the ankles.

"The boys were on their way to the Lazy E Arena for the competition. They decided to drop by for a few days," Nash said with a casual shrug.

"Drop by, hell!" one of the cowboys snorted. "I could smell Bernie's smoked ribs and charcoaled steaks all the way down in Texas."

"I smelled his famous barbecue sauce all the way from Montana," the bulldogging star insisted.

"After we exercise our horses and enjoy a little friendly competition in Griffin arena, I'm gonna chow down on half a hog, all by myself," the burly calf roper from New Mexico announced.

Hal Griffin glanced discreetly at his brother and then winked at Levi. "Why don't you come down to the barn, Dogger. We're doing a little roping to get in condition for the next rodeo. Nash brought in a load of sand from the river this morning and worked out the mud holes. The turf is in good shape."

Levi nodded. "I intend to do just that, as soon as I make a phone call. I'll have to reschedule my hospital therapy."

When the men trooped out to unload their horse trailers, Levi smiled gratefully at Nash and Hal. "Thanks. I always enjoy those guys. It does wonders for my morale."

After the brothers ambled way, Levi wheeled himself around and made a beeline for the phone.

"J.C.," Levi said in a hushed voice. "I can't get away for a couple of days. You're going to have to cover for me."

He paused to listen to his associate on the other end of the line. "Now look, damn it, I can't leave with a bunkhouse full of cowboys here to visit me. It would invite too much suspicion. Nash and Hal will start asking questions. If they find out what's going on, they'll put a stop to it. I won't let that happen . . ."

When Levi caught sight of a movement beside the office door, he swore viciously before returning his attention to the phone. "I'll get back to you tonight.

"Damn it to eternal hell," Levi seethed as he replaced the receiver. Furious that he had been overheard, he spun his chair around to deflect the glare directed at him. "Damn it to hell," he muttered again.

Crista was silently fuming after hearing the incriminating conversation. She had arrived shortly after the convoy of pickups and trailers converged on the barn to unload horses. Although this wasn't the scheduled day for her visitations, she had made time so she could squeeze in tomorrow's consultation with the social worker in Keota Flats.

Detective Pine had finally trailed Janelle Chandler long enough to catch her in the back seat with Red Cameron, smoking a joint, after fast and furious sexual athletics in the parking lot at Mangy Dog Saloon. The tips Crista had given the detective had led to an arrest. Red Cameron, worthless creep that he was, had been eager to point an accusing finger at Janelle in order to get himself a reduced sentence for drug possession and soliciting a prostitute.

Crista had been in a grand mood when she arrived at the ranch, knowing young Lisa Chandler had been removed from her mother's custody. And now this! Crista was certain Levi was making suspicious arrangements, playing on the Griffin brothers' sympathy so he could deceive them.

"How could you, Levi?" she hissed as she surged into the office. "What kind of scam are you using on these devoted men who have bent over backward for you?"

"I don't have the faintest idea what you're talking about," Levi snapped at her, his blue eyes flashing with hostility.

"Oh, yes, you do," Crista snapped right back. "I overheard a conversation a few weeks ago that aroused my suspicions. This one confirms them. What is it? Embezzlement? Since the Griffins put you in charge of finances, did you decide to filch money from the accounts and make a few side investments of your own?"

"Get the hell out of here," Levi growled, his arm shooting toward the door like a bullet. "You are officially off my case."

"Sorry, pal, but you're going to discover that I'm going to be all over your case from now on. I've already told Hal and Nash that they've given in to you too often. After all they've done for you, I should think you would be appreciative, not spiteful enough to cut their legs out from under them!"

Levi rolled forward to wag a finger in Crista's fuming face. "You'll keep your damned mouth shut about this if you know what's good for you. If you screw things up, I swear I'll have your job and ruin your reputation. And don't think for a minute that I can't get it done. Hal and Nash will believe whatever I tell them, and you can bet I'll tell them plenty if you try to interfere in something that's none of your damned business. I've spent three years making plans, and I'll be goddamned if I'll let you foul this up. Now get out of here!"

Defiantly, Crista marched toward the desk, intent on retrieving the financial ledger and insisting Nash take a close look at it. When she reached for the ledger on the edge of the desk, Levi snarled and flung himself out of his chair to snatch the book from Crista's hand. With it clasped protectively to his chest, Levi crashed to the floor.

"Get out of here, damn you!" he growled furiously.

"What the devil is going on in here?"

Crista whipped around to see Nash poised in the doorway. She was quick to note that his accusing gaze went directly to *her*, not to the invalid sprawled on the floor.

If there was any question as to where she stood with Nash, his automatic reaction left no further doubt. She had known she was at the bottom of his list of priorities, but it still hurt to have it verified.

"What are you trying to do to Levi?" Nash growled at her.

"I didn't do—"

"The hell she didn't!" Levi cut in frantically, jerking up his head. "I want her out of here, Nash, and I don't ever want to lay eyes on her again."

"Nash . . . ?" Her beseeching tone was wasted on him.

Without another glance in Crista's direction,

Nash stormed over to lever Levi upright and then hoisted him back into the wheelchair.

Chest heaving, clutching the ledger, Levi sneered at Crista, determined to sway Nash to his side. "She told me I was wasting my time and your money with all these exercise contraptions. She said I would never walk again, no matter how hard I tried."

Nash rounded on Crista, his rugged features twisted in outrage at her cruelty. "Damn you. How could you say such things? What the hell are you trying to do? Ruin five years of rehabilitation? And don't give me any shit about this being some innovative psychological motivation to stimulate patients, either. Because I won't buy it!"

"Nash, you've got to listen to me—"

"Don't you see what she's trying to do, Nash?" Levi interrupted. "She thinks she can come between us, but she doesn't know we're like family. She told me she was going to concoct some story about how I've been embezzling money from the ranch in an attempt to turn you against me. She probably wants you all to herself.

"I've thought she had the hots for you for quite some time now. Hell, I even encouraged it—for your sake at first, because I thought you needed to enjoy your life more than you have been. But now I realize she's poison wrapped in a pretty package!"

Nash jerked upright, his back rigid as a steel fence post. His glittering golden eyes burned into Crista like lasers. Condemnation and disdain were written all over his face.

"I never said any of those things," Crista said in her own defense. "You have to believe me."

"Do I?" Nash scoffed disdainfully. "Don't bet on it, Curly."

"She was trying to get her hands on the ledger so she could alter the expenditures," Levi insisted, spitting out explanations as fast as he could think of them. "She promised she'd authorize the paperwork to have me stashed in some hospital for invalids if I didn't keep my mouth shut."

Crista stared at Levi as if he had become a two-headed monster right before her very eyes. The easygoing demeanor he adopted for the men who cared and provided for him had crumbled like *papier-mâché*. Crista knew Levi had to be guilty of fraud or embezzlement—maybe both. He wouldn't have become so desperate to convince Nash of his innocence if he weren't.

Levi had twisted the truth, and trusting friend and protector that Nash was, he was going to find *himself* financially crippled because he had become accustomed to believing everything Levi said without hesitation or question. Nash's most admirable qualities were about to become his downfall. He was playing right into Levi's hands, and nothing Crista could say would stop him.

"You conniving little bitch," Nash sneered. "Did you think just because you and I—"

He snapped his mouth shut like an alligator. The muscles of his jaw leaped in barely restrained fury. He looked as betrayed as Crista felt.

"You knew the rules, damn you. They haven't changed. They will *never* change. Hal was right. The minute you start trusting a woman she'll betray you one way or another. What the hell did you hope to gain from this?"

"You, probably," Levi was quick to reply before Crista could get a word in. "I've seen the way she

looks at you when she doesn't know anyone is watching. You know how divorcées can be—hot to trot. I'll bet Crista is used to crooking her finger and having any man she pleases. She even admitted she can be a royal bitch when the mood suits her. We should have taken her at her word.

"The accountant she has sniffing after her was probably too tame to satisfy her," Levi added with a disparaging smirk. "She's just like the groupies who hang around the beer stands at rodeos, looking for a ride with a real cowboy. And after she gets rid of me, she'll probably start trying to worm her way onto this ranch for the profit to be gained from it."

Levi's smoldering gaze drilled into Crista's flushed face. "Well, it won't work. We're more than family and we take care of each other. Now get out of here before I tell Nash what else you promised to do if I stopped you."

That comment left Nash staring at Crista with blatant mistrust. "Get out of my sight," he hissed between clenched teeth.

"And good riddance," Levi seconded.

"I have the feeling that incident at Mangy Dog and the *supposed* prowlers in your home was all a set-up," Nash hurled at Crista, furious at his own gullibility. "No wonder Detective Pine didn't take you seriously. And just what the hell was I to you?" he went on in disgust. "Just another game you played for your amusement? God, and to think I swallowed all that crap about you being the victim of a bad marriage. It was probably a pack of lies to get my sympathy. I'm beginning to understand why your husband found better things to do."

Crista staggered back as if Nash had slapped

her. He had slashed her pride to ribbons, and he was so furious that he couldn't distinguish truth from deception. He had twisted the truth to convince himself of *her* guilt, because his unswerving devotion to Levi simply would not permit him to believe anything else. Nash's own guilty conscience and fierce sense of obligation were conspiring against him to condemn her.

"Hey, are you guys coming down to the arena or not . . . ?"

Hal's voice trailed off when he blundered into the office to see his brother standing rigidly beside Levi's wheelchair, glowering at Crista.

"Get her out of here," Nash ordered gruffly.

When Hal grabbed her arm, Crista pulled loose, her livid green eyes flashing. "Don't bother crawling on your knees to apologize when you discover who's really at fault here," she spat through her tears. "If you could believe for even a moment that—"

"She's trying to prey on your sympathy, Nash," Levi quickly broke in. "I would never betray you, not after all you've done for me."

Nash turned away. He couldn't bear those crocodile tears glistening in those deceptive green eyes. He should have listened to Hal from the beginning. Whatever was on Crista's hidden agenda, Nash would never forgive her for making such demoralizing comments to Levi.

Hal clenched Crista's elbow and uprooted her, ignoring her choked sobs as he towed her through the entryway and out the door.

"You're really a piece of work, honey," he muttered. "What did you do? Set your sights on my brother, hoping for a juicy cut of this ranch? And that modified saddle you dragged here for Levi?

What was that all about? Were you trying to make the rest of us think you were sincere in your attempt to do what was best for Levi?"

Hal swore viciously as he shepherded Crista toward her car. "God, you really should meet my ex-fiancée. You're two of a kind. A couple of tramps who'll say and do anything to get what you want, ought to be best friends.

"Well, you can forget about getting your devious hands on my brother or on Chulosa Ranch. And if I have my way, you'll be looking for a new place to rent at the end of this month. When Uncle Jim learns what you've done, he'll toss you out."

Hal jerked open the car door and thrust Crista beneath the wheel, ignoring the river of tears that bled down her cheeks. "If you've got any sense, you'll take a wide berth from now on. And if you send Levi back into the kind of fits of depression he suffered in the beginning, you'll goddam answer to me. Nash and I have busted our butts to keep his spirits up. We're not going to watch him go to pieces and give up because of a deceptive little bitch like you!"

"I hope he takes you for you the ride of your life," Crista spitefully flung back. "If I were you—"

"You're not—"

"—I'd take a close look at that ledger," Crista warned before she cranked the engine and sped off.

Crista managed to keep a grip on herself until she reached the rise of ground overlooking Chulosa Ranch. And then her hard-won composure shattered. Hot tears spilled down her cheeks, making it difficult to see where she was going. And where she wanted to go was home, as quickly as she could get there.

Six months earlier Crista had been hurt, mortified, and betrayed when the details of Jonathan's infidelity and his attempt to embezzle from his client's trust funds and insurance settlements were made public. It was true that their relationship had been doomed from the onset, but Crista had tried to honor her vows and commitments. In that, she could understand Nash's fierce loyalty to his friend. But for Nash to twist her feelings for him into something sordid, devious, and manipulative was simply too much!

It was glaringly apparent that Nash had found nothing but physical pleasure with her. It was all he would allow himself to have, because . . . she meant nothing to him . . .

Crista broke down and cried uncontrollably at the humiliating thought.

And with Hal Griffin, the world's greatest cynic, living under the same roof, Nash would constantly be bombarded with advice and warnings— all of which he would unquestionably heed. If this afternoon's nightmare was any indication, Crista's feelings counted for nothing in Nash's book. He was prepared to conform to the gospel according to Levi Cooper and accept counseling from Hal— the woman-hater.

Damn them all! She should stand aside and let the whole lot of them sink like rocks in the ocean. They were all about to learn an expensive lesson about blind trust—compliments of Levi Cooper.

Thank God Crista hadn't been foolish enough to actually fall in love with Nash . . .

A sob burst from her lips. Crista was very much afraid she already cared too much. She had told herself she wasn't going to become involved with a man for a long time to come—if ever. Jonathan had left too many scars on her heart.

"God, Delaney, you can really pick 'em, can't you?" Crista asked herself with a sniff. "If this doesn't teach you that you have the absolute worst taste in men, and that good intentions are the bane of your life, I don't know what will!"

Levi slumped into his chair and swore colorfully. He wasn't proud of himself for what he'd had to do. But damn it, Crista could have blown the lid off his carefully-laid plans. Levi had felt threatened to the extreme, especially when he knew Nash had developed a fond attachment for the attractive therapist.

Nash's interests had been clearly evident the night he had tramped off to rescue Crista from Mangy Dog Saloon. He had been so restless during the domino game that he couldn't sit still, couldn't concentrate. And everybody in the house knew he'd come home late. What he and Crista had been doing until all hours of the night was the subject of great speculation.

Hell, Levi had noticed the way Nash had looked at Crista the first time she showed up. Levi had even played on that preoccupation and insisted she make regular visitations. She had distracted Nash, allowing Levi to make his necessary arrangements.

Unfortunately, things had gotten way out of hand.

Heaving an angry sigh, Levi rolled around the desk to stuff the ledger in the bottom drawer. He was going to have to smooth things over tonight, making sure the Griffins and the other cowboys had a grand time. He had to make Nash forget about the unpleasant encounter with Crista.

Another twinge of regret nipped at Levi's conscience. Well, he would have to wage that battle later. Right now he would roll down to the barn to spring the surprise on Nash that inclement weather had postponed.

Everything would work out for the best, Levi convinced himself as he rolled away. It *had* to. He had spent three years making triple-damn certain his plans would come off. Crista had to be sacrificed. Levi had convinced himself that the end justified the means, in this case.

Nash spewed a raft of curses as he strode into the barn. A knot of frustration coiled in his belly as he reached for the saddle to toss on Bowleg's back. He couldn't believe Crista would to sell Levi out. But he couldn't think of one reason why Levi would lie to him.

It hadn't been easy to choose between the man he had dedicated his life to protecting and the woman who . . .

The woman who *what?* Nash asked himself harshly. The woman he'd had sex with? Why, Nash wondered as he shoved his booted foot in the stirrup, had Crista believed she could get away with accusing Levi of wrongdoing?

What could she have been after? The money she had lost when her ex-husband drained her savings? Or was that another of her deceptions? Had Crista decided to remove the one obstacle that stood in her path in hopes of getting her hands on the Chulosa Ranch?

He didn't know what to think. And who could

understand the workings of the female brain? Certainly not Nash Griffin. He had been in an all-male environment too long to second-guess Crista's motivations. He wasn't sure he had been around women enough lately to recognize their lies when he heard them.

Nash shook his head, trying to clear his jumbled thoughts. He didn't have time to sort it all out right now. The barn and corrals were crawling with cowboys who had arrived to lift Levi's spirits. That was the purpose of this party. Nash couldn't allow his frustration to spoil the three-day visit he'd planned for Levi. Nash was going to pretend to enjoy himself, even if it killed him. Later, when he could be alone with his thoughts, he would sit himself down and try to untangle things.

"Hey, Good Time," Rooster Anderson called out. "I hear you made a grand showing in Fort Worth. Let's see if you still have a knack with a calf and lariat. Five bucks says you've lost your touch."

Nash halfheartedly returned Rooster's challenging grin and trotted Bowlegs from the barn. It shouldn't be too hard to cast an accurate loop, he encouraged himself. He would just pretend he was tossing a noose around Crista's lovely neck. From all indications, he functioned best when he and Crista Delaney were at odds. If the confrontation in the office was anything to go by, Nash was going to be hell-on-horseback during the upcoming competition with old friends.

Levi punched the stopwatch and checked the time after Nash had roped his calf, bounded from the saddle, and tied the animal with pigging string. "Damn, Nash, you came on like gangbusters."

Levi glanced at Rooster, who sat on a prancing black gelding, a pigging string clamped in his teeth, his lariat poised and ready. "You've got your work cut out for you, Rooster. Good Time was down and dirty in ten seconds flat."

"Damned good thing Good Time gave up the circuit," Ace Ketcham said with a snicker. "None of us would get any glory these days."

When Rooster gave Choctaw Jim the nod to release the calf in the chute, Rooster gouged his horse and tore off. As skilled as Rooster was, he was no match that afternoon for Nash Griffin. It took Rooster twelve seconds to flip and tie the calf.

"Who'd you say had lost his touch?" Hal taunted the bulky cowboy from South Dakota.

Rooster shrugged good-naturedly and retrieved his pigging string from the calf's hind legs. "Okay, Good Time, double-or-nothing in my main event—bulldogging . . ."

His voice trailed off when Bernie Bryant led Popeye from the barn, equipped with the modified saddle. Heads turned in synchronized rhythm toward Levi, who handed the stopwatch to Hal. All conversation came to a standstill as Hal, Bernie, and Choctaw Jim lifted Levi onto the horse.

Nash stood there, his jaw dropped, watching Levi Cooper clamp the pigging string in his teeth and flip the kink from the lariat. Nash's heart twisted like a pretzel as he stared at the man who had been named Rodeo Rookie of the Year, and had been on his way to stardom before the tragic accident at Glitter Gulch.

Nash resisted the urge to dash forward and pre-

vent Levi from taking the risk of riding—and falling. But another part of him thrilled to the sight
of Levi back in the saddle, even one with metal
bars and velcro straps.

The grin on Levi's handsome face, when he
glanced at Nash, was enough to cut the knees out
from under the sturdiest of men. Nash felt a lump
welling up in his throat.

Cheers resounded around the arena when Levi
gave that old familiar nod, indicating he was ready
to chase down a calf. Nash held his breath when
Popeye gathered himself behind and lurched off
with the kind of lightning speed that had earned
the horse the title of Best Roping Horse—four
years running.

In pride and satisfaction Nash watched Levi cast
his loop. The lariat settled neatly over the calf's
horns, and Popeye set up like a good mount was
trained to do, keeping the rope taut.

Although Levi couldn't bound off the right side
of his horse and wrap the pigging string around
the calf's legs, instant applause filled the arena.

Levi beamed like a floodlight.

"Damn, boys, I can't tell you how good it feels
to be one of you again." Levi glanced down at
Nash, who was staring up at him in silent admiration. "What do you say about some team roping? Any takers for some friendly competition?"

Nash swung onto his horse and reined up beside Levi. "When did you—?"

"While you were away at the rodeo," Levi cut
in, chuckling. "It's a borrowed saddle." He didn't
dare say where he'd gotten it. For the moment,
thoughts of Crista Delaney had escaped Nash. "I
practiced riding and roping while you were gone

so I could surprise you. This seemed like the perfect time."

Nash swallowed a second lump in his throat. "You sure as hell did that, Dogger. I wasn't certain you would ever want to ride again, but the look on your face is answer enough."

Levi nodded. "I'll take the calf's heels. I'm not quite steady enough to rope the horns and drag the calf while the heeler casts a loop. I don't have the use of my legs to guide the horse."

"I'll serve the calf up to you," Nash promised. "Just don't miss the legs."

"I'll make the double rocker—both legs wrapped in the loop," Levi promised.

Nash glanced toward his brother and Rooster, who had teamed up for the competition. "Hal's roping with tender ribs, but Rooster's pride is smarting right about now. He won't want to be outdone by—"

"A *cripple* and a so-called *has been*?" Levi finished for him.

"Use that term again, and I'll knock you off that damned horse myself," Nash growled, but there was entirely too much affection in his voice to sound threatening.

"Good Time?" Levi's gaze focused momentarily on Nash before flitting away, unable to look him in the eye.

"Yeah, Dogger?"

"Aw, never mind. Let's go beat the pants off our competition."

That was not to happen, Nash discovered a half-hour later. Although Nash and Levi made their catches without a hitch, Hal and Rooster had the best time in the group.

Nash decided that coming in third wasn't all

that bad, considering the best cowboys on the rodeo circuit were competing. What was most important was the fact that Levi was back in the saddle, laughing and joking with the rest of them.

After Levi had the chance to polish his skills, they might even enter a rodeo, just for the sport of it. Nash would look forward to that day. It would give him the chance to escape the memories of a certain woman . . .

Nash shut away the thought that had sneaked into his mind. For the duration of the cowboys' stay at Chulosa, he was going to forget Crista—she didn't exist. Whatever her motives for tormenting Levi, they were unforgivable. The tender affection Nash had begun to feel for her was going to die a quick death—here and now.

The sight of Levi's face flushed with anger and frustration during the scene in the office incited too many unpleasant flashbacks from five years past. Nash couldn't bear to see Levi upset. It nearly drove him to his knees.

And, Nash told himself firmly, he could not, would not, ever divide his loyalty again. Today's fiasco served to prove what could happen when he did . . .

Sixteen

Crista stood beneath the shower, sobbing like a child, her emotions churning uncontrollably. Only when she had drained the hot water tank did she finally reach for a towel.

One minute she swore she should march herself back to Chulosa Ranch and demand that Nash and Hal take the ledger to Jack Forrester for a thorough examination. The next minute she told herself that Nash and Hal deserved whatever resulted from the scheme Levi had concocted. She had certainly taken it on the chin when Jonathan filched money from her accounts and left her with a stack of bills that had taken months to settle.

It would damned well serve Nash right if he discovered—firsthand—how naive and humiliated *she* had felt during the court trial and the months of struggling to get her financial legs beneath her.

Crista wrapped the towel around herself and padded toward the bedroom, her gaze straying to the bed where she and Nash . . .

Crista squelched the thought. Whatever she and Nash might have had together—even while foolishly playing by Nash's rules—was over and done. She had been cured of all her ideals where men were concerned. The third time must be a charm, all right, she thought miserably. She could name three ways for a woman to ruin her life—Cole Delaney, Jonathan Heywood III, and Nash Griffin.

Muttering, Crista stuffed her head through the neck of a T-shirt and pulled on her jeans. Lord, this was one evening she would have given anything to take Choctaw Jim up on his offer to ride. She was more than ready to climb on the back of a horse and thunder off into the sunset, letting the wind scatter her tormented thoughts. But after the incident at Chulosa, Crista doubted Jim Pryce would provide her with a horse, much less let her continue renting his farmhouse. It looked as if she would have to relocate—to another planet, maybe.

Crista ambled down the hall and then pulled up short when she noticed a shadow drifting along the living room wall. Her pulse leaped to her throat as she cautiously retreated, bracing her hands on the walls in case her wobbly knees gave way.

Crista ducked into the bathroom—it was the only interior room with a lock on it. If she was lucky, she could crawl through the window and make a run for it.

The instant Crista twisted the lock she heard muffled footsteps in the hall. In sheer panic she made a lunge for the window. Her hands were shaking so badly she could barely get the window unlocked.

Hardly daring to breathe, she eased open the window and then shoved the screen aside.

The thud at the door nearly gave her heart failure. Crista stepped up on the edge of the bathtub and thrust her upper body through the escape hatch. She was halfway to safety when the door rattled on its hinges and she heard a muffled curse.

Her pulse pounding in her ears, Crista dived to the ground, then struggled to kick free of the window. Her bare feet hit the ground and she bounded off in a dead run, headed for the trees and underbrush that lined the creek below the house.

In the distance Crista heard the splintering of wood and a loud curse. Crista never looked back as she ran for her life . . .

An hour later, having followed the meandering creek that flowed toward the river, Crista spotted a herd of horses grazing in the twilight. Glancing in every direction at once, she inched from the shelter of the trees and then sprinted toward the horses. She would make better time on horseback than on foot—especially barefooted.

Too bad her closest neighbors were the Griffins at Chulosa.

The *peaceful retreat,* Crista reminded herself. She doubted it would be anything but peaceful when—if—she showed up there.

Well, tough, she thought defiantly. She had to reach a phone to call the police. Of course, Nash probably wouldn't let her near the house, certain this was just another of her plots.

"Damn him to hell and back," Crista muttered bitterly. He couldn't have hurt her worse if he had shot her between the eyes.

Halting twenty yards from the horses, Crista gave a whistle. Several equine heads turned toward her, but none of the horses responded.

As the sun melted into the autumn horizon, casting its flaming reflection on Fire River, Crista calmly approached the nearest mare. She wondered if any of these horses was broken to ride. Probably not. She would have to break one on the run—without bridle and saddle. Great!

Speaking softly, Crista closed in on the piebald mare. When she reached out to stroke the animal's broad neck, the mare sidestepped. Crista wasted no time, tossing her leg over the horse's back and clamping both hands onto the mane.

Although she braced herself for a leaping buck, the horse merely trotted off, tossing its head a bit.

Squeezing her legs against the mare's belly, Crista urged her into a trot and then into a gallop. Anxiously, Crista stared down the line of fence posts that stretched eastward. No way would she attempt to leap an unsaddled, unfamiliar horse over a fence. There had to be a gate somewhere. Crista needed to find it—fast.

When she finally found the gate, she leaned out to unhook the loop of wire without dismounting. The horse's rump slammed against the corner post, sending the mare prancing sideways. Crista put a stranglehold on the mane and clamped herself to the horse. With considerable coaxing, she managed to guide the horse close enough to the fence post to relatch the gate.

Mission accomplished, Crista aimed the paint pony toward the rolling hill and the ranch house beyond.

The sound of bawling cattle caused the mare to prick her ears. Crista stared into the distance, seeing the flood lights surrounding the Griffins' private rodeo arena. She was more than a mile from the ranch house—in the dark, riding bare-back.

Not for the first time she was thankful for her years of training with horses. If nothing else, this ordeal had provided her with a sense of inde-pendence and accomplishment. She could damned well take care of herself when times got tough. She didn't need Nash Griffin any more than he needed her.

In fact, she thought defiantly, she could have devised a way to evade Red Cameron at Mangy Dog Saloon without Nash's help. She wished he had stayed home that night!

Thirty minutes later, Crista was close enough to the barn to hear the drone of conversation, the occasional outbursts of laughter, and smell the smoke drifting from Bernie's oversize char-coal oven. The cowboys were probably having their private rodeo, sipping beer and swapping stories.

Crista decided to circle around to the back of the house. She wanted to avoid all contact with Nash. She sure as hell didn't want or expect his assistance, just the use of his phone.

With a sense of relief, Crista walked the mare toward the kitchen door and slid to the ground. Casting a cautious glance toward the barn, she headed for the abandoned house. To her dismay, she strode inside to see Nash hunkered over the refrigerator, retrieving two six-packs of beer.

Well, damn, she had successfully managed to rescue herself and ride blindly through unfamil-iar pastures. Then, at trail's end, wouldn't you know she would have to meet up with the wolf-dragon. She'd be lucky indeed if he didn't throw her out of the house before she had the chance to beg the use of his phone.

When Nash spied the barefoot blonde standing at the kitchen door he jerked upright, hitting his head on the edge of the refrigerator. She looked as thrilled to see him as he was to see her.

"You have a short memory, Curly. I told you to go away and never come back," Nash growled.

She braced herself against his abrasive tone and ominous glower. "I would like to use your phone, if it isn't too much to ask."

"Anything you ask is too much," Nash sneered, slamming the refrigerator door with a loud thump.

Crista matched him glare for glare. "If this wasn't an emergency I wouldn't bother asking at all."

Nash smirked sardonically. "Emergency?"

His condescending stare had Crista gnashing her teeth as angry frustration burned in her stomach. "Are you going to let me use your phone or aren't you?"

Nash nodded curtly. "If it will get you out of here any faster, then go ahead."

Despite his irritation, Nash took note of the way Crista limped toward the phone. He couldn't imagine what ploy she was using now. Probably another of her damsel in distress routines, but he'd be damned if he'd ask any questions or offer assistance.

Plucking up the phone book, Crista found the number and then dialed the sheriff's department. When she asked for Detective Pine, Nash was on his way out the kitchen door. He wasn't hanging

around to eavesdrop, because he didn't give a
damn what was going on.

When he spied the piebald paint pony that belonged in the pasture on his uncle's farm, Nash
whipped back around. Despite his firm resolve he
found himself straining to hear Crista's conversation.

"Could you give me a number where Pine can
be reached?" she questioned. "I would like him
to follow up on a previously reported incident."

When Crista received Pine's home number, she
redialed. "Well, damn," she muttered when she
heard the busy signal.

Nash braced his shoulder against the doorjamb, the six-packs dangling from his fingertips.
"Staged another break-in to report to Pine, did
you?" he scoffed.

Crista slammed down the receiver. "No, not
that you care or have bothered to listen to anything I have to say. I didn't stage anything. I had
to lock the bathroom door and climb out the window to escape the prowler in my house. I managed to get here—bareback—and all I ask of you
is the patience to let me wait until Pine gets off
his damned phone!"

Nash appraised Crista's appearance once again,
reluctant to believe anything she said after the
events of that afternoon. Damn it, so much for
attempting to put her out of sight and out of
mind—before he went out of his! How the hell
was he supposed to forget her when she kept popping up faster than bread from a toaster?

When Crista turned her back on him to redial,
Nash pushed away from the door and headed toward the barn, carrying the fresh supply of beer
for the visiting cowboys. He tried to convince

himself he didn't care what Crista was up to and that he wasn't going to be lured back to her against his better judgment. But when he heard the phone ring, he broke stride.

"Nash?" Crista called after him. "This call is for Hal. The woman wants to hire him to round up her stray cattle."

"Take down the number and I'll have Hal return the call later," Nash said as he pivoted toward the barn once again. He halted in midstep, swore foully, and then reversed direction. He should have better sense than to let Crista prowl around his house, considering her accusations against Levi. For all he knew, this might be her attempt to swipe the ledger. She knew there was a crowd in the barn. She could be using the distraction to her advantage to sneak into the house. Hadn't he already caught her at it?

When Nash stepped inside, Crista was slamming down the phone, spitting a few curses of her own. Nash heaved a resigned sigh and called himself every kind of fool. "I'll take you home and you can use your own phone to reach Detective Pine."

"I'll go back home only if you'll loan me your shotgun," Crista insisted.

Nash snorted sardonically. "Lady, I sure as hell wouldn't trust you with a loaded gun."

"Not surprising. You don't trust me—period."

"You've got that right."

"Not that I care, I might add," she flung back at him.

Nash replaced the beer in the refrigerator and then shepherded Crista toward the front door. Jiggling the key in the faulty ignition, Nash waited for the rattletrap truck to sputter to life.

Without so much as one word of conversation, Nash drove to Crista's home. When the truck rolled to a stop in the driveway, she opened the door and stepped gingerly onto the gravel. Her feet were killing her, after traipsing along the creek and through the pasture to retrieve the mare. Her bruised pride and battered heart weren't in such good condition, either.

"Well, hell," Nash muttered, climbing from the cab.

In swift strides he overtook Crista, sweeping her up into his arms. He held her as far away from him as he could without losing his balance. When he reached the porch he promptly set her on her bare feet.

"I know it will probably ruin the effect you were hoping for, but next time you decide to play one of your charades for my benefit, wear shoes."

"There won't be a next time, because you're a lost cause. You and your cynical brother."

Nash's chest rose and fell in exasperation. He supposed he should at least have a look around, just in case Crista hadn't concocted this story. His overworked conscience would get the best of him if she was actually telling the truth and had fallen victim to attack after he left her alone.

Nash reached for the doorknob, finding it locked. He glanced inquiringly at Crista.

"I don't have the key," she grumbled. "I'll have to climb back through the bathroom window." She spun around and walked off. "Thanks for the ride. Go back to your party, cowboy. I'll take care of this by myself."

When she disappeared around the corner, Nash scowled sourly. He scowled again, realizing his footsteps were taking him in the same direction Crista had gone.

Light sprayed through the bathroom window, spotlighting the shapely female attempting to climb through the opening. The light accentuated every curve of a body Nash had learned by sight and touch . . . and heart.

Nash cursed the wayward thought as he surged forward to give Crista a boost. When he wrapped an arm around her hips to hoist her off the ground, he found himself scowling all over again.

It only took one touch to set off a flood of forbidden memories. Damn, he was an idiot. When it came to this green-eyed, curly-headed woman, he felt like a damned kite on a string, being tugged every which way.

He was still tied to a lifelong obligation to Levi, and yet he was being tossed around by this whirlwind of a woman whom he was beginning to think was a fruitcake. He was also beginning to have serious reservations about Crista's version of the incident involving her jailbird of an ex-husband.

It could well be that Crista had been a party to the fraud and embezzlement and had escaped unscathed. Now she was accusing Levi of the very same thing. Was it an ironic coincidence or a carefully staged scheme?

Before Nash could cram Crista through the opening, he heard her phone ringing. Whoever had placed the call gave up while Crista was making her way through the bathroom.

When she pivoted and then poked her head back out the window, Nash swallowed a grin. He did *not* want to have one damned thing to do with this woman. Too bad the mere sight of her set off so many conflicting emotions. Even while he was angry and mistrusting, she still had the ability to make him smile—to bring him a moment of pleasure amid his confusion and frustration.

How could he hate her and desire her with simultaneous and equal intensity? Lord, she would drive him nuts if he wasn't careful.

"Go home," Crista demanded. "If the prowler is still in the house it's no skin off your back. If I wind up murdered, make sure Detective Pine is fired before he can collect his retirement pension."

Nash tamped down another unwanted smile as Crista shut the window in his face. If nothing else, he had to admit his association with her was nothing if not interesting. She certainly triggered the full spectrum of his emotions. But then, maybe he had needed to be shaken from his customary rut.

And maybe not . . .

Gawd, Nash thought. What a shame he didn't drink much these days. He could have used a few belts. The other cowboys in the barn were guzzling suds like it was going out of style. Nash and Choctaw Jim were the only sober men in the bunch.

Spinning about, Nash tramped back to the porch and pounded on Crista's door. "Open up, Curly. I want to see the evidence of this alleged break-in."

"Go to hell, Griffin!"

Where, he wondered, did she think he'd been for the past five hours?

Nash banged on the door until Crista finally let him in. He took quick inventory, finding nothing out of place in the living room. He did, however, notice the footprint on the bathroom door, the splintered wood and bent hinges. He glanced back at Crista, frowning thoughtfully.

"I staged this myself, of course," she said flippantly. "All this, just to lure you over here so I could wrestle you to the bed and ravish you."

While Crista blinked back angry tears Nash studied her astutely, trying to decide if she was on the level or lying through her pearly whites.

"Just leave, will you?" she sputtered. "I'd like to grab something to eat and get a few hours of sleep before I have to go to work in the morning."

"Crista . . ."

When he reached for her, she reeled away, refusing to let him touch her. "You don't want me in your home and I don't want you in mine. There's already one kook running around the place . . . and it's not me! So stop looking at me like that, damn it!"

When Crista lurched away, Nash latched onto her arm, pressing her against the wall. He leaned full length against her when she squirmed. Her lashes swept up, and Nash's body stiffened when he found himself tumbling into those hypnotic green pools.

"Damn you, Curly. I don't need this. Don't you understand? You're tearing me apart!"

His mouth came down hard on hers. His hands slid around her hips to haul her against him. Crista resisted him—for all of one second and then melted like butter on a hot biscuit.

Nash hated what Crista did to him, hated himself for wanting her without reason or rhyme. But the bottom line was that he *did* want her, *did* care about her. She made him feel things he never had, something much more than superficial satisfaction. If he didn't, he wouldn't be in such torment now!

A quiet moan rose from Crista when she felt the old black magic once again transforming her anger into breathless desire.

Even while Nash hated and mistrusted her, she still longed to be a part of his life—a vital, necessary part. But that was never going to happen, and it was killing her to know it. She may have acquired the power to arouse Nash and he may have surrendered the pleasures of his body, but she would never have his heart . . .

Crista told herself that she should resist Nash's kiss, the tantalizing feel of him against her, but her traitorous body was paying no attention whatsoever to the good advice from her brain. And her emotions weren't helping the situation, either.

Oh, the hell with it, Crista thought as she slid her arms around his broad shoulders. They were both hopeless causes. So why fight it?

Crista arched into him, accepting the roiling hunger in his kiss, returning it. When his hand swirled around her ribs to delve beneath the hem of her T-shirt, Crista was sure her legs had turned to sand.

His impatient yet tender touch stripped all sensible thought from her mind. She almost wished he had been rough with her, as her husband usually was. Perhaps then she could have mustered the will to push him away.

Instead, she practically begged for his caresses, the plunging thrust of his tongue and the possessive heat of his lips. He was burning her alive, and she could do nothing but respond to him, as if wanting him was a basic instinct that knew no master save itself.

Crista's breath broke when he teased her nipple with thumb and forefinger, sending wild sensations spiraling up from her very core like molten lava. When his lips migrated down the column of her throat, she struggled to draw breath and found none to sustain her. His mouth settled on one beaded nipple while his fingertips continued to tease the other. Shamelessly, Crista moved toward his body, craving more of the sweet torment that sent her world spinning into oblivion.

She knew she would regret her shameless reactions later—when she could think straight. All she was doing was proving to Nash that she wanted him desperately, that she was willing to do anything to have him. But she was too far gone to consider the repercussions. The floodtide of sensation had drowned all sense of reason.

She felt his hand drift to the band of her jeans, heard the rasp of the metal zipper gliding down to admit his prowling fingertips. Her ragged breath hitched as he curled his hand around her hip, pushing her jeans down to a pool at her feet.

Crista closed her eyes and moaned aloud when he traced her heated softness through her bikini panties. She was a hopeless wanton where Nash was concerned. She all but begged for his touch, reveling in the feel of his hand trailing along the elastic leg band, teasing her, arousing her, tormenting her with anticipation of pleasures to come.

And all the while his hand skimmed her most sensitive flesh, his lips brushed over her breasts, holding her suspended in splendorous torture. His muscled legs shifted, nudging her feet apart, granting him further access to the sensitive flesh of her inner thighs.

When he knelt before her, his mouth drifting down her belly to the silky fabric of her panties, Crista's legs felt like cooked oatmeal. She could feel his hot breath on her skin, feel his fingers gliding, tugging, arousing until she shivered in helpless spasms.

With one quick sweep of his hand, Nash peeled away the fabric that formed a flimsy barrier between his moist lips and her dewy flesh. Crista cried out at the first searing touch of his tongue and lips, his swirling fingertips. She could feel the hot-burning fire explode inside her, feel her femininity answering each caress. She felt the convulsions claim her with each stab of his tongue, felt the empty ache of wanting him—all of him—clench so deeply inside her that she had to bite her lip to restrain a wild cry.

Shudders wracked her body, even as he rose in front of her, still stroking the fires of her passion. When his lips feathered over her mouth, hot with the scent of her, Crista felt another spasm of pleasure ripple through her.

She had never experienced such intimacy, never dreamed such bone-melting sensations existed . . . until Nash taught her.

"Once and for all," Nash whispered against her parted lips. "And when this sweet poison runs its course, I'll be free of you. One last time, Crista. And then never again will my heaven and hell be one . . ."

The quiet hiss of another zipper broke the silence. When Crista felt the hard length of him pressing into her, she peered up into golden eyes that reflected all the passionate torment that roiled inside her.

He watched her intently, while she watched him. And when he buried himself deeply inside her she could feel the throbbing pulse of his desire.

When Nash drew her leg over his thigh, Crista's eyes widened, startled by the indescribable sensations that burgeoned inside her, taking her beyond the pinnacle of ecstasy she had visited a moment earlier. The empty ache was gone; he was sheathed inside her, thrusting and withdrawing in a slow, gentle rhythm that drove her over the edge.

When Crista would have closed her eyes against the torrent of sensations that buffeted her, Nash's husky voice demanded what little attention she had left to give.

"Look at me," he rasped as he moved rhythmically against her. "If I can't distinguish truth from lies anywhere else, I want to see it in this, at least. I want to watch you while you burn around me. I want to look into your eyes when you lose all control . . ."

Crista gasped aloud when another spasm of inexpressible pleasure swirled through her.

Nash smiled at her response. "One truth, Crista, only this one. Could you really have loved me if I had let you—?"

Nash cursed himself when his body buckled to overwhelming need. He couldn't demand an answer to his question because he was being swept into the eye of passion's turbulent storm. His lips found hers, clinging in desperation, sharing each breath. Desire—hot and explosive—consumed him, body, mind, and soul.

His hands glided down her hips, clutching her so tightly that he feared he would unintentionally leave marks on her. But he was a man driven to obsession. When they were one, sharing the same heartbeat, the same last breath in a world of total sensation there was no other reality but this one damnable, undeniable truth: Despite everything, he wanted Crista like hell blazing . . .

The world reeled and tilted, and Nash braced one arm against the wall before his balance escaped him. He withdrew from her petal-soft mouth to snatch a breath and then buried his face in the cascade of blond curls that spilled over her shoulders. His body moved on its own, driving into her until he could go no deeper and yet, still feeling as if he were too far away to satisfy himself.

Dear God in heaven! Was there no way to break this spell that robbed him of the good sense he had spent thirty-three years cultivating? How could he keep reducing himself to a creature of insane lust, when Crista had become a threat to everything he was trying to protect?

One of them must surely be mad, Nash decided. He just couldn't figure out which one. *Her* for spinning a web of deceit—for reasons he couldn't understand—or *him* for wanting to believe her . . .

Pulsation after helpless pulsation wracked his body, reducing him to a mass of bubbling flesh and melted bone. Crista's name tripped from his lips as he half collapsed on her, crushing her against the wall.

Countless moments later, Nash drew a fortifying breath and lifted his head. He had fallen into the deepest reaches of those captivating evergreen eyes . . . and he cursed himself a thousand times over for letting desire do his thinking for him. If he didn't get the hell out of here—now— he was going to start questioning Levi's version of the incident in the office. He would be hearing what he wanted to hear, instead of listening for the truth from those poison-coated lips.

Nash fastened himself into his jeans and swore soundly. He was still fully dressed, while Crista was wearing nothing but the T-shirt that barely covered her hips.

Good Lord! He had just treated her like a second-rate slut, taking her up against the wall in the damned hall—of all places!

Maybe it was what she deserved—hell, he didn't know. But what he *did* know was that he regretted what he had done, resented his inability to control himself when he was alone with Crista.

One thing was for sure, Nash decided as he wheeled away. He had figured out which one of them was crazy—he was. He had obviously been kicked in the head one too many times.

With his jaw clamped shut, Nash stalked toward the front door. He was not coming here again. He always regretted it when he did—or rather afterward, when he had recovered his sanity. All he had proved was that even anger and mistrust couldn't stop him from craving this woman until even hell wouldn't have it. She was turning out to be the curse of his life!

When the door clicked shut, Crista slid down the wall, clutching her discarded jeans. A hysterical sob broke from her throat when she realized how infuriatingly vulnerable she was to Nash.

Lord, if she was in love with him—and she had every reason to fear she was, given her utterly shameless abandon—she wasn't enjoying it very much.

Except for their phenomenal lovemaking, Crista amended. The physical pleasure she experienced—could have been born of nothing but love. There was no question about that.

"You're doomed, Delaney," Crista whispered to her empty house. "You know damn well you're so much in love with the man that nothing else matters, even if he refuses to believe it . . ."

Seventeen

Hal scooted sideways on the hay bale to make room for his brother. "Where the hell have you been? Did you have to *brew* the beer yourself?" he questioned as he accepted the drink Nash offered him.

Nash settled himself inside the circle of men lounging in the barn. When Leon nudged his legs, demanding attention, Nash reached down to give his faithful dog a pat on the head. "I took a call while I was in the house," he hedged. "It was for you."

Hal stared ponderously at his brother, his onyx eyes probing deeper than Nash would have preferred. "It doesn't take forty-five minutes to answer a call for me. Unless you've started *speaking* for me, too."

Nash popped the lid and downed the first swallow of his one-drink limit. "I started speaking for you when you started keeping tabs and time clocks on everything I do."

Hal muttered under his breath. "The bitch-goddess again," he bitterly presumed. "I figured she must be around somewhere after I spotted the piebald mare that's supposed to be pastured at Choctaw Jim's. The mare came clomping in here to socialize with the rest of the horses.

"What game is Crista playing now? I thought we were well rid of her."

Nash was beginning to wonder if he would ever be well rid of Crista Delaney. And damn it, he didn't know who or what to believe after the confrontation in the office.

Dogger kept insisting Crista was trying to break the bond between him and the Griffin brothers for her own selfish purposes. Crista kept warning Nash that Dogger was up to no good with the accounts . . .

A round of laughter reverberated through the barn. Nash glanced up to see Levi Cooper's face light up with amusement. He suspected Rooster Anderson was spreading one of his wild tales about his extracurricular activities—after regular rodeo hours.

Likable and reliable though Rooster was, he hadn't come by his nickname without reason. He did his share of crowing around hen houses, and he could be a hell-raising renegade when the mood suited him. Nash should know. He had raised plenty of hell with Rooster in his glory days.

"Hey, Good Time." Levi rolled himself across the circle to wedge in between Nash and Ace Ketcham. "Would you and Hal mind putting clean sheets on my bed and tidying up the room while I say my good nights to the other men?"

Nash frowned in concern. "You're turning in already? Are you feeling okay?"

Levi shrugged his shoulders. "I'm fine. I just went overboard with the riding and roping tonight. I think I'm going to have to get in condition. My muscles are starting to cramp."

Hal and Nash automatically came to their feet

to do Levi's bidding. When Nash turned away, a silent voice niggled him. He didn't appreciate what Crista kept saying about spoiling Levi rotten and jumping the instant Levi snapped his fingers.

"Hal?" Nash murmured as he and his brother ambled up the sidewalk. "Do you think we cater to Levi too much?"

Hal grumbled and shot his brother an accusing look. "She's gotten to you, hasn't she? What's that little witch doing, anyway? Working on your mind while she's playing with your body? I keep telling you that you better be careful which head you let do your thinking for you."

"Zip it, Hal," Nash snapped.

"It seems to me that *you* should be the one doing that."

"Don't push it, little brother," Nash warned darkly.

"Why? Because you're too damned sensitive when the topic of Crista Delaney comes up?" Hal smirked in question. "Sometimes I swear you're on the verge of taking her word over Levi's. Why in the hell would Levi try to cheat us? We've always been like the three musketeers."

True, Nash reminded himself. Why would Levi bite the very hands that fed him? It made no sense. And yet, why would Crista lie to him? What could she be up to?

Hal strolled through the kitchen and glanced down at the message beside the phone. "Who the devil is Andrea Fletcher?"

"Some lady who wants to contract you to round up her missing cattle," Hash replied.

"A woman?" Hal snorted derisively. "The last thing I need is to get tangled up with some female who thinks she can tell me what to do and how to do it, just because she's paying me to do what she can't do herself. I've got a rodeo coming up in a few days. I don't have time to go a few rounds with a female."

Hal snatched up the phone to reject the offer and then glanced pointedly at his brother. "Considering the woman trouble you seem to be having, I'm not going to test the Griffin luck. I've sworn off women—except in the necessary sense. Too bad you aren't doing that."

Leaving Hal to call his rejected female client, Nash ambled off to find some clean sheets and spiff up Levi's private quarters. Since Bernie had been busy preparing for the surprise party, Levi's quarters were in disarray. Glasses and plates had been left on the end tables and on the office desk . . .

Nash halted in front of the desk, recalling Crista's plea to double-check the financial ledgers. He didn't want her clouding his mind with suspicion, damn it. Not after he and Hal had entrusted Levi with the management of the ranch.

Hesitantly, reluctantly, Nash veered around the desk to locate the ledger that had been tucked into the bottom drawer. He supposed it wouldn't hurt to have a quick look-see, just to reassure himself that Levi would never betray them.

"Well, son of a bitch," Hal muttered from the doorway.

Nash jerked up his head to see his brother glaring at him.

"She *has* gotten to you, hasn't she?" Hal's disgruntled gaze darted from the ledger in Nash's hand to the grim expression on his face. "I suppose you're going to tell me that our good friend Dogger has been taking his profit from the ranch as well as the money you and I have made leasing our horses, and has been feathering his own nest."

Nash made note of the sizeable sums of money paid for hospital therapy. The expenditures to keep the ranch in operation were less than the cost of Levi's rehabilitation programs.

And for what? Nash asked himself with a scowl. It wasn't the first time he had wondered if the hospital staff was making a killing off Levi Cooper. Considering the cash paid for gait therapy treatments at Kanima County Hospital, Levi shouldn't have been *walking* by now, he should have been *running!*

"Do you have the slightest idea how much cash we've paid for rehabilitation, not counting the cost of home health care and in-house physical therapy?" Nash asked as he swiveled the ledger in his hand. His forefinger tapped at the astronomical figure recorded and documented each month.

Hal's brows soared in astonishment. "Damn! We probably could have built our own hospital."

"And paid in full," Nash agreed. "Those sons-a-bitches are hanging us out to dry. Either that or—"

Hal reached over to snap the ledger shut. "I refuse to believe Levi is embezzling money. And you wouldn't be giving it a thought, either, if that well-stacked female hadn't put suspicious ideas in your head—or the one below your belt."

Nash was as close as he ever wanted to come to punching his brother in the mouth. With great effort he kept his doubled fist clenched at his side instead of cramming it down Hal's throat.

Hal stuffed the ledger in the drawer and rose

to his full stature, sternly appraising his brother. "You've been screwing her, haven't you, Nash?"

"Butt out, Hal. What I do and don't do is none of your business, unless it pertains to this ranch," Nash said firmly.

Hal expelled a harsh breath. "In other words, yes," he speculated. "You may as well admit it. Jeezus, the next thing I know you'll be telling me you've fallen in love with that devious little tramp. And don't get me wrong—I think she's a tempting piece. I've looked her over a few times myself, wondering what it would be like to take a joy ride—"

Nash's fist collided with Hal's jaw, spinning him around like a top. In stunned disbelief, Hal staggered for balance and grabbed his throbbing cheek.

"Don't you ever make me have to throw a punch at you again, damn you," Nash snarled at him. "We're supposed to be on the same side."

Hal spun away to snatch up the sheets Nash had laid on the edge of the desk. "Yeah, we are on the same side, only now there's a little blonde wedged directly between us. I'm starting to get an uneasy feeling of *déjà vu*, big brother. Only this time it's happening to *you*, not *me*. But don't think joining the army and putting as much distance between you and Crista will prevent having your heart ripped out. My brand of therapy for that didn't work worth a damn."

Hal paused beside the bed and glanced back at Nash. "They shoot horses with broken legs. To my way of thinking, they may as well shoot men with broken hearts. Heart don't mend any better than a horse's busted leg. At best, hearts scar over.

"But you never forget a woman's treachery.

Whatever Crista Delaney is really up to, you can bet it isn't in your best interests. Women can't see past their own motives, and that's a fact."

Nash didn't bother coming to Crista's defense. Hell, he couldn't swear she *had* a defense. But still . . .

Nash halted the thought and concentrated on erasing every image of Crista from his mind while he helped Hal strip the bed and replace the sheets.

Once the overhead bars and hand rings were shifted back into position above the bed, Nash followed his brother to the door.

Levi rolled through his personal quarters, smiling tiredly. "Thanks for the pleasant surprise. You made my day. It was good to see the other cowboys again and be a part of the friendly competition."

"Our pleasure," Hal insisted, sidestepping to let Levi pass. "Your room is all set. Anything else we can get for you before you turn in?"

Levi shook his head. "Nope. I can handle it from here."

When Hal ambled off, Nash hesitated, watching Levi roll toward his bedroom. He wanted Levi's assurance that there were no discrepancies in the ledger, but he didn't have the heart to upset Levi. The paraplegic cowboy was riding high after the party, after making his return debut in the arena. Nash couldn't bring himself to spoil the evening for Dogger. The man didn't deserve Nash's suspicion, especially not tonight . . . and probably not ever . . .

"Are you finally going to join the party?" Rooster Anderson teased Nash when he sank down on the hay bale. "We still have a few wild oats to reminisce about. I was just telling the boys about that cowgirl you hooked up with in your younger days."

He took a long swig of beer and then chuckled. "Talk about a little lady who could fill a tight pair of jeans. And wild as a March hare, as I recall. She could race barrels with the best of them, but when she set her sights on Good Time . . ."

The other men snickered when Rooster waggled his bushy brows and grinned devilishly.

"She took Good Time for a few spins and bucks, I'll bet. What the hell was her name? I've forgotten."

Nash silently drank his warm beer and said nothing.

"Of course, Good Time never was one to kiss and tell—"

"That's enough," Nash cut in gruffly.

As was Rooster's custom, he began exaggerating to get a rise out of his intended victim. The truth was often sacrificed when Rooster was in the mood to crow.

"I bet that barrel racer taught you a few different ways to do it—"

"I said . . . that's enough, Rooster."

Rooster downed the rest of his beer and reached for one of the cans that had been iced down in the metal tub beside him. "Hell, yes, it was enough. You ruined that cowgirl for the rest of us. After the rodeo in Sikeston, Missouri, she wouldn't have a thing to do with anybody else." His twinkling gaze darted to the dark-haired cowboy beside Nash. "Well, except for your brother here. She didn't mind keeping it in the family."

Hal shrugged nonchalantly. "I never was one to turn down hot sex or a fast horse."

The other cowboys guffawed.

"As I recall, you did ride off on a fast horse to avoid a certain redhead," Ace Ketcham put in.

While the other men chuckled, Hal glanced pointedly at his brother. "Take it from me, fellas. You're a helluva lot better off making fast getaways. Entanglements with women lead to trouble. We would probably all be better off if cowgirls stuck to barrel racing instead of chasing blue jeans. As for me, I don't like to get caught with my pants down for too long at a time."

Nash swallowed a curse when Hal aimed the barb directly at him.

"Speaking of barrel racers, you should see the little lady who rents Choctaw Jim's farmhouse. She can turn on a dime and burn leather," Bernie Bryant said.

Nash could feel the color drain from his face. His startled gaze swung to Bernie, who had casually propped himself on the stack of hay, his deformed arm draped across the straw.

"It's a good thing you horny rascals didn't get a look at her. This party would have packed up—lock, stock, and beer barrel—and moved down to her place hours ago."

"What the hell are you talking about?" Nash demanded.

"Crista," Bernie answered slurrishly and then chugged his beer. "Even wearing Nikes instead of boots, she can cut corners and thunder toward another barrel—lickety-split."

"I think you've been drinking so much you're hallucinating," Nash retorted.

Bernie lifted his stubbled chin. "The hell I am. I saw her myself—right through the kitchen window. You were at the rodeo in Fort Worth while

Hal was recuperating," he reminded Nash. "If you don't believe me, just ask Choctaw Jim. He was in the arena with her."

Nash's glittering gaze swung to his uncle, who had suddenly become fascinated with the saddles and bridles draped over the nearby stalls.

"You didn't tell me Crista had a rodeo background," Hal muttered at Nash.

"I didn't know it myself."

Hal smiled sardonically and sipped his beer. "You two must have never gotten around to discussing that, you were so deeply involved in other activities."

For the second time in an hour, Nash wanted to knock Hal's runaway tongue down his throat. This time he managed to restrain himself, but it wasn't easy!

When the party broke up two hours later, the cowboys wandered down to the bunkhouse. Nash dogged his uncle's footsteps.

"Why didn't you tell me about Crista?"

Choctaw Jim shrugged a sturdy shoulder as he strolled toward the house. "It was supposed to be between her and me. I didn't know Bernie saw her riding Bandit."

"Bandit?" Nash's brows jackknifed. "Christ, that gelding isn't a barrel racer."

Jim grinned wryly. "He sure as hell is now."

"She could have been hurt! That horse has entirely too much strength and spirit for a woman to ride."

"Crista handled Bandit just fine, and you're making too much of nothing," Jim told his nephew. "I wouldn't have put her on Bandit if I didn't think she could handle him."

Nash had wondered how Crista had managed to catch the piebald mare in Uncle Jim's pasture. He had figured it had simply been luck that prevented her from taking a tumble while she rode through the darkness to reach Chulosa Ranch.

Obviously luck had nothing to do with it.

"Why is she keeping her riding experience a secret?" Nash queried.

"You're asking a question I can't answer." Jim strode into the house, unsnapping his shirt on his way to bed. "She asked me to keep it under my hat so I did." He stared somberly at Nash. "Hal told me you had ordered her off the premises and that I should evict her from my rent house. Nobody has bothered to tell me what's going on, though. Would you like to explain?"

"No," Nash grumbled, glancing away.

When Jim strode off, Nash cursed under his breath. He could think of absolutely no reason why Crista hadn't mentioned her riding skills, unless she had a specific reason for keeping it a secret.

Then he found himself wondering what other secrets she was keeping from him—and why.

Nash tossed his hat on its hook by the door and raked his fingers through his rumpled hair. It was becoming glaringly apparent that he had kept his nose to the grindstone so long that he couldn't see what the hell was going on around him. He simply didn't know how to deal with women these days. And he didn't know what to think about the confrontation between Crista and Levi, not to mention her claim that someone was prowling around her home.

Whatever was seething beneath the surface at Chulosa Ranch would damned well have to wait, Nash decided. There was a bunkhouse full of cowboys to be fed and entertained before they continued on the next leg of the circuit. Until the crowd had thinned out, Nash wouldn't have time to sit down and decide *what* might possibly have motivated *whom*.

One thing was sure, though, Nash mused as he prepared for bed. He was going to feel betrayed either way. If Crista was lying, he was the world's biggest fool, just as Hal said. And if Dogger was lying . . .

Nash squeezed his eyes shut and blocked out the thought. He was simply unable to accept that possibility. It simply could not be. If Levi was dirty-dealing behind his back, then everything Nash believed in would come tumbling down like a house of cards.

To double-cross a long-time friend simply was not the cowboy way. They looked out for each other, protected each other, defended each other. What could possibly be worse than being sold down the river by the man Nash considered his trusted friend . . . ?

Nothing . . . except discovering the woman who turned him wrong side out, making him want things that could never be, had thoroughly and purposefully deceived him.

That, Nash thought bleakly, would be every bit as bad . . .

Crista had spent the past two days preparing for the hearing at Kanima County Courthouse. If nothing else, it was a welcome distraction from thoughts of the man who obviously perceived her as a femme fatale—or something to that effect.

Although Detective Pine had taken his duties on Lisa Chandler's behalf seriously, he had not proved helpful concerning the incident with the prowler. Pine claimed his wife and his sister-in-law had been yammering on the phone for hours on end the night Crista tried to get in touch with him. More than likely, he had taken the phone off the hook and caught a nap in front of the television.

The detective had come tramping out to take note of the damaged bathroom door the following evening, boasting about how he had caught Janelle Chandler and Red Cameron whooping it up in the back seat of Red's car.

At least Pine had accomplished *something*, Crista consoled herself. Janelle Chandler had ranted and threatened when she discovered Crista had shadowed her and sicced the detective on her. It had been an ugly confrontation, with constant curses from Janelle's foul mouth. But Crista tolerated the insults, knowing the Department of Human Services had made arrangements to place Lisa in competent care.

Of course, Lisa might not thank Crista for the good deed. And certainly Nash Griffin hadn't been the least bit appreciative when she warned him to keep an eye on Levi.

Crista didn't know why she had bothered. She had enough problems of her own, what with an unidentified prowler stalking her home, keeping her in a constant state of alarm.

As if Crista didn't already have a dozen irons in the fire, there was always the Inspector-Admiral

to contend with. Old Ironsides was due to dock
in Crista's office any day now.

From the minute Crista awakened to the alarm
clock that morning, she had been hounded by a
sense of impending doom. Probably just a bad
case of nerves, she supposed.

It had been a trying two months, she thought
to herself. She had left Oklahoma City to take a
new job and then found her personal life in turmoil and conflict. Her ill-fated attraction to Nash
Griffin had been eating her alive.

Lord, Crista thought as she pulled on her skirt,
she could use a vacation—already. Or maybe she
should make arrangements to meet Cynthia Marrow. Cyn understood frustration. Perhaps she
could offer some advice . . .

The jingling phone was a welcome disruption
of Crista's thoughts. Tucking her silk blouse into
her skirt, she scurried off to answer the call,
oblivious to the drifting shadow that hovered beside her bedroom window.

"Hello?" Crista frowned at the noticeable hesitation on the other end of the line. A prank call?
Probably. "Hello?" she demanded irritably.

"Crista, it's Levi Cooper. I need to talk to you."

Crista checked her watch. She was due in her
office, where a stack of evaluations, medical forms,
and staff schedules awaited her. She didn't have
time to discuss any tricks Levi had up his sleeve
this time. But curiosity got the best of her.

"So talk, Levi. I'm listening."

"I can't discuss this over the phone," he whispered. "I'm coming to your place so we can speak
in privacy."

"Now?"

"It can't wait."

The line went dead. Crista cursed at the receiver. Before she had time to replace the phone, a hand shot out of nowhere and clamped over her mouth.

"Put it down, nice and easy. Keep your fingers off the buttons. If you try to call 911, it will be the last call you ever make."

Crista's heart stopped beating when she felt the barrel of a pistol prying between her ribs. Very carefully, she set the phone in its cradle. She had the unshakable feeling she was about to discover who had been stalking her the past few weeks. She wondered if she would live long enough to convey the information to someone who cared . . . or *if* there was anyone around who *did* care . . .

Levi Cooper stared momentarily at the receiver, gathering his thoughts. He intended to have every line well rehearsed by the time he confronted Crista Delaney. She could cause him a great deal of trouble if he couldn't cut a deal with her. The sooner the better.

Even if he had to buy her silence, it would be worth the price. All that mattered was the plans he had made, the dream that had been three years in the making. Crista Delaney was not going to throw a wrench in his plans, and that was all there was to it.

"Where are you off to in such a hurry?" Nash questioned as he watched Levi roll through his living quarters.

Levi cursed under his breath when Nash followed him out the front door. "Since the cowboys have been here for the past three days, I had to

reschedule my hospital therapy for this morning.
I'll be gone until lunchtime."

"Hal and Choctaw Jim are loading up to leave
for the rodeo in Guthrie," Nash informed him.

"I'll drive down by the barn before I head to
town," Levi promised, forcing a casual smile.

At least Hal and Jim would be out of his hair,
Levi mused. It was bad enough that Nash was still
hovering around. Levi had done his best to convince Nash to make the trip, too, but as usual, he
wouldn't budge.

When Levi rolled down the ramp toward the
handicap van, Nash trailed behind him. "I want
you to know I trust you, Levi, but I—"

"You want to believe Crista," Levi interrupted.
"I made a mistake when I insisted she take my
case. I should have seen this coming. I guess I
can't blame you for wanting her. She would be a
temptation for any man."

Nash stared down at his long-time friend, watching Levi lower the hydraulic lift so he could roll
into the back of his van. "All I want from you is
the truth, because right now, I don't know what
the hell to believe."

Levi positioned himself on the lift, avoiding
Nash's searching gaze. "I'm already late for my
appointment and I want to see Hal and Choctaw
Jim off. This is going to have to wait until this
afternoon, Good Time."

Leaving Nash staring pensively after him, Levi
wheeled down the aisle to lock himself into place
in the van. In a cloud of dust, he whizzed to the
barn to wish Hal and Jim good luck at the rodeo.

Nash was still standing in the driveway when
Levi drove off. Glancing into his rearview mirror,
Levi watched Nash vanish into the cloud of dust.

"Damnation," Levi scowled. He was so close. So goddam close! He had to stall Crista, had to find a way to prevent her from arousing Nash's suspicions. If she didn't cooperate, Levi would have to take a risk . . .

The very thought of having his plans foiled put a determined clench in Levi's jaw. He was simply going to have to make sure Crista Delaney didn't botch anything up. Somehow, some way, he had to secure her silence, and that was that!

Nash mentally kicked himself all the way to his jalopy. He hated himself for what he was about to do. He had waited until Hal and Jim drove off before leaving the ranch. He had given Levi time to drive to the hospital, and now Nash was going to see for himself just exactly why the out-patient therapy on the gait machine was so damned expensive.

And it had better be worth every cent of those documented expenditures in Levi's ledgers. If the fee for the therapy didn't match the amount in the ledger, Nash would know Levi had betrayed his trust. If the fee was the same, Crista was deceiving him for reasons he still couldn't imagine.

Nash wasn't sure he was going to like facing the truth—he was the loser either way.

Eighteen

"Sit down—carefully, no false moves," came the gruff voice from behind Crista.

Crista swallowed hard. She knew that voice! Startled, she swung her head around to stare at the man wearing a ski mask. "Jonathan?"

Jonathan Heywood III didn't ease his grasp on Crista's arm. Still holding her at gunpoint, he removed the mask. "None other."

Crista's jaw dropped as she appraised the new creases and noticeable scar on the chin of Jonathan's once-handsome face. There was a cold glaze in his hazel eyes; life in prison had definitely left its mark.

"What are you doing here?" she questioned, bewildered.

Since the last time she had seen her ex-husband he had gained at least twenty pounds and had dyed his blond hair black, along with the mustache that made his upper lip look like a fuzzy caterpillar. The beard that rimmed his jaw looked like dyed wool.

"I guess you don't take time to listen to news broadcasts," he smirked. "Either that or this podunk of a town doesn't get Oklahoma City TV stations."

Jonathan relaxed slightly, flashing that arrogant

smile Crista had come to expect—and hate. "I escaped from the correctional center three weeks ago.

"Walked out, actually. It isn't all that difficult in minimum security places. All you have to do is snow the warden and kiss up to the guards until you have them thinking you've found that old-time religion. When you have them believing you've turned over a new leaf, they find jobs for you. Then you can take your walk without some guard breathing down your neck."

"Would you please put that pistol down," Crista requested as calmly as she knew how. "What do you want from me?"

Jonathan's cocky smile was suddenly replaced by a glare. "I want the damn key, Mary Crista. I've torn this place inside out trying to find it."

"You're the one who's been prowling around here?" she croaked. "How did you even find me in the first place?"

"Your friend Cynthia Marrow told me where you were."

Crista blinked in disbelief. "Cyn would never—"

"She didn't know it was me, of course," Jonathan cut in as he eased a hip onto the edge of the sofa. "I told her I was one of your doctor friends at the City hospital and I needed to confer with you about one of your former patients."

That was Jonathan through and through, Crista reminded herself. He was a devious, silver-tongued fox. Crista ought to know. She had fallen for his line more times than she cared to remember, before and during their two years of marriage.

"If you think I'm going to hide you here, you're mistaken."

Jonathan snorted. "I never expected you would.

Why do you think I tried to find the key without letting you know it was me?"

Crista frowned, bemused. "What key are you talking about?"

"The one that's going to get me out of the country before those thugs I got tangled up with can find me," Jonathan muttered, absently tracing the scar that marred his jaw. "They swore if I didn't tell them where to find the money, they'd hire someone in prison and I wouldn't live long enough to spend the cash. I had to get out—and fast."

His explanation finally began to soak in. During the trial, Jonathan had declared under oath—not that an oath would faze him—that he had lost all the embezzled money in bad investments. Crista had the uneasy feeling Jonathan had stashed a nest egg somewhere, hoping to make a fresh start when his sentence had been served. Obviously his life had been threatened and he had been pressured into a premature release—of his own making.

"Who are these thugs you made the mistake of doing business with?"

"Believe me, you don't want to know. They're hardly in my social class."

In Jonathan's opinion, he was the sole graduate of his social class. Too bad Crista hadn't realized that before she married him. The man who had courted her and the man she had married turned out to be two entirely different people.

Jonathan glanced restlessly around him. "I'd love to stay and chat, but I've got to get the money and book a flight to my favorite South American country. Things are going to get a little hot around here when my former business associates find my trail.

"Now where the hell did you put that damned jewelry box I gave you?" he all but shouted.

"The jewelry box," she repeated stupidly. "You tore my house upside down and chased me through the bathroom window because of the jewelry box?"

Jonathan threw her a withering glance. "I taped the key to my safety deposit box on the underside of one of the drawers of your jewelry box. Until I can get to the money, I'm stuck in the States. And until you hand over the box, you're stuck with me." He smiled sarcastically. "I'm sure you're as delighted with that prospect as I am."

The hum of a motor and the crunch of gravel caused Jonathan to bound to his feet, though he kept the pistol trained on Crista's chest.

"Who the hell is that?" he grumbled irritably.

Jonathan inched toward the window, still holding Crista at gunpoint. She cringed apprehensively. Finding herself at gunpoint with the last man she ever hoped to see again had derailed her train of thought. She had forgotten Levi Cooper was on his way over.

"It's one of my patients," she explained, rising to her feet.

"Stay where you are," Jonathan demanded gruffly.

Crista froze to her spot and stared at the one-eyed deathmaker pointed at her chest.

In stunned amazement, Jonathan watched the fire-engine-red van back up against the porch. In less than a minute, the back door of the vehicle swung open and a man in a wheelchair appeared.

"Well shit, just what I need . . ." Jonathan's sour tone evaporated abruptly and a diabolical grin tugged at the corner of his dyed mustache.

Crista didn't have a clue what Jonathan was planning, but she knew for sure she wasn't going to like it, not if that calculating smile was any indication. "Leave him out of it. He's a paraplegic, for heaven's sake. Even *you* wouldn't stoop that low."

"Honey, considering the company I've had to keep the last few months, you'd be shocked at what desperation can do. You'd also be surprised how many tricks of the trade you pick up from people who have no business being in *minimum* security. It makes you wonder what our justice system has come to."

Crista suddenly remembered the nondescript, tan-colored car she had noticed beside the road half a mile from her home—and that it contained a change of clothes. No doubt the older car was in Jonathan's possession. And unless she missed her guess, it was the same car that had practically run her off the road during the rainstorm. She had returned home that night to find her house a shambles. She suspected Jonathan had been in the process of making his getaway.

If stealing a car had posed no problem for Jonathan, Crista doubted he would have much trouble finding a way to unlock her bedroom window and gain access to her home. Ah yes, Jonathan had indeed become an accomplished criminal while doing time.

"Crista!" Levi called as he rolled his wheelchair across the porch.

Crista's gaze darted frantically toward the door. She couldn't risk involving Levi in this nightmare.

He probably deserved to pay penance for whatever he was planning to do to Nash, but Nash would never forgive her if this man came to harm.

Just as Jonathan yanked the ski mask over his head, Crista made her move. She charged at Jonathan like a bull, her hand swinging up to knock the pistol sideways.

"Get out of here, Levi!" she screamed in warning.

"You stupid fool," Jonathan snarled, lashing out at her with the pistol.

The weapon caught Crista upside the head, sending her stumbling against the end table and crashing to the floor.

"What the hell's going on in there?" Levi shouted.

"RUN . . . !" The sharp blow to Crista's skull turned her world upside down and shaded her eyes with black. She felt her knees buckle as she struggled to remain conscious. "R . . . u . . . n . . ."

Crista intended the last warning to be a shout. It was no more than a whisper.

She collapsed atop the upended table like a discarded doll.

"Goddam it," Jonathan muttered as he raced to the door to overtake the unexpected guest.

A tremor of panic snaked down Levi's spine—as far as the sensation would go—when he heard the crash of furniture and the mutter of a man's voice. He wheeled his chair around, hoping to roll into the van and make his escape, cursing his inability to move as swiftly as he once had.

Before Levi could maneuver into the van, the front door banged open. Levi swiveled his head to see the man in the ski mask charging toward him, a pistol clamped in his fist.

"Shit," Levi hissed, wheeling back around to face trouble head-on. His only hope was to use his upper body strength to catch the bastard by surprise. If Levi could get a hand on that pistol, there was an outside chance he could wrest it loose and get the drop on this creep.

"Sit tight, pal," Jonathan growled. "You're coming inside with your therapist. I always did think she had too much concern for her patients."

Levi glanced through the storm door, seeing Crista's limp body draped over a fallen piece of furniture. His conscience beat the hell out of him, realizing Crista had tried to protect him even after he had lied through his teeth.

When Jonathan made the mistake of reaching for the handle behind the chair, Levi sat poised and waiting to pounce. He may have been confined to a wheelchair, but his reflexes were still as acute as ever.

Levi's arm snaked out with the quickness of a coiled snake, putting a hatchet-like blow to Jonathan's wrist. The pistol bounced and skidded across the porch—out of reach.

Jonathan's furious curse hung in the air like black rain when he found two sinewy arms clamping around his shoulders, twisting him, turning him, and taking him to the floor like a downed steer.

There was only one thing Levi hadn't considered when he attempted to wrestle Jonathan to the porch. He no longer possessed the ability to maneuver himself around to level a blow that would send Jonathan cartwheeling off the elevated porch and into unconsciousness. Levi's swinging fist grazed Jonathan's dyed mustache and cheekbone, whipping his head backward.

Hissing furiously, Jonathan latched onto the wheelchair in hopes of steadying himself. The chair reared up and rolled backward, clipping Jonathan's feet as he tried to upright himself. In a tangle of wheels and legs, both men crashed against the open door of the van and tumbled down the porch steps.

Snarling, Jonathan shoved and kicked to free himself from the limp weight that pressed him into the ground. Levi's head had snapped back against the concrete steps, instantly bringing blood. Dazed, he tried to wrap his arms around Jonathan's legs before he could escape, but Jonathan slammed his heel into Levi's chest and shoved Levi's skull against the step a second time.

When Levi slumped, his eyes rolling back in his head, Jonathan kicked himself free. "Just what I needed. A goddam hero on wheels—"

"No," came a deliberately calm voice from the doorway of the house. "What you need is a prayer, Heywood. That's all you've got left."

Jonathan whipped around to see the two burly figures in ski masks who kept their pistols trained on his heaving chest. "Sonofabitch," he muttered in disgust. "Son . . . of . . . a . . . fucking . . . bitch."

That was another thing Jonathan had learned in the pen—how to cuss with the best of them, especially when it was appropriate.

Now, it was most appropriate . . .

* * *

Nash took his time driving to the hospital. He had every intention of giving Levi time to reach his destination and begin his exercises on the gait training machine. While Levi was stretching his legs in a simulated walk, Nash was going to check the cost of the exercise program—just to assure himself that Levi wasn't pulling a fast one, as Crista claimed.

With a puzzled frown, Nash veered into the front parking lot. Levi's van was nowhere to be seen.

Don't go jumping to conclusions, he cautioned himself. He wasn't familiar with Levi's routine here at the hospital. It could be that he was accustomed to unloading himself at the rear of the building, which might be closer to the rehabilitation ward.

Striding through the front entrance, Nash requested directions to the rehab wing. The older, frizzy-haired woman at the computer didn't even do him the courtesy of looking up from her monitor. She hitched her thumb over her bony shoulder, instructing Nash to follow the fluorescent arrows on the floor.

Nash hiked off, making a left turn at the intersecting hallways, then slowed his pace and scowled. He felt like a damned traitor, trailing after Levi, sneaking around to avoid being seen by his best friend.

Glancing at the posted signs above the doors, Nash spotted the rehab center. He positioned himself beside the door to scan the equipment and patients.

Wilma Elliot, the therapist he had run off his ranch before Crista assumed the duty of visitations, was wandering around the room with a clip-

board in hand. A teenage boy was hooked up to
what Nash assumed was the gait machine, while
an aide pushed the computerized cart and attach-
ing gadgets behind him.

Nash could hear the drone of conversation in
the corner, but he couldn't see who waited a turn
on the equipment. Removing his hat, he quickly
poked his head inside the room. To his dismay,
Levi wasn't waiting in line. Nash told himself there
was no need to panic just yet. There had to be a
reasonable explanation. Levi might be elsewhere,
taking his vital stats, filling out those infernal, un-
ending medical forms that he always dragged
home for Nash and Hal to sign. Levi had to be
here—somewhere.

When Nash saw the two young female technicians he had previously ordered off his property
coming toward him, he decided to get some answers.

Jill Forrester blanched when she recognized
the brawny giant, dressed in a threadbare shirt,
jeans that bespoke of excessive washing, and
scuffed boots. "Good Lord, the dragon cometh,"
she groaned.

Wendy York halted in her tracks. "I hope I'm
not on his hit list this time. He chewed me up
and spit me out once already."

Nash stopped directly in front of the two apprehensive young women who clamped their clip-
boards to their chests—for whatever protection
that might provide. "Where's Levi?" he demanded
without preamble.

Jill glanced uneasily at Wendy, who shrugged
her stiff shoulders.

"He isn't here," the women chorused.

"What do you mean *he isn't here?*" Nash muttered. "He was scheduled for rehab this morning."

"Scheduled for rehab?" Wendy echoed.

"For gait training."

Nash's temper was roiling. Both women were staring up at him as if they were ready to cut and run at the first sign of danger.

"Levi comes in twice, sometimes three, times a week to work on that high-powered machine, which—as far as I can tell—hasn't done him a damned bit of good. Now where do you have Levi stashed?"

Jill winced at the snarl in Nash Griffin's voice. "I . . ."

Nash was at the end of his tether. He was getting nowhere fast. "Where the hell is Crista's office? At least she has the courage to stand up to me."

Wendy's arm shot toward the office a few paces down the hall. "It's right there, but she—"

Nash surged off, growing madder by the second. He had a growing feeling he'd been lied to, but he was not going to believe that until he had no other alternative.

When Nash rounded the corner, Crista was not seated at her desk. Out of the corner of his eye, he noticed movement beside the file cabinets. He veered inside to see a middle-aged woman rummaging through the drawers.

"Where's Crista Delaney?" Nash demanded to know.

The woman performed an about-face, her unappealing features puckered in a frown. "That's what we would all like to know," she said with a snort. "Our incompetent department head hasn't bothered to show up for work or call in. She hasn't even begun to work on next week's staff-patient schedule, either. Nor has she filed the forms scattered all over her cluttered desk. But she is definitely going to hear about it when she arrives, on that you can depend."

Nash took an instant dislike to the old battle-ax. He wasn't sure why. Probably because she was standing there in her orthopedic shoes, looking down her hooked nose at the world—and everybody in it—while verbally crucifying Crista. That was one luxury Nash suddenly realized he had reserved for himself. He had taken offense when his brother made derogatory remarks about Crista. He had even yielded to the temptation of popping Hal in the bazoo when his sharp tongue overran his brain.

"Now then, Mr. . . . ?" Daisy Darwin paused, expecting Nash to fill in the blank.

"Griffin," he supplied gruffly. "I'm looking for Levi Cooper."

Gathering her bravado, Jill stepped forward. "I already told Mr. Griffin that Levi isn't here. He doesn't make hospital visits."

Nash half turned, feeling as if he had been kicked in the gut. *"Never?"* he gritted out.

"Never," Wendy confirmed.

"I want to see his evaluation charts," Nash insisted.

Jill spun around to retrieve the file from the cabinet, and then dropped it in Nash's outstretched hand. He studied the forms, noting each documented visit to the ranch. There were no notations of gait training at the hospital. And even worse, the copies of the supposed medical forms that contained a legal-size paper on the bottom of the stack—the ones Levi claimed required Hal's and Nash's signatures—were not among the papers.

Nash felt his mind reel when Crista's words came back to haunt him in a rush. The ledger, Nash thought frantically. If all the money he and Hal had worked and slaved to collect had not gone toward exercise training, where the hell had it gone?

In the past three years, the total expenditures had to have amounted to over a hundred thousand dollars. And what about all the money Nash had funnelled into the accounts after making TV, magazine, and newspaper ads for Western wear and promoting pickup trucks? What about his share of the profit from the ranch that he donated to Levi's funds, rather than keeping it himself? Nash had been living like a pauper to make sure Levi lived like a prince.

Damnation, Nash had made one sacrifice after another to cover Levi's *supposed* expenses. Hell, he was still wearing the same clothes he'd worn for over five years, the same damn boots that had been resoled at least three times and could use another trip to the shoe shop! Nash had been driving that beat-up bucket of rust he called a truck so Levi could have that hand-operated, fully automated handicap van and Hal could afford to pull the horse trailer behind the dependable, extended-cab truck on his way to and from rodeos.

Gawd, Nash hadn't even allowed himself much in the way of enjoyment the past five years, hoping to compensate in every way possible for his negligence. He had worked and skimped and scratched and clawed. And for what? What the hell could Levi had done with all that money?

With a furious snarl, Nash lurched around, sending the technicians scattering. Damn it, he had cut Crista to shreds and treated her like dirt. As it turned out, she had been right all along. Levi was definitely up to something, and Nash's blind loyalty had been a disastrous mistake!

How was he ever going to make amends to Crista after the cruel and humiliating way he had treated her? And worse, she had been stalked by prowlers and Nash had shrugged it off—just like the lackadaisical Detective Pine!

Nash was sure he must have looked like a crazed maniac when he stalked down the hall, swearing under his breath. People kept darting wary glances and scampering out of his way.

He hit the front door of the hospital with the heel of his hand, sending it slamming against its protective guard with a snap and a groan. Nash was absolutely furious with himself, with Levi, and even with Crista for being right!

With great effort, Nash battled to get himself under control. He inhaled several deep breaths as he stalked toward his truck—that pile of junk metal he drove so Levi could have the very best!

Nash hoped he could get himself in hand before he confronted Levi. At the moment, he felt like strangling the man he had centered his life around the past five years.

Nash had treated Crista so badly, and all because of Levi. He had taken Levi's side during the argument in the office. He had shouted Crista out of his house and shown no compassion when she had to run for her life to escape the prowler.

She had been out to protect Nash's best interests all along and he had refused to believe it.

Crista . . . Nash gritted his teeth when the image of her face blazed across his mind. He had all but turned his back on her, and still she continued to come to his defense, trying to protect him from the man he had considered a trusted friend.

Nash had been afraid to become more involved with her than he already was, afraid *he* would betray *Levi*. Boy, was that a laugh! Look *who* had ultimately betrayed *whom*. Levi had turned his back on his most devoted friends—the only family he had. He had broken the sacred cowboy creed, big time.

Well, things were going to change around Chulosa Ranch—starting now. Nash was driving to downtown Kanima Springs to buy himself the first new clothes he'd had in five years. Tonight, after he had it out with Levi, he was marching himself over to Crista's in his new duds and offer her the apology she deserved, even if she refused to see or speak to him again . . .

Another frustrating thought flashed through Nash's head as he sped home, making him groan aloud. The last night he had spent with Crista, he had taken her, standing up in the hall, and then walked away without looking back.

God, after all she had probably been through that night—having been scared half to death—he hadn't shown much sympathy or gentleness. He had simply taken her in the heat of lust, hoping to burn his fever for her out of his system—forever. Not that he had accomplished that, he thought with a self-deprecating smirk. He was hooked on that woman, and he knew it.

And even if his words fell on deaf ears, he was still going to apologize all over himself.

Nash pressed harder on the accelerator as he sped toward town. If nothing else, his life was going to change dramatically. He had never asked for so much as a thank you for his personal sacrifices to Levi, but neither had he expected out-and-out betrayal. Geezus! It was enough to tempt Nash to make a pit stop at Mangy Dog Saloon to guzzle beer until he couldn't think, see, or feel.

Nineteen

Jonathan Heywood III was sweating blood. He had been motioned back into the house, but it was difficult to do when his self-preservation instincts urged him to turn tail and run like hell. That tactic would probably earn him two bullets in the back.

No, Jonathan reminded himself nervously. Dave Winston and Freddy Miller wanted to keep him alive long enough to locate the cash he'd stashed in a safety deposit box—under an assumed name—in a small town west of the City.

Jonathan had had the presence of mind to hide the money before investigators could get their hands on it. These loan sharks were the only ones who knew the money hadn't been lost in bad investments. If Jonathan could keep his cool, maybe he could devise a way to escape this latest predicament and recover the cash to pay for a permanent vacation away from the jurisdiction of the States.

Freddy clenched his beefy fist around Jonathan's arm and shoved him onto the sofa. "All right, pal, where is it?"

"I don't have a clue," Jonathan insisted.

Freddy backhanded Jonathan, causing a trickle of blood to ooze from his puffy lip. "Bullshit!

We've trailed you around this area for more than a week. We know that money has to be here somewhere."

"If I knew where it was, don't you think I would have gotten hold of it long before you found my trail?"

Dave looked down at the woman sprawled facedown on the end table. "Is this your ex-wife or one of your girlfriends?"

"The ex." Jonathan removed his mask and wiped the blood off his lip. "As you can tell, she wasn't all that thrilled to see me. I had to knock her out before she called the cops."

Dave eyed Jonathan speculatively. "She has the money?"

Jonathan Heywood III—who had been raised in the lap of luxury, spoiled by his family's power, and obsessed by acquiring a lofty, prestigious position all his own—didn't believe that the rules and regulations the rest of the world lived by applied to him. He looked out for number one, even if it meant Crista would have to suffer for it. After all, wasn't it her fault Jonathan hadn't met the goals he had set for himself?

Although he had married Crista because she had the class, beauty, and style to fit the image he wanted to maintain, she also hailed from money. Lots of it. Her father had leased oil rights to hundreds of acres of his property in northern Oklahoma. The only problem was that Jonathan hadn't counted on Cole Delaney being quite so stubborn. Cole had all but disinherited his daughter and had not provided a cent of financial support for her marriage.

Jonathan was sure he'd be set for life by age thirty, but since Cole was nowhere near as generous as anticipated, Jonathan had to resort to other means—investing in stocks that could pay off quickly.

His mistake was dealing with the likes of Miller and Winston, who turned out to be as devious and cunning as he was. Now these two goons were breathing down his neck—there was even a warrant out for his arrest. He had no cash to buy an airline ticket to freedom, much less spending money when he got there. All he had was the measly cash he had stolen from Crista.

Jonathan was accustomed to thinking shrewdly and talking fast. Now it was imperative that he cover his highly exposed ass. His future—or lack thereof—was at stake and he was desperate enough to do whatever it took to save his skin.

"Crista knows where the money is," Jonathan declared, watching his ex-wife stir groggily. "But she isn't talking. I was going to hold her paraplegic patient hostage until she retrieved the money. That's when you two showed up—via the same bedroom window I came through, I guess."

Dave neither affirmed nor denied the assumption. "What's the story on the slug who's out cold, sprawled beside his wheelchair?"

"Like I said, he's one of her patients. She always was a sucker for a sick-o." She certainly didn't waste much sympathy on me, though."

"Can't blame the broad for that," Freddy smirked sarcastically.

When Crista began to regain consciousness, Freddy and Dave fished their black ski masks from their coat pockets. Freddy, who was accustomed to providing the muscle, scooped Crista off the floor and propped her on the opposite end of the couch.

"Okay, honey, where did you hide the cash?"

Crista blinked, attempting to clear her vision and focus on the faces looming before her.

When Crista was unable to gather her wits fast enough to suit her interrogator, another ominous shadow towered over her.

"Make no mistake here," Dave growled. "We aren't leaving without the cash. Your friend in the wheelchair is going to suffer worse than he already has if you don't start talking."

Crista winced when she remembered that Levi had arrived. She had no idea where he was or what had happened to him. All she knew was that she was responsible for whatever injury he might have sustained. Levi may have deserved what he was getting, but he obviously possessed a few good qualities or Nash and Hal Griffin wouldn't be so devoted to him. Levi, like Jonathan Heywood III, had been corrupted by greed. What a pity that there were those in this world who were at the mercy of their obsession for power and position.

"Come on, honey," Freddy growled, shaking Crista loose from her sluggish thoughts. "We don't have all day. You give us the money and you and your friend will be rid of us. If not, everybody loses—you and the slug, mostly."

Crista stared at the oversize ape who towered over her, wearing a black mask, keeping the spitting end of his pistol pointed right between her eyes. "It's in my office."

Dave glanced behind him, frowning. "What office? There isn't one here, not that I noticed."

Crista swallowed and licked her bone-dry lips. "At the hospital."

"You're going to have to send her inside the place," Jonathan insisted. Then an inspiration hatched. This was the chance he'd been hoping for! "That's one place that doesn't close down for the night, you know. I'll go with her to make sure she doesn't double-cross us."

Dave snorted. "Forget it, Heywood. I don't trust you not to double-cross us, either."

"Then which one of you guys has enough balls to march through the hospital with her? Not only could Mary Crista identify you, but so could the entire hospital staff. Somebody has to be there to make sure she doesn't send off a call to the cops. You can bet she'd do it in a minute if you give her the chance."

Jonathan knew he had Dave and Freddy eating out of his hand when they exchanged pensive glances. "I'll make you two a deal. If you let me walk, the money is yours. Minus the cost of a plane ticket to get me out of the country."

When Dave and Freddy eyed him warily, Jonathan quickly added, "Come on, boys, I'm not trying to double-cross you. I can't turn you in without incriminating myself, now can I? The only one around here reluctant to cooperate is Mary Crista, but her friend outside will provide incentive. If she doesn't do as she's told, the guy lies out there until he rots. She may wish the rest of us in hell, but she won't let the paraplegic come to harm. That's just the way she is."

After a long moment, Dave and Freddy nodded consent. They hauled Crista onto her wobbly legs and propelled her toward the door.

"We better take my car," Jonathan suggested. "I hid it in the barn. Better to leave the place looking as if Mary Crista is giving a therapy session, so we don't arouse suspicion."

"It looks pretty suspicious with that slug
sprawled by the steps," Freddy smirked.

"We'll drag him to the barn. He can't get into
trouble down there." Jonathan spun around, taking the precaution of yanking the phone from its
jack and setting it on a shelf in the kitchen, out
of Levi's reach.

With ski masks in place, the three men emerged
with Crista. While Dave and Freddy dragged Levi's
limp body to the barn to deposit him in a pile of
loose straw, Jonathan discreetly retrieved his forgotten pistol.

Smiling to himself, Jonathan drove up the graveled path and headed toward Kanima County
Hospital. He wasn't out of the woods yet, but the
details of his scheme were taking shape. If things
went according to his expectations he would be
worshipping the sun on the sandy beaches of Rio
in a couple of days.

The instant the old two-tone car zoomed from
the barn, Levi Cooper levered onto his elbows.
By playing possum he had not only been allowed
to overhear the conversations in the house and
barn, but he had been left alone. He had also
seen the driver of the car pull off his ski mask
before speeding away. Levi didn't know Crista's
ex-husband by name, but he could recognize the
bastard on sight.

Squirming around, Levi dragged himself off
the pile of straw and slithered from the barn. Although Crista's ex-husband had unhooked the
phones in the house and placed them out of
reach, Levi's cellular phone was tucked in the

pocket of his wheelchair. If he could haul himself back to the house he could call for help.

Levi grimaced as he dragged himself over the graveled path leading to the house. He had driven to Crista's home, hoping to make a deal with her. Now there was no telling what would become of her. And though she may have been out of his hair permanently, his conscience was nagging him to death.

Despite the trouble she would undoubtedly cause him, Levi wasn't so cold-blooded that he didn't recall how Crista had hunted down the modified saddle that allowed him to compete with the other cowboys. Neither could he forget her generous but spirited nature, her giving heart.

Although Crista had interfered in his plans, she had been a bright spot in his days. He had looked forward to their therapy sessions. And furthermore, there was something going on between her and Nash. In spite of Nash's growling and snarling, he wouldn't take it kindly if Crista came to bodily harm at the hands of hired muscle.

Huffing and puffing for breath, Levi slumped on the ground to rest. He had made good progress toward the house before his arms gave out. His lungs were burning like a forest fire and the sleeves of his shirt were in tatters, revealing the scraped skin on his elbows and forearms. He didn't have a clue how his lower body was faring, but if his legs were suffering the same abuse as his arms and chest, he would be completely raw by the time he reached the house.

Gathering his determination, Levi estimated the distance to his overturned wheelchair that they'd stashed behind the van. He had come fifty yards—it felt like ten miles—and he had a good thirty yards to go.

"Time to *cowboy up,* Dogger," he told himself resolutely. He broke into a rueful smile, remembering the countless times Nash had used that familiar phrase on him during his rodeo days. When the going got tough and injuries left weary muscles screaming in pain, a man had to grit his teeth and challenge himself to his very limits.

This was one of those times when he had to get by on *cowboy ways.* You simply did what you had to do, when there was no one around to help you get the job done. Levi would be damned if he'd lie here helpless on the cold ground, waiting for help that might not arrive. He had to reach that damn phone before he had Crista's death on his conscience. And not for the first time did he remind himself that his attempt at heroics, and his battered physical condition, would reinforce Nash's loyalty. When Nash got a look at Levi, sympathy would be overflowing.

Funny, wasn't it? Levi mused. Who would have guessed that this ordeal would wind up working to his advantage, even if he was going to look and feel like hell by the time he was rescued.

Crista tried to think past the throbbing pain in her skull. She had always considered herself hard-headed, but the butt end of Jonathan's pistol proved her wrong. To add to her discomfort, she was sandwiched in the back seat between the two men in black ski masks, the barrels of their pistols stuck in her ribs. She wondered if she would survive this ordeal and what condition Levi would be in by the time someone located him.

Thank you, Jonathan, you bastard, Crista silently fumed as she glared at the back of her ex-husband's dyed-black head. Jonathan was whizzing down the road at excessive speed, gravel pelting the underside of the old car like hailstones. As usual, he was looking out for himself. All that concerned him was saving his neck. Well, it was his own fault that he was keeping such undesirable company. He had brought this on himself with his unsuccessful get-rich-quick schemes.

Since their marriage, Jonathan had been out to show the world and his pompous father—especially his pompous father—that Jonathan was the better man. All he had proved was that he was foolish enough to get caught.

Jonathan Heywood *II* hadn't. And Crista imagined the shrewd counselor had pulled a few underhanded deals in his time. She knew about one of her father-in-law's maneuvers. He had boasted about it to her. He had managed to acquire the mineral rights as his legal fee for handling the estate of a wealthy rancher. Since there was no next of kin, Jonathan II had cut himself a deal that earned him millions. Oil wells had cropped up on the property—what a convenient coincidence.

The churches and schools near the deceased rancher's property were supposed to have benefitted from the estate, but it was Jonathan II who reaped the financial rewards in a big way. He had gloated all the way to the bank.

Now his only son, who had become obsessed with outdoing his father, was running his latest scam and Crista was suffering for it. Jonathan had told his cronies that she was in on this scheme. If she knew Jonathan—and she knew him only too well—he was considering his options at this very moment. The almighty dollar had always meant more to him than Crista did.

Her thoughts trailed off when Jonathan veered into the parking lot and glanced back at her.

"Which exit is nearest your office?" he questioned.

"The west one," Crista said dully.

Jonathan parked a good distance from the other vehicles and left the motor running. "We'll be back as quick as we can," he assured Dave and Freddy.

Dave stared Jonathan down as he slid from beneath the steering wheel, then handed Crista over to her ex-husband. "Don't think for even one minute that we trust you, Heywood. If you try anything, you'll pay for it—with your life."

Jonathan flung his suspicious associate a withering glance. "I'm the one taking the chances here. And for nothing more than airfare. All you have to do is sit tight while *I* show my face all around this place. If you want to be the one to keep an eye on Crista, you sure as hell have my permission."

Dave muttered sourly as he sank down on the seat Jonathan had vacated. "Make it snappy. And no funny business or I'll blow you to pieces the first chance I get."

Grabbing Crista's arm, Jonathan shepherded her toward the west exit. "One word from you, Mary Crista, and I'll make sure your paraplegic doesn't live to see tomorrow—and you may not, either."

"Provided *you* live past sunrise," Crista flung at him. "Forgive me if I don't include you in my prayers."

He pulled her closer, assuring her that his weapon was handy, should she make the situation difficult. "There are also your friends at the hospital to consider," he grimly reminded her. "If you don't cooperate, I'll find myself another hostage."

Crista winced at the threat, noting the cold steel in his strained features matching the cold steel of the weapon in his pocket.

Jonathan flashed her a feral grin when he saw her expression change from defiance to defeat. "I thought you'd see it my way," he said, as he ushered her through the door.

Hissing and cursing, Levi slithered along on his left elbow until the bloody scrapes burned intolerably. He switched to his right forearm to provide the power to heave himself forward.

Only a few more yards, he encouraged himself. He could crawl across grass instead of gravel in a few more minutes. That wouldn't be so painful.

Levi heaved a gusty sigh of relief when he left the wide span of the gravel driveway behind. His gaze focused on his overturned chair, ignoring the stinging abrasions covering his arms and chest. He breathed in huge, see-sawing gulps, hoping his overworked heart wouldn't go into cardiac arrest before he reached his cellular phone.

If Crista Delaney didn't appreciate the efforts to which he had gone to aid her, Levi swore he'd make things more difficult for her than he already had. She definitely owned him now. But damn it, things would have run so much smoother if that blond bombshell-of-a-therapist hadn't overheard his private conversations with J.C. and blabbed her suspicions to Nash.

Even if Levi had been mad enough to spit nails, he still didn't want Crista to come to physical harm. He wasn't that spiteful. Hell, all Levi really wanted was to quietly conduct his business without Crista's interference.

If she ended up dead . . .

Levi decided not to dwell on that possibility. He chose, instead, to review the conversation he had overheard. Jonathan had claimed Crista knew where some money was stashed, but Levi couldn't believe she was in the con. It didn't jibe with the woman Levi had come to know.

If it was true that Crista was sitting on a nest egg, why would she be in Kanima Springs, tending patients? She could be living high on the hog on some tropical island. It made no sense to Levi.

His speculations evaporated when he finally reached his overturned chair. With one scraped-and-bleeding arm, he fished into the leather pocket to retrieve his cellular phone and dialed the ranch.

He may have been confined to a chair, but he had proved to himself that he wasn't completely helpless. That meant a lot. And Crista Delaney would be forever in his debt if he managed to help her. He wondered if she would keep that in mind when he tried to cut a deal with her. He would be sure to remind her—just in case she forgot.

Bernie Bryant shut off the vacuum sweeper when he thought he heard the jingle of the phone. Sure enough, the phone rang again. In three quick strides he scooped up the receiver.

"Chulosa Ranch. Head cook and bottle washer speaking."

"Bernie?"

"What are you doing, calling me at this time of the morning, Dogger?" Bernie asked in concern. "I thought you were doing gait training. Is something wrong?"

"I took a detour," Levi said breathlessly. "Is Nash there? I need help."

"No, he left shortly after you did. He said he was going to town to pick up feed for the horses."

"You're going to have to come get me, Bern. I'm at Crista's."

"What the hell are you doing over there?" Bernie asked, bewildered.

"Just get over here as fast as you can, will you?" Levi muttered impatiently. "I've got big trouble. And before you leave, call the cops. Tell them to pick up three guys in a two-toned tan Chevy at the hospital. They're armed and dangerous."

"Will do." Bernie hung up and dialed the police. In less than a minute, he shot out the front door. He was in mid-leap off the porch when it dawned on him that he had no mode of transportation. Hal and Choctaw Jim were driving the truck and Nash was in the jalopy, hauling feed. Bernie would have to walk the five miles to Crista's or rely on horse power—literally.

Bernie dashed toward the barn, his deformed arm churning like a wheel. He had just thrown a saddle blanket over his horse when he heard a roar of bad mufflers announcing Nash's return.

"About damn time," he grunted, switching direction.

When Bernie appeared at the barn door, Nash was stalking forward with a feed sack over each shoulder. The scowl on his bronzed features did not invite conversation, though that had never stopped Bernie before—nor did it now.

"Levi's got trouble," Bernie blurted out hurriedly.

"More than he knows," Nash muttered in a resentful tone.

"I'm not kidding around, Good Time," Bernie insisted as he followed Nash into the barn to unload the sacks. "He called from Crista's house, saying he needed help. I was saddling up to ride over there when you showed up."

Nash stopped short and glanced back at the stocky cowboy. "He's at Crista's?"

Bernie nodded. "That's what he said. He was panting for breath. I don't know what's going on over there, but he told me to send a patrol car to the hospital to track down three armed men in a Chevy."

Nash tossed the feed sack in the corner and spun around. He wasn't sure he could face Levi just yet without giving in to the urge to strangle him. Levi had been lying through his charming smile for years, damn him. He had betrayed Nash's trust, his loyalty. What the hell kind of friend was Levi anyway? And what the hell was he trying to pull now?

When Nash hopped behind the wheel of the old truck, Bernie bounded into the passenger side. Although Bernie rattled on nonstop, speculating on the problems awaiting them, Nash said not one word.

His emotions were hopelessly tied in knots. His world had tilted sideways when he discovered Levi had lied. Nash had given that traitorous bastard the best of years of his life—first, training Levi to be a top-notch rodeo competitor, then providing for him after the disaster in Las Vegas.

Nash had made more personal sacrifices than he cared to remember—all for a man who had been stockpiling cash and doing who knew what else.

And worse, Nash reminded himself as he squirmed in his skin, he had treated Crista horribly. Lord, how could he even begin to compensate for the hurt he'd caused her? If Crista felt anywhere near as bitter and angry as Nash did—after the shattering realization of Levi's betrayal—he would have one helluva time coaxing her to listen to him.

Nash swore inventively. It was humiliating to realize the person he thought he could trust completely was the one he could trust least. And if Levi thought he could continue to prey on Nash's sympathy, he was in for the greatest shock of *his* life!

Crista was thankful that the hospital halls were abandoned—at least for the moment. With Jonathan clinging to her like English ivy, she made a beeline for her office. When he closed and locked the door behind him, Crista watched him take inventory of the small room. When his gaze landed on the two purses tucked beside a file cabinet, Crista frowned worriedly.

"Those belong to your technicians, I presume." Jonathan smiled craftily. "Get me a set of car keys from one of the purses, Mary Crista."

Crista's chin tilted in stubborn defiance. "You aren't dragging anyone else into this. I'll get the jewelry box, but that's all. I want you out of here."

Jonathan shook his head and grinned devilishly. He ambled forward to pluck up the phone, earning another of Crista's wary frowns. "Get me the police," he said to the operator.

Crista stared at him, puzzled. "What are you up to?"

"You'll see," he said with a devious chuckle. "Now get the jewelry box."

When the police dispatcher came on the line Jonathan gestured for Crista to do as she was told. "Yes, ma'am, I want to report a stolen car *found.*"

To Crista's amazement, Jonathan gave the make, model, and license plate number of the car he had been driving, informing the dispatcher that the vehicle was sitting in the hospital parking lot. He had sicced the cops on his associates while they were lounging—unsuspecting—in the idling car!

When Jonathan hung up, he snatched the jewelry box from Crista, pulled open the second drawer, and retrieved the small key taped beneath it. Since Crista had refused to grab one of the purses in the corner, Jonathan snatched up the nearest one and rummaged for car keys. Then his gaze slid to the box of adhesive tape and bandages stacked atop a file cabinet. He quickly snatched up several rolls of tape and crammed them in his coat pocket.

"Let's go, Mary Crista. I'm not through with you yet."

Crista found herself shuffled out the door. She considered breaking and running, but she was afraid Jonathan would do as he threatened—latch onto an innocent hostage.

"Get us out of here without taking us past the nurses' desk," Jonathan demanded in a hushed tone. "I intend to be in your friend's car and long gone when the cops show up to arrest those goons."

Crista ignored her hellish headache and veered toward the back exit to locate Wendy York's car in the staff parking lot. "Jonathan, why don't you just let me go before you get yourself into more trouble than you're already in. There's no need to add kidnapping to your list of crimes."

Jonathan snorted at the suggestion. "No way, honey. You're my insurance."

He unlocked the door of Wendy's compact car and stuffed Crista onto the seat, holding her arm so she couldn't scramble out the passenger side. He rammed the key into the ignition, smiling triumphantly as the small car purred to life. "You'll be rid of me soon enough, Mary Crista," he assured her as he backed out of the parking space.

Crista glanced toward the tan car where the two men unknowingly waited for the trap to close around them. "How did you get that stolen car anyway?" she questioned for lack of much else to say.

Jonathan smiled proudly. "I told you, prisons are training grounds. I heard one of the other convicts boasting about how he had swiped a car and used it for a robbery. He just hung around the post office until some lady in a big rush left her kid in the idling car and ran inside to grab her mail."

Crista gaped at Jonathan. "You kidnapped a child, too?"

"No, I just snarled at him a couple of times, set the kid on his feet, and he tore off to find his mother. I hotfooted it out of town, using country roads so I couldn't be easily spotted."

"God, Jonathan—"

"Don't start with me, Mary Crista," he snapped as he veered onto the graveled road. "I don't need another of your lectures. Besides, the honest do-gooders of the world are the ones who get screwed."

He flashed her a ridiculing smile. "I never dreamed your father would turn out to be as stingy as mine."

The thought caused Jonathan's attractive features to pucker in resentment. "This is his fault, too, you know. I spent my childhood listening to my God Almighty father brag about how he could make money hand over fist, how clever he was. I wanted to do him one better."

"You did that, all right," Crista smirked unsympathetically. "*You* got caught swindling. *He* never did."

"Just shut up," Jonathan muttered.

His severe expression changed to a wicked grin when he spotted two patrol cars heading toward the hospital. "I know you'd like to see me tucked away for life, without parole, to avoid the shame and embarrassment. But you'll still get part of that wish, Mary Crista. We'll both try to forget we were married to each other. I forgot on a number of occasions with several somebody elses." He tossed her a haughty glance. "All of whom were better in the sack than you ever were, by the way."

Crista let another of his degrading insults slide off. In the past, his ridicule had cut deeply, leaving her with painful feelings of inferiority and self-doubt. But these days, she knew better. She responded to Nash Griffin openly, freely, eagerly, even if he didn't have any more respect or concern for her than Jonathan did. If she lived long enough, she would thank Nash for that—at least.

When Jonathan veered onto an access road leading to a pasture, Crista glanced at him warily. She reached for the door handle, but Jonathan held his fingers on the electric door lock.

"We can do this one of two ways, Mary Crista," he told her grimly. "I can pistol-whip you unconscious again or you can—"

Crista lunged at him, claws bared. If she was going out of this world, she was going in a blaze of glory, not like a whimpering child. Her nails clawed into Jonathan's beard. When his hand flew up to protect himself, she launched herself against the door, groping for the electric door lock. Before Jonathan could react, she shouldered her way out of the car and bounded off like a jackrabbit.

"Damn you," Jonathan snarled as he scrambled from the car, giving chase.

He dashed after her, pistol poised. When Crista thrashed through the tall Johnsongrass in the ditch, Jonathan lunged forward to tackle her. His arms clamped around her knees, sending her sprawling in the ditch. Crista tried to squirm loose, but Jonathan flipped the pistol in his hand, bringing the weapon down hard on her head.

The blow she had already received, compounded with this one, caused flashes of silvery light to explode in her skull. A wave of nausea rose in her throat as the world spun furiously around her. Inky blackness swallowed up the painful throb in her head as she felt herself sink into pitch-black silence . . .

With Crista effectively incapacitated, Jonathan dragged her limp body toward the culvert. Passersby wouldn't be able to spot her, not with the overgrown weeds and grass forming a barrier. Complimenting himself on the clever handling of what might have been a catastrophe with the two goons, Jonathan fished the adhesive tape from his pocket and wrapped Crista up nice and tight.

Then he scurried back to the car and drove off. He had one more trick up his sleeve, just in case the car he had stolen was discovered missing before he could dispose of it.

Too bad Mary Crista had been so daring, he thought fleetingly. He hadn't intended to be so brutal, but she had all but invited it.

Shrugging away the thought of how, when, and if Crista would be rescued, Jonathan drove away. He smiled wryly, wondering what explanation Freddy and Dave would offer the police. Those two muscle-brained clowns should be cursing him up one side and down the other right about now. And while they were being locked away, Jonathan would retrieve the cash from the safety deposit box and then soar off into the wild blue yonder.

One more stop, Jonathan told himself. Once he had changed cars again, no one would have a clue about where to find him. Even Jonathan Heywood II couldn't top this. Dear ole Daddy could screw unsuspecting clients out of their money, but he couldn't have pulled this off!

The thought made Jonathan smile broadly as he turned up the radio and sang his way down the gravel road.

Twenty

"Holy shit!" Bernie crowed.

All Nash's resentment evaporated when he saw Levi sprawled beside the concrete steps of Crista's house. The side of Levi's face was caked with blood, his sleeves ripped to shreds, his buttonless shirt hanging open, and his chest scraped raw.

Nash was out of the truck in a flash, with Bernie a half-step behind him.

Seeing Levi in this state triggered flashbacks of the tragic fall in Glitter Gulch. Nash dropped to his knees to inspect the gash on Levi's skull, the abrasions on his body. "What happened?"

Wearily, Levi pushed himself up against the side of the porch. "I met up with more trouble than I could handle." He swallowed hard, his throat parched. "Could I have a drink?"

"On my way," Bernie said as he clambered up the steps.

"Good Lord! What happened in here?" Bernie called out.

"Three men," Levi tried to explain through his dry mouth and puffy lips. "They—"

"Just wait until Bernie gets you a drink," Nash insisted as he levered Levi onto the ground to check his legs.

Grimacing, Nash surveyed the raw flesh beneath the holes in the knees and thighs of Levi's jeans. He looked as if he'd been dragged behind a horse for miles. Nash glanced up, seeing the smoothed track across the grass and the graded gravel that led up from the barn. Frowning, he stared at the overturned wheelchair. What the hell had gone on here?

Bernie dashed out the door, slopping water from a glass. Kneeling, he offered Levi what was left. "Where's Crista? And what three men are you talking about?"

Levi gulped the water and then half collapsed on the ground. "I came by to see Crista, but her ex-husband was already here. I guess he must have knocked her out before he wrestled with me."

Nash felt as if an unseen fist had slammed into his belly. "Her ex-husband? I thought he was in prison."

"He isn't now." Levi hoisted himself up on a skinned elbow and then reached down to reposition his legs in front of him. "He came after me with a gun. Something about holding as hostage while he forced Crista to fetch his stash of cash."

Nash felt nauseous, remembering the prowler who had invaded Crista's home and then sent her running scared. Nash could have kicked himself to Kanima Springs and back for refusing to take her concerns seriously. It was apparent that Jonathan Heywood III had escaped from the correctional center and had tracked his ex-wife down.

"I tried to take the pistol away," Levi continued after several gulps of water. "He wasn't expecting me to be so strong, but then, I wasn't expecting him to shove my chair down the steps, either."

"Good Lord," Bernie wheezed. "You could have—"

"Broken my back?" Levi cut in, smiling bleakly.

"Well, you should have been careful anyway," Bernie muttered, flustered.

"Go on, Levi," Nash urged. "What happened after that?"

Levi sighed and then continued. "I played possum after that. Two other men showed up. I guess they'd been tracking the ex-husband. They went after the money the ex claimed Crista had hidden, except he kept calling her *Mary* Crista."

Nash frowned. For some reason that name rang a distant bell. Why? He wasn't sure. But for certain he had heard it somewhere before.

"When Crista regained consciousness, the men in ski masks dragged me down to the barn and loaded her into an old car that had been hidden in there. As soon as they drove off I crawled back to my chair to reach the phone."

"Did they say where they were taking her?" Nash queried worriedly.

"To her office at the hospital."

"Bernie, help me get Levi into his chair," Nash ordered.

Together, Nash and Bernie hauled Levi up and settled him in his chair. The crashing fall had bent the left wheel, causing it to scrape noisily against the side of the chair. Rolling Levi into the van proved difficult, since the wheel stuck and held on each roll. Once the hydraulic lift had been lowered, Bernie and Nash had to hoist the inoperable chair into place and leave it in the back of the van.

"Take the van," Nash told Bernie. "I'll pull around the driveway to get out of your way."

"Where are you going?" Bernie asked as he climbed behind the steering wheel.

"To find Crista."

Nash jiggled the ignition switch and swerved around to the back of the house, giving Bernie plenty of room to turn the van around.

The fog of dust that rolled above the row of cedar trees lining the lawn heralded another arrival. Nash held his breath, hoping Crista had returned, unharmed.

A sporty blue compact car wheeled into the driveway. Suspicious, Nash gunned his truck, pulling out from behind the house. When the car tried to whip around to leave as hurriedly as it arrived, Bernie thrust the hand-operated accelerator forward, using the van to block the escape route. With his bushy head poked out the window, Bernie waved at Nash.

"Dogger says that's the man who attacked him!"

Nash glared down at the dark-haired man trying to clamber from the car. Nash mashed on the accelerator, pinning the man between the truck and Crista's red sports car parked in front of the house.

Nash could see Crista's keys dangling from Jonathan's fingertips. The bastard obviously intended to switch vehicles in case he was being followed. But Nash would be damned if he'd let Heywood escape!

Jonathan lunged toward the car door, trying to lock himself inside before the brawny cowboy overtook him. With surprising agility for his size and stature, the man grabbed the door before Jonathan could slam it shut. Frantic, Jonathan reached for the pistol tucked in his pocket, but a meaty fist snaked around the partially opened door to collide with Jonathan's wrist. The pistol tumbled off the console and wedged between the seats.

Jonathan choked for breath when he was grabbed by the nape of his jacket and plucked up, as if he weighed no more than a sack of potatoes. His knees and elbows scraped against the door as he was roughly hauled out and then slammed up against the side of the car.

"Where is she?" Nash snarled ominously.

"Where's who?" Jonathan croaked. "Argh!"

Jonathan's breath was ripped from his chest when the looming giant smacked him against the car.

"Wrong answer, smart ass," Nash growled, tawny eyes glittering. "You'll find yourself in worse condition than the paraplegic you knocked down the goddam steps if you don't watch your mouth."

"I don't know where Mary Crista is, I swear to God!" Jonathan wheezed. "I barely managed to escape those gorillas myself!"

"Don't believe him," Levi called from the van.

"Hey, pal, you've got this all wrong," Jonathan burst out. "My ex-wife has the cash those goons were after. I still don't know where the money is. Those other two men—"

Nash coiled like a spring and struck with killing force. His doubled fist caught Jonathan in the mouth, whiplashing his head against the top of the sports car. When Jonathan's knees folded like a tent, Nash clamped hold of his jacket, holding him upright.

"Bernie, bring me the lariat from the back of my truck."

Bernie scurried from the van to do as he was ordered.

"What are you going to do, cowboy?" Jonathan smirked. "String me up like a one-man lynch mob? This is the 90's, you know."

Bernie handed Nash the rope, his grim expression focused on Jonathan. "You need to know that when Nash Griffin gets riled he's the meanest son of a bitch you'll ever want to meet. If I were you, I'd tell him what he wants to know—fast. He goes loco when he gets furious." Bernie glanced at Nash's wolfish snarl. "Yep, I'd say he's already furious and I'm glad I'm not in *your* shoes, tenderfoot."

In hurried strides Nash marched Jonathan to the pasture fence and tied him to the sturdy corner post. Nash was getting some answers—the right ones—even if he had to resort to the most drastic measures.

When Nash wheeled around and stalked away, Jonathan squirmed inside the tightly bound lariat. "You're wasting my time and yours, cowboy. I told you I didn't know where Mary Crista was. More than likely she took the money she stashed for safekeeping after I was sent to jail."

Nash climbed into his truck and lowered the hydraulic-operated hay fork that was bolted to the bed. In spiteful satisfaction he watched Jonathan's hazel eyes pop as the truck shifted into reverse.

Bernie shook his head as the spear of the hay fork zeroed in on Jonathan, aimed just below his belt buckle. "I told you he goes crazy when he loses his temper. But I guess it will take being impaled to convince you. Too bad you city boys are so thick-headed."

"He wouldn't dare!" Jonathan hissed as the pointed prong of steel inched toward his body.

Bernie smiled devilishly, exposing the gap between his teeth. "Wanna bet your life on it, tenderfoot?"

"Shit!" Jonathan howled in agony when the hay fork prodded the most tender parts of his anatomy.

Hydraulics whined as the fork inched lower.

"Now there's a sight," Levi chuckled as he watched from the opened door of the van. "Prick to prick."

"Looks like Nash is planning to roast your chestnuts on an open fire," Bernie noted. "Leave it to Nash to invent a new technique of castration." He whistled in mock sympathy. "I'd say that's bound to hurt. Glad my pecker isn't stuck on that prong."

Jonathan screamed bloody murder when the hay fork rammed between his legs, pinning his male parts against the post behind him. Nash kept easing back until Jonathan was pinched so tightly he couldn't suppress another shriek of agony—in a voice one octave higher than normal.

"All right, damn it!" Jonathan wailed through clenched teeth. "I know where she is."

Nash killed the engine, leaving the hay prong wedged between Jonathan's legs, granting him no breathing space whatsoever. Climbing down from the truck, Nash stalked over to ease his hip onto the spear, prompting another squeal of pain as the point of the prong shifted beneath Nash's weight.

"Now that I've made my point, city boy," Nash growled sarcastically, "I want the truth, and you better be as convincing as you were while you were lying. After what you did to Levi, I'd just as soon crush your nuts flat as flounders as look at you."

"At least give me room to breathe," Jonathan whimpered.

"You've already got all the space I'm giving you," Nash snapped. "If I climb back into the truck, it'll be to run you through. I'm not in a charitable mood."

Nash folded his arms across his chest and stared intently at the whitewashed face, set inside a mass of artificially-darkened hair and beard. "Now then, Heywood, exactly what happened after you left Levi in the barn and drove off?"

Jonathan swore viciously as Nash shifted his weight on the hay fork, scraping his balls raw.

"Still don't want to talk? I can fix that quick enough." Nash hopped from the prong, causing the metal point to bounce against the inside of Jonathan's legs.

When Nash stalked toward the front of the truck, Jonathan blurted out. "I drove to the hospital to get the key to the safety deposit box where the money is stashed."

Nash pivoted slowly, deliberately. "Does Crista know where the money is?"

Jonathan shook his head. "No, I taped the key under the drawer of her jewelry box before I was incarcerated. She didn't know it was there. I tore her house upside down trying to find the damned thing."

"That's not what you told those two apes," Levi put in.

"I was trying to save my ass," Jonathan snorted defensively.

"So you drove to the hospital with Crista as

your hostage," Nash presumed, his voice a deadly growl.

Jonathan nodded slightly. "I talked Freddy and Dave into waiting in the car I stole after I escaped from the correctional center. When Mary Crista and I were in her office I called the cops to pick up Freddy and Dave so they couldn't follow us."

"Us?" The word swirled through Nash's mind like smoke.

Jonathan had taken Crista with him when he drove off in the blue compact car. He had Crista's car keys.

Nash reached over to grab Jonathan by the collar, bending him into the prong. "Now, I'll ask you one more time," he snarled ominously. *"Where . . . is . . . Crista?"*

Jonathan swallowed audibly, his Adam's apple bobbing like a fisherman's cork. "I tied her up and left her in a ditch on a country road."

"Alive?" Nash growled viciously, his golden eyes so intent that even Bernie took an involuntary step backward.

"Alive," Jonathan squeaked.

"Where, exactly," Nash demanded ruthlessly.

"Three miles south and two west of the hospital."

Nash released his stranglehold on Jonathan, shoving him back as if touching him were repulsive. Jonathan yelped when his lower torso slammed into the metal spike—again.

"Get me off this goddam prong. I told you what you wanted to know."

Nash glanced grimly at Bernie before turning away. "Heywood stays where he is until I get back. If he's lying, I'll poke him so full of holes he'll leak like a sieve."

"Gotcha, boss" Bernie complied. "I won't let him off the hook."

"Levi, call Sheriff Featherstone and get him out here," Nash instructed on his way toward Crista's car.

Cursing, Nash wrestled his way beneath the steering wheel and struggled to slide the seat back far enough to give himself leg room.

Shoving the car into gear, Nash wheeled across the lawn and then flung gravel, pelting Jonathan—for good measure. If that bastard had harmed one hair on Crista's head, Nash would return to do his worst. Hell, he might be tempted to do it anyway!

Crista moaned into the tape that was plastered to the lower portion of her face. After Jonathan had knocked her silly, he had wrapped her up like a mummy. She lay half submerged in the stagnant water that filled the culvert.

A shiver rippled down her spine when she felt something crawling in the mass of tangled hair that spilled around her. Ticks! she thought with a grimace. If she didn't die of exposure or starvation, those blood-sucking little beasts would make a meal of her. She had to get out of here . . .

After worming and squirming for five minutes, Crista sagged in exhaustion. Jonathan had taken the precaution of twisting a roll of adhesive tape like a braided leash, securing her to a jagged piece of metal on the rim of the culvert. She couldn't move more than six inches without reaching the end of her tether.

Lord, what was the use? Crista asked herself dispiritedly. If she hadn't suffered a concussion, she'd be surprised. She had all the symptoms—nausea, headache, and the constant urge to fall asleep.

Might as well, Crista mused. It wouldn't do much good to remain awake while ticks had a field day with her. And who would miss her? Certainly not Levi, who had been wheeling and dealing. Not the Griffin brothers. Hal had no use for women—period. And Nash . . .

Crista blinked back a mist of tears. The thought of him hurt worse than the bumps on her noggin. She had given her heart away, but all Nash really wanted was her body—even when he *didn't want* to *want* it. He didn't trust her, he didn't really want her and he sure as hell didn't need her in his life.

Well, one day soon he would discover that his best friend was his worst enemy. Too bad Crista wouldn't be around to gloat. She would be rotting in a culvert, infested with ticks and fleas, waiting for the inevitable circling buzzards . . .

The crunch of gravel brought her head up. When the vehicle decreased speed, Crista dared to hope. By some miracle, had someone apprehended Jonathan before he reached his cursed safety deposit box?

Crista discarded the thought. More than likely, someone had stopped to relieve himself on the side of the road. This was her big chance to get help and all she could do was mumble—and not very loudly, either.

Nash stopped by the side of the road, staring at the overgrown ditch. "Crista?" he bellowed at the top of his lungs.

He pricked his ears, trying to hear over the whistle of the wind. A faint sound caught his attention and he called out Crista's name again. He thought he heard something in the distance.

The culvert. Nash broke into a run and leaped down the steep incline to tunnel through the Johnsongrass. There, nearly invisible in the thick matting of weeds, was a mass of blond hair and a body half in, half out of the culvert.

A spark of hazy memory leaped up at Nash, causing him to break stride. He remembered a similar scene somewhere in his past, something familiar, something . . .

Nash shook off the thought and dropped to his knees. Carefully, he dragged Crista from the culvert and hugged her bound body to him as if she were a long-lost treasure. Damn Jonathan to hell! Crista could have starved or drowned before someone found her. She was drenched from the waist down, her clothes were damaged beyond repair, and the knots he felt on the back of her head were immense.

When Crista squirmed away, Nash jerked himself to attention and then unwound the adhesive tape covering her mouth.

"Ticks!" Crista blurted out. "They're crawling all over me!"

Nash spotted one offensive brown pest crawling up the side of her neck and flicked it away. Another blood-sucking, disease-transmitting little menace was perched on her shoulder, looking for a juicy place. Nash shuddered to think how many parasites were making themselves at home in that thatch of blond hair. Crista would be lucky if she didn't get Rocky Mountain Spotted Fever or Lyme Disease.

"How did you find me?" Crista asked.

"Your ex-husband must have decided to switch cars in case the one he was driving was reported missing," Nash explained. "He pulled into your driveway just before Bernie and I hauled Levi home."

"Is Levi okay?"

Nash nodded as he fished out his pocket knife to cut Crista loose. "He's scraped raw from dragging himself across the gravel to reach the cellular phone in his wheelchair."

"And Jonathan?" Crista inquired as Nash freed her numb arms.

"I left him pinned between my hay spear and a fence post," Nash was delighted to report. "I all but crushed his . . . um . . ."

"You shouldn't have stopped," Crista muttered. "I wanted to do that myself."

"Giving him the nutcracker treatment was the only way to pry the truth from that lying son of a bitch," Nash muttered as he pulled away the tape that encircled Crista's knees and then reached down to free her ankles. "You can really pick 'em, can't you, Curly?"

Crista stared at Nash's face, shadowed by the blazing sunlight behind him. "Can't I, though," she murmured. "I've decided to swear off men indefinitely."

"Small wonder why." Nash considered himself a first-class jerk, ranking right up there with Jonathan Heywood III. They had both made Crista's life miserable.

Truth to tell, Nash was surprised Crista was even speaking to him. She was obviously punch-drunk from too many blows to the head. She was also in a state of shock. When the daze wore off,

Crista would start cursing him—and most deservedly.

Feeling helplessly inadequate, Nash watched Crista dig into her hair, plucking out the disgusting insects. He knew he should apologize here and now, but hell, he didn't even know where to start. Not that she was expecting an apology. From all indications, Crista's foremost concern was climbing into the shower and scrubbing her scalp . . .

"Ouch . . ." Crista flinched when her fingers scraped against one of the knots on the back of her head.

"Let me see." Nash carefully parted the thick mass of hair to inspect the bloody gash.

"Well? Does it look as bad as it feels?"

"How bad does it feel?"

"Awful."

"That's how it looks."

"You'd make a lousy nurse," Crista muttered. "The idea is to cheer up patients, not depress them further."

"Sorry. I always was too blunt."

"That's a fact. And sympathy has never been your strongest suit, except where Levi is concerned."

Nash grimaced at the mention of the traitor's name. "If it makes you feel better, I'm very sympathetic toward you at the moment."

Crista glanced over her shoulder, studying his inscrutable expression. "Funny, it doesn't show."

"Can you stand up?" Nash inquired, clutching her arm to steady her. "Are you feeling dizzy or nauseous?"

"No, yes, and yes . . . I think," she answered

sluggishly. Her shoulders slumped and she bit at her lower lip before she looked the other way.

Nash suspected Crista had plunged from the adrenaline high that had sustained her during her ordeal. She looked fragile, vulnerable, though she was valiantly trying not to succumb to the sea of tears swimming in her eyes.

Coming to his feet, Nash hoisted Crista up beside him. Gently, he reached beneath her knees and lifted her into his arms. "You'll feel better when you get home."

Crista made a sound that could have meant anything. Nash felt her holding herself away from him, as if she was refusing the comfort he offered.

Not that he blamed her. He had shown little concern or compassion the past few days. She didn't expect it from him. Why should she? The men in her life weren't known to be there when she needed them.

No wonder Crista prided herself for being independent. By necessity, she'd had to be. There had been no one to count on but herself.

When Nash carefully set Crista on her feet, she opened the car door and sank gingerly onto the seat. She stared straight ahead while Nash circled around her car to slide beneath the steering wheel.

In silence, Nash drove back to the house, with more care than speed on the rough roads. He cast Crista an occasional glance, certain her composure was barely held together. If he wasn't mistaken, she was waiting until she arrived home to fall to pieces.

Admirable. Nash never had all that much respect for overly sentimental women who cried at the drop of a hat and went to pieces in a crisis.

Talk about *cowboying up,* he thought with a smile. Crista Delaney could really roll with the punches.

"Nash?" Crista murmured two miles later.

"Yeah, Curly?"

Crista swallowed and blinked repeatedly, battling for control. "Thanks for the help."

"Don't mention it. It wasn't much."

His tone was purposely devoid of emotion. He was trying to lure her out of her shell. She was keeping him at bay, holding herself at a distance. She would feel ten times better if she simply exploded, the way Nash did when he was frustrated. He was subtly prodding her, offering himself as a scapegoat.

"You're a genuine bastard," she erupted suddenly.

Nash swallowed a satisfied smile. Now they were getting somewhere. "I know, Curly. Twenty-four karat."

Temper could be a wonderful thing in appropriate situations, Nash reminded himself. This was one of them. And besides, Crista was right. He *was* a genuine bastard. He couldn't even begin to apologize for all the times he'd done her wrong, rejected her, mistrusted her.

The words were still stuck in his throat like a fish bone. Hell, she wasn't the only one around here who was on the edge. Nash had discovered his best friend had purposely lied to him. And what Levi had been doing at Crista's house, Nash sure as hell intended to find out.

Nash silently cursed himself for his inability to communicate what he was feeling. Words rumbled through his mind in disconnected phrases.

It was better this way, he convinced himself. He

had nothing to offer anyone, not when he had all but stopped living, stopped dreaming, five years ago. Not when Levi's deviousness had probably stripped Nash of what little money he had. He would probably do Crista a great favor if he dropped her on her doorstep and never went near her again.

Problem was, Nash would've had to stop breathing, stop living, if he tried to keep his distance now. Having come so close to losing her had taught him how much he cared about this curly-haired woman whose evergreen eyes had mesmerized him, a woman whose generous heart was the size of Oklahoma. Nash couldn't imagine what the world would be like without Crista in it—somewhere . . . even if she would always be beyond his reach . . .

Twenty-one

When Nash pulled into her driveway, the place reminded Crista of a three-ring circus. Here she was, at the end of her emotional tether, fighting for composure, her head pounding in rhythm with her pulse. She had to make a statement to the sheriff. And worse, Jonathan was speared to the fence post, glaring at her as if *she* were at fault.

"God, I don't think I can—"

Nash folded his hand around her fingertips, giving them a quick, reassuring squeeze. "You'll make it, Curly. You've already been through so much, this will be a piece of cake."

Crista stared into his bronzed face, finding comfort in his strength, compassion in the glowing fire of his amber eyes, tenderness in the touch of his hand. She managed a feeble smile.

"I'm sorry I called you a bastard. I was lashing out, but I shouldn't have said that to you."

Nash shrugged a broad shoulder. "Why not? I've been taking my frustration out on you since the day you set foot on my ranch. Turnabout should be fair play." He glanced at her inquiringly. "Do you want me to handle this for you? I will, you know. All you have to do is ask."

Crista stared at him for a long moment. It

would be so easy to let Nash Griffin fight her battles for her.

"No. Like you said, after the morning I've had, this is just a piece of cake."

"I'll be right beside you, all the same," Nash assured her, giving her hand one last comforting squeeze.

Crista climbed from her car. Her gaze darted to Jonathan, wishing she could finish what Nash had started. Watching the three-timing, lying, cheating Jonathan Heywood III become a eunuch had tremendous appeal.

The selfish son of a bitch, Crista fumed silently. And to think she had wasted two good years of her life on that worthless excuse of a man.

The sheriff, who had been immersed in conversation with Bernie and Levi, pivoted to survey Crista's frazzled appearance. "Ms. Delaney?"

Crista nodded, holding herself rigid, restrained.

"I've taken Bernie's and Levi's statements. I'll need to hear your version of the story, and Nash's as well."

"You can speak with Crista after she showers and changes clothes," Nash said. "I found her bound up in a culvert where Heywood left her. The ticks were having a picnic at her expense."

"Sure, sure, take all the time you need, ma'am," Sheriff Featherstone offered. "I'll get our prisoner settled while I'm waiting."

Nash flicked a glance at Jonathan. "He's as settled as he deserves to be."

The sheriff bit back a grin. "I won't argue with that, but the law allows him certain rights."

"Yeah, go figure," Nash retorted.

"The disbarred attorney has been spouting the

law at me since I got here," Featherstone grumbled. "I've been stalling, keeping him on the prong as long as I could. I'll buy a little more time by inspecting the barn where Levi claims the getaway car was stashed."

Crista breathed an enormous sigh of relief when she entered her house, away from the watchful eyes of people swarming around like ants.

"Can I fix you a Coke or coffee?" Nash murmured.

"Wine," Crista requested on her way down the hall.

"The whole bottle, Curly?"

"That will do for starters," she called over her shoulder.

Crista gasped at her reflection in the mirror. She looked awful! Her hair stuck out like an enormous cotton ball. Her face was smeared with mud, her clothes were ruined, and her milky-white pallor could have startled a ghost.

After turning on the shower, she pulled off her wet clothes and tossed them in the trash. The pulsating shower massage was a godsend. For a moment she simply stood beneath the riveting streams, letting the water sluice over her.

Crista didn't even react when the glass door slid open and a hand appeared, offering her the requested glass of wine. Her nerves numb, reflexes worn, Crista simply raised her head to see Nash's eyes locked on her face—and nothing more.

At that moment, Crista was absolutely certain

that she was hopelessly, helplessly in love with this man.

"Drink up, Curly," he said. "There'll be another full glass waiting when you're finished."

Crista promptly drained the glass and handed it back. As the shower door eased shut, she practiced deep breathing before dumping half a bottle of shampoo on her head.

Ten minutes later, Crista emerged to find an oversize sweatshirt, panties, and sweatpants neatly folded beside the sink. A faint smile played about her lips. She could love that man long past eternity if he'd consent to let her become part of his life.

Ah, well, Nash had always been a dream away, Crista reminded herself ruefully. She seemed destined to spend her life chasing unfulfilled dreams, skimming the surface without exploring the depths.

Her wet hair pulled back in a pony tail, Crista padded into the living room to find Nash waiting with the promised glass of wine.

"Better?"

"Better," she confirmed, accepting the glass.

"Shall I invite the sheriff inside, or would you like a few more minutes to catch your breath and gather your thoughts?"

"I'd like a few minutes."

Nash sank down on the sofa and pulled her onto his lap. For a long, quiet, comforting moment, he simply held her, his arms protectively around her. Shifting slightly, he tucked her head against his shoulder.

Crista closed her eyes and relaxed, feeling an inner peace and tranquility she had never known. It was comforting and yet heartbreaking to know the simple pleasure she enjoyed with Nash was only temporary.

She wanted forever with Nash.

All she was getting was a lousy five minutes.

"Ready, honey?" Nash whispered, brushing a kiss across her pallid cheek.

Crista nodded. When he set her down beside him, she curled her legs beneath her, sipped her drink, and collected her thoughts. Her head still thudded painfully, but the nausea had subsided. Nash had predicted she'd make it—and she had. The ordeal was just one of many pitfalls life had thrust at her, another challenge to overcome.

Some people endured worse, Crista reminded herself. Lisa Chandler, for instance. The poor kid was only thirteen and had survived an automobile accident—which her doped-up mother had probably caused. Lisa had undergone two surgeries, not to mention being relocated to a foster home while her mother awaited trial.

Oh, yeah, some people definitely had it worse.

When the door creaked open, Crista glanced up to see Sheriff Featherstone lumbering toward her. He parked himself in the chair across from her and attempted to put her at ease with a smile. But, as always, it was Nash's presence that gave her the strength she needed to present a precise account of the incidents leading up to her rescue. Nash stood in his familiar stance, holding up a wall, his face expressionless.

"So you're saying you still don't know where the money is?" Featherstone frowned. "According to Heywood, you *do* know, because you were in on it with him."

Crista gnashed her teeth. That son of a bitch never missed a chance to tell to lie! "I suspect

Jonathan has every intention of pulling the same stunt that enabled him to escape from the correctional center, so he can retrieve the money he stashed. He hid the key to his safety deposit box in my jewelry box, which was in my office at the hospital. He told me he had used an assumed name to rent the box."

"Did he tell you what name?" Featherstone questioned.

Crista gave her wet head a shake. "No, and he didn't tell me the name of the South American country he planned to escape to, either. If the key and the assumed name aren't discovered, Jonathan will be planning another break for freedom.

"I also expect his father will pull a few more strings to make sure his incorrigible son gets off lightly again. Jonathan Heywood II knows lots of low people in high places. And being a well-known attorney, it would be bad publicity for my ex-father-in-law to have his only offspring sentenced to maximum security."

"So you're telling me that your ex-husband has the key and not you?" Featherstone repeated.

"He took it from the jewelry box while we were at the hospital," Crista insisted. "What he did with it after he knocked me unconscious and left me in the ditch, I can't say."

The sheriff jotted down a few more notes and then heaved a sigh. "We may never be able to recover the money unless we know the name and location of the deposit box. Heywood is contradicting your story. He maintains that he doesn't know where *you* put the key, and that he was forced to admit—at the point of a hay spear—to things he didn't do."

"The only confession I forced Heywood to make had to do with revealing Crista's whereabouts. Her life was in danger," Nash spoke up, pushing away from the wall. "It seems to me that he's lying to protect his own worthless hide and he'll continue to do it if he thinks it will get him a lighter sentence."

"I expect you're right," the sheriff agreed. "But my hands are tied by the very laws I'm obliged to uphold."

"Well, mine sure as hell aren't," Nash muttered.

Crista massaged her throbbing temples. It seemed she may never be rid of Jonathan Heywood.

When Nash strode toward the door, Crista glanced up. She had no time to wonder where Nash had gone or what he was planning to do, because Featherstone was taking her through her statement one sentence at a time. She had the unshakable feeling the sheriff was still trying to make up his mind about whether she was involved.

A few minutes later, Crista heard a revving engine, followed by a wild shriek and a raft of curses. Before Featherstone could set his notebook aside and trot off to investigate, Nash re-appeared.

Without preamble, he slapped the small silver key into Featherstone's hand. "The assumed name is Everett Parker and the safety deposit box is in Union City."

Featherstone blinked, his gaze bouncing back and forth between the key and Nash's face. "Heywood told you that?"

Nash stared over the top of the sheriff's head, focusing his full attention on Cristas. "Eventually . . . I think you should swing by the hospital before taking your prisoner to jail," he suggested, glancing down at Featherstone. "I accidentally put my truck in the wrong gear while I was trying to get Heywood off my hay spear."

Nash's grin widened and his eyes twinkled with mischief. "I must have stuck him pretty good. Quite by accident, of course. But all of a sudden Heywood started volunteering information. And sure enough, I found the key under the seat of Crista's car, just where he said it was. Heywood must have stashed it there before he could make his getaway."

The sheriff reversed direction to retrieve his notebook, a smile tugging at his lips. "In that case, we'll call this a wrap and I'll see that my prisoner gets proper medical attention. I'm sure he'll remind me that he's entitled to it."

When Featherstone strode away, Nash called after him, "Oh, and be sure to tell Heywood I'm dreadfully sorry, but accidents do happen."

When the sheriff exited, Crista peered questioningly at Nash. "Accidents?"

He shrugged nonchalantly. "I didn't see the sense of dragging things out. Enough was enough, so I applied my own rules of justice. The system bends over backward to protect the accused. I advocate a more sensible approach that *protects* the innocent instead."

"Thank you, Nash," she murmured, tears welling in her eyes. "I was nearly at the end of my rope—"

Her voice trailed off when the phone erupted. Nash sorely wished he had left the damn thing unplugged when he found it on the kitchen shelf.

"Go lie down, Curly. I'll take the call," Nash volunteered.

"It's nice to have you running interference," she murmured as she headed for her bedroom.

"Look, lady, Crista isn't coming to work today, and maybe not tomorrow, either. I don't give a shit if her evaluation forms are incomplete. Have the technicians fill them out or do it yourself.

"Instead of sniffing and snorting about those damn files, you should be asking how Crista is managing after what's happened. It's too damn bad you weren't taken hostage instead. And don't think for one minute that I won't report this call to administration. If anybody's butt is going to be in a sling, it'll be *yours!* Now don't you dare bother Crista again with more of your petty complaints while she's recuperating!"

Crista smiled when she heard Nash's gruff response. It didn't take a genius to figure out who was on the other end of the line—Admiral Darwin, the nitpicking grouch.

Nash's tongue-lashing had sunk that persnickety old battleship-of-a-medical-inspector, Crista decided as she sprawled on her bed. Old Ironsides had met her match in the wolf-dragon of Chulosa Ranch. Too bad Crista couldn't sic Nash on Daisy more often to keep her shipshape.

When exhaustion and the sedating effect of the wine overtook her, Crista drifted into deep, welcome sleep. But a smile played on her lips as the dream of *Nashoba,* the wolf guarding her gates, flitted across her mind. Crista would eagerly choose the golden-eyed wolf-dragon over a nice guy any ole day of the week . . .

* * *

While Levi lay in bed, Nash worked silently, tending the numerous scrapes and abrasions. Conflicting emotions warred inside Nash. On the one hand he wanted to shake Levi until his bones rattled for lying about his therapy. On the other hand, he was grateful that Levi had risked severe personal injury by crawling to the cellular phone to aid Crista. If he hadn't, Heywood would have accomplished his mission and Crista might still be lying in that tick-infested culvert.

And just exactly what had Levi been doing at Crista's home that morning? Had Levi intended to buy her silence with the money he'd been filching from the ranch?

Levi hissed in pain when Nash administered antiseptic to the raw flesh on his left elbow. "Damn, that stuff burns like fire. What the hell is it? Straight alcohol?"

"Nope, just the usual stuff we always use," Nash said as he applied another dab.

"Geezus, Nash, you can smear that crap all over my legs if you want, since I can't feel it, but go easy on my arms, will you?"

Amber eyes glittered down on Levi's skinned chin and flushed face. "I am going easy on you, Dogger. I feel like knocking the living shit out of you."

Levi stopped moving, his curious gaze scanning Nash's menacing expression. "What are you talking about?"

Nash set the antiseptic aside and rose from the edge of the bed. "For starters, you can tell me how you happened to be at Crista's home this morning when trouble broke out."

Levi glanced down at the abrasions on his belly, purposely avoiding Nash's piercing gaze. "I . . .

uh . . . wanted to apologize for that scene in the office last week. I . . . um . . . said a few things I regretted and decided to make amends and ask her to take my case. Without the massages and therapy I haven't been as comfortable as usual. Too many muscle cramps."

"You thought Crista would take your case after the accusations you made?" Nash smirked. "I find that a little presumptuous, Dogger. We practically ran her out of here on a rail. Considering the treatment she received here, I wouldn't set foot on this place again if I were Crista."

Nash crossed his arms over his chest and propped himself against the wall, staring grimly at Levi. "Don't try to feed me more of this horseshit. I want the truth."

Closing his eyes, Levi sucked in a deep breath. "I'm really exhausted, Good Time. It took all I had to make that crawl to save Crista. I did it for you, because I know you care about her." He paused for effect, then added, "Could we discuss this later?"

Nash leaned over, bracing his arms on the edge of the bed, a dark scowl on his rugged features. "We are going to discuss this *now*. I want straight answers."

"Straight answers about what?"

"About where you've been going all these years when you claimed to be at the hospital rehab center, taking gait training."

Levi's blue eyes popped open and his jaw dropped.

His reaction confirmed Nash's worst fears. Levi had purposely deceived him and now he knew he'd been caught. "After you left this morning, I drove to the hospital to check on your therapy."

Levi turned a lighter shade of pale. "Nash, I—"

"Funniest damned thing," Nash cut in, snarling, "the technicians—every damn one of them—informed me that you had never been scheduled for gait training sessions, not even once the past three years that you've driven off in that expensive damned van Hal and I bought for you!"

Nash clamped his lips together, fighting for control of his temper. "Did Crista know the truth? Is that why you went to see her, to buy her silence? She knows more than you'd like, doesn't she? What did you think you could do? Pay her off with the embezzled money?"

"Nash, you've got things all wrong," Levi hurriedly inserted.

"Do I?" One thick black brow rose. "I think I'm just beginning to get things right. Now I'll ask you again, Dogger." His face became a mask of steel, his eyes glittering like polished gold. "What have you been doing when you were supposed to be going to gait training and I've been paying out the ass for the rehabilitation you aren't taking!"

His baritone voice exploded like a sonic boom. Levi winced.

"Damn her for putting those suspicions in your head."

"Damn *her*?" Nash snorted derisively, jerking upright. "Because of your lies and deceptions I've treated Crista hatefully! As it turns out, *she's* the one who deserves my courtesy and consideration."

"Nash, if—"

Nash was too furious to listen to more of Levi's lies. He wanted to finish this—and now. "I've busted my butt for five damn years for you," he all but yelled. "I took every endorsement I was offered to make extra money. Hell, Levi, I even endorsed jock straps—and modeled them! The money for your handicap van, the remodeling for your private quarters, and this damned therapy you *aren't* taking has cost a fortune."

"I can explain—"

"And what about Hal?" Nash raged on. "And Uncle Jim? And Bernie? We all made a commitment to you, because you had no family. *We* were your family—or at least I thought we were.

"Hal and I even deeded a third of the ranch over to you and I've given *my* third of the profit to you, not to mention the money I've made for giving rodeo clinics. Geezus, Levi, what the hell kind of friend would lie like that?"

Levi turned away from the wolfish snarl and livid golden eyes that burned down on him. "I need to rest," he muttered.

"And I need to make some changes around here," Nash snapped unsympathetically. "From now on, you get no preferential treatment. I'm through making personal sacrifices for a man who doesn't appreciate everything everybody has done for him!"

Nash lurched around, his chest heaving. "From here on out, Hal and I will be looking over your shoulder while you're doing the accounts for this ranch. You'd better be able to document every expenditure. And if you want Crista Delaney back on your case, then you'll have to crawl back to her. I'm not taking your side against her ever again. Do you understand!"

"I understand better than you know," Levi murmured.

Swearing, Nash stormed out, taking inventory

of every contraption, every expensive exercise
machine he had made available for Levi.

The shrill ring of the phone broke into his
troubled thoughts. Nash rounded the corner into
the modestly furnished living room he never had
time to enjoy.

"Hello," Nash said more gruffly than he intended.

"Is Hal there? I want to speak to him."

Nash frowned at the sultry but forceful feminine voice. "No, he's hustling two rodeos and
won't be back until tomorrow. Can I take a message?"

"Yes," the woman said abruptly. "You can tell
that male chauvinist cowboy that I think he's a
lily-livered coward."

Nash couldn't suppress a grin. Hal had been
called many things in his life—and most deservedly—but *coward* had never been on anybody's
list.

"Anything else while you're on a roll?"

"As a matter of fact, yes," the young woman
huffed into the phone. "You can tell the big
chicken that I'm offering good money to round
up the cattle that keep breaking loose on my
ranch. And just because I happen to be a
woman is no excuse for that unmanly, cow-
hearted—"

Nash nearly chuckled aloud as the irate female
searched for a few more adjectives. "Yellow-bellied?"
he supplied helpfully.

"That, too," the woman muttered. "What the
hell is wrong with that man? Well, you can tell
the big coward that I'm not in business just to
hear myself crow! And if Hal won't take this job,
just because he can't deal with taking orders from

a woman—especially one who's paying good money for his services—then he is absolutely, positively the most insecure man ever to walk the face of the earth. If I could do this job all by myself I would, but I can't. I'm running out of time and I've got more trouble than I can handle without having Hal drag his feet!"

Nash knew the feeling of having more chores and trouble than he had time to handle. "Would you like me to give your name when I deliver the message to my brother or do you wish to remain anonymous?"

"He knows who I am. I called him last week and he rudely dismissed me. And I feel sorry for you if that bean-brained billy goat is your brother!"

Nash broke into a full-fledged grin. This fiery female was exactly what the cynical Hal Griffin needed to shake him loose from his rut.

"Just what is your name, ma'am?"

"Andrea Fletcher."

"From Fletcher Ranch, southwest of Kanima Springs?" he questioned in surprise.

"It won't be Fletcher Ranch for long if I don't get some help around here," she grumbled. "I don't have much time left."

The line went dead and Nash frowned at the receiver. He had half a notion to take the job himself.

The creak of the front door caught Nash's attention. He stepped into the hall to see Bernie Bryant lugging a new wheelchair inside.

"Dogger is back in business," Bernie announced. "Did you tend his injuries?"

Nash nodded. "He's patched up and resting in bed." Pivoting, Nash headed for the door. "I have a few calves to doctor before dark. I'd appreciate it if you would fix a supper tray for Crista. I'll take it over to her when I'm finished in the corral."

Bernie shook his head sadly. "That poor woman had one helluva day, didn't she? If not for Dogger I shudder to think where she would be right now."

"Yeah," Nash murmured.

And if not for the heroic act of kindness—on Crista's behalf—Nash probably would have strangled his supposed friend hours ago. Nash grimaced every time he remembered hurling harsh accusations at Crista during the confrontation in the office. A simple "I'm sorry" wouldn't cut it, not after all the misery he had caused her.

Although Nash's perspectives had changed dramatically since this morning, he still felt a strong sense of responsibility to Levi. Though he had become spoiled and selfish the last five years, it was *Nash's* fault. Crista had pointed that out several times, as he recalled. In short, Nash had probably gotten what he deserved for going overboard. But Nash still had a debt to pay to Levi. He just wasn't going to be as blindly loyal as before, Nash promised himself. But nothing had really changed.

Nothing could ever change, not as long as Levi was without the use of his legs.

Twenty-two

The insistent chiming of the doorbell brought Crista awake. She glanced around groggily, trying to get her bearings. With a tired yawn, she crawled from bed and padded down the hall. She opened the door to find Jack and Jill Forrester poised on the porch, toting two bouquets of flowers.

"I'm glad to see you're holding up so well after your ordeal," Jill said as she breezed through the door. She set the flowers on the end table and turned back with a smile. "Wendy sends her gratitude and best wishes. She would be here in person to thank you for seeing that her car was returned, but she took your patient visitation schedule after she finished her own."

Dully, Crista accepted Jack's sympathetic hug and murmured a thank you for the dozen red roses.

"According to Jill, you're the heroine of the day," Jack murmured, pressing a light kiss to her forehead.

"For some reason, even Old Ironsides has backed off," Jill added.

Crista had Nash to thank for that. He had taken Daisy Darwin to the cleaners when she had called that afternoon.

"I took it upon myself to request a couple of

days off for you, so you could recuperate," Jill announced. "Wendy and I are going to split your workload."

"That's very kind of you, but—"

Jill flung up a well-manicured hand. "No buts, boss. You'll probably want to drop in to see Lisa while you have the time off. She was taken to the CART house, where she'll have round-the-clock care after her last surgery. The physicians assured me she'll be good as new. They also performed plastic surgery on her face."

That piece of news lifted Crista's spirits. She could only hope Lisa didn't blame her for intervening. Crista had dealt with enough bitterness lately—enough to last a lifetime.

"I have something else I need to discuss with you," Jill requested, motioning Crista onto the couch. "We had a most peculiar visit from Nash Griffin this morning."

Crista took a seat. "When was this?"

"About nine o'clock. He was looking for Levi Cooper. For some reason, Nash was under the impression that Levi had been taking gait training in the rehab center."

"Gait training?" Crista parroted. "His medical records indicate he chose not to participate in ambulatory exercise, except as a method of stimulating circulation. Where did Nash get the idea Levi made hospital visits?"

Jill shrugged. "I don't know, but he was stunned by the news."

Crista wondered how long Levi had deceived Nash. And where, she wondered, had Levi been while he was supposedly at the hospital?

Filled with suspicion, Crista wondered if Levi had used phony financial records and was siphoning money into his private account. Dear Lord, there was no telling how much cash he'd swindled from the Griffin brothers.

The doorbell chimed again, much to Crista's chagrin as her tender skull amplified the sound.

"I'll get it," Jack volunteered.

The door swung open and Jack retreated swiftly when a cowboy's dark profile loomed in front of him. Balancing a covered tray in one hand, Nash Griffin invited himself inside.

"I brought supper," he announced, his gaze zeroing in on Crista, taking note of her waxen features and the dark circles under her eyes. "Have you eaten yet?"

"No, I was asleep when Jack and Jill dropped by."

"To fetch a pail of water?" Nash asked straight-faced.

"To bring flowers," Crista said, directing his attention to the bouquet.

Nash scowled. Why hadn't he thought of that? It would have been a chivalrous gesture. But then, he never had much practice at being a gentleman.

Jack Forrester obviously knew—and practiced—all the little things that could melt a woman's heart. Nash glanced discreetly at the attractive, well-dressed accountant and then at Crista. He really should do Crista a favor and vanish from her life. It was glaringly apparent that Jack had an interest in her—even if the young accountant wasn't her type. But Jack did treat her with the respect she deserved. Maybe Nash should simply make his apologies and get the hell out of here.

"We should be going," Jack murmured as he ambled over to pat Crista's hand. "We just wanted to check on you. If you need anything, don't hesitate to give us a call."

"Thanks, but a few hours of sleep should help. I appreciate the flowers. They perked me up."

When the Forresters made their exit, Nash strode into the kitchen to reheat the barbecued ribs, baked beans, and potatoes Bernie had heaped on the tray. Crista lounged against the doorjamb—a habit she had unconsciously picked up from Nash. She watched him make himself at home in her kitchen.

"This is very generous of you."

"Not as thoughtful as flowers, though," Nash replied without glancing at her. "I guess that's why Jack makes the big bucks. He keeps up with the important details. As for me, I only remembered to cover the basics—like food."

"I appreciate the effort," she assured him.

"I still wish I had thought of flowers," he grumbled as he pulled the steaming barbecued ribs from the microwave and shook the sting from his hand.

Crista watched him covetously, wishing . . . She sighed inwardly. She wished for things she knew Nash couldn't give, things she swore she'd never want again.

Just what *did* she want these days? Her independence? That seemed so hollow when her heart whispered for more.

"Have a seat, Curly. It's ready," Nash declared.

Crista parked herself at the table while Nash served dinner. As usual, Bernie's smoked ribs were out of this world. Crista hadn't realized how starved she was until the succulent meat practically melted in her mouth.

She was attacking her second rib when Nash

said out of the blue, "Have you got a thing going with Forrester?"

Crista slammed the rib onto her plate and glared at him. What a stupid question! "Yeah, sure I do. That's why I've been making love with you, because I have a *thing* for him!"

Nash raised his gaze to meet hers. "Is that what we've been doing? Making love?"

"I'm sure there's some crude rodeo term cowboys use. What's the faddish phrase nowadays? Is it still a roll in the hay? A joy ride?"

"Don't get your feathers ruffled, Curly, I was just—"

"And quit calling me Curly, damn it!" she sputtered.

"I never call you *Curly Damn it*. Just Curly. I didn't know it offended you."

"Well, it does." She plucked up her rib. "You think I like having you call attention to this blond Brillo pad I have to wear on my head? Maybe I should shave it off and wear a wig."

Nash bit back a grin. Even when Crista was grumpy she had the ability to amuse and entertain him. That was one of the things he liked about her.

"Don't cut it off. It burns like sunshine in daylight and glows like gold at night. Just like you do. I love all those curls."

The rib hung in her fingertips, inches from her mouth. She studied him intently, noting the unexpected sparkle in his eyes, the lopsided curve of his lips. "You do?"

"Yep." Nash munched on his rib. "Among other things."

Crista cocked her head, appraising him from a different angle. Was this the same hard-ass cowboy she thought she knew? She swore he was teasing her with that dry humor he usually kept under wraps.

"Oh? Among other things? Like what else?" she dared to ask.

"You've got a great body, Curly."

"Thanks," she said with a disgruntled sniff. "That's what we modern women love to hear. All body and no brains. We slept our way to the top." She threw him a narrowed glance. "If you're trying to perk me up, you're failing miserably."

"Good food is supposed to perk you up," Nash pointed out. "I was only trying to provide dinner conversation."

Crista's shoulders slumped. She was entirely too defensive, too sensitive and aware of this man. She was put out with him, because he didn't love her back. As far as she knew, there was no law about such things. But that didn't stop her from wishing he cared as deeply as she did.

"I know this isn't any of my business," Nash said a few minutes later, "but I'm curious why Heywood called you Mary Crista."

"Because that's my name. I dropped the first name and took my maiden name back after the divorce. Surely, you can understand why I wanted no connection to that jerk."

Mary Crista . . . The name tinkled like a distant bell. Somewhere in the clutter of his past that name sparked a dim memory. Nash wished he could make the connection . . .

He glanced up suddenly, surveying the wild tangle of hair surrounding that lovely but weary face. A more recent memory flashed before his eyes and then catapulted itself back through time, linking up with a gone-but-not-forgotten image.

Nash distinctly remembered seeing Crista lying facedown on the ground, left in a culvert filled with stagnant water. The scene reminded him of another incident—clouded by time—until now . . .

As the hazy memory shifted like a kaleidoscope, Nash suddenly found himself staring into his past—visualizing an outdoor arena at one of those countless rodeo clinics he and his brother had given while they were on the college rodeo team.

He remembered that pretty little girl with the tangled snow-blond hair, the one the boys teased and pestered unmercifully. She had ridden and roped with the best of her male counterparts. That group of adolescent boys had done everything except stand on their heads to get that cute little girl to notice them. But she had kept to herself. She had seemed lonely and isolated and Nash had taken a special interest in her, fondly referring to her as . . . Little Orphan Annie . . .

"Mary Crista . . ." Nash breathed in disbelief.

Crista frowned at Nash's stunned expression. "Don't call me that . . . and why are you looking at me like that? Do I have ticks crawling in my hair again?"

No wonder Bernie claimed Crista could turn and burn around barrels at full speed on horseback, and Choctaw Jim said she could handle a horse so well. No wonder she was familiar with the saying that rodeo grit could become as familiar to cowboys as toothpaste. That's where she learned how to imprint foals, too. She was that lonely little cowgirl whose daddy had dumped her off at the college dorm without so much as a hug or good-bye, and then picked her up with the same lack of affection.

But why didn't Crista want Nash to know they had met years earlier?

"Little Orphan Annie . . ." Nash whispered, stunned. "Why didn't you tell me?"

Crista flinched. Damn, he had remembered! She had taken great pains to be sure he wouldn't make the connection.

Flustered, Crista stamped away from the table and headed for her bedroom, hoping Nash would take the hint and go home. No such luck.

When Nash grabbed her arm, Crista jerked away and marched into her room.

"Crista—" Nash braced his hand when she tried to slam the door in his face. "What the hell's wrong with you? And don't give me any crap about having a bad day. *That* has nothing to do with *this*. I asked a simple question and all I want is a simple answer."

Crista wheeled on him, fighting the tears that blurred her eyes. "It's not that simple."

"Fine, then give me a complicated answer."

"No."

"What do you mean *no?*" Nash asked, baffled.

"I mean I don't want to answer the question," she blurted out stubbornly.

When he reached for her again, Crista hastily retreated. Her emotions were in turmoil. She didn't trust herself with him. She was liable to tell him the truth—something Nash didn't really want to hear.

Nash watched tears bleed down her cheeks and dribble onto the front of her wrinkled sweatshirt. Hell's bells, she had held up admirably through the frightening ordeal with Heywood and his goons. Now here she was, crying because he had asked her a simple question.

Women—who could understand them? They could drive a man crazy if he let them—And Nash was sure he didn't have very far to go to get there!

Nash did the only thing he knew to do. He opened his arms. "Come here, Curly. You cried on my shoulder before. It wasn't so bad, was it?"

"It was bad before, but now it's infinitely worse!"

"Why? Because I finally made the connection between you and that curly-headed kid I scraped off the turf all the time at some nameless rodeo clinic years ago?"

That was obviously the wrong thing for Nash to say. Crista jerked back as if he had stabbed her. Another flood of tears spilled from her eyes.

"To you it was just some faceless kid, one of hundreds," she flung back on a sob. "But to me, it was one of the few precious memories of a barely tolerable childhood, with a father who never had time for me. Except to find fault."

Nash frowned, puzzled. "That clinic was a precious memory for you?"

"No, *you* were, damn it!" Crista railed. "I fell head over boot heels for that young cowboy. He was my first and fondest love. And you just spoiled everything, because it meant *nothing* to you and *everything* to me! Until now, I could always pretend there had been a special bond between us those long years ago. At least I had *that!*"

Nash had always claimed that women's tears had little effect on him, but Crista's tears were another matter entirely. When she cried, he bled. But then, everything she did affected him, reluctant though he had always been to admit it. Hearing her confession left him feeling like the world's most insensitive clod.

When he advanced to gather her in his arms and comfort her, she backed away. "Come here, honey," he coaxed.

"Just go away, Nash. I'm planning on having a well-deserved breakdown. I prefer to do it alone, if you don't mind."

"I'm not leaving," he said softly but firmly. "We have to talk—about a lot of things. And just so you know, I'm flattered that you had a crush on me."

Crista swatted him on the shoulder. "It wasn't a crush, you idiot, it was love—first love—and you spoiled it!"

Nash used her flailing arm to tow her to him— the last place she seemed to want to be. Well, tough. That was the only place he wanted her to be.

And furthermore, Nash was through making personal sacrifices for everybody else. For once he was going to think of himself and what *he* wanted. And what he wanted was to spend one uninterrupted night with Crista. He wanted one night with no holds barred. Just the two of them.

Crista felt her traitorous body surrender the instant his arms encircled her. When he molded her against his muscled body her defenses evaporated.

"You just don't understand, Nash," she said brokenly, tilting her flushed face to his. "Everything has changed and yet it's still the same. I could no more help loving you *then* than I can keep from loving you *now* . . ."

The instant the words were out Crista yearned to call them back.

That's what happens when your emotions go into a tailspin. You just open your big mouth and out it all comes.

Now Crista had to face the humiliating conse-
quences of expressing her love for him. This kind
of vulnerability could shatter the strongest heart,
and hers was so brittle.

"You love me?" he asked huskily, probing into
her soul with eyes intent and piercing "Why?"

Crista looked away and sniffled. "I don't know.
I'm hysterical. I don't even know what the hell I'm
saying. It's the first phase of this breakdown I mentioned. Next I'll probably claim I *imagined* being
taken hostage by my ex-husband and those two
goons. I can't distinguish reality from hallucination. It's a symptom of mental imbalance, you
know."

Smiling, he curled his callused fingers beneath
her chin, forcing her to meet his twinkling gaze.
"Why do you think you love me, Mary Crista?"

"What kind of question is that?" She tried to
glance away, but Nash held her head firmly but
gently in place.

"It's an honest one that deserves an honest answer." With a tender smile he stared into her
green eyes. "What could I possibly have done to
deserve your love? I turned against you when you
tried to warn me about Levi. You were right, you
know. And I haven't even apologized for taking
his side. But I am now and I'm sorry as hell.

"I wasn't here for you while Heywood was
prowling around the place, scaring you half to
death. And I haven't even made love to you properly. The way a woman like you deserves. And I
didn't even think to bring you flowers to cheer
you up. So why do you think you love me?"

"It's the little things," Crista managed to get
out without her voice breaking. "The things I
never had with Jonathan. The moral support at

crucial moments—like this afternoon when I was
about to come apart and you reminded me that
the worst was over and I could get through the
rest. It was the way you stood at a distance while
the sheriff questioned me, just to be there if I
needed you. The way you dealt with Jonathan and
his lies, when it looked as though he might get
away with blaming me."

Crista relaxed and smiled a watery smile as she
continued. "It's the way you came to my rescue
at Mangy Dog Saloon. The way you handed me
a glass of wine while I showered. The thoughtful-
ness of providing supper when I was too tired to
fix it myself. And even the way you prodded me
this afternoon until I vented my frustration. You
let yourself be my scapegoat. And it's that dust-
dry sense of humor."

Nash stroked her back, feeling her settle contentedly against him. He was oddly satisfied to
hear he had done at least a few things right with
Crista—*for* Crista.

"You deserve to have the world at your feet,"
he murmured. "I wish I could give you that."

"I don't want the world, I only want—" Well,
thank goodness! At least she had the presence of
mind to button her lip before she begged for his
love.

"What *do* you want, Crista?" he whispered as
he framed her face in his big hands, lifting her
petal-soft lips to his, admiring those fascinating
eyes that spoke of such generosity and spirit.

"It would be enough to know that carefree yet
caring young cowboy who stole a little girl's heart
and brightened her world with his smile—for just
one night."

Only for her, Nash reached deep inside himself, reached back to a time when a world of dreams still lay ahead of him. That part of him which had been alive—a part unburdened by hard living and free from responsibility—longed to be what Crista had once seen in him. He wanted to be her champion, that dashing white knight who saved the day and fulfilled a damsel's dreams in the dark of night.

Nash brushed his lips over hers gently. The salty taste of tears, and Bernie's smoked meat, wrapped themselves around his senses. The feel of her body cried out to everything masculine in him, but Nash reined in his need. He was going to make love to Crista—slowly, thoroughly, even if it damn near killed him. He was going to give of himself in ways he never had before.

For the first time in years he would step outside that shell he had grown around himself. He would become the man he had been a lifetime ago—for Crista.

That sad, isolated little girl would have everything that she believed love *should* be—pure, sweet, satisfying, and fulfilling.

Nash slowly lifted his head and smiled. "Do you know where we are, Mary Crista?"

"In my bedroom," she warbled, lost to the tantalizing effects of his kiss.

He gave his head a shake as he traced the tracks of her tears. "We're in *Kanima*—that mystical place, that magical somewhere that knows no other time and space."

When he smiled down at her Crista saw the harsh lines that life had etched in his face fade away. That ornery grin—the one that made his eyes glisten like gold nuggets—transported her back to that day eons ago when she had landed flat on her face and then looked up to see that handsome cowboy squatting on his haunches in front of her. The precious memory opened like a window, beaming with bright promise.

Crista moaned softly when his gliding caress wandered down her rib cage.

"Mmm . . . now here are the kind of *ribs* a man could feast on to his heart's content," Nash teased playfully.

His hands moved deliberately higher, sketching the curve of her breast beneath the oversize sweatshirt. He felt her tremble, and he ached to share her every sensation.

His thumbs brushed her taut nipples and he watched passion flare in those expressive eyes, knew the thrill of excitement that rippled from her body and his.

Arousing Crista aroused him, and Nash marveled at how the giving of pleasure could bring him such immeasurable satisfaction. When Crista shivered beneath his hands and lips, his male body hardened and clenched, taut as a bow.

Slowly, deliberately, he drew the sweatshirt over her head and let it drop to the floor. In the soft glow of the night light he savored the sight of her full breasts beneath his caressing fingertips.

"I could make a study of you, Crista," he murmured huskily. "Every soft, silky inch of you. Maybe you don't want to hear it, being the 90's woman you are, but you are absolutely lovely."

He bent his head, pressing moist lips to the pulsing curve of her throat, the sloping contours of her collarbone and, finally, to the lush swell of her breast. Her breath caught at the feel of his tongue flicking against her nipple and he smiled against her satiny flesh.

"Is it another insult to confess that I enjoy touching you, tasting you?"

Crista made a soft sound and Nash smiled again. "Is that no or yes? Or aren't you sure? Maybe I should give you time to think it over while I do that again."

His mouth hovered over her sensitive skin, his tongue gliding in a lazy circle. When he gently suckled at the dusky crest, her nails bit into his biceps and clung there, squeezing tighter with each languid stroke of his tongue. And while he held her on tenterhooks, his hand paid tender tribute to the other beaded peak until he made her breath break in a quiet moan.

With skillful ease, his hand inched downward, swirling over her ribs and belly. He traced the elastic band of her sweatpants, heightening her anticipation—and his.

His hand shifted again, slipping beneath the fleece fabric to follow the lace border of her bikini panties. Ever so slowly he pushed her clothes out of his way, letting them glide down to her bare feet.

"Nash . . ." Her gasp of pleasure was his name . . .

The telephone picked the most inappropriate and frustrating moment to ring, breaking the sizzling mood of the moment like a stone crashing through a stained glass window.

"Alexander Graham Bell can take his damned invention and stick it up—"

Crista's forefinger pressed against his lips. "Give the man a break," she rasped. "He's long gone."

The phone blared again and Nash muttered, "I wish he had taken his telephone with him

when he went. It's ruining the only love life I've
had in five years."

Nash guided Crista to bed and tucked her beneath the sheet. "I'll be back as soon as I get rid
of whoever it is."

Tormented by a craving that was impossible to
ignore, Nash forced himself to answer the call.

"Delaney residence." His voice rumbled with
impatience.

"Nash? It's me, Bernie."

If Nash could have reached through the phone,
he would have cheerfully choked Bernie.

"You need to come home," Bernie added ur-
gently.

The tone of Bernie's voice caused a knot of
apprehension to coil in the pit of Nash's belly.
"What's wrong?"

"It's Levi. He's gone."

"What do you mean he's gone?" Nash repeated
incredulously.

"I mean exactly what it sounds like I mean,"
Bernie grumbled. "I went in to check on him
after supper and he was just lying in bed, staring
at the ceiling. When I walked down to the barn
to feed the supper scraps to Leon and toss hay
to the horses, I heard the van roar off. When I
checked his room, I discovered he had taken
nothing with him—not a suitcase, not the mobile
phone, nothing."

"Where the hell did he go?"

"I don't know. He didn't leave a note."

Nash cursed in helpless frustration. He had
read Levi every paragraph of the riot act that evening, refusing to let him apologize, refusing to
let him explain.

Damn it, Nash had hoped to make Levi see the error of his ways, not oust him from the ranch!

Where the hell did Levi think he was going? What was he going to do? God, if something happened to him, Nash wasn't sure he could bear any more guilt.

"I'll be home in a minute," Nash murmured before he dropped the receiver into its cradle.

Reluctantly, Nash paced back to the bedroom door. He hated doing this to Crista, teasing and pleasuring her—and himself—and then walking away.

Because of Levi. Always because of Levi.

Nash was doing it again, damn it—placing Levi ahead of Crista.

"Nash? Is everything all right?"

"No, I'm afraid not. I confronted Levi before I came over here and told him I knew he'd lied about taking therapy and that he'd taken money from the ranch funds. That was Bernie," Nash reported. "He said Levi has left without a word. I've got to find him."

Nash stared at sweet temptation in the bed— where he wanted to be, with Crista. "I'm sorry . . ."

"I hope he's okay," Crista commiserated.

"Yeah—me, too," Nash said as he turned away. "I'll be back tomorrow night to give you the latest on the Levi Cooper Caper. Maybe then we'll have our night together."

"Nash?"

He swiveled his head, tormenting himself one last time. "Yes, Curly?"

"I love you . . ."

Nash walked out into the night, cursing. He could barely tolerate leaving Crista . . . and yet

he'd become so conditioned to watching out for
Levi. If Levi did something drastic, because Nash
had lit into him, Nash wasn't sure he could live
with himself.

Twenty-three

Exasperated, Nash jerked off his hat and slapped it against his thigh. He had spent most of the night driving around the countryside, trying to locate Levi's red van, hoping and praying he hadn't decided to end it all. But Nash hadn't found hide nor hair of Levi anywhere. Neither had Sheriff Featherstone. It was as if he had vanished in the space of a few hours.

Though he tried, Nash couldn't forget the tempting sight of Crista lying in bed, awaiting his return, offering her love. He hadn't been able to spend even one long, uninterrupted night with her. He'd had to forsake his own pleasure to track Levi down.

Damn it, how could the anticipation of one night of pure heaven become hellish so quickly? Lord, there were times when Nash caught himself wishing Crista had never walked into his life. Even though he'd only been going through the motions of living the last five years, at least he'd accepted the limitations of his life and had learned to be content with them. Now he knew what it was like to want and desire something very badly.

Even when Nash was feeling the worst effects of Levi's betrayal, he had never once planned to turn him out in the cold. Nash could never have sacrificed Levi, not even when he ached for Crista with every part of his being.

The rattle of an approaching pickup and stock trailer jostled Nash from his troubled thoughts. He automatically wheeled toward the front door, aware that the familiar clatter heralded Hal's and Choctaw Jim's return from the rodeo.

By the time Nash, with Bernie on his heels, reached the barn, Hal had climbed from the cab to work the kinks from his back.

"How'd it go, little brother?" Nash questioned.

Hal massaged his tender ribs. "It went well."

"Better than well," Choctaw Jim amended as he stepped down. "You're looking at the undisputed leader in the All-Around standings. Hal has already come close to qualifying for the National Finals in Las Vegas."

"How did he do in bronc riding?" Nash questioned his uncle.

"First place," Jim announced proudly.

"And calf roping?" Bernie asked.

"Second."

"Saddle bronc?" Nash queried.

"Another first. Hal rode and roped like a man possessed," Jim reported. "Our horses were nothing to scoff at, either. Cowboys were lining up beside the chutes, begging to use our livestock. Everybody who rode Popeye, Blue Duck, and Bowlegs placed in the money, and we got a sizable cut of the purses. It was a productive rodeo—now Hal can take a few weeks of vacation from the suicide circuit."

"I'm going to start my vacation with a long, hot shower," Hal said tiredly.

Nash glanced grimly at Bernie when Hal pulled the paycheck from his shirt pocket, intending to deliver it to Levi. "Bern, why don't you help Uncle Jim unload. I need to talk to Hal."

Nodding agreeably, Bernie strode around to the back of the stock trailer to fetch the horses and gear.

"Don't tell me, let me guess," Hal snorted. "More trouble with that damned therapist. What kind of problems is she causing now?"

"Crista isn't the problem."

Hal trudged up the front steps, scoffing at his brother's remark. "She's a woman, therefore she's trouble. And Crista Delaney is sure as hell all woman."

Before Hal started raking women in general—and Crista in particular—over the coals, Nash cut to the heart of the problem. "As it turns out, Crista's suspicions about Levi were right on target."

Hal arched a black brow as he opened the door. "I'm sure a good screw convinced you of that—Hey! Watch it, big brother! My ribs are still tender!"

Nash reacted instinctively to the crude comment. He slammed Hal up against the doorjamb and held him there. "No, *you* watch it, smart ass."

"Better to be a smart ass than a dumb shit . . . like somebody's *brother*," Hal snorted.

"You owe Crista an apology," Nash gritted out. "While you were gone, I decided to follow Levi to the hospital for his therapy session."

Hal stood perfectly still, wedged painfully between the doorjamb and the sinewy forearm. "And?"

"And Levi wasn't there. When I questioned the technicians, come to find out Levi has *never* been in gait training therapy, not even once the past three years."

Hal's brows jackknifed. "What? Are you sure?"

Nash nodded bleakly. "I talked to everyone on staff in the physical therapy department. Levi has never been on that computerized machine that's supposedly costing us so much money."

"Then what happened to all the cash we shelled out for his exercises? It has to amount to over a hundred thousand dollars."

Nash backed off, giving Hal breathing space. "Well over *two* hundred thousand, counting the endorsements and advertising I handed over to Levi after I won my last title," he amended.

Hal sagged back against the wall of the entry-way, his onyx eyes wide with disbelief. "What the hell did he do with all that money? Why would he lie to us?"

Shrugging, Nash led the way into Levi's private quarters. "I asked him those same questions last night. When I left to check on Crista, Levi tore off in his van before Bernie could stop him. We haven't seen him since. I had Featherstone send out an APB, but he hasn't turned up anything, either."

Hal smothered a curse—barely. "What the hell did you do? Threaten to toss Levi out in his wheel-chair so you could set up housekeeping with that curly-headed blonde?"

Nash snarled at his snarling brother—it was like staring at his reflection in the mirror. "Crista happens to be in love with me—"

"And you believe her?" Hal cut in sarcastically. "Son of a bitch, Nash. After five years of celibacy you think you have obligations to the first hot item who comes along and claims she loves you?"

Hal shook his head. "Let me tell you something about love. There ain't no such thing. It's nothing but an illusion."

"Crista's different," Nash protested, "and one day you may have to eat those words."

"Yeah," Hal smirked. "That'll be the same day I roll over and die. I let a woman make a fool of me once, all because she claimed she loved me. It'll be the same for you if you don't watch your step. She's even managed to come between you and Levi. *Levi*, for heaven's sake. He's like our adopted brother. We've been hauling him around with us since the day he finished his junior year of college—"

"And to repay us he's been embezzling the money we gave him for the therapy he hasn't taken."

Hal let out his breath in a rush. "I'm still having a hard time believing it."

"You think I want to believe it?" Nash muttered sourly. He grabbed the medical files and thrust them at Hal. "I checked every document and evaluation form, trying to tell myself there had to be a logical explanation."

Nash stared grimly at his brother. "Do you remember those two legal-looking papers Levi had us sign six months ago and the ones he shoved under our noses three weeks ago?"

Hal nodded. "I remember. They were to approve financing and permission for another round of hospital sessions."

"So Levi said, but those forms weren't in the files."

"I'm sure there's a reason for that. Maybe they're filed at the hospital," Hal said, thumbing through the stack of papers.

"There's a reason, all right," Nash grumbled. "I have the uneasy feeling we were manipulated into signing something Levi didn't want us to know about. The financial statements *we* saw are in the file, but there were only two pages of medical mumbo-jumbo. If you recall, our signatures were on legal-size documents—the ones Levi obviously *didn't* want us to see. He camouflaged them."

Hal staggered back, bracing himself against the edge of the desk. "Geezus, what did we do, Nash? Sign the goddam ranch over to him? That's the only thing we have that would require all three signatures, since the property is undivided." Hal raked his hand through his hair and stared worriedly at his brother. "Holy shit—surely Levi wouldn't try to sell the ranch out from under us!"

"Then *you* tell *me* why Levi left the minute I confronted him. The more I think about all the phone calls he's been making and taking, those concealed documents he needed us to sign, and his attempt to lay the blame on Crista, the more I believe he went behind our backs.

"Does it seem a little ironic to you that Levi pulled up stakes and left without a word or a forwarding address, immediately *after* I told him what I found out? Why would he bolt and run if he wasn't guilty of something? And why would he drive over to Crista's place, after he had accused her of trying to cause so much trouble?"

Hal frowned in confusion. "When was this?"

Nash motioned for Hal to follow him. "Maybe you'd like to hear about it over a cup of coffee."

"Maybe I would," Hal mumbled, following Nash into the kitchen. "Hell's bells, I leave this ranch for a few days and it all comes tumbling down. I don't recall having so much trouble before Crista showed up."

Nash flung his brother a withering glance. The Cynic of Kanima Springs was quick to blame women for anything and everything. Nash had hurt Crista more than enough without his bitter-minded brother cursing her every chance he got.

When Crista heard the rap at her front door, she quickly checked her appearance in the mirror. Nash had promised to come by this evening, updating her on Levi's escapade. Although she was concerned about Levi, she had enjoyed a leisurely day away from the office. She had checked on Lisa Chandler, finding the girl in good spirits and on the way to recovery.

Crista had driven up to Keota Flats that afternoon to make a wickedly impulsive purchase—which she was presently wearing in honor of Nash's arrival. She hoped Nash appreciated it, even if he had arrived earlier than expected, depriving her of a half hour of primping.

The slinky silk negligee, with its plunging neckline and provocative slit to the hips, was by far the most erotic purchase Crista had ever made. She wanted to make a new beginning with Nash, hoping he'd return to being that fun-loving cowboy once known by the nickname of Good Time.

Crista had seen occasional glimpses of the man less restrained, less inhibited. She longed to coax Nash back into cherishing life, rather than being imprisoned by it. Hopefully, knowing that she cared very deeply for him would bring him out of his shell and give them both a chance at happiness.

This gown was therapeutic as well as seductive, Crista told herself, smiling impishly as she approached the door. She wanted to set a playfully romantic mood, to enjoy their evening together, even if thoughts of Levi still hovered in the back of both their minds. . . .

The man Crista struck a provocative pose for—in the open door—was *not* Nash Griffin!

It was his brother . . .

"Good Lord!" Hal croaked when a vision to torment even the most cynical of men appeared before him in a slinky green fabric the exact match to her hypnotic green eyes.

Her face flaming with embarrassment, Crista slammed the door and groaned in humiliation. She was vividly aware of Hal Griffin's low opinion of her and the rest of those of the female persuasion. He had cut her to the quick once already.

Once had been plenty.

Hal pounded on the door. Crista winced, unsure she had sufficiently composed herself to confront Hal again.

"What do you want?" she demanded.

"I hate to spoil this steamy tryst you were obviously planning for my brother, but there's been a change of plans." Hal paused for an impatient moment. "Are you going to let me in or do I have to explain through this damn door?"

"Give me a minute." Crista made a mad dash to the bedroom to change into something presentable. When she re-entered the living room, she discovered Hal had invited himself inside and had sprawled on her sofa, munching on the snacks she had prepared for Nash.

Crista watched Hal appraise her western shirt

and jeans through hostile eyes. Even her modest attire didn't seem to suit him.

"Now I know what kind of hold you have on my brother." Hal came to his feet, looming over her. "And just so you know, *sweetheart*—"

The phony endearment dripped with sarcastic overtones, Crista noted.

"—If you cause my brother the slightest misery, you'll answer to me," he finished in a distinctly menacing tone.

"Just so *you* know, I care very deeply about your brother," she assured him. "I only want the best for Nash."

"And I'm sure you think you're the very best," he snorted sardonically.

Crista took a bold step forward, tilting her chin upward. "Don't mess with me, buster. Surely I don't need to remind you how quick I am on the draw with a loaded syringe. You better back off before I'm tempted to put you under sedation and prep you for a personality transplant."

A reluctant smile tugged at one corner of Hal's mouth, ruining the effect of his ominous glare. "I swear, lady, you must take daily injections of sass."

"It helps when dealing with cantankerous men like the Griffin brothers." Crista raised a curious brow. "Now what's this about a change of plans? Or do you want to waste more time hurling insults and threats at each other?"

Hal flashed her a warning frown. "Don't think I've decided to like you. But I *will* give you a short grace period before passing final judgment."

Crista smiled in mock gratitude. "Your generosity overwhelms me. Should I drop to my knees now? Or are we pressed for time here?"

Crista wasn't sure, but she had the feeling Hal had backed down slightly. He had decided to call a truce—however temporary. He relaxed his rigid stance and his dark eyes took on a less formidable glitter. Though his expression hinted at seriousness, he appeared less threatening than before.

"We haven't been able to locate Levi," Hal reported.

Crista squeezed her eyes shut. She hadn't meant to come between the Griffin brothers and Levi Cooper. God, where could Levi have gone? Why did more complications have to arise, just when she and Nash were on the verge of making a new start?

Sure as the world, Nash was blaming himself for Levi's unexpected exodus. Nash's overactive sense of responsibility was probably eating him alive. Though she admired that trait, she secretly wished *she* could be the recipient of such unfaltering devotion. But she had decided to accept whatever Nash could offer.

"I'm sorry," Crista whispered. "Although you probably won't believe it, I want what's best for Levi, though not at your and Nash's expense. I couldn't bear to see Nash hurt."

Hal made a sound that could have meant virtually anything. Crista didn't ask for a translation. The best she could hope for was a civil relationship with this cynical cowboy.

"We got a call an hour ago from Rooster Anderson and Ace Ketcham, two of the professional cowboys who paid us a visit last week," Hal explained. "They were on their way back to Texas when they happened onto Levi, somewhere south of the City."

Crista held her breath, fearing the worst. "Is Levi all right? Has he been hurt?"

Hal shrugged noncommittally. " 'Still in one piece' was all Bernie could get out of Rooster. He said we better bring Levi's therapist along when we came to pick Levi up. It doesn't sound too good, especially since Levi is still recuperating from crawling across your driveway."

"I'll get my medical bag." Crista wheeled toward the closet. "Where's Nash?"

"He was vaccinating and branding the weaning calves when the call came in. He asked me to come and get you while he was finishing up in the corral and taking a fast shower."

Crista grabbed her bag and jacket to ward off the autumn chill. Lord, she was never going to forgive herself if Levi had come to serious harm. He might be suffering because of her, because she had dared to voice her suspicions to protect Nash.

Crista felt guilty and ungrateful. If not for Levi, she could have suffered an awful fate. She might still be hog-tied and stuffed in that disease-ridden, tick-infested culvert, while Jonathan flew off into the wild blue yonder with a suitcase of embezzled cash.

Despite the fact that Levi had taken unfair advantage of Hal and Nash, the man had come to her rescue, indicating he still possessed a few saving graces. If Levi had been bad to the bone—like Jonathan—hating him would have been simple. She could understand why Nash was having a difficult time coping with his emotions where Levi was concerned.

Crista prayed for some kind of reconciliation, prayed that Levi hadn't allowed himself to be-

come as selfish and corrupt as Jonathan. She
wouldn't wish the kind of humiliation she had
endured at Jonathan's hands on her own worst
enemy. She would, most certainly, spare Nash that
torment if she could.

Nash was poised by the front door when the
truck rolled across the gravel driveway. His hair
was still damp from his shower and he had but-
toned himself into his clothes on the way down
the steps. A sense of urgency rippled through
him, and it had since Bernie had delivered the
message from Rooster and Ace.

Guilt and frustration were eating at Nash like
a worm in an apple. If Levi was injured, especially
after he had suffered the effects of his long crawl
the previous day, Nash didn't think he could forgive himself.

God, Levi, what have you done to us and to yourself?
The question played over and over in Nash's
mind. He felt betrayed by the incriminating evidence he had uncovered at the hospital and yet
torn by his long devotion to a friend. He couldn't
wait to haul Levi back home and talk this whole
damned mess through—once and for all . . .

Nash's tangled thoughts trailed off when he saw
Crista's silhouette inside the truck. He hoped Hal
had taken the opportunity to apologize for his
misconceptions about Crista. But knowing Hal,
Nash doubted his brother's cynical opinions
would allow his generosity to stretch very far.

But if nothing else, Nash promised himself, Hal
and the other men would come to understand
that Nash would not tolerate any hostility toward
Crista. Luckily, though, Bernie and Choctaw Jim

didn't hold all women in contempt—on general principle—the way Hal did.

Before Nash could descend the steps, Crista bounded from the truck and dashed toward him.

"I hope Levi hasn't done himself harm," Crista murmured as her hand folded comfortingly around his. "I guess I should have handled the situation differently . . . somehow . . ."

Nash bent his head, pressing his mouth to her parted lips—with God and everybody else as witnesses. He considered it statement enough for his family and friends. Nash was making his feelings known—here and now.

Before Nash broke the kiss he heard Hal muttering in the background. When Nash glanced over the top of Crista's head he saw his uncle wink and Bernie break into a toothy smile.

At least *they* approved. Nash wished he could say the same for his grumbling brother.

"I'm sorry about the change of plans," Nash apologized to Crista.

"You'd be even sorrier if you could have taken a gander at that little green number she was wearing when I got there," Hal snorted.

Nash glanced curiously at Crista. Her face had turned fuchsia in the porch light.

Crista pivoted to flash Hal a homicidal glare. "I wonder if Nash would mind all that much if he suddenly became an only child."

"Don't threaten me with that damned syringe again," Hal flung back.

"I thought we had called a truce."

"This is as good as the truce gets, sweetheart—"

"Hal!" Nash's clipped voice rumbled in warning. "Butt out."

"Yeah, yeah, I know, and I'm supposed to mind

my manners and all that, too." He flicked his brother a quick glance. "If you can pry yourself loose from Goldilocks we need to get this show on the road. We've got a forty-minute drive ahead of us. I don't know about the rest of you, but I'd like to get to the bottom of this thing with Levi. The sooner the better."

Grabbing Crista's hand, Nash towed her toward the truck.

"I suppose the two of you want the back seat all to yourselves," Hal speculated—with blatant sarcasm.

Nash bared his teeth as he breezed past his surly brother. "Just keep your trap shut and drive," he said for Hal's ears only.

With Hal poised behind the steering wheel and Uncle Jim and Bernie, sitting three abreast— broad shoulder to broad shoulder—in the front seat, Nash settled his arm around Crista's shoulders. He drew her familiarly against him, giving her a discreet hug. Having her beside him felt right, natural, necessary, even if Hal was about to burst his pearl-studded snaps in objection.

As the truck pulled away, Nash brushed his lips against the unmanageable locks that curled at Crista's temples. "I can't wait to get a look at that sexy green number Hal mentioned. But since Levi—"

Crista nuzzled contentedly against him. "It really wasn't all that scintillating. It can wait."

Nash winced inwardly at her acceptance of her position on his priority list. Damn it, he wasn't being fair to Crista. He balked at his divided sense of loyalty, knowing she deserved better, wishing he could offer her more.

She claimed to love him, but how long would

RIVER MOON

it be before some other man came along to offer
Crista more than a few stolen moments? And who
knew what Nash and Hal would have left when
this situation with Levi was resolved?

The Griffin brothers could be flat broke and
homeless. Then Nash sure as hell would have
nothing to offer Crista, and damn it, he hadn't
even had the chance to take her out on an official
date. If Levi had taken control of the ranch *and*
the cash, Nash might not be able to afford to buy
Crista a hamburger and Coke at a fast-food joint.

Levi had thrown everyone's life into turmoil.
Nash didn't have a clue what to expect when they
reached their destination. The only thing that
hadn't been vague in Rooster Anderson's explanation was directions to wherever the hell Levi
had holed up.

Twenty-four

Following Rooster's instructions, Hal exited from the interstate and veered west for half a mile. The five occupants stared, bemused, at the lighted parking lot in front of a gargantuan metal building.

"What in the hell . . . ?" Nash's voice dried up when Hal applied the brakes, pausing beside a row of pickups hitched to stock trailers.

"What is this place?" Hal questioned.

"You've got me," Bernie replied. "It looks like a spanking new indoor arena or something."

Piling out of the truck, the entourage strode toward the entrance to find Rooster Anderson and Ace Ketcham awaiting them. Rooster stuck his head inside the door and then spun back around, his face splitting in a broad smile.

"About damned time you got here," Rooster declared.

"Where's Levi—?" Nash gasped when floodlights flared to life above him. He glanced up to see fifteen-foot-tall neon letters beaming down at him.

"Holy Moses!" Hal croaked.

In stunned amazement, the honored guests stared up at the sign that could now be seen from the interstate—half a mile away.

GRIFFIN BROTHERS RODEO ARENA

Nash staggered back, clinging to Crista, who was holding on to him for balance and support.

Like ushers at a Broadway show, Rooster and Ace swung open the double doors to reveal the man in his wheelchair.

Nash's eyes popped like kernels of corn. "What the hell's going on?"

Levi rolled forward, beaming with amusement and satisfaction. "Nothing's going on yet. We couldn't have the grand opening without the guests of honor."

The smile faded from Levi's features as he focused his attention on Crista, who stood before him with her mouth hanging open. "I owe you an apology, Crista," he said humbly. "I had to let you take all the heat in order to make the final arrangements. I was on my way to explain the need for secrecy when we both met with trouble in your front yard."

Crista tried to speak but nothing came out. Nash, however, recovered more quickly than she did.

"You sold our ranch to build this arena?" he questioned in wary trepidation.

Levi gave his sandy-blond head a shake. "Nope, you and Hal *bought* this arena with the money you've been forking over for my therapy for more than three years. The papers I had you sign—letting you think they were medical forms—were the deed to this property and a permission form for me to mortgage my third of the ranch so I could make the final installment for building costs."

"What are you saying?" Nash asked hoarsely.

Levi stared at the dumbstruck Griffin brothers.

"For five years the two of you—all of you, Bernie and Choctaw Jim included—have provided and cared for me, because I had nowhere to go after the accident. When I hit rock bottom, wondering if living in this wheelchair was worth the effort, you were there to boost my spirits with cowboy reunions, card and domino games—whatever it took to ease my depression.

"You handed your hard-earned money over to me, buying everything I could possibly need. You insisted I take therapy, hoping I could learn to walk again. But I had already been told there was no chance. *I* knew years ago what *you* refused to accept."

Levi grinned at the stupefied men. "And despite what you've probably been thinking the past few days, I'm well aware of every sacrifice you made for me, because of me. The only way I could repay you for all you've done was to invest the money in this arena. I've already seen to it that the scheduled events were approved by the rodeo association. J.C. Winters has been making the arrangements and promotions for me."

Nash staggered back, overwhelmed, stunned, disbelieving. "God, Levi, you didn't have to do this."

Levi's blue eyes glistened with admiration and sentiment. "Ah, but I did, Good Time. You stopped living for yourself, because you shouldered the blame for what happened to me.

"Hell, it wasn't your fault. I never blamed you, not even for a second, but you were ready to accept full responsibility for something you really had no control over. I was the one who wanted a little personal glory after you made a clean sweep of the National Finals. I got reckless, took a risk that you and Hal warned me not to take on a horse that wasn't trained for bulldogging.

"You've been beating yourself black and blue for five years, trying to compensate for something that simply was *not* your fault."

Levi rolled his chair forward, handing sets of door keys to Nash and Hal. "This is my way of repaying you for always being there when I needed you, for sacrificing so much for the orphan kid from Nebraska who wanted to be as skilled and successful as his famous mentors."

He dropped a separate set of keys in Nash's hand. "And this is the key to the shiny red extended cab pickup I had J.C. drive up here for you. Now you can put that bucket of rust out to pasture."

With tears swirling in her eyes, Crista dropped to her knees in front of Levi. "I'm so very sorry I complicated things for you, Levi. The conversations I overheard on the phone led me to believe—"

"I know." Levi cut her off, smiling regretfully. "I know you were trying to protect Nash, because you care as much about him as I do. But I couldn't risk having the Griffin brothers discover what I was planning to do until the arena was completed. Knowing them, they would have tossed the cash right back in my lap and insist that some miracle cure might come along in the future.

"And because the plans were so close to completion, I became frantic and came down hard on you. I've waited over three years for this, eager to see the looks on Hal's and Nash's faces when I could return part of their generosity."

Levi glanced back at Rooster and Ace before

returning his attention to Crista's tear-streaked
face. "I had decided to let you in on the secret,
the same as the cowboys who came to visit last
week, the same ones I invited here tonight. But
yesterday turned out to be a disaster. I never got
the chance to explain."

More tears tumbled down Crista's cheeks when
Levi reached out to squeeze her hand affection-
ately.

Quietly Levi added, "Believe me, Crista, I don't
blame you for anything. I only hope *you* can forgive *me* for forcing you to endure Hal's and
Nash's damnable tempers. I've waited a long time
to spring this surprise. And I guarantee that seeing the looks on their faces tonight was worth
everything."

"But I don't know how to repay you for the
trouble I caused, for my misguided suspicions,"
Crista whispered miserably.

Levi curled his hand beneath her chin and
grinned boyishly. "I'll take your out-of-this-world
massages as payment. Best I ever had."

His gaze focused momentarily on Nash before
returning to Crista. "If you can help me turn
Good Time Griffin back into the man he used to
be, back when he was quick with a joke and a
smile, I'll call it even if you will."

"Are we gonna get started on the competition
tonight or just stand around jawing?" Rooster
crowed. "It isn't manly for a hard-ass cowboy like
me to be hanging around here with a lump the
size of Oklahoma in my throat. Before I get all
choked up, what do you say we go buck some
broncs?"

Rooster surged inside. In a matter of seconds,
bright lights flickered to life above the turf, which

was surrounded by a restraining wall and elevated grandstands. A cheer resounded through the arena as old friends converged to congratulate the new owners.

Crista stood aside, mopping tears with her shirtsleeve while the surging crowd of cowboys descended on Hal, Nash, and Levi. She was thoroughly appalled at herself for believing the worst about a man who turned out to be as self-sacrificing and generous as the Griffin brothers.

Knowing Nash as she did, Crista had a pretty good idea why Levi had insisted on secrecy. Nash would have loudly and stubbornly objected to the project from the onset, demanding that his hard-earned money be spent on Levi. But Levi had taken it upon himself to provide for his adopted family's future security, making preparations for the day when Hal and Nash were ready to slow their hectic lifestyle.

Warm, indescribable pleasure skittered down Crista's spine when Nash threw back his head and laughed heartily at something one of the cowboys had said to him. The cracks in Nash's veneer indicated that the fun-loving man he had once been was emerging again. Learning that Levi's deception was born of gratitude had lifted a great burden from Nash's shoulders. He could breathe easy for the first time in five years.

Crista backed away when the boisterous crowd swarmed into the arena to enjoy their private rodeo among old friends. Nash needed this time with the other cowboys, the chance to recapture the lifestyle he had enjoyed so much and then given up in order to care for Levi.

Crista didn't belong here with them. This was a time for Levi, Hal, and Nash to become the close-knit family they had been before Crista had unintentionally caused so much conflict.

"Where the hell do you think you're going, Curly?"

The deep baritone thundered across the parking lot.

Crista pivoted to see Nash's massive silhouette framed by the lighted indoor arena behind him. "Home where I belong," she called back to him.

Nash strode determinedly toward her, pausing only long enough to scoop her into his arms before reversing direction. "Not on your life, lady," he growled down at her. "Levi already has the barrels set up for your exhibition ride. According to my uncle and Bernie, you can turn and burn on horseback better than a race car can on four wheels."

"I'm not going to run barrels," Crista told him firmly.

Nash smiled that devastatingly handsome smile that catapulted Crista back through time. "The hell you say, Little Orphan Annie. I fully intend to see if that kid I scraped off the turf learned anything."

"Nash—" Her voice evaporated when he carried her through the door and planted her on the horse Choctaw Jim held by the reins.

Choctaw Jim's black-diamond eyes twinkled up at her. There was quiet confidence and encouragement in his gaze, his knowing smile. "You were always poetry in motion, Mary Crista. Nash has his life back. Now go find the best of your own past out there on the turf. I think maybe you gave up this part of your life for some of the same reasons Nash did—to be there when your friend needed you most."

Crista's misty gaze locked with Jim's. She had always thought he possessed an ability to see beyond what appeared to be, to what really was. This perceptive Choctaw certainly lived up to his namesake—the wise old owl.

Jim was right on the mark, Crista realized. Her loyalty to Cynthia Marrow after the crippling accident had given Crista's life new purpose and direction, providing her with the ability to break free of her father's domination.

"And something else, Mary Crista," Jim murmured as he handed her the reins. "Do you remember the philosophy I discussed with you on our way to Mangy Dog Saloon?"

Crista nodded. "I remember."

"Good," he said softly, "because I'm beginning to see the loving bond my wife and I had come back to life." His dark-eyed gaze drifted to Nash. "I can see it in *him* . . . because of *you* . . ."

Stirred by Jim's poignant words, Crista settled herself on the saddle, focusing her undivided attention on the three barrels that were set one hundred feet apart. She let herself go back through time, back to the days when rodeo competition had been her life, her father's grandest expectation for her—and recognition for himself.

Crista rode for her own pleasure, for the challenge and inner thrill of racing as one with the powerful pony beneath her. She was going to do what she had once loved, because she *had* loved the thrill and excitement of the rodeo, not because her father said it must be so.

Leaning forward, Crista put her boot heels to the horse's flanks, lunging off in a burst of speed, moving in practiced rhythm, shifting her weight in smooth precision as she took the first turn . . .

while a cheering crowd of cowboys serenaded her . . .

"She's pretty damned good . . . for a woman," Hal begrudgingly admitted as he watched Crista give the horse time to collect its balance before starting toward the second barrel. He glanced at his brother and groaned. "For God's sake, wipe that disgustingly lovesick smile off your face. You're making me nauseous."

Nash felt an extraordinary sense of pride burgeoning inside him as he watched Crista's skillful performance. When the bay gelding's hip was directly beside the second barrel, she reined sharply, banking a perfect left turn. The horse lunged off, dirt splattering beneath its hooves. Crista looked right at home, racing across the turf with the reins in her left hand. She expertly guided her mount around the last barrel in the cloverleaf pattern, and then she took the route again, for the sheer pleasure of it all.

"I wonder why she gave it up," Nash mused aloud.

"For much the same reason you did," Choctaw Jim confided, watching with the same fascination as every man in the arena. "For an injured friend—the one Crista borrowed the modified saddle from so Levi could be one of us again. Is it any wonder she understands the kind of devotion you've given to Dogger?"

Nash frowned pensively. "How is it that *you* know so much about her past and *I* don't?"

Choctaw Jim smiled his enigmatic smile. "Maybe it's because I asked her. And maybe it's because I remembered her from the high school rodeo finals in Oklahoma City. She had several titles to her credit—barrel racing, breakaway roping, pole-bending racing. She even won the goat-tying event for cowgirls. I've seen her cast a rope every bit as well as you and Hal."

Jim nodded thoughtfully. "Seems to me she'd make a fine addition to the family—"

"Damn it, don't put ideas in that mushy head of his," Hal said and scowled. "He's turned as soft as pudding already."

Without taking his eyes off Crista, Nash grinned. "Maybe I am softening up, but at least nobody accused me of being a lily-livered, male chauvinist pig of a coward who's afraid to contend with a woman."

Hal jerked upright, his broad shoulders flung back, his chin tilted at an angle. "Are you saying I am?"

"Nope, but Andrea Fletcher of Fletcher Ranch says you are," Nash clarified. "She called and asked me to relay that message. According to her, you aren't man enough to take the job she offered because you can't deal with a woman in a position of authority, you big overstuffed chicken."

Hal's chest puffed up like a bullfrog's. "Oh, she did, did she?"

"Yep," Nash confirmed before he strode forward to grab the reins when Crista halted in front of him.

Crista's eyes sparkled with pleasure as another round of applause and whistles resounded around her. Nash stared up at her with so much pride and affection he almost burst.

"Good God," Hal muttered when his brother reached up to scoop Crista into his arms. When Nash slid Crista provocatively down his torso, bestowing a steamy kiss on her lips, Hal rolled his eyes. Cowboys snickered and tossed teasing remarks, which Nash was obviously too far gone to hear.

"Come crawl on a rank bronc," Hal insisted, prying his brother loose from the clinch. "If you won't listen to me, maybe a few wild bucks will jar some sense back into you."

"Do you mind, Crista?" Nash questioned as Hal towed him away.

"Christ, you're asking for *her* permission?" Hal grunted disdainfully. "You need your head examined."

Nash was paying no attention whatsoever to his brother. His thoughts and his gaze were focused on a bewitching face framed by a mane of long, curly hair. Crista was staring back at him with a smile that spoke volumes, promising the love that was his for the taking.

In the grandstands, Levi Cooper observed the interplay with supreme satisfaction. He lifted his glass of champagne in toast, and Nash felt humbled and grateful for his long-standing friendship with Levi.

Nash was sure he was the most fortunate man on the planet, in the universe. Words couldn't express the emotions coursing through him as he met Levi's twinkling gaze.

Levi glanced at Crista and then back at Nash. "Be happy, Good Time. You deserve it. No one could be a better friend than you've been to me."

A lump knotted in Nash's throat. Levi's unexpected surprise had gotten Nash right where he lived. He wasn't sure he deserved the inexpressible happiness that consumed the very depths of his heart and soul. But he wasn't going to argue with it—not anymore, not ever again.

Crista was right when she said it was a waste of the present and future to live in the past. Levi had followed that philosophy and had planned for the future—for all of them. He had accepted what could not be changed and he had gotten on with life.

Of course, Nash would have had a conniption fit if he had known what Levi had been doing the past three years. But Levi had built a dream, making an investment to benefit his adopted family. He was one helluva cowboy, even if tragedy had cut his rodeo career short. Levi had taken his position as the head of financial management at Chulosa Ranch very seriously. Nash had the unmistakable feeling this business venture would be successful with Levi wheeling and dealing from his chair. He had all the necessary connections, plus the initiative and assertiveness required to produce results. He was brimming with purpose and enthusiasm. It was written all over his face . . .

"Climb aboard, Good Time," Hal ordered, dragging his brother from his musings. "Try to get your head on straight during this eight-second ride or you'll be doomed for all eternity."

Nash glanced over the top of the chute to see Crista sitting in a box seat beside Levi. "Eternity . . ." he murmured. "I like the sound of that."

Hal shook his head. "If I ever start acting as pitifully lovesick as you are now, get a rope. And for God's sake, pay attention to business here, man! If you don't, this bronc will throw you all

the way into next week. Hell, every cowboy in the
arena can see you've gone nuts over that blonde."

Nash grinned the way he used to, before tragedy took the light from his golden eyes and wiped
the smile from his lips. "Get the hell out of my
way, little brother. I'm taking the ride of my life,
and one for Dogger while I'm at it."

"Lost cause," Hal said as he hopped down from
the chute.

When Nash and the bronc erupted from the
chute like a launched missile, Rooster Anderson
leaned against the rail beside Hal. "Damn, but
he's good. He makes it look easy. I always did like
to watch him ride."

"Yeah," Hal murmured, his gaze drifting to the
pretty blonde in the stands. "I just hope Nash remembers how hard the ground is when he takes
the big fall."

Rooster followed Hal's gaze. "I'd say he already
did—head over boot heels."

Nash Griffin, Hal decided, may have been old
enough to know better, but he was too far gone
to care . . .

Twenty-five

Crista sat on her couch, her booted feet propped up in front of her. Since the men from Chulosa Ranch had dropped her off thirty minutes earlier, she had been reliving the memories of the glorious evening she had just spent at the new arena. All her fears and suspicions about Levi had taken a surprising turn. Crista couldn't have been more relieved—or pleased.

Hearing the sound of an approaching pickup, Crista made her way out to the porch to see Nash climb from the new vehicle Levi had purchased for him. As he ambled toward her, she glanced curiously toward the truck. "What? Hal didn't accompany you to make sure you didn't succumb to the wicked wiles of a woman?"

Nash strode across the porch to loop his arm around Crista the instant he was within arm's reach. "No, I managed to sneak away without Hal."

Evergreen eyes twinkling, Crista pushed up on tiptoe to greet Nash with a welcoming kiss. "Roped and tied your little brother, did you?"

"Didn't have to," Nash replied, grinning devilishly. "There was another message from Andrea Fletcher on the answering machine when we returned." Nash nuzzled against Crista's throat, inhaling the scent of her, brushing his lips across her satiny skin.

"The same woman who called the night I came to use your phone?" Crista questioned, her voice fracturing in response to Nash's feathery kisses.

"Yeah, the one who called Hal a chicken-hearted coward."

Crista leaned back, bubbling with laughter. "I'll bet that went over well."

Chuckling, Nash opened the door and ushered her inside. "Hal stalked down to the barn to load his horses in the stock trailer and flew off to show—and I quote—'that smart-mouthed she-cat' that eagles have sharper claws."

Crista blinked in surprise. "You mean Hal decided to take the job rounding up her missing cattle?"

"Either that or he plans to trample Andrea Fletcher on horseback," Nash said with a snicker.

"I don't see how Hal can gather cattle at night, even if he does have eyes like an eagle."

"Me, either. He must be going for the woman's throat tonight and her cattle tomorrow . . ."

Nash's voice trailed off when he reached the bedroom door and noticed the slinky green negligee that had been hurriedly tossed on the bed. He glanced from the seductive bit of silk to the woman he had tucked possessively beside him.

"Hal saw you in *that?*" Nash chirped. "Damn, he must have seen quite a lot of you, Curly. I'm feeling envious and deprived."

Glittering golden eyes swept possessively over her. A warm flush of pleasure stole through Crista. She had wondered if Nash would make an appearance after he had dropped her off at the house. Since Hal had raced off to show some un-

fortunate female who's boss, Crista would have
Nash all to herself. The prospect made her smile
in anticipation.

"Thinking wicked thoughts, Curly?" Nash
growled, his voice husky.

"Certainly not." Crista tried to look properly
affronted. She must have failed, because Nash was
grinning scampishly at her—just like the old days.

"I'd like to see you in that flimsy little thing
before I strip you down."

"And then?" she questioned as she sauntered
over to pluck up the garment in question, mim-
icking Janelle Chandler's strut-your-stuff walk.

"And then we're going to spend one uninterrupted night together," Nash promised. "If that
meets with your approval."

Crista nodded before Nash turned around and
made himself scarce while she changed into the
negligee she had bought with him in mind, with
only him in mind.

Crista wriggled into the green silk, feeling the
fabric glide over her skin like a lover's soft caress.
She, however, longed for the real thing—the
touch of the man she had given her heart to—
generously, freely . . . and someday, perhaps forever . . .

Nash strode down the hall, carrying two glasses
of red wine. His footsteps halted at the bedroom
door when an angel in evergreen appeared before him.

Good Lord! Nash thought as his hungry gaze
took in the shimmering green bit-of-nothing Hal
had ranted about. Talk about a knockout! No won-

der Hal thought Nash was in heap big trouble. He
was. Nash wanted to gobble Crista alive.

"Well?" Crista prompted when Nash simply
stood there with a stranglehold on the wine
glasses. "Does this meet with your approval?"

"Oh, definitely," he choked, trying to plug his
eyes back in their sockets. "If you wear that getup
for anyone but me, the green monster of Chulosa
Ranch will be on a rampage."

Crista smiled. "I'm glad you like it."

Nash strode over to deposit the wine on the
makeup table, and then came to stand directly in
front of her. "The only thing I would like better
is having you wear nothing but me . . ."

His voice frayed the instant his hands settled on
the curvy slope of her hips, feeling the lush silk
fabric teasing him, concealing what he wanted
more than he wanted to breathe.

All playfulness vanished in the space of a heartbeat when Crista stared up at him with so much
love shining in her eyes that he was sure he could
see all the way to eternity. Hal was right—Nash
had it bad—or rather, far better than he deserved.
But Nash wasn't arguing with his fate.

"I love you," Crista whispered as her arms ascended his chest and looped over his broad shoulders. "Please believe it, Nash, because it's true. I've
never loved anything or anyone the way I love
you . . ."

Nash nearly went to his knees when she spoke
so openly, so generously, so sincerely.

With a soft moan he took the invitation. Dip-
ping his head downward, he drank his fill of the
dewy nectar of her kiss and felt the floor shift
beneath him. He could barely breathe but he was

already past caring if he could. He would survive just fine on kisses.

Nash carried Crista to bed, easing his knee onto the quilts to lay her down gently. When she shifted to make room for him, Nash felt his body aligning itself to her like a piece of puzzle sliding perfectly into place, exactly where it belonged.

"If you've ever believed, for even a moment, that all I've wanted was just to have sex with you, Mary Crista Delaney, I'm here to tell you that you're very much mistaken," Nash whispered as he teased the puckered peaks of her breasts through the silky fabric. "It's always been more than physical between us. I knew that, even the first time when I was so hungry for you I nearly burned alive. I would never have broken a vow that had lasted five years if I hadn't gotten in over my head. I tried to fight it, for all the good it did. But the truth is I couldn't walk away from you then and I can't now . . ."

He eased the thin straps out of his way to greet every inch of her flesh with reverent caresses. His lips drifted down her body like the flutter of a butterfly's wings, skimming her belly, her hip, the sensitive skin of her inner thighs. His thumb traced her heated softness, feeling the hot rain of desire he had so quickly, so easily called from her.

With slow, penetrating strokes of his fingertips he caressed her, aroused her with patient tenderness. When he withdrew, her body cried out to him, longing for the physical expression of her love for him.

Nash felt Crista's hand clench around his wrist, her nails biting at him while she fought for control. His mouth moved downward as he inserted two fingers, spreading her, teasing her. And when his lips grazed her scented flesh, he felt her shimmering around him, tasted the very essence of her passion and heard her cry his name on a shattered breath.

Making her want him with every fiber of her being brought him unbelievable pleasure. He loved making love to this wildly responsive woman.

"Come here . . . please . . ." she whispered as the throes of passion consumed her again.

Nash denied her plea, too enthralled by the sweet intimacy of her body caressing him as delicately as he caressed her. He wanted to see her come to life in his arms, over and over again, to feel the whispering tremors of ecstasy claim her.

He lived for those helpless sounds of her surrender. His body clenched in its own instinctive response, but Nash vowed to drench her in waves of splendor before he came to her, giving all of himself to the one woman whose spirit called out to his heart and soul.

"No . . ." Crista breathed shakily. "No more . . . I need you desperately . . ."

"Not yet," he whispered against her quivering flesh. "We've only just begun, Crista. I want to discover every way imaginable to make you burn . . ."

Still holding her intimately in his hand, Nash shifted up beside her. His mouth descended on her parted lips, imitating the slow, languid penetration of his fingertips. He was rewarded for his tenderness with yet another shimmer of ecstasy, one that left no part of her—or him—untouched by passion.

With hands trembling, Crista reached up to tug at the pearl snaps on his shirt. Nash smiled at her need to undress him. He savored the loving sweep of her fingertips across the dark hair on his chest. But his smile faltered and his breath broke when her hand glided down beyond the band of his jeans to find him hot, hard, and eager for her touch.

"Mmm . . . the man of steel," she purred impishly, her lips skimming over the muscles of his belly. "Shall we see if you can *take* as wondrously and patiently as you *give*?"

"I can't take much," Nash rasped. "I'm already on fire."

"Then we'll see how hot *you* can burn . . ."

Nash felt his breath hitch, stalling somewhere in the cavity of his chest, when the mass of curly blond hair swept down his torso and hands and as gentle as a whisper freed him from the confines of his jeans. He held himself in careful control while she worked her maddeningly sweet magic on his ultrasensitive flesh.

Ah, the kind of torture to die for, he decided as Crista kissed and caressed him. Her lips skimmed his flesh, exciting and arousing him to the very limits of his control, causing him to groan aloud.

Nash was beginning to understand the meaning of willing defeat. He knew the weightless sensations of floating in space. Every bone and muscle in his body melted beneath her tantalizing touch. Her fingertips were like drifting threads of silk, spinning a tangled web of inexpressible pleasure, weaving a cocoon of erotic splendor.

"Good God, Crista . . ." Nash gasped at the delicious feel of her hands and lips cherishing him, crumbling the last vestige of his control.

When she traced his throbbing length with gliding tongue and nipping teeth, a silvery drop of

need eluded his willful restraint. Nash couldn't
survive much more. She was killing him with wondrous sensations that uncoiled and engulfed. He
wanted to feel her fitted around him like a silken
glove, moving with him toward wild release in the
circle of his arms.

Nash rolled to his side. Hands trembling, he
drew Crista onto her hands and knees. When he
moved behind her, Nash felt the helpless thrust
of his body taking intimate possession. A quiet
moan escaped him as they blended into one,
sharing the throbbing impulses of perfect passion.

With each thrust he felt her response, heard
his name whispered like a chant.

Before desire robbed him of all thought, Nash
eased away. He relished the raspy protest Crista
made before he gently pressed her to her back.
He came to her again, watching the dim light
glisten in her eyes as he positioned himself between her open thighs. When her lashes fluttered
down, Nash pressed gently against her, holding
himself just beyond her welcoming warmth.

"Look at me, Crista," Nash commanded
hoarsely. "For all the times I've hurt you unnec-
essarily and unintentionally, for all the times I
failed or disappointed you, I want to heal every
pain by giving you all I have to give.

"That little girl I met so long ago wasn't just
another tarnished vision from the past. She was
the picture of beauty, innocence, and endearing
spirit. I will remember her as I will always remember you . . ."

He came to her then, as softly as sunshine
blending into twilight, feeling her holding him
with such profound tenderness that it stripped

away his willpower, as if it never existed. "And I can't help but love you, Crista. You send my heart up in flames . . ."

Nash offered his quiet confession and then lost himself to the white-hot tingles that coursed through him like a raging river. What he had known since that very first time he and Crista made love was again confirmed. She was his perfect match, the missing half of his soul . . . *the right fit* . . .

The thought whipped through his mind like a whirlwind. Uncontrollable passion billowed and consumed, converging and then scattering in shards of burning pleasure. Nash clutched Crista to him, holding on for dear life while ecstasy spilled from him in shuddering release. He buried his face in that soft cloud of curly hair, breathing in the unforgettable scent that was so much a part of her, and now of him.

For the longest time Nash simply held her to his heart, his body, and his soul. He didn't want to break the spell. He wanted to drift off into that timeless dimension where the feel of Crista's body joined with his was the only reality he needed.

She was his life force, the very breath he breathed, the quintessence of pleasure.

She was his heaven on earth—pure and sweet and unbelievably fulfilling . . .

"I can't stop loving you," Crista whispered as she stroked the contours of his back. "I've spent too many years being reminded of what love *isn't*. I don't ever want to stop enjoying what love really *is*."

"Crista—"

"No, let me finish," she insisted. "I won't even ask for promises you can't keep, or commitments you don't want to make. I just want to be with you as often as I can, to hold you, love you—"

Nash pressed his index finger to her lips, shushing her. "I wish I could be that generous of heart, but I can't." He smiled into her passion-drugged features before dropping a kiss to her lush lips. "I want you with me always. I want you to be the first thing I see each morning and the last thing I see before I fall asleep at night. Being away from you has taught me the difference between alone and lonely. I need you with me, Crista. Will you marry me? Will you share your life with me?"

Crista peered up at him, smiling radiantly, her heart in her eyes. "I can't think of anything else I'd rather do." Her smile turned utterly impish as she moved provocatively beneath him. "Except this . . . because it's just the right fit . . ."

Husky laughter rumbled in Nash's chest as he traced the mischievous curve of her lips. "Little lady, no self-respecting cowboy would argue with that . . . In fact, I've been thinking the exact same thing myself . . ."

And that was the very last thing Nash thought before the overwhelming need to make wild, sweet love to Crista all over again consumed his mind, body, and soul.

Dear Readers,

I hope you enjoyed Nash and Crista's story. The life of rodeo cowboys has always been near and dear to me. My husband's uncles, Bill Feddersen and Don Feddersen, are world champion rodeo title holders. I want to honor the Feddersen brothers and other cowboys like them who keep the thrill and romance of the Old West alive. They were my inspiration for writing this story—and its sequel.

Please join Hal Griffin in February, 1997, when his story will be continued in *CRIMSON MOON*. You can rest assured that Hal's cynical theories on women are going to be tested and purged by the fiery Andrea Fletcher.

Until we meet again . . . in *Kanima* . . .

Carol Finch

Carol Finch